Amanda Cinelli was born into a large Irish Italian family and raised in the leafy green suburbs of County Dublin, Ireland. After dabbling in a few different careers, she finally found her calling as an author after winning an online writing competition with her first finished novel. With three small daughters at home, she usually spends her days doing school runs, changing nappies and writing romance. She still considers herself unbelievably lucky to be able to call it her day job.

Louise Fuller was once a tomboy who hated pink and always wanted to be the Prince—not the Princess! Now she enjoys creating heroines who aren't pretty push-overs but strong, believable women. Before writing for Mills & Boon she studied literature and philosophy at university, and then worked as a reporter on her local newspaper. She lives in Tunbridge Wells with her impossibly handsome husband Patrick and their six children.

STOLEN IN HER WEDDING GOWN

AMANDA CINELLI

ITALIAN'S SCANDALOUS MARRIAGE PLAN

LOUISE FULLER

MILLS & BOON

First Published in Great Britain 2021
by Mills & Boon, an imprint of HarperCollins*Publishers* Ltd,
1 London Bridge Street, London, SE1 9GF

www.harpercollins.co.uk

HarperCollins*Publishers*
1st Floor, Watermarque Building,
Ringsend Road, Dublin 4, Ireland

Stolen in Her Wedding Gown © 2021 Amanda Cinelli

Italian's Scandalous Marriage Plan © 2021 Louise Fuller

ISBN: 978-0-263-28245-0

05/21

MIX
Paper from
responsible sources
FSC™ C007454

STOLEN IN HER WEDDING GOWN

AMANDA CINELLI

MILLS & BOON

For Sarah
The best friend a girl could ask for

CHAPTER ONE

EROS THEODOROU RAISED the single glass of ouzo into the air and made a silent toast to the night sky above his Athens penthouse. His mother stood by his side, a haunted darkness in her eyes as she stared out into nothing.

'I didn't expect you to play the grieving widow.' He placed his glass down on the ledge with unnecessary force, not bothering to mask his irritation.

'I may not legally be his widow…but I loved him.' Arista sighed, turning to face him with a hint of steel in her pale grey eyes. 'I was with him until the end.'

The thought of his formidable mother playing nursemaid, kneeling once again to the whims of such a man…it was enough to make Eros see red. The world knew Arista Theodorou for two things, her powerful career as legal adviser to the global elite and her disastrous on-again-off-again relationship with Zeus Mytikas.

'The bastard always knew how to manipulate you.' Eros cursed swiftly under his breath and felt his fists tighten as an old darkness threatened to resurface—the resentment and hatred that he'd long ago learned to keep buried.

'You didn't come to the memorial,' Arista said, her tone laced with disapproval.

Still pulling strings from beyond the grave, the old man had arranged for his body to be returned to his home country. Over the past week, it seemed the entire capital city had turned out in mourning for their most powerful ex-citizen. Eros felt his lip curl in revulsion. 'If I wished to attend a public spectacle, I'd go to the circus.'

'He was your father.'

Her cool hand touched his forearm, a rare show of affection. He allowed himself a moment to savour the novelty before calmly removing it.

'*No*. He wasn't.'

The taut syllables seemed to sit in the air between them, silently daring his mother to contest his words. As he expected, she averted her gaze. Eros had long ago learned that the title of father was one that needed to be earned. The blood that connected him to Zeus was only that. A genetic link that could not be erased, no matter how much money or power he amassed.

'Why are you here, Mother?'

'Our schedules never seem to have us in the same city at the same time...' she said quickly, avoiding his eyes as she touched the small briefcase at her feet. 'I thought we might have dinner... Talk.'

'The truth.' Eros rolled his eyes, despising the use of niceties to conceal hidden motives. With Arista, there was always a hidden motive.

'Fine.' All traces of kindness vanished from her eyes. 'There are some urgent matters that we must discuss.'

'Make it quick, I have a date in half an hour.'

'Of course you do.' His mother's expression tightened. 'You talk of his philandering ways, and yet—'

'If you finish that sentence you can show yourself out,' Eros warned.

'I didn't mean to touch a nerve.' Arista shrugged, her tone flat and lacking its usual bite.

'If you must know, unlike your darling Zeus, I actually respect the women I entertain. They are quite aware that

I am not in the habit of long-term arrangements, so there are no misunderstandings or accusations. It's called communication, Mother, you should try it.'

'Are you really so arrogant as to believe you haven't broken women's hearts simply because you told them not to give them to you?' Arista scoffed, lifting a slim black folder from the depths of her designer handbag.

Any retort to her words was lost as Eros eyed the official documents, a dull roar building in his ears. 'What is this?'

'Zeus's last will and testament.'

He remained deathly still, controlling the violent reaction that boiled in his veins. 'You have got to be joking.'

He leaned against the balcony edge, a harsh bellow of laughter escaping his chest. 'After he tried to ruin my businesses, after the threats and reminders that I walked away from leading his empire...'

Disbelief warred with rage within him as he tried to focus on the sweeping view over the city that stretched all the way to the Acropolis. He was vaguely aware of his mother as she heaved a sigh and took a seat beside him. Her dark blond hair was identical to his own, a feature he'd always been grateful for as it put him another step away from the sleek black darkness of the powerful Mytikas family. He was not easily recognised as one of them, even if his cerulean blue eyes were a permanent reminder of the man who'd done the bare minimum in contributing to his birth.

Eros sat back, kicking his heels up onto the table in front of him. 'Let me guess, he had a change of heart and decided to leave everything to me and nothing to his other by-blows.'

Arista stiffened at the reminder that she was not the only woman to produce an illegitimate child by one of the wealthiest men in the world.

'It's not quite that simple.' She shook her head. 'There are stipulations…'

'Look around.' He gestured to the penthouse suite that sat atop the high-rise tower he owned in the centre of Athens's financial district. 'Why would I want to take his poisonous empire when I've built one of my own? I have no need to jump through his hoops.'

He was merely the second born of three bastard sons that Zeus had chosen to acknowledge in his lifetime. The image of Xander's face came unbidden into his mind and he pushed it away. His traitorous half-brother had made it clear where his loyalties stood the moment he took Zeus's name and stepped into the role of prodigal son.

As for the third and youngest of their merry trio, a reclusive member of one of the oldest dynasties in Italy, Nysio Bacchetti had made it impossible for anyone to connect his powerful family name with that of his hidden paternal link.

'This stipulation…it applies to all three of us?' Eros fought to keep his tone even. 'What have the others had to say on the matter?'

Arista shook her head. 'The Italian didn't even answer my calls. He will not risk the link being made public. But Xander has long known what he stood to lose if Zeus changed his mind…mainly his majority shareholder position and his place as acting CEO.'

He took the documents from his mother's hands and read through the highlighted text. Silence descended upon them and he could feel his mother's anxious gaze.

The first to remain in a valid marriage for one year, inherits all.

The words settled like lead in his gut. Marriage? He had walked away from Zeus's fiercely traditional values and control, but he had to admit that attempting to enforce matrimony from beyond the grave was an impressive feat.

'So Xander knows about this?'

'He knows…and he is already engaged. No announcement in the paper, no engagement party, it's all been kept completely under wraps.'

'Very convenient,' Eros murmured, still skimming down the legal pages spread out before him. Sure enough, the document made clear that of the three illegitimate sons Zeus had fathered, whoever married first and completed the terms would take everything. He sat back in his seat, tension building in his temples.

'Eros, don't you see…he's already acting like he has won. Our last board meeting was dominated by talk of his plans to purge the company of excess.' Arista's voice turned cold. 'He made it clear that my position in the company would fall under that category.'

He turned to his mother, fire in his veins and all thoughts of his date firmly forgotten. 'This conversation is futile. You know that I will never marry.'

'Not even to spite Xander?' Her voice raised an octave as she continued. 'I need to retain control at Mytikas and the only way I can achieve that is with my own son at the helm. Please, Eros.'

He saw her expression soften and knew this was a part of her act. It was always this way with Arista. For such a powerhouse of a woman, he had often seen her reduce herself to theatrics to achieve her goals. She would promise the stars, only to walk away once she had got what she needed.

He thought of his childhood spent watching her manipulate the one man who had loved her for the one who never would. His stepfather, a proud man who'd craved a simple family life, had died expecting her to change. Once upon a time, Eros had expected her to change too.

He turned to stare out at the starlit sky, his mind struggling to remain on track, as it often did with sudden shifts of information. Decades overcoming an embarrassingly inconvenient childhood stammer made him hyperaware of moments that might trigger a relapse. His jaw tightened and he carefully inhaled and exhaled a breath before speaking, just in case.

'What do you expect me to do? Barge into the church and object? Surely you can do that yourself.'

'I can't risk my position, you know that. Plus… If we want to make sure this marriage doesn't go ahead, it's not just the ceremony that needs to be ruined.'

'Ah… I see.' He forced his tone to remain calm, not belying the flash of anger that seethed in his veins. 'You don't just need my help, Mother. You need my reputation.'

'I need this bride to become suddenly, irrevocably unmarriageable. At the very least, it will give me time to contest the will. If you are determined not to fulfil it yourself.'

'I must admit, the thought of ruining Xander's perfectly laid plans is quite tempting,' Eros mused, running a hand along his jaw.

'Will you do it or not?' Arista snapped, her loss of patience sudden and sharp against the stillness of the night air. 'I just…want your brother to pay for how he betrayed you. I don't want him to win.'

Eros felt his fists tighten at her impatience, knowing that his mother had never once tried to stand up for her only son in the past. She had remained at Zeus's beck and call while Eros had gone out into the world, using nothing but rage and bitterness to forge his way alone.

The memories remained under the surface of his control but he drew upon the emotion they evoked as he stood up and took his mother's hands in his own. He saw her eyes light up with barely restrained hope.

It was rather poetic that her fatal error would so perfectly mirror that of the man she'd loved so much. Arista believed him weak, just as Zeus had, but now she was unwittingly inviting a ravenous wolf into the hencoop.

'Rest easy. I will stop the wedding.'

'You will?' she said hopefully. 'And the bride?'

'Consider her already taken care of.' He kept his features neutral. 'You just focus on contesting the will. I will do the rest.'

'This deal remains confidential between us?' she said sharply. 'If I succeed, the house in the Hamptons and the seat on the board will be mine but everything else is yours for the taking.'

'Of course,' he said silkily. 'Have I ever given you a reason not to trust me?'

Her expression softened, her objective met, and she sipped on her own ouzo like a cat who had just got the proverbial cream.

It was only once she had gone and Eros was alone with the stars once more that he allowed the ghost of a smile to touch his lips. Using his phone, he searched for the name of the woman his mother had given him before she'd left. His brother's bride.

He had long imagined what he might do if he ever got the opportunity to seek revenge on those who had wronged him...but he had never considered there might be collateral damage. He would go to New York and he would destroy his brother's plot and ensure that in a matter of weeks there would be no Mytikas Holdings for them to fight over.

He would destroy everything. Divide it up and sell it off piece by piece.

He looked at the photo on his phone once again, running his finger across the image. His big brother had chosen a pretty bride. He wondered if the beauty knew of the world she was entering into. Even if she didn't, he could not allow himself to feel guilt. It wasn't his fault if his brother had drawn an innocent into the crossfire.

In this family…all was fair in love and war.

'What do you think you're doing?'

Priya Davidson Khan jolted upright in her seat at the sound of her best friend's voice in the doorway of the office, her surprise causing her to knock over the neat stack of documents she'd been studying. 'I had a few things that needed my attention.'

'On a Sunday?' Aria strode into the room and stopped to glare down at her with obvious disdain. 'Don't you have somewhere rather important to be?'

'Money never sleeps,' Priya grumbled, furiously gathering the scrambled pile of pages. After another sleepless night, she'd come into the deserted office to calm herself by double-checking the most up-to-date figures for the company she would soon own. She'd set her plan in motion, lining up all the various parts she required until her inheritance finally became her own. She just needed to survive the next few hours first…

'Step away from the spreadsheets.' Her friend's feet appeared in her peripheral vision as she scooped up more of the errant papers under the vast mahogany desk.

Priya looked up, properly taking in the extravagant dusty pink bridesmaid's gown that Aria wore and the long white garment bag in her hands.

Her stomach sank as she took in the elegant black script on the front that read Bride.

'Sweetheart…if you were planning to run from a wedding again, you could have chosen somewhere a little more glamorous.' Aria smiled good-naturedly.

Priya swallowed hard, feeling her anxiety peak at that single word.

Again.

Her best friend wasn't trying to be cruel. They often joked of her disastrous first engagement and the society scandal that had come from her abrupt departure mere hours before the ceremony. But that had been in the past, when she'd believed herself free of this world with all its expectations and power plays. She pushed away the sinking feeling of dread and stood up, wiping down her moist palms on her tailored black suit trousers.

'What time is it?'

'Just past two.' Aria's expression softened as she stepped into the office suite and closed the double doors softly behind her. Frustration she could have dealt with, but the look of kind concern on Aria's pretty face was too much.

'Are you *sure* you want to go through with this? With… him?'

Priya thought of the *him* her friend referred to and felt the urge to growl that of course she wasn't sure. Xander Mytikas had been a last-minute choice, a deal brokered by her uncle as part of their family's desperate bid to avoid ruin. Where else was she going to find a temporary husband willing to walk away from a woman of her fortune without demanding a pay-out?

She had met the powerful financier for dinner a few times over the week before, and he had his own reasons for their arrangement, which suited her just fine. There was no attraction between them, no risk of complications. So why did she still feel this stifling sense of suffocation every time she thought of their agreement?

Perhaps it was the two-page newspaper spread he had already ordered to announce their union once it was made public, a small voice whispered inside her. She pushed the thoughts of the media away, feeling her anxiety climb. Of course the news of his wishes for a public marriage had come as a shock. Who wanted to take part in a society marriage after publicly proclaiming their lifelong spinsterhood to the world? She could already imagine the headlines.

Let them call her a social climber, let them focus on the scandal...no one could know the truth behind her hasty nuptials.

'Just help me get this on, please?' Priya exhaled a long breath and took the garment bag from her friend's hands, avoiding her questioning gaze as she undid the zip and revealed the extravagant white gown that had been selected by the top stylist in charge of the event. That was how she'd thought of it in her head until this moment, a nameless event to tick off on her weekly agenda. Only now, feeling the silk under her fingertips, she felt the first rumblings of panic under the smooth facade of her infamous ice-queen composure.

The closure of tiny hooks and buttons threatened to cut off her circulation and she'd barely caught a glimpse of her reflection smothered in expensive white silk before she forced herself to look away.

'Could you go ahead to the ceremony and tell them I'm running late?' Priya avoided her friend's eyes. 'I just... need a moment.'

Aria embraced her in a quick hug, her mouth opening but then closing on whatever words she had wished to say. With one last frown, she closed the doors behind her and Priya let out a shuddering breath. On unsteady feet, she looked around her at what had once been Arun Davidson Khan's domain. The last piece left of her father's legacy.

The New York headquarters of Davidson Khan Financial was all that remained of what had once been an international empire. The building was a slice of gilded history and had always been a favourite haunt of hers with its grand vaulted ceilings and unrivalled views of the Hudson in the distance through the sash windows.

Remembering what she'd always done as a girl, she placed her hands on the cool glass and listened to the hum of the city, trying to draw the white noise into herself to block out the chaos of her thoughts. All too soon she forced herself to move backwards, back towards the private elevator that would take her down to her fate.

Like a woman on her way to the gallows, she clamped her hands by her sides, mentally preparing to take the first step back into the flames she'd spent seven years escaping.

New York society was vicious at the best of times, but to the heiress who had publicly spurned it... She would never know true peace again.

As a young girl growing up amongst Long Island's elite, Priya remembered planning her fairy-tale wedding day with her friends. With a silk scarf for a veil and an illicitly obtained bouquet from Mama's prized rose garden, she would imagine herself to be a grand society bride just like her perfectly polished mother had been.

But it turned out her mother had been far from perfect, and her love had only ever been conditional upon Priya doing as she was told and following the rules expected of an upper-class heiress.

For seven years, she had taken time to just be herself. But once she got married...she would be a billionaire.

Closing her eyes tightly, she fought to inhale, but every attempt seemed to only serve to tighten the bands forming around her ribcage.

The private elevator came to a stop far too quickly for her liking and as the doors opened into the empty executive atrium, her path was blocked by a broad figure in a sleek black suit. She was momentarily transfixed by a pair of ce-

rulean blue eyes framed by the kind of angular bone structure and full lips that were usually reserved for the catwalk.

For a long, ridiculous moment all she could do was stare.
Beauty was not a word often used to describe men...but
there was no other word to accurately encompass the *force*
of viewing such a face. His dark blond hair was pulled back
into a neat style, but she could tell that it would fall almost to his shoulders unbound. Coupled with the perfectly
groomed shadow of stubble along his jawline, the overall
effect gave him a rather dangerous quality that seemed
quite at odds with the serene smile on his lips. As though
he'd heard her thoughts, that smile tilted up to one side and
his features were transformed anew.

'You must be the bride.' His voice was deep and slightly
accented.

Priya's heart thumped against her breastbone and she
swallowed hard, her throat suddenly parched even as she
pressed her lips flat and reminded herself that she was not
a swooning teenager. She *was* the bride and she was currently late to her own wedding.

'Did the white dress give me away?' she asked tartly.

'I think it was the overwhelming aura of excitement,'
he replied, copying her tone.

A dimple appeared in one of his cheeks and she studiously ignored it, focusing on the slim white access card in
his hands, a card that was only given to security guards
or drivers.

'I didn't order a car.' She frowned; she hadn't even
thought of it. 'Xander really did think of everything.'

Something briefly darkened in his gaze but the smile on
his face remained intact as he opened the doors that led to
the rear street access of the building. He turned, tipping his
head to one side. 'Do you need assistance with the gown?'

'I'll manage,' she said stiffly, not knowing why his innocent attention felt discomfiting, and not entirely appropriate. He was handsome, but she had met countless handsome men during the years she had worked abroad in foreign investment firms. She had never exactly gravitated to any of them but, still, she noticed.

She was about to get married to one of the most powerful men in New York and she was being distracted by some very inappropriate thoughts for her *chauffeur*.

They emerged into the gloomy autumn drizzle and she was suddenly grateful for the broad male shoulders that shielded her from view of curious pedestrians as they passed under the canopy to where a long silver limousine waited.

Huffing out a breath, she tried to slide gracefully onto the butter-soft leather seat but only succeeded in falling in very slowly. How women were expected to move freely in these ridiculous haute couture creations was completely beyond her. If it had been up to her, she'd be saying her vows in something far more functional.

Without comment, the driver leaned down and rearranged the silk, which had been trailing towards the wet ground, carefully around her feet. The angle of his head made her stiffen, her body tingling with what she hoped was just nerves. When he finally straightened and closed the door, she could breathe. What on earth had got into her?

She may not be in an actual romantic relationship with her groom but she had promised that she would play the perfect society bride. That meant maintaining the appearance of a blissfully married couple for the next year. She had no need for such a lengthy time frame, but Xander had insisted. There could be no scandal, no accusations of a staged union. It needed to look real.

Twelve months was a small price to pay to unlock her

inheritance. As much as she hated it, she had grown up a part of this world so she could easily play the part of the blushing bride for a time. It was no big deal, really…

Closing her eyes tightly, she focused on her breathing and the sound of the engine being brought to life, so much so that she missed the sound of the opposite door opening and closing quickly, before the car began to move.

'Champagne?'

Her thoughts interrupted by that smooth accented voice, her eyes snapped open to find she was not alone and she jolted back in her seat.

'Who on earth is driving the car?' She shook her head, feeling the very definite sensation of the vehicle beginning to move.

'The driver, of course.'

Priya felt her mouth slacken with dismay as her surprise guest nonchalantly pressed a button to reveal two chilled flutes and a bottle of expensive champagne.

'You…you deliberately misled me.' She sat up straighter in her seat, realising with a sharp tug of horror that she'd been so distracted she'd left without alerting the security guard that had been assigned to her.

'I never said that I was your driver.' His eyes had that same amused glow again, as though he found the situation highly entertaining.

'Who are you and why are you here?' She narrowed her gaze.

'I'm here to talk to you, of course.' Strong golden-skinned hands carefully popped the stopper and poured. 'I've been told I resemble a fallen angel. Maybe today I'm yours.'

She deliberately ignored the glass he offered her.

'That's not an answer.' She slipped her phone out of her small handbag and gave him her best glare. 'You have ten seconds to tell me your purpose here before I call the police.'

'What will you tell them, Priya?' he said silkily, his exotic accent seeming to caress each syllable as they passed his lips. 'What kind of terrible things are you imagining I might do to you? I'm curious.'

Her skin instantly prickled with gooseflesh. Who on earth was this man and why did everything he say sound like a lover's bedroom whispers? Tightening her fists, she tried and failed to conceal the sudden tremor in her body.

'Relax, princess. You are not in danger from me.' He exhaled sharply, as though her reaction had deeply irritated him. Without breaking eye contact, he reached across to press a small button on the side panel. 'You recognise Ennio, yes?'

The screen behind him was lowered and Priya felt her chest ease slightly as she took in the kind face of the man who had chauffeured her around the city many times in the past weeks. His smile held a hint of guilt as he waved once and raised the screen again, leaving her alone with her mystery guest once more.

'Did you bribe my driver?' she asked.

'*Bribe* is such an ugly word, don't you think?' He slung one powerful arm along the back of the seat, surveying her over the rim of his glass. 'I prefer to think of it as…offering a preferable incentive.'

'Who are you?' she repeated with as much steel as she could muster, considering the thousand butterflies currently using her stomach as a cage.

'You mean he didn't tell you about me?' He feigned being wounded in the centre of his chest, tutting softly. 'Seems my brother is hiding more from you than just his true motive behind this marriage. You're lucky I'm here to set the balance right before you make it down the aisle.'

His *brother*. Priya felt her mouth open slightly before she closed it again. Being part of New York society, it was impossible not to know about her groom's powerful father and his infamous indiscretions but nothing about the man in front of her was anything like her finely polished and serious fiancé. Xander was dark and lean where this man was golden-skinned and had shoulders that seemed to fill the entire seat. His collar was open and his long golden hair brushed back in the kind of effortless style that only looked good on a man of his calibre. He practically oozed sex appeal and vitality, so much so that she forced herself to look away from his knowing gaze and remind herself of what was at stake.

She knew that Xander had ulterior motives that he hadn't revealed but she had ensured that their prenuptial agreement was ironclad. She'd read through the papers herself, their arrangement was crystal clear. Everything was under control.

'You're clearly here to make a revelation of some sort, so kindly get to it. I'm already running late.' She smoothed her hands down flat in her lap, gathering her expression into a cool mask.

'Do you love him?'

'That's…none of your business,' she responded tautly, her jaw tightening with barely restrained irritation. As though he hadn't got the answer he wanted, her mysterious guest simply frowned and took another slow sip of champagne.

'I've seen the prenuptial agreement…you certainly have a routine mapped out. Dinners in public, social events… You seem quite eager to bolster your reputation now that you've returned to society.'

'You don't know me.' Priya spoke through clenched teeth.

'I know enough.' He downed the remnants of his champagne in one movement, the golden liquid glittering for a moment on his lips. 'I know that one sordid photograph with me would be all it takes for my brother to discard you and whatever deal you've made.'

Priya fought past the sudden dryness in her throat, hardly able to process such a scandalous threat. 'What benefit could possibly come from ruining this wedding in such a dramatic way?'

'Oh, no, princess... I'm not just here to ruin the wedding.' He leaned forward, his full lips stretching into a sinful smirk. 'I'm here to ruin *you*.'

CHAPTER TWO

'YOU ARE THE one Xander was worried about.' The realisation hit her with sudden clarity as she remembered a conversation she'd overheard as they'd navigated the complicated terms of their prenuptial agreement.

There are members of my family who may pose a problem.

She'd heard mention of her fiancé's feuding Greek family but she hadn't taken them too seriously. She took in the man seated across from her once more, this time seeing his ethereal beauty for what it was. A colourful trap designed to lure a woman to her doom.

'You must be the one they sent away... Eros.' She breathed deeply, almost afraid that she was correct in her assumption. She'd only ever heard whispers of Eros Theodorou, a powerful Greek investment banker and property mogul. His reputation amongst the elite of Europe was one of the work hard, play hard variety.

'In the flesh.' His lips smoothed into a perfect smile as the word fell silkily from his lips. 'It seems my family did not manage to completely erase me from their history.'

'Unfortunately not.'

'That's an impressive skill you have.' He sat forward,

bracing his hands on his knees. 'I almost feel the chill of your disapproval in the air.'

'You expect me to be pleased that I'm being kidnapped on my wedding day?'

'Such dramatics.' His brows rose as one hand pressed against the centre of his chest. 'What possible reason would I have to necessitate kidnapping you?'

Priya kept her features impassive, not entirely sure how to interpret her situation. Whatever his reasons for getting her alone this way, her gut told her that it was not good.

'For all you know, my plan is to simply escort you to your handsome groom myself.' He spoke with thinly veiled amusement.

'There would be no need for theatrics if that was the case.' She raised one brow.

'True.' He tilted his glass in her direction. 'I'll admit my intentions are not so noble. But I assure you I have no need to steal you away. I have every confidence that once you know the truth behind this rather sudden union, you will walk away all by yourself.'

'You're despicable.' She exhaled sharply.

'Believe it or not, I'm the least of your problems.' He looked impressively villainous all of a sudden, watching her from the shadows. 'I'm simply here to serve a warning that this family thrives on deception.'

'You expect me to heed a warning from you?' she said tautly, feeling her nails dig into her palms. 'I read that you were caught selling company secrets. You're a criminal.'

'So the stories say.' He sighed with an air of boredom.

'So that's not true?'

'I don't know what amuses me more, that people believe me a white-collar criminal or that they believe I allowed myself to get caught.'

'You find it funny to have your reputation precede you?'

'Do you?' His eyes seemed to turn a shade darker as his gaze momentarily caught on the large diamond ring on her finger. 'Does my brother know about what happened to your last groom?'

His words hit her square in the chest and she fought to regain her composure for a long moment. 'Do you have to practise being so offensive or does it come naturally?'

'It's one of my many talents.' He sat forward, his cerulean eyes meeting hers with such intensity she fought not to squirm. 'So, let's get to the point. Did your uncle force you into this little marriage bargain of yours or did you offer yourself up willingly?'

Priya narrowed her eyes, feeling her heartbeat quicken. 'Why would I satisfy you with an answer to such a ridiculous question?'

'I've done my research, Miss Davidson Khan.' He tilted his head to one side, studying her with quiet focus. 'For one of the wealthiest heiresses in the country, you have been living a rather modest lifestyle. You're on track to come into your inheritance in three years, so you have no pressing reasons to enter into such a bargain. Your uncle, on the other hand...'

He flipped open the case of a slim tablet computer by his side and it sprang to life, filled with rows upon rows of numbers. Priya feigned nonchalance as she peered closer, praying it wasn't what it seemed to be. Praying that he was bluffing.

He was not.

'How did you get access to this?' she asked in shock.

'Let's just say it's a talent of mine, hunting down secrets that powerful people wish to keep hidden from the world.' He snapped the case shut, making her jump. 'A wealth management firm with a CEO secretly drowning in debt. Quite a headline, don't you think?'

'Is that what this is? You're here to blackmail me on my wedding day?' She felt anger rise within her at his serene expression as he remained silent, slowly swirling his index finger around the rim of his champagne flute.

He continued. 'I was just curious why you would wait so long to inherit the shares in your father's company, only to hand them over in a buyout.'

'I have not agreed to a buyout.'

'Are you sure about that?'

His words held no amusement now as he drew up another file for her perusal, the contract that she had signed days before. Only now her uncle's signature had been added, along with one particular amendment. Xander Mytikas was vying for a merger…and Vikram planned to give it to him.

Blue eyes watched her, his full lips pressed into a hard line. 'My brother has a poor track record when it comes to promises. And your uncle has already proved where his loyalties lie.'

Priya felt her thoughts swirl out of control, the pressure of the past week finally threatening to overwhelm her. This was too much. From the moment she had agreed to this ridiculous marriage bargain, she had inwardly fought against it. She had walked away from this life seven years ago for a reason and now she was being dragged back into it kicking and screaming.

She didn't have to save her uncle; she could leave him to his own fate. But would she ever forgive herself if she let the last of her father's beloved company disappear, absorbed into some faceless conglomerate? She'd promised that she would make him proud. She'd vowed to carry out the plans he'd begun, once she had gathered enough experience to earn her place.

'I've already agreed to the deal. Even if this is all true…'
She shook her head, frustration and anxiety making her
pull and fuss with the folds of silk that swamped her. 'I
suppose you are here to warn me out of the goodness of
your own heart?'

'Of course not.'

'Then why?' she urged. 'Revenge?'

'Something like that, yes.' His eyes turned dark with a
flash of malice, his gaze moving to look out the window.

'Quite a theatrical notion for a self-professed villain.
Why on earth should I trust you?'

'You shouldn't.' He ran strong fingers along his jaw.
'Someone as wealthy as you stand to become should trust
no one. Especially not people who place conditions on their
false concern.'

'Ah, so your concern is genuine?'

'I don't make a habit of caring for the plight of small
investment firms that are utterly irrelevant to my business
interests.' He met her gaze, no trace of remorse on his beautiful features. 'I can offer you something else. Freedom.'

'I am free. I chose to accept this deal with my eyes open.
Despite your flattering appraisal, I am not some damsel in
distress in need of rescue.'

'I am not here to rescue you. The single term of my offer
is simple,' he interjected smoothly. 'Walk away from this
wedding. Publicly. Abandon my brother and his precious
image…and I will buy your father's company myself and
hand it to you, no strings attached.'

'Revenge would be worth that much to you?'

'My brother once caused me a great deal of public shame
and ridicule. I can think of no situation more perfect for
him.'

Priya sucked in a sharp breath, unable to look away from
that dark smile on his lips. How could a man with such

striking beauty be so cold and calculating? She closed her eyes briefly, feeling her pulse thrumming in her ears. How had she got into this situation where she was tempted by such an unlikely escape?

The man she'd agreed to marry had a reputation for being ruthless in the boardroom, true, but he had never given her reason to mistrust him. Still, thoughts arose, memories of his evasion of her questions behind his motives. He would only say that he needed the marriage for his own private legal reasons.

The idea that Vikram had conspired to secretly force through a merger was not so farfetched. The only reason she'd even found out about his debts was because he'd been busily selling off all of his own shares. But Xander had seemed so earnest in his sympathy for her plight. Was it possible that she had once again completely misjudged a man claiming to have her best interests at heart?

Maybe he would be relieved if she called everything off…

Hearing the selfish direction of her thoughts, she mentally shook herself. No. She couldn't walk away from this… no matter how far out of her comfort zone she was. She had to at least speak to him first.

The car came to a sudden stop and Priya looked sideways, shocked to see that they had arrived at the courthouse already. Blue eyes remained trained on her, waiting for her answer to his offer.

Waiting for her to put her faith and the future of hundreds of employees into the hands of a stranger.

'I… I can't trust you. I'm sorry.'

Without waiting for assistance, she threw the door open and used every ounce of strength she had to lift herself to a standing position and step carefully outside. The sidewalk was eerily empty and the grey stone building looked even more imposing under the murky grey clouds that blanketed the sky above them. There was a heaviness to the air, as though the heavens above were set to burst at any moment.

A cab careened to a stop nearby and she recognised the furious figure of her bodyguard emerging from the passenger seat. She shivered, looking back down to find Eros's lightening gaze still intensely focused upon her.

'Let me make this clear, this offer expires the moment you turn your back on me,' he warned darkly.

She took a step back and slowly turned, hearing a dark chuckle emerge from behind her. For a moment she wondered if Eros Theodorou was going to follow through on his threat to accompany her into her wedding ceremony himself. But moments later she heard the door being pulled shut with a final click.

The bodyguard came to a stop by her side, panting and agitated. 'Are you unharmed, Miss Davidson Khan?'

'I'm fine.' She pressed her lips into a thin line but inside she was furious at herself for making such a glaring lapse in judgement. She was the queen of details, she never missed a step. Yet with one mere flash of a charmer's smile, she'd gotten into a car with a stranger like a wayward child.

Squaring her shoulders, she resisted the urge to look back and began scaling the steep steps. It was unusually quiet for an afternoon in Manhattan.

Her thoughts threatened to consume her and drag her further away from the quiet, resolved demeanour she'd adapted in the past days. She was no longer able to ignore her roiling thoughts. Her calm sea had been ravaged by the storm that was Eros Theodorou.

She suddenly wished she hadn't been so intent on doing this alone. Perhaps this was why brides were walked into a wedding by their fathers, so that they were less likely to run.

But her father was dead and her mother was already inside with her uncle, watching to make sure she followed through on her promise to save them.

She wasn't just walking alone, she *was* alone.

She was so distracted by her melancholy thoughts that she didn't see the cameras until the first flash blinded her. She halted mid-step, her gown forming a stark white cloud against the dark stone. As if in horrifying slow-motion, the entire platform at the top of the steps became swarmed with reporters.

Priya froze.

A couple dozen eyes fell upon her with laser focus. Pedestrians slowed down in her peripheral vision, craning their necks to get a good look at the spectacle she presented. A tableau of perfectly polished fear and uncertainty.

Just walk, she urged herself, feeling the panic rise in her throat. Fewer than ten steps separated her from clearing up the details of the prenup, unlocking her inheritance and saving her family's name from ruin. Just a few more steps and she would have done her duty to her father. She would be on the pathway to freedom.

But the crawling claws of fear grew inside her chest, making her feel like she was trapped underwater and being pulled downward. A quick look behind her revealed an empty space where the limousine had been. The knowledge that she was truly alone intensified her panic. Her lungs felt like they were filling with water with each second that passed. She needed to move. She needed to breathe.

One quick glance upward revealed her uncle pushing past the shoulders of the paparazzi and journalists who had overrun the courthouse entrance. Vikram moved towards her and she held up a hand to stop him.

'Did you amend the prenup?' she asked shakily, watching the immediate play of guilt and anger across his dark features.

'This is not the time or place to cause a scene, Priya,' he growled. 'Get inside.'

She immediately took a step back, out of his reach. 'Even after I came to save you, you still couldn't help yourself?' She shook her head with disbelief.

'The company is dead in the water anyway,' he hissed under his breath, eyes darting towards the reporters eagerly flashing their cameras. 'This way we all win.'

'How dare you.' She felt her legs begin to shake as she stumbled backwards, feeling the eyes of what seemed like a thousand onlookers follow her. A quick glance showed Xander emerging from the doorway, only to be blocked by a wall of people. He met her eyes, one dark brow rising in silent question, and Priya felt the final knot of indecision lock into place.

Shaking her head slowly, she tried to convey her apology without words. He may have been swayed by a bad deal with Vikram but no one deserved this kind of humiliation. She should never have agreed to their marriage in the first place.

As he realised her intention, his face hardened with concern and he seemed to try to push through the crowd. Priya didn't wait to see if he succeeded. She turned and fled down the remainder of the steps.

As she made quick progress down the street, the earlier mist suddenly gave way to a steady downpour. She felt her hair and shoulders become soaked instantly but had no time for vanity. Without her purse, which she had somehow dropped, she couldn't even hail a cab. The reality of her decision seemed to hit her with finality as she came to a stop in a narrow alleyway and felt a sob threaten to choke her.

Thinking of the humiliation she'd just caused made her throat clench painfully, so she forced herself to focus on how on earth she was going to navigate the streets of New York in pouring rain wearing a giant haute couture wedding gown.

As she tried to clear her mind and formulate a plan, a familiar sleek silver limousine appeared at the opposite end of the alleyway and came to an immediate stop. A tall, broad frame stepped out into the rain, blond hair darkening instantly under the heavy downpour.

Priya felt a shameful mixture of frustration and relief as she watched Eros move towards her with leonine grace.

'You're faster than I anticipated,' he said as he reached her side, his face strangely devoid of either triumph or judgement.

She hated the fact that he seemed so confident that she would run and that he had tracked her with such ease. In the brief moments of their meeting, he'd done his best to show her exactly what he knew would make her want out of her ill-fated deal. The knowledge made her fists tighten with anger.

She was vaguely aware of a dark coat being draped around her body, cocooning her in warmth and the unusual scent of mint and sandalwood. She hesitated, unable to decide if, by accepting his help, she was accepting everything he had offered. She looked up, meeting his eyes for the first time and feeling her stomach clench at the intensity she saw there.

She may have just walked away from her best chance of unlocking her trust fund and saving the firm by herself, but if she was actually considering accepting an offer of no-strings help from a man with his reputation, she had certainly lost her mind.

'I just need to get out of here, please,' she said with as much strength as she could muster, feeling the cold of the rain seeping into her skin through his coat. The wedding gown was a dead weight now, sodden and dark with mud at the hem. She didn't care. She needed him to know that just because she had run from the wedding—just because she was getting into this limo—it didn't mean she was trusting him.

Liar, something whispered deep within her.

'Your rescue comes at a price.' His words were tight with what sounded like irritation. 'But we can discuss that once we're somewhere less wet and freezing.'

What happened to no strings? she thought with sudden anger. Did all men believe that they could simply change the rules on a whim?

Before she could challenge him, a buzz of voices sounded out behind them and Priya turned her head just as a bulb flashed brightly in her face, momentarily blinding her.

A growl, low and feral, came from her side and she was lifted over one powerful shoulder. He moved fast down the alley, his face a mask of calm as he dropped her unceremoniously into the darkness of the limousine interior, the door closing with a sharp thud behind her.

Through the tinted glass, she watched as Eros loomed over the small group of photographers that had pursued her like dogs on a blood trail. His threats were dark and muffled by the window, but effective considering the crowd seemed to shrink away immediately. The door opened and he slid in with ease, taking the seat directly beside her and filling the car with his overwhelming presence.

She felt the change in the vibrations around her as the car began to move away from the tangle of gridlock that surrounded the courthouse, but she couldn't force herself to open her eyes and look back. She felt like she'd run a marathon, but it had been less than five minutes since she'd stepped out of this limousine in front of the courthouse.

Her body shook and jerked in earnest now as the adrenaline coursed through her. Even her teeth chattered as she tried to inhale and exhale smoothly. It was useless, she knew this feeling far too well. She was headed for a full-scale panic attack and nothing would stop it. She leaned forward into the cloud of white silk and heard a pathetic whimper escape her lips as her breathing accelerated with brutal force.

She was vaguely aware of a sharp curse coming from nearby, but the sound was drowned out by the noise of her breath struggling to exit and enter her lungs.

When it came to comforting women, Eros would admit that most of his experience existed solely in the post-love-making glow of the bedroom. Comforting a woman he had just stolen away from her own wedding was another matter entirely.

She'd chosen to walk away on her own, he reminded himself. Perhaps if he repeated that to himself enough he might actually believe that his original plan hadn't begun to change from the moment he'd set eyes on Priya Davidson Khan in that hotel lobby. A new idea had begun to form, one that both excited him and filled him with unease.

He looked down at his stolen bride, her body swamped in his favourite tailored suit jacket and her ruined white gown and he felt something within him tighten uncomfortably. He'd come to New York intent on revenge. Intent on ruining his brother's precious public image and finally finding a way of dismantling the throne of corruption and lies his father had ruled for decades.

But then he'd laid eyes upon the woman he'd been sent to ruin and a wild idea had formed in his mind. A terrible, brilliant twist to his plan where he would not simply ruin his brother's chance at wedding his perfect bride.

He would steal her…for himself.

He was not in the habit of drawing innocent people into his plans and playing by the rules had never been his style but if a bride was what was required to fulfil the terms of the will fastest, he saw no better choice than the woman in front of him.

She was exactly the kind of bride his pompous, perfectionist brother would choose for this production he was putting on. The dutiful protégé, stepping into power with his society bride by his side. He probably planned to create an army of perfect little heirs to further lock up his hold over the empire he had no right to.

In planning his brother's ruination, he had dug into Priya's past enough to see that she had grown up in luxury, trained to move in only the most polished circles. Apart from an embarrassing engagement and messy break-up at eighteen, she was scandal-free. Perfect for an elitist fool like Xander.

But the past seven years of her life since her disastrous first failed jaunt down the aisle were strangely devoid of gossip, as though she'd ceased to exist. Now she had her face turned away from him as she calmed herself. Her hands were clasped in her lap, crushing a fistful of silk as though she wasn't sure if she wished to cry or throw a tantrum. Somehow, he didn't think she would allow herself to do either. She had quickly assumed a mask of complete control.

What would it take to unravel that glacial resolve?

Why was he so utterly fascinated by it?

He watched as she calmed herself down, using some kind of breathing exercise, and he decided that now was not the time to inform her about his original plan to have her photographed with him. He had dealt with the paparazzi and if they dared to defy him, they would regret it.

The world may think him a wild and reckless playboy but that was only because that was the image he presented to them. If Zeus had known the true power he possessed, how much wealth he had accumulated during the past fifteen years, he would have long ago turned his corrupt focus on him.

He had planned his careful takedown of the Mytikas empire for more than a decade, then, at the last hour, his bastard father had to go and die. Zeus had long ago chosen Xander, the oldest of his three by-blows, to be his sole heir. The idea that he would offer up the position to be easily snatched away by one of his rejected spares at the last moment was exactly the kind of power move Eros should have expected.

The car slowed down as they entered the sleek rows of residential towers that bordered the south end of Central Park. The driver manoeuvred them down a narrow alleyway to a discreet private entrance, partially hidden from the street.

Priya looked up as they came to a stop, her eyes glazed and unfocused. 'Where have you brought me?'

'Somewhere you can dry off and wait out the media storm.' He stepped out of the limousine and extended his hand to her, trying and failing not to notice the delicious display of skin on show as she struggled to gather the gown. It must weigh a significant amount, judging by the awkwardness of her movements.

Almost the moment the thought crossed his mind, he looked down to see her wrestling with the lower layer of silk, which had got stuck in the doorway.

'This is why I hate wearing dresses.' She punctuated the last word with a sharp pull, which quickly resulted in a loud ripping sound. She froze, wide-eyed and still completely trapped against the doorway.

Eros moved closer, surveying the gown. 'Allow me?'

After a moment she nodded and Eros leaned down, tearing the rest of the fabric free with one easy tug. But instead of stepping away, he pulled again, ripping the lower edge of the skirt from below her knees. The movement completely detached the heavy cloud of silk and netting from the underskirt, which still fitted snugly against her thighs. He stood back, surveying his work with a satisfied smirk.

'That was…completely unnecessary,' she said in horror.

'Forgive me, princess, were you planning on wearing it again?'

With a thoroughly unladylike growl, she stepped out of the larger mass of material and kicked the mud-splashed silk to one side.

'That's better.' He ensured his words were dry and disinterested as he avoided staring down at the perfect toned skin of her long legs.

Wide, molten chocolate eyes narrowed up at him with anger and Eros felt a flash of something suspiciously akin to enjoyment. No, he corrected the errant thought, attraction was what he felt. And why wouldn't he be attracted? She was a beautiful woman and he was a red-blooded male. He'd met plenty of beautiful women, but that didn't mean he had so little control as to act on it every time his libido roared to attention.

They remained in silence on the long ride up to his penthouse suite, for which Eros was grateful. The woman was a distraction and right now he needed to focus on his game plan. Once his mother realised what he was now planning to do…she would do everything within her power to put a stop to it. Time was not on his side…but maybe he could pull it off.

It all depended on whether or not he could convince the woman by his side that marriage was the most logical course of action for them both. A sentence he had never dared to think, let alone speak aloud.

The brand-new luxury tower was a pet project of his and comprised a series of condominiums with price tags that would make even the wealthiest magnate's eyes water. The lobby was a cavernous marble hall that dated back more than a century.

Antique mirrors and sumptuously dark fabric lined the hallway walls of his penthouse, accented by warm glowing sconces.

'I can't tell if this place is a restoration or brand new.' Her eyes widened as she stepped into the bright open-plan living space and gazed up at the bronze ceiling feature.

'It's one of my favourite things to do, to take a slice of history, preserve it and put it on show within something modern.' His architects had been given free rein to complete a building that was worthy of note in the history books. When he had seen the final plans, how the rest of the tower rose behind the original structure like a gleaming sword slicing into the sky, he'd been speechless.

He had never planned to live in Manhattan again, but he had taken the top-floor suite on impulse, having been bewitched by the warm stone floors, bronze details and the perfectly centred views over the park.

A strange chattering sound emanated from the woman beside him and he looked down to see her stubbornly trying to hide her discomfort as she stared around at the wide open-plan living space.

'It's b-beautiful.' She shivered.

Cursing under his breath, he decided to forgo a tour, taking her by the hand and guiding her into the spacious guest suite before ushering her into the bathroom.

'You're turning blue. That dress needs to come off.'

He heard Priya's swift intake of breath.

'I have nothing else to wear.'

'I have no wish to have you contract pneumonia under my watch, princess. You need a hot shower and dry clothing. Turn around.'

'Don't be ridiculous. I can manage.' She breathed shakily, staring down at the sodden gown with stubborn determination.

'I doubt you got into that dress alone.' He pointed to the layers of silk ribbons and loops, criss-crossing to hold the back of the gown together.

'You seem to know a lot about corsetry—are you a dressmaker?'

'I'll admit I have an appreciation for delicate lingerie. Mainly the act of removing it from a woman's body.' Eros didn't know whether to laugh or groan as he watched her absorb his words and unconsciously bite her lower lip.

'Okay, then,' she said, rather breathlessly. 'Try to be quick. I am quite cold.'

He was tempted to make another double entendre until she exhibited another racking shiver and he noticed her lips had taken on a dark tinge.

The dampness of the silk was a hindrance he hadn't foreseen, with each sharp pull only serving to slide the fabric a scant few centimetres. Cursing under his breath, he opened the drawer of the vanity and pulled out a small penknife. A few quick slides of the blade and the material began to sag open, revealing the smooth expanse of her bare back.

'Is it done?' She turned to look in the mirror, catching his eye as he slid his blade under the final loop.

'I'm afraid you won't be winning any fashion awards, but you can probably breathe again. How tight was that thing?'

'It's an object of torture.' She turned just as he moved outside the doorway, momentarily losing her grip on the dress so that it slid dangerously low on her chest.

Eros felt like the world moved in slow motion as inch by inch of creamy brown skin was revealed to his suddenly starving gaze. She was the perfect mix of softness and muscle, round in all the right places. She quickly covered herself back up to her chin.

'I should probably get warmed up too.' He watched her in the mirror and began to unbutton his shirt, noticing her eyes following the movement.

Her eyes widened and her tongue snaked out to moisten her bottom lip. As though realising he'd seen her reaction, she shook her head, slamming the bathroom door closed and turning the lock.

Dear God, if he didn't know better he would think she was a weapon sent to destroy his control. Women had always been his weakness, his preferred company and comfort. He had devoted his adult life to becoming a master of pleasure. Women seemed to seek him out for his supposed talents, then left in search of men they respected to settle down with, and that suited him just fine. But the last few months had been hectic with a slew of unexpected projects and he'd found he didn't have the usual time or energy to devote to seduction.

Then, the moment he'd arrived back in Athens and had been poised to revive an old acquaintance, his mother had arrived with her news.

He just needed to get laid, he told himself with a laugh as he disappeared into his own comfortable master suite, thankful for the brief reprieve from their sparring. He needed to regroup and reset his plans. He was a master of details but right now this all felt like an impulsive mess. He knew he was making the right move—he trusted his intuition, it had never steered him wrong—but what he didn't trust...was her.

Or was it that he didn't trust himself around her?

Hardly taking a moment to examine the space he'd spent an exorbitant amount of money on, he moved to the long floor-to-ceiling windows and gazed out into the distance. It had been such a long time since he'd set foot in this city that he'd almost forgotten about the breath-taking beauty that Manhattan had to offer.

He'd been raised in Greece but as a child of divorced parents he'd spent almost half of every year travelling with his jet-setting mother. Coming to prefer his mother's lax method of parenting over his stepfather's severe style, he'd spent much of his teenage and early twenties with New York and other major financial cities as his playground. Regret was a familiar pang against his breastbone as he let his eyes wander over the tall giants of steel and glass that formed the iconic skyline in the background and the lush green of the park spread out below.

He imagined what his stepfather would think, knowing Eros was about to do the one thing he'd warned him against. Though he had only been married to Arista for less than a decade, Stavros Theodorou had remained a constant presence in Eros's life and had given him more than any blood relative ever had. He was the man from whom he had taken his family name, the man who had taught him to value loyalty above all else.

Marriage is a trap, he would growl, his voice pure gravel from years of chain smoking.

Unable to sit with his thoughts for another moment, Eros walked into the slate-walled bathroom and stripped, stepping under the harsh spray of the waterfall shower.

A groan of pure pleasure escaped his throat as the heat unravelled some of the knots in his shoulders. The image of a certain pair of delicate hands, kneading his muscles, entered his mind and he pushed the thought away with an impatient frown.

His promises to his stepfather had driven him for the past ten years. His regrets over how he had treated the only person who had ever had his best interests at heart still shamed him, but he was determined to undo some of his wrongs. Double-crossing Arista and teaching her a lesson was the first step. Then, once he had inherited the majority shares of Mytikas Holdings he would move his focus on to Xander.

Images of Priya bathing on the other side of the wall entered his mind unbidden and he indulged himself for a moment, imagining what it might be like to unravel that polished stone exterior and reveal the molten heat he could sense beneath.

CHAPTER THREE

PRIYA STARED AT her reflection in the floor-length mirror and wondered how on earth she had ended up in such a precarious position. She'd been so relieved to be free of the wedding gown she'd hardly even thought of what she would wear once she got out of the shower until a quick peek outside the bathroom door had revealed a freshly pressed white shirt laid out on the bed.

It was clearly excellent quality and expensive but it was designed to fit six feet plus of muscular Greek male, not her own meagre five and a half feet. The hem was respectable at least, covering her to just above her knee. And with few small adjustments, rolling up the sleeves and tucking in the collar…it almost passed for a chic dress.

Almost.

She walked back out into the open-plan living area and was relieved to find it empty. A polished wooden drinks bar took up one side of the dining area and she immediately busied herself, looking through the various vintage and luxury brands of whiskey. Selecting one she recognised as having been one of her father's favourites, she poured a glass and felt a familiar ache within as she inhaled the familiar scent. The sun had begun to set fast, setting the room ablaze with colour and drawing her gaze outside to the red and gold hues of the park far below.

Her body was tight with nerves as she felt the stillness of

the cavernous apartment settle onto her like a dead weight. The amber liquid did nothing to ease the growing whirlpool of guilt and uncertainty swirling like acid in her gut.

'What have I done?' she whispered, hearing her heartbeat threatening to burst from her chest.

'You've recognised a poor investment and changed course.'

She turned, taking in the man who stood a few feet away and felt her stomach clench in response. His hair lay wet and curling upon his shoulders, only serving to accentuate the sharp cut of his cheekbones and that dangerous jawline. Gone was the three-piece suit, replaced now by a pair of form-fitting black jeans and a stone-grey sweater that looked luxuriously soft. He looked so effortlessly put together and here she stood in just a shirt, like a woman who had just fallen out of his bed. Of course he didn't even try to hide his perusal of her makeshift dress as he stalked towards her, closing the distance between them.

Priya stood her ground, despite the urge to run, or worse, to move closer. She couldn't have chosen a worse time to be struck down by something so inconvenient as an attraction. He eyed the glass in her hand, leaning forward until he was close enough to inhale the scent of the whiskey.

'You have excellent taste. This one is my favourite.' Their eyes met for a moment before he moved to pour himself a glass. He hummed low in his throat after the first taste and Priya felt a shiver run down her spine. Shaking off the uncomfortable sensation, she forced herself not to retreat as he focused on her once more.

'Come. We have things we need to discuss.' With effortless grace, he lowered his powerful frame onto a long leather sofa and gestured for her to take a seat by his side.

The move felt strangely intimate and Priya felt her brows rise in the face of such bald arrogance. Now that the adrenaline of the afternoon had begun to recede, anger bubbled just beneath the surface of her control. Taking another long sip of the vintage whiskey, she fought the urge to throw the liquid into his lap. 'I'd prefer to stand, thank you.'

'Suit yourself.' His fingers drummed a sharp rhythm on the arm of the chair.

'I'm not being ungrateful,' she said quickly, not quite able to look directly at him. Not unlike the blazing heat of a summer sun, Eros Theodorou was a risk to be approached with caution. The man exuded the kind of scorching male energy that she had always made a point of avoiding. But there was no avoiding her current situation and the fact that his vengeance-fuelled proposition was the only remaining chance she had to save her father's legacy.

The resentment left a bitter taste in her mouth. This was not a moment for pride, she reminded herself. There were people's livelihoods at stake.

With a single fortifying breath, she met the eyes of the man who was both tormentor and saviour. 'I'm very thankful for your assistance today, though I know your motives weren't exactly pure. Still… I've thought about it and I'd like to accept your offer.'

He was silent for a moment, his eyes focused on the amber liquid he swirled around in a glass on his knee. 'It's a pity…because that particular offer has now expired.'

Priya felt that single word reverberate in her mind with all the force of a thousand drums. *Expired.* 'Is that supposed to be a joke?'

'You walked away from me, Priya. You wounded my very fragile male pride.'

'There is nothing fragile about you or your ego,' she blurted, anger taking hold of her tongue. She took a single step towards where he sat, the injustice of it taking her breath away. 'Was this a part of your plan? You picked me up in front of all of those reporters…'

Something dark flickered in his eyes that looked suspiciously like guilt and Priya felt her insides drop with sudden realisation. '*You*. Of course, it was you who arranged for the paparazzi ambush. Now you've got exactly what you wanted without even paying a penny.'

'In my world, this is how business is done. I was not lying before, I would have paid your uncle's debts without any further action.'

'But now you have the upper hand.' She felt her lips twist with the realisation, cold fear sliding down her spine. 'Do you wish to make me beg for your help? Is that why you brought me here?'

She vaguely saw him place his glass on the floor and stand. The air felt too hot, the pressure in her chest growing by the second. This hadn't been a rescue; it had been an attack of conscience. He had no intention of helping her—why would he? She had refused his scandalous offer but then she'd still gone and jilted her groom. She'd been a pawn in someone else's game once again.

'I need to leave… I can't stay here.' She began walking towards the foyer and he was upon her in an instant, his big frame moving around her to block her path. He was close. So close that she could see a few rogue droplets of water slide from his slicked-back hair and down his neck. The drops disappeared down into the vee of his sweater and she felt herself swallow convulsively past the dryness in her throat.

'You will not run from me, Priya,' he grated out, something wild and untameable glowing in his eyes.

'Why would I stay here a moment longer? So you can threaten to send scandalous pictures to the press and ruin me even further?' she challenged, pushing past him but having her progress hampered by the obstruction of one very large, very muscular male hand against the wall beside her head.

'The reporters were there purely to anger my brother and further the scandal. Once they'd chased you I called them off. As it stands, there will be no mention of your connection to me in the press. But if you go running from my building wearing only one of my shirts… There is only so much damage control I can do.' There was no amusement in his tone now, only thinly veiled anger that made her skin prickle with awareness. Her breath came in sharp bursts, his proximity not helping matters. Almost as though he'd heard her thoughts, he released her from the cage of his arms and put some space between them.

'Surely the whole point of it was to have them target me, as well.' Priya closed her eyes. 'You tricked me into that limo, knowing exactly what you planned to do.'

A muscle ticked in his jaw. 'Originally, yes.'

She felt despair settle upon her like a dead weight, making her shoulders slump back against the wall as her heart continued to pound against her ribs. She felt like she had entered a fever dream where nothing made sense. She needed to leave and get back to the tiny apartment she'd rented in the East Village and try to find a way to regroup.

'I'm handling this poorly.' Eros spoke from a few steps away.

'You think?' She forced her eyes away from him, feeling her pulse pound uncomfortably at his proximity. Her awareness of his blatant male energy was just another source of irritation to her overloaded mind.

Eros mimicked her posture, leaning one broad shoulder against the opposite wall. But while she imagined that she looked fragile and exhausted, he looked fresh and virile, a man who knew he held all the power. God, what she would give to shift that balance back where it belonged. To take control of her own destiny once and for all.

'I don't want to make you beg, Priya. You're far too valuable for those kinds of games. I want to offer you an alternative,' Eros said. 'A way that we can both get what we want.'

'You're quite optimistic that I'd believe you.'

His words held no amusement now as he watched her, his full lips pressed in a hard line. 'You are probably aware of the stipulations of the last will and testament left by my dear father?'

She didn't answer his assumption, allowing him to continue.

'You see, I find myself in a similar legal situation to my dear brother. One that also requires the immediate acquisition of a bride.'

Priya felt the shock of his words hit her in the chest. Had she heard him correctly? Was this why Xander had been so adamant on rushing their wedding?

'Are you suggesting that I fill that position?' she asked.

'Suggesting…advising…' He made a rough gesture with his hands, his posture relaxed. 'Marriage to me would be infinitely more entertaining, don't you think?'

'Why would I marry you?' The words burst from her lips unbidden.

'It's the perfect solution. We are both equally bound by the need for a hasty wedding.'

'I can't imagine you being bound by anything.' She saw a glimmer in his gaze and immediately regretted the picture her own words evoked. Clearing her throat, she shook off the image, hardly believing she was entertaining this offer at all. 'Why on earth would I trust you?'

'Because a man in my position can provide the financial backing and influence you need to force your uncle to do exactly as you ask. I can clear his debts and relieve him of his shares in the process while also ensuring the information is kept confidential. I have powerful lawyers in my employ who would be at your disposal. After one year, once we have both achieved our separate goals, we would part ways.'

'You honestly think it's that simple?' she asked, wondering why she was even listening to another offer from a man who'd already proved himself to be untrustworthy.

'Anyone in your situation would jump at the chance.'

'You admitted to seeking revenge on my fiancé today, hardly a great basis for a new partnership of any kind.'

He took a step closer, not quite crowding her but still setting her nerves further on edge. 'My paragon of a brother is no longer your fiancé.' His voice was a low purr. 'I'll admit that I am largely motivated by revenge on your former groom. I have made no secret that I pride myself on winning, Priya.'

'I am not a competition to be won,' she snapped, awed by his sheer audacity.

He had been raised to believe he was a god, no doubt, and so was utterly unable to perceive the idea that a mere female like her might not want him. 'I know my worth. I know that by marrying me you would have access to my fortune to do with as you wish and, quite frankly, from what I know of you… I cannot take that risk.'

'I have no need for your money or your father's firm and its history of dwindling assets. Accept my terms and I will have a prenuptial agreement drawn up tonight and signed by morning. It would be a private agreement. No theatrics, no publicity of any kind.'

'A prenuptial…' She frowned, her thoughts becoming scattered as she fought to process the possibility in his words. 'This is insane.'

'You say you know your worth, well, there we are well

matched. I am willing to offer you a short-term, equal partnership whereby you can turn the tables on your uncle and
take control of your fortune yourself. Alone.'

Priya froze, hardly believing what he was saying. She'd
always planned to take it slowly and earn her place at Davidson Khan. Was she ready for that kind of power? She'd
only graduated with her master's degree four years ago but
her reputation as a talented mind in the financial world was
already well known from her time working for major firms
in London and Dubai.

'Marriage to me would be a business contract, Priya. I
have no need for a society bride and I suspect you would
not enjoy the public scrutiny of jilting one groom for another while you attempt to take the helm of Davidson Khan.
There would be a gag order in place to protect both of our
interests, but I would need to take measures one step further. If you agree to become my bride, we leave New York
and you can't return or have any contact with the outside
world until I allow it.'

Priya blinked, her brain struggling to process all the
information. 'Are you actually proposing to lock me away
until you decide when I will be released? Like I'm some
kind of prisoner?'

'It would only be for a few weeks at most, but there
would be no actual chains involved…unless you're into
that kind of thing?' He raised a brow in her direction, his
lips quirking.

'Be serious.' She straightened her shoulders, ignoring
the image his words conjured up. 'What exactly would I
be expected to do for that length of time? Where would
you take me?'

'That I can't reveal either. Not until you've signed a
prenup.'

'You expect me to blindly agree to your outrageous terms and yet you don't trust me with your own plans?'

'I have never offered you my trust, Priya. Neither do I expect any from you. It's human nature for people to hold their own best interests at heart.'

'That almost passed for philosophical.'

'I'm full of surprises.' He smirked, extending his hand to her. 'So, do you agree to my terms?'

She hesitated for a long moment, mulling over his words. Could she really allow herself to be whisked away to some unknown location, like a stolen prize? She thought of her uncle's face and the rage he'd no doubt flown into once he'd realised she was running from the wedding. If she didn't stop him, he'd destroy everything her father had worked so hard for. He would destroy the legacy that was always meant to be hers.

Suddenly, a dangerous thought occurred to her.

She didn't have to trust Eros Theodorou to accept his offer. She could use him, just as she'd been used so many times in the past. She could accept his offer and use his wealth and power as a stepping stone. Even his ridiculous terms could serve as a valuable period to feign her own defeat while she regrouped and formulated her plans. She didn't need to know where he was taking her, only that it was far away from Manhattan. Then, once the time was right, she would return and lay claim to everything that was rightfully hers.

'Okay, I'll do it. I'll marry you.' She heard the words escape her lips on a breath while her heart pounded. 'What happens next?'

Eros's expression was filled with a dark glimmer of triumph as his gaze lowered to take in the glittering diamond she still wore on her left hand. 'You can start by taking his ring off.'

She looked down, flexing her fingers in the low light. She'd almost forgotten about the delicate princess-cut diamond that had been delivered to her home days before the wedding along with a bouquet of beautiful yellow roses. There had been no note, nothing to make it seem more than the simple business arrangement she'd agreed to. But the idea of wearing Xander's ring had filled her with such anxiety she'd left it in the box, only sliding it onto her finger for the handful of public appearances they'd made in the week before. Being seen with her on his arm had been very important to her former groom.

'I'd planned on returning it.' Priya toyed with the platinum band, not quite liking the tone in Eros's voice, or the idea of being commanded to remove the ring as though it were a symbol of ownership. She was not passing from one man's hands to the next. She was a smart businesswoman with autonomy who had decided to swap a poor deal for one with less risk.

The thought that perhaps her formerly intended groom may not have known the extent of Uncle Vikram's duplicity made her pause. But the damage had already been done. She twirled the ring around and around, feeling the guilt she'd been suppressing finally rise to greet her. 'I feel like perhaps he is owed an explanation.'

'Give me your hand.' His voice was like a sharp whip in the silence, snapping her focus back to him. His features hard and unyielding, he stepped forward and extended his hand to her. She surprised herself by following his order, placing her left hand in his before she had the good sense to question herself. With surprising softness, he opened her palm out slowly and slid the ring from her third finger with one smooth movement. The sensation made her shiver involuntarily...or was it the intensity in his eyes as he pocketed the small piece of metal and rubbed once over the bare skin left behind?

A long silence spread out between them and Priya found herself completely unable to look up, needing a moment to gather her thoughts without the intensity she knew she would find in his gaze. He seemed to do everything with such purpose, such bold confidence, she couldn't help but feel a bit steamrollered with every new interaction. And yet he gave her the space to make her choice with almost infuriating consistency. She might tell herself she'd been backed into a corner but the reality was it had been she who had done it. If anything, he'd offered her a way to get out with her dignity intact.

The memory of running from the crowd of onlookers in her giant gown was still fresh. As was every moment leading up to her scandalous exit. Feeling all those eyes upon her, judging her...

A stern voice jolted her from her thoughts. 'Look at me.'

She looked up and was met with barely restrained fury blazing behind the blue depths of his gaze.

'You owe him nothing, *me akous*.' His voice seemed to deepen, slipping into what she presumed to be his native Greek. He shook his head once, catching himself. 'Do you understand me, Priya?'

She hesitated, chewing on her lower lip as she fought against the urge to simply agree. He was effortlessly authoritative with his impressive height and stern brooding glare. But she had never been the kind of woman to sit back and submit to anyone's orders, especially not those of a man she had only just met.

Shaking off the spell he seemed to have put her under, she moved away from him, seeking the airy freedom of the balcony as she tried to conceal the tremor of anxiety that threatened to overtake her composure.

* * *

Eros fought not to smile as Priya silently seethed with rage in the wake of his commands. He knew he had been pushing too far by issuing an outright order but hearing her talk of owing Xander anything had lit a fire of anger within him. His brother was a calculating bastard, and he had no doubt the other man knew exactly what he'd been doing when he'd accepted the deal with his fiancée's uncle without her explicit consent.

'Why do I get the impression that you are far more trouble than I anticipated?' he mused.

'Because I prefer to know my own mind rather than nod and go along with every testosterone-charged request you make of me?' she responded. 'If I had known that by accepting your help I was entering into some kind of tug of war between you and—'

'You know nothing about the situation.'

'Seeing as I've just agreed to marry you, perhaps you could enlighten me?'

Eros felt familiar anger seethe and roil just beneath the surface of his control. He had long ago learned that anger was just as vulnerable to manipulation as love or trust. Anger was far more unpredictable and far more easily incited. He looked down at the woman before him, this beautiful lamb who had unknowingly stepped into the middle of a battlefield. She may be innocent in all of this, but that did not make her his ally.

Less than a few hours ago she had been set to become the bride of his enemy. He had seen the play of emotions over her face, the guilt, the care. She had no idea of the truth of the man she'd been about to wed. She had no idea the truth behind their family name, the lies and the greed.

The legacy of Zeus was so potent he had ensured he caused chaos even after his death. Of the three sons he'd sired, Xander Mytikas was the most like their father. Cruel, calculating and obsessed with his precious image.

'I wasn't prepared to sacrifice my humanity in the quest for my father's approval. Let's just say that my brother made a very different choice. He chose the prospect of power over the chance to do the right thing. Just as he planned to do with you.'

Fury pulsed within him, pushing against his control. Tightening his fists, he forced a smile to his lips and sighed with practised nonchalance, forcing himself to look away from the beguiling effect of the sunshine reflecting in the deep amber of her eyes.

'Marriage may be a binding legal agreement, but there is nothing in the vows to influence morality.'

'Is that your way of telling me not to trust you either, Eros?'

Hearing his name on her lips for the first time distracted him momentarily and he found himself looking back once more, getting drawn into the steady, serious force of her gaze. She didn't look away, remaining utterly still as she assessed him. When had a woman ever looked at him this way? As though she was trying to unravel the outer shell he presented to the world in order to see beneath. For a man who prided himself on using his charm to control every interaction, it was…uncomfortable.

'Blind, open trust is a myth. Without incentive or consecquences, people will always act in their own best interests. I plan to apply both to our situation effectively.'

'You're talking about a prenup?'

He nodded once. 'I have spent a decade building my own empire on my own terms, free from the corruption and sacrifice required under the rotting logo of Mytikas Holdings. I may be many terrible, scandalous things…but in business I protect my own. Once we're married, like it or not, you fall under that term.'

'So, as your wife, I'd be on par with your employees? I'm honoured.'

'It's a hazardous position.' He leaned against the stone balustrade. 'Many women have tried and failed to get my ring on their finger. The backlash may become dangerous.'

His words carned the tiniest flicker of humour on her full lips, and he forced himself to look away. 'I received word that your friend has been causing quite a stir, attempting to hunt you down.'

She stood up straight. 'Aria? I should speak with her.'

Eros met her eyes with silent warning. 'You remember our bargain? No one can know about our deal until I choose it.'

She folded her arms across her chest and her eyes darkened with anger but she managed to keep the same coolness to her voice. 'You can't plan to lock me away immediately? I have things I need to get from my apartment, my clothes and my planner. I have a life too, Eros. I need to tell my friend that I'm okay.'

Eros considered her words for a moment, then slid his phone from his pocket and placed it in her palm. 'You have three minutes.'

After instructing her to keep the call on loudspeaker, Eros kept his eyes on Priya as she paced the foyer with her back turned to him.

The call was answered after barely one ring and a woman's voice filled the room. Priya winced as her friend immediately began berating her for disappearing.

'Relax. I'm fine, I'm safe.' She took a quick look over her shoulder. 'I found another way to solve my problem but I need to leave town for a few weeks.'

'Another way? Another groom, you mean?' the woman asked. 'Where are you going? Where is he taking you?'

Priya's voice flattened. 'Look, it's complicated and I can't go into it for legal reasons…but Vikram lied. This is the only way I can still save the company.'

Her friend was quiet for a long moment and he noticed Priya looked down at the screen to make sure the call hadn't been disconnected. 'You still there?'

Her friend's voice was filled with emotion. 'I don't like this. I don't like any of it.'

'I don't like it either, but it's what I need to do.'

Eros felt something dark rise within him at her words. He tapped the dial of his watch with pointed impatience, seeing her eyes narrow in response. She spoke quickly into the phone. 'Look, it will all be fine. I'll explain everything once I'm back.'

The other woman's voice lowered slightly. 'If you can't talk, just say yes or no. I heard Xander send guards in pursuit of his brother…there was this really intense, dark-haired man with a European accent. Italian, I think. Are you with him?'

Eros moved quickly, capturing Priya's hands and ending the call with one touch to the screen.

'That was rude.' She levelled an angry gaze at him, dark brown eyes filled with fury, and tried to pull her hands free from his grip.

'You were going to answer her question.'

'I don't break my word,' she gritted. 'But who was she talking about? Who did Xander see if it wasn't you?'

Eros thought for a moment, a wry smile pricking at one corner of his lips. 'I suspect that perhaps I am not the only of Zeus's bastard sons who came to break up your wedding. A fact that may work in my favour.'

'There are more of you?' Priya's eyes widened.

'It's not our concern. From now on, you will have no contact with your friend or anyone else until I allow it. This may not be a traditional marriage but I do not tolerate disloyalty in any form.' He looked down at his phone screen, seeing messages that had come in from the team of lawyers he'd kept on standby for the night. He had many things that needed to be done if he was going to pull this off. Many separate pieces to juggle before he staged his quiet retreat to Greece.

His retreat…with his stolen bride.

His eyes seemed to gravitate to the smooth skin of her long legs of their own accord, drinking in the beauty of her shape before finally reaching her face. She was the picture of quiet fury and he could understand why.

A woman of her intelligence and accomplishments being bound by such an archaic inheritance clause was akin to caging a wild tiger and expecting it to play the docile house pet. Her uncle deserved to lose everything and he would take pleasure in meting out the first step of that punishment.

He was slightly uneasy about the seeming calm she'd shown since accepting his offer. He wasn't as vain as to think she would be jumping for joy but he'd at least expected a little resistance.

Realising he was late to the emergency meeting he'd called with his legal team, he pulled on the leather jacket he'd slung over a nearby chair and took a moment to slick back his still-damp hair in the mirror. In the reflection, he saw Priya watching him.

'You're leaving?' She spoke with feigned nonchalance but he saw the small furrow that appeared between her brows. 'You expect me to just wait around this apartment alone until the ceremony?'

'I will need to move fast if we hope to be married by tomorrow night.' He pressed the button for the ground floor, using fingerprint technology, and leaned against the open doorway of the elevator.

'Tomorrow night?' He heard the shock in her voice. 'How is that even possible?'

'I make it my business to achieve the impossible. In this instance, however, it's nothing so miraculous, just a simple waiver and the right connections.' He took in the tightness of her features and almost laughed. Most of his past entanglements would have been overjoyed at the prospect of nabbing him as a husband but this woman looked like she might bolt at any moment.

'This building is security-protected. I will know if you attempt to break our terms and I do not appreciate being double-crossed.'

'I'm the one who usually gets taken for a fool so I could say the same to you.'

He chuckled to himself, taking a step back and pushing the button for the ground floor. 'I will have your things collected and couriered here. In the meantime, princess, get some rest.'

CHAPTER FOUR

WHEN PRIYA STEPPED out of the shower the next morning, she found her luggage had been delivered and placed just inside her bedroom door. Still dressed only in her towel, she dug out her trusty planner and sat down to write a quick entry, crossing off the date before marked 'Wedding' and adding a new one. She knew it was strange, how she needed something as silly as a planner, but it worked. She had long ago learned to embrace anything that quietened the hum of her own mind.

Her father had always called her a worrier, while her mother had proclaimed her only child to be self-centred and highly strung. She now knew that anxiety was simply something she managed. But the night before, in the darkness of Eros's guest bedroom, without a cell phone or laptop to busy herself with, she had been forced to endure the hum of her own mind and its attempts to grasp the unexpected turn her life had taken.

As a result, her eyes now burned from the scant few hours she'd managed to sleep and her shoulders were so tense they ached. But she was fine, she told herself sternly as she focused on dressing in her favourite skinny jeans and a soft woollen sweater. The apartment was silent as she padded barefoot out of her room in search of food. She hadn't eaten a thing since lunch the day before and now her body was in full rebellion. Feeling a little shaky, she opened the fridge and grabbed the first thing she saw, a large platter of perfectly sliced cantaloupe. Without a second thought, she bit into the first piece and groaned with relief as the sweetness hit her tongue.

The sudden clearing of a throat directly behind her almost made her choke. She turned, expecting to see a particularly irritating Greek smirk, but instead was greeted by the sight of a tall grey-haired man, flanked by a younger man and woman who calmly revealed that they were there to finalise the prenuptial agreement.

The prospect of doing anything remotely resembling work made her synapses light up with glee and she spent the next hour reading the agreement and questioning and ensuring there were no loopholes in it. Once Eros had discreetly paid her uncle's debts and purchased the majority shares, he would be legally obliged to transfer them directly into Priya's name. As they finished the process, a phone call was made and the grey-haired man began speaking in what sounded like rapid Greek. After a moment he extended the phone towards her. 'He would like to speak to you.'

Priya stood, moving quickly out onto the balcony for privacy.

'Everything is to your satisfaction?' a familiar accented voice rumbled on the other end of the line.

'I've agreed to all of your terms, and I'm officially bound by the law not to reveal your evil plans.' She shivered in the cool air, wrapping her arm around herself. 'The lawyers mentioned that I will need my passport. I'd like to know where I'm being taken once we are married.'

'Patience, Priya.' His voice was playful but underlined with steel. 'I've left a gift for you in the foyer. I'll see you at six.'

The line went dead and Priya fought the urge to curse aloud in the most unladylike fashion. She was irritated by his obvious mistrust, but reminded herself that he had warned her that she would be kept in the dark. It was fine, she told herself as she escorted the lawyers to the elevator, smiling tightly until she was once again left alone. There was no reason to worry.

She hadn't even officially begun working at Davidson Khan, yet they had an excellent structural team already in place. Once the shares had been transferred, there was no reason the company wouldn't just continue to run as normal.

It would be just like taking a vacation. She closed her eyes and stretched the tense muscles in her shoulders. Of course, she hated vacations, but she would deal with the boredom by planning her strategy for stepping into her new role. Judging by the amount of time her new fiancé had chosen to spend with her so far, she would most likely be left to her own devices, which suited her just fine.

Her thoughts consumed by the future, she almost missed the large parcel that had been left on the side table. The packaging was expensive and marked with the name of one of her favourite Fifth Avenue boutiques. A sleek black card bearing a golden archer logo lay on top:

Don't rip this one.
E

She frowned as she took the box into the bedroom and opened it up, pulling away layers of tissue paper. Inside she found a pair of butter-soft ivory silk tailored trousers and a matching fitted blazer. The sizing was perfect and she wondered if he had guessed just by looking at her or if he'd had someone go digging for that information. Pushing that uncomfortable thought away, she looked through the rest of the packages and found a detailed ivory corset and matching thong.

Of course he would buy her lingerie. Still, the corset was clearly designed to show at the apex of the blazer to soften the look. It was a pity she couldn't wear it. Wearing this suit would be a show of submission and the balance of control was already sliding uncomfortably beyond her reach.

More than likely he hadn't even chosen it himself, she told herself as she undressed and quickly showered, deliberately leaving the package out of her eyeline. She didn't really have anything appropriate of her own, other than one of her plain black work suits, but maybe keeping this professional was a good course of action. Yes, that was a good plan.

Throughout her short, sparse dating history she had been given compliments on her dark eyes and curvaceous body, but she had never been called a great beauty. Her Indian heritage and serious expression had always made her easily recognisable next to the rows of smiling blonde heiresses at society balls and she'd got some attention, but she'd never cared much about what she wore or how she looked.

Eros had openly assessed her attributes and what she had seen in his gaze led her to believe that he found her physically appealing but he had not objectified her in the way she would have expected from a man with his reputation.

She may or may not have lain awake until dawn, agonising over her decision and searching her mind for information on the man she'd just agreed to marry. Would she be foolish for believing the media narrative without asking the man himself? Even as the thought entered her head she brushed it away. One could not possibly fabricate a reputation of wild nights out and strings of affairs with beautiful women.

As her father had often told her, if it walked and talked

like a duck, it was a duck. As uncomfortable as it made her feel to tie her name to a man like him, the worst thing she could possibly do was start imagining that perhaps he wasn't what he said he was.

She took some time fixing her hair into a sleek chignon at the base of her head, finishing it off with a delicate gold slide that was encrusted in tiny pearls and diamonds. The piece had belonged to her great-grandmother and had been brought to the United States from Mumbai almost eighty years previously. She still remembered the look of pride in her father's eyes when he had presented it to her at her first debutante ball.

It had been traditionally worn by brides in their family and although the wealthy Khan family had since joined their name with the elite Davidsons and become steadily less bound by the traditions of their ancestors as each generation passed, this one had somehow stuck. After her first disaster of an engagement she had put the piece away, never believing she would wear it again. She still didn't know quite how she had allowed herself to be pushed into such an agreement. But sometimes that was how it worked, wasn't it? You believed that you were still in control but the control had been taken from you so slowly you didn't notice until it was too late.

Eros had casually mentioned her first attempt at matrimony, not knowing how powerful a weapon he had wielded. That dark moment in her history had shaped everything that she was and had been the catalyst for her walk away from the sizeable inheritance that had been hers. It had forced her to discover who she was without her father's wealth and had made her the woman she was now.

The decision to step back into this world and manipulate the stipulations in her father's will had not been taken lightly. She had thought she'd found the best solution to save her father's legacy and keep her fortune out of her mother's and her uncle's hands. Eros had been an unwitting angel in disguise, really. Even though she was not maintaining full control of her fortune, she knew that she would never allow herself to be controlled or manipulated in that way again.

She had just finished applying some basic make-up when the intercom buzzed, heralding the arrival of a driver to take her to the ceremony. Evidently, Eros was not planning to see her until they were face to face at whatever altar or judge's desk he had commandeered this late on a Monday evening.

Her plain black trousers and blazer lay flat on her bed, ready for her to make a statement of her own, but she couldn't stop her eyes from gravitating once again towards the garment box she'd pushed to the side.

What exactly would a secret wedding to Greece's most scandalous playboy entail? Perhaps a show of faith and compliance might suit her better than such an early rebellion. She needed to keep him on her side if he was to rescue her company from ruin after all. Before she could rethink it, she grabbed the box and pulled out its lavish contents once more.

The silk slid over her fingers as she quickly dressed and stepped in front of the floor-length mirror in the corner of the room. For several minutes the only sound was her own shallow breathing as she stared at her reflection.

She looked at herself from all angles, awed at how the lines transformed her into something very soft and feminine while still maintaining its power-suit appeal. She almost wished she had hated it, just so she didn't give him the satisfaction of admitting how perfect his selection had been.

The intercom buzzed once more, jolting her from the

moment and forcing her into action. Her stomach flipped over as she took a deep breath and stepped into the elevator. There was no turning back now.

Eros told himself that having the quick ceremony at sunset in Central Park was functional and easier to contain on short notice than booking a venue or walking into City Hall. The semi-darkness and leafy foliage provided cover, as did the handful of guards he had ordered to block off the pathway to the pavilion and the judge who had agreed to marry them under special licence.

The delicate light green and grey iron structure known as the Ladies Pavilion sat nestled in between the trees and the rocky descent to the water, providing a spectacular view of the lake and the skyline beyond. This wedding may be a business deal but she had already run from two grooms, and he had no interest in becoming the third. So he had taken a calculated risk, sending her the ivory suit as a gift and allowing her the freedom of walking herself down the aisle. Or rather the dirt path, in this case.

He frowned down at the muddy edges of the path and hoped that she didn't have an aversion to nature. He had chosen neutral ground, an open space where they were not trapped, and this place had been the first one to come to mind.

As he looked out at the sun over the skyline reflected in the still surface of the lake, he listened to the sound of the city just beyond the trees. There was nothing peaceful about Manhattan, but this small corner of the park was probably the closest to solitude that one could get.

There had once been a time when this city had been his playground, with his older brother at his side and the world at their feet.

But there was no risk of his older brother coming to play

his best man. Not now when Eros had stolen Xander's perfect bride for his own.

'Your paperwork is in order and we are ready to go. Are you sure she is on her way?' the elderly judge asked. Her husband had accompanied her, standing silently in the background, prepared to act as witness.

'She'll be here.' He gave her his most charismatic smile, trying not to look back towards the lamp-lit path. He was not worried about Priya running from *this* wedding, he reminded himself. He had made sure that she had nothing to run from, but he had also made it impossible for her to disappear without his knowledge. He had assigned a skilled bodyguard to escort her for her own safety as well as his. If she had decided to go back on their deal, he would know.

His temples throbbed from a night of little sleep. Along with the task of keeping tabs on both of his brothers, his company, Arcum Investments, had just leased brand-new premises in New York and with an impromptu honeymoon planned, he had many loose ends to tie up before he disappeared with Priya. He had also had his team put on the case of acquiring Davidson Khan and clearing its CEO of his rather sizeable debts. Just like with every other investment they undertook, Arcum would need to make sure all the paperwork was airtight before they made their final move.

Just as he began to feel tension build within him, the judge gasped softly beside him. Eros turned to follow her gaze and saw an ethereal vision in white appear at the end of the lamp-lit path.

She was all long legs and high heels, gliding towards him with her piercing dark gaze and full pursed lips. Yesterday, when she had stepped out of the elevator in her haute couture wedding gown, he had been struck by the sadness in her expression in the moments before she'd seen him and put her shields up. She'd seemed smaller, somehow. Like the force within her had been quietened. She had been obviously out of her comfort zone in the wedding gown and now he could see the difference with his own eyes.

In this bridal outfit, she didn't just walk, she strutted. She stood tall, the ivory silk seeming to hug every curve and dip of her body as she walked towards him. The pearls and beading on the undergarment that covered her chest seemed to glitter like diamonds as she passed under the golden glow of the lamps.

He saw the briefest bit of confusion and surprise on her face as she took in the setting he'd chosen but she shut it down quickly, adopting a serene expression as she navigated the steps in her heels. Bright red heels that seemed to be a perfect match for the intricate little ornament she wore in her hair.

He didn't know why but it gave him a small flare of pleasure that she had dressed for the occasion even though they both knew that this was not a true wedding. He allowed himself the briefest moment to take her in, noting her face was free of the elaborate make-up that had adorned her the day before, and her hair was a simple sleek style. He got the feeling that this was her true preference…simplicity.

Was it possible that she truly did not care about the wealth she had inherited?

Perhaps they were not so different after all. She intrigued him with her unreadable expression and fierce passion for what she cared for. Perhaps this short time they would be forced to stay together would not be quite unbearable.

The judge quickly moved forward to greet her, shaking her hand and guiding her towards the spot where Eros stood still and watching.

'You're late,' he heard himself say.

'It's customary for the bride to make her groom wait.'

A small smile graced her lips but he saw the subtle flare of irritation in her eyes.

Eros smiled and felt himself relax for the first time in hours as they both turned and listened to the words that the judge began to say, reaffirming their prenuptial agreement.

Their vows were short and to the point, but still contained the usual promises to love and honour. When the moment finally came to slide the ring onto his bride's finger, he was surprised to feel his throat contract around the words, stopping him.

He had sworn he would never do this. That he would never make these kinds of impossible promises to another human being. Promises of the loving kind were just asking for disappointment and heartbreak. He'd had enough of both to last him a lifetime. Inhaling a deep breath, he forced himself to refocus and concentrate on the goal at hand. To remind himself that there were no hearts on the table and therefore no risk in that regard.

He took the smaller of the two gold bands and slowly slid the ring onto Priya's finger. Despite the placid, disinterested expression on her face, he felt her fingers tremble beneath his own. When it was her turn to place the larger ring on his finger, claiming him as her husband and vowing to honour him, he found he was unable to look away.

The rest of the ceremony passed in a haze of signatures as the judge ensured everything was above board. Priya kept her gaze downward but swore she could feel Eros watching her. He could have chosen anywhere for this part of their arrangement. They could have worn sweatpants to City Hall and it wouldn't have made a difference. Unless... A thought occurred to her just as a gentle flash illuminated them in the cocoon of lamplight they'd been under.

Priya looked behind them and, sure enough, a single

photographer stood at the steps of the pavilion. Her eyes flew to Eros, but his expression was unreadable. The guards did not move to stop the photographer, which meant…he had been invited.

He had said they needed to make this look real in order for it to be accepted as a true marriage. But every second of the ceremony made something within her ache.

The judge had been speaking, she realised with a jolt, pulling her attention back to the very real moment she was living.

'I now pronounce you husband and wife,' the older woman declared, a wide smile lighting up her face as she took a step back. 'You may now kiss the bride.'

Priya felt every muscle in her body tighten in response to such a simple, common sentence. She was wearing white, he had put a ring on her finger. A kiss was the natural next step. And yet their agreement had seemed so theoretical until now. Suddenly everything seemed very, very real.

'We don't need to,' she said quickly, already feeling far too warm from the heat of the strong hands that still held hers. 'I mean…it's not necessary.'

The judge frowned and Priya immediately cursed herself for her own sharp tongue.

'She is nervous,' Eros purred in that low tone she'd now come to recognise as one of intense enjoyment of her discomfort. 'I'd love nothing more right now than to kiss my beautiful bride.'

Priya forced a serene smile on her face as she took one bold step forward. She was not a coward. One meaningless kiss would not jeopardise their arrangement. She told herself that she was still in control…until Eros took a step forward to seal the space between them. She felt the air whoosh from her lungs as one powerful arm wrapped around her waist, holding her much too close. Not close enough, that dark voice within her protested. Inhaling on a gasp, she forced herself to look up, to meet the heat of his gaze as he dipped his head towards hers in what felt like slow motion.

At the same moment his lips touched hers, his other hand reached up to cup the side of her neck with a firm sensuality that felt far too heated for a judge's gaze. His skin seemed to set her aflame with that touch, holding her in place as he gently increased the pressure of his mouth on hers. Even without words, she felt like he was goading her, trying to get a reaction. She tried to remain dispassionate, telling herself that she wouldn't give in to such a blatant challenge. But her body didn't seem to get the memo in that regard.

He was simply proving his point about attraction, she told herself. But, still, her body was crying out to deepen the kiss… She tightened her hands into fists to resist the insane urge to wind her fingers into his hair.

He was the enemy, she reminded herself. He had taken charge of her destiny and intertwined it with his own.

The tiniest touch of his tongue against her lips made her body shiver, involuntarily pressing against him. The strong heat of his hand flexed hard on her hip and the delicious pressure sent pulses of electricity down every nerve ending. Suddenly she could no longer resist. She opened to him, all rational thought leaving her as she gloried in the scent of him, the heat of their kiss. She slid her own tongue against his and thought she heard a low growl coming from deep in his throat.

A faint cough came from nearby, along with the sound of the judge's amused chuckle, and just like that, it was as if a spell had been broken. Priya froze, realising how completely she had been swept away. Eros immediately released her from the shockingly sensual clinch they'd fallen

into. She could still feel the heat of his hand on her neck…
on her hip…

Had she *moaned*?

'Now I see why you were in such a rush to wed.' The
judge smiled and shook their hands, walking them to the
edge of the pavilion before wishing them a long and pros-
perous future together.

Priya's heart hammered in her chest as she studiously
avoided looking at the man by her side while she tried to
get a firm handle on her runaway libido.

That had not been how this was supposed to go.

She'd spent the past seven years of her life completely
unaffected by the handsome, powerful men she'd encountered daily. They'd barely been married two minutes and
she was already letting down her boundaries? What on
earth had got into her? Like a wild dream, the past couple of minutes replayed in her mind and she fought not to
turn away and hide her discomfort at her own loss of control. Instead, she met his gaze head on. Daring him to say
something. To her surprise, his face was utterly devoid of
expression.

They walked in silence through the park, flanked by a
trio of discreet bodyguards to where a limo waited for them.

'Are the guards really necessary?' she asked, needing to
redirect the subject as he slid into the dark interior of the
car beside her, bringing with him the subtle scent of spice
and sandalwood.

'In marrying me, my enemies are now yours.' He closed
the door with a sharp thud, turning to face her. 'Let's just
say that you are a very valuable investment.'

'And the photographs? Are they for my protection too?'
She tried to remain calm but her heart still skittered uncomfortably in her chest from his kisses and she felt totally
off balance. She hated feeling off balance. 'Eros, you might

not care for your reputation but if I am going to be taking the helm of Davidson Khan I need to care about mine.'

'The photographs are to assure the legitimacy of our marriage can't be contested. They will not appear in the media. I told you, this arrangement remains between us until I choose to reveal it.'

'In going into hiding, do we not appear weak?'

'Patience, Priya. There is a difference between hiding in fear and controlling the narrative as one prepares for a full-scale attack.'

She thought on his words for a moment, then realisation dawned. 'You plan to make a play for control of Mytikas? But…how?'

'What better way to destroy a kingdom than from the throne itself?' He sat back lazily in the seat, watching her from beneath hooded lids. 'Don't worry, I don't plan to change the terms of our agreement. You will not be required to play the role of my wife in public over the next year. Unlike your former fiancé, I have no need to foster a good reputation.'

She exhaled a hard breath, still not able to shake the knots in her stomach. The lights of Manhattan passed by in a blur and she realised that they were not going back in the direction of the apartment but moving out of the city entirely.

'Are you going to tell me where we're going?' She sighed.

'We leave New York tonight,' he said simply.

His silence following the declaration was a reminder of their bargain. No details until they had arrived at their destination. Until she was locked away.

CHAPTER FIVE

THE MIDNIGHT COMMERCIAL flight to Athens provided Priya with a brief reprieve as Eros busied himself with a series of video conference calls and stacks of paperwork emblazoned with that same golden bow and arrow symbol, which she now knew was his company logo. She knew very little about Arcum Investments other than that they were a quiet and predatory investment firm that had swept the European markets over the past decade, but she'd heard tales of their exponential growth and daring risks.

Fitting, she'd thought to herself. Considering she felt like she had been targeted by a hunter. The realisation that she had been cornered so well still stung, but there was no going back now, she thought with ferocity.

The next few weeks would give her the time she needed to regroup and formulate her plans to take her place at the helm of the company she had been born to run. After that, she could simply pretend that this marriage had never happened until their divorce was finalised. They'd agreed to a date, one year in the future. One year and she could forget Eros Theodorou and forget that kiss.

Three engagements, one wedding and still her love life was non-existent. Considering her reaction to a simple kiss, she should have tried harder not to neglect her own needs. She wasn't even sure if she had any, considering the amount of contact she'd had with the opposite sex in the past seven years.

Since her embarrassing public failure of a wedding to her high school sweetheart, Eric, she'd avoided all men, which had been easy. Even when she'd realised she was obligated to feign a loving marriage with her former groom, she'd felt nothing. Not even an ember of desire.

One look at Eros Theodorou and it was as though her poor neglected libido had staged an outright protest. The moment his lips had touched hers tonight she had lost all coherent thought other than *yes* and *more*.

Irritation flared as she realised she had unconsciously raised her fingers to trace her lower lip as her thoughts whirled. She swore they were still hot and swollen from his skilful ministrations. A shiver ran down her spine and she forced herself to keep her gaze focused on the book she had bought while slowly ambling through the airport stores to avoid her groom.

He may have elicited a response in her, but she knew better than anyone that sexual attraction was easily stirred and discarded.

She would not become one of the notches on his bedpost. He was exactly the kind of man she'd spent her entire life avoiding and now she wore his ring on her finger. Closing her eyes, she tried to focus on the vibrations of the plane around her and not the deep baritone of Eros's voice as he spoke in rapid Greek a foot away from her. She found her eyes drawn to his side of the aisle far too often.

She'd noticed that he was left-handed, and that he kept a small pad of paper just out of sight where she was pretty sure he was doodling. Did billionaire playboys doodle? The thought had made her thoughts wander even more. She'd regain focus on the page once more, only to be distracted again by a loud outburst from his side of the aisle.

The man was a force of energy as he worked, constantly moving even while seated.

From the one call he'd taken in English, she'd heard mention of his shares in Mytikas Holdings and a meeting planned, but then he had noticed her attention and moved to the other end of the aircraft. On the next call he'd switched into rapid Greek, but she was sure she'd heard his brother's name mentioned more than once. He used his hands far too much as he spoke, spreading them wide and making gestures that were so thoroughly Mediterranean... Catching her thoughts, she turned away, irritated with herself. He was just a man. A very tall, golden and perfectly structured man but...a mere mortal nonetheless.

Whatever strange stirrings of attraction he'd unlocked within her would have to go unanswered.

She'd managed to drift off into a dreamless sleep at some point, her glasses still on and her book still open on her lap. When she awoke, the cabin was in darkness and someone had reclined her seat and tucked a blanket around her. Her book had been placed on the side table, glasses neatly propped on top.

She looked immediately to her left and found Eros in the same position, his face completely relaxed in sleep.

Somehow she'd slept for almost five hours, almost half the flight time, and the pilot was readying for their descent into Athens. The view from her window showed the late evening sun inching across the ocean below towards the ancient capital city.

When they finally landed and she looked to her side it was to see Eros alert and serious, looking like he'd just stepped off the runway. His blond hair was once again neatly tied back and he had barely a wrinkle in his designer shirt. Meanwhile, she was pretty sure she had mascara clogged under her eyes and the comfortable shift dress and leggings she'd donned for travel were more than a little the worse for wear.

They exited the aircraft first and were met on the tarmac by their own private car. The only time Eros spoke was to explain that he was taking her to his own remote private island and that the only way to get there was via seaplane as the winds were far too treacherous for helicopters. He seemed distracted and suddenly lacking the charming vibrant energy she'd come to expect from him. When they finally arrived at the docks and he stepped onto a small white plane alone, however, she froze.

'Where is the pilot?'

'You're looking at him.' He placed one hand on his hip, his expression hidden behind a pair of mirrored aviator sunglasses. 'Is there a problem?'

'I assume you have a licence?'

'Of course.' He reached into the plane and pulled out a black folder, opening it to reveal some official papers. 'Ten years of experience enough for you?'

She watched as he placed their luggage in the back of the plane himself, noticing that for the first time there were no assistants or staff in sight. A strange sense of foreboding sizzled within her, but she brushed it off.

Her body remained clenched tight with anxiety as Eros guided the plane into a swift ascent and they moved out smoothly over the Aegean Sea. Strong hands gripped the controls and his eyes remained trained ahead, unerringly confident and at ease as he guided them higher above the waves and scattered islands below.

She quickly forgot her nerves and lost herself in the beauty of the view all around them. He pointed to a few larger islands, giving her an idea of where they were, until eventually he announced their descent. Priya felt her eyes widen as she took in a small island ahead that was vaguely in the shape of a heart. Or possibly a butterfly. She squinted as they dropped down and began to coast on the water, feeling the pull and shift of the seaplane as Eros guided it to a stop at the long marina that jutted out at an angle from a pebbled beach.

Ahead, the land seemed to climb upward to a high plateau where she could vaguely see the outline of a large villa nestled in a grove of myrtle trees.

When Eros began unloading the cases from the plane, Priya frowned, covering her eyes to peer up towards the house and grounds.

'I assumed you would be the type to insist on staff at every turn.' She reached across him to grab her own bag, not wanting to saddle him with all the heavy lifting.

'You believe me to be spoiled?' He met her eyes with one brow raised.

When she simply shrugged, he let out a low chuckle and moved to settle a few last matters on the plane. She almost missed his words as he walked away, his back turned to her.

'I'm afraid we must make do. There is no staff here, *agape mou*.'

Priya froze at the endearment, then once again at the words that preceded it, wondering if perhaps she had misheard him. Surely there was staff—he was a billionaire, for goodness' sake. He had been born into the kind of luxury that most people could only dream of. A private island this size would need a staff to maintain the house and the grounds…

Surely there had to be *someone* else on this tiny island other than the two of them. He couldn't possibly mean for them to remain here alone. She watched as he closed the side door of the plane with impressive strength, his muscles flexing under the golden sun.

'The couple who usually live here and maintain the land have been given a much-deserved holiday at my request.'

'What...? Why?' She half spluttered the words.

'I told you there would be no contact with the outside world.'

Priya turned her face away from him to hide her irritation but as she did so she saw his lips twitch with amusement. Taking a deep breath, she tamped down the urge to turn around and demand to be taken back to the airport. To admit defeat in the face of his shameless attempts to set her off balance.

'If you wanted to lock me away, you could have at least had the decency to do it in a place with an internet connection.'

Eros watched the play of emotions cross over Priya's features and felt the tiniest sprinkling of guilt bubble up to the surface of his long-forgotten conscience. He hadn't thought of this isolation period as locking her away, but now that they had arrived...

He sighed, hefting his case under one arm and watching as she grabbed her own and stalked ahead of him along the whitewashed wooden marina. His reason for waiting until they were already on Greek soil before revealing the truth of their honeymoon was obvious, and judging by the look on her face as she stared out at the endless expanse of sea that surrounded them she had realised that her choices had been effectively limited.

Eros was a man used to getting exactly what he wanted and he had made sure that his bride had absolutely no chance to double-cross him. Of course, if she truly wished to walk away now, he wouldn't stop her. He would take her back to Athens himself, no questions asked. He was not her jailer. But she had agreed to stay by his side until both of their deals were complete and he would not apologise for safeguarding his own interests, considering her track record so far.

He guided her to a wide metal hatch in the rock face and entered a code on the panel by the door. The door slid upward, revealing a deceptively large hangar within that housed a second seaplane and a few smaller electronically powered vehicles.

Eros walked to his sleek white Jeep, which had the fastest land speed, and held the door open, but looked back to see Priya inspecting a small two-seater roadster.

'I have never seen this model. Is it electric?' she asked, running her hand along the hood with obvious reverence.

Eros was curious as he watched her slide her fingers along the seams in the rear of the vehicle and pop the hood to peer inside. 'It hasn't been released yet. I allowed my team to use the island for testing their prototypes. The plane too.'

'You own the brand?'

'I invested in them as a start-up. I liked the idea of cleaner travel between the islands. The land toys were a bonus.'

'They're all electric?' she asked, following the wires to the panel in the wall of rock beside them.

'The island is mostly run on solar and wind, yes.' He walked towards her, looking down at where her delicate hands stroked and prodded at the intricate inner mechanisms of the million-euro toy he'd invested in on a wild hunch. He liked cars—of course he did, he was a red-blooded male—but, unlike a lot of car fanatics he knew, he had very little interest in the actual workings of the vehicles he drove. He was far more interested in the inspiration behind the designs and shape and left the maintenance to his mechanics.

'There isn't really much room in this one for luggage.' He hovered behind her, fascinated at her obvious interest and seeming knowledge.

As though she'd realised he was staring, she straightened and took a step back, popping the hood closed. 'My papa was a classic car collector.'

'I can't imagine you getting your hands dirty,' he mused.

'My mother tried her best to make me into the stereotypical society princess. But Papa told me I could be whatever I wanted to be. I decided I wanted to be…him.' She shrugged.

'Did he put you under all that pressure, or did you do it to yourself?'

She looked up sharply at his words. 'I wanted to work alongside him and join his vision to turn our family's banking empire into a force of good rather than evil.'

Her words stunned him for a moment, a jarring echo of his own youthful self. At twenty-seven she was only seven years younger than him but she was full of positive energy. So seemingly sure of her own path. The urge to tell her about what had brought about his own exile from Zeus's empire rose in him but he pushed it away. This was not some kind of therapy circle.

She didn't need to know about the details of his own naivety, just as she didn't need to know the history that this island held for him. Named Myrtus for its wealth of lush pink Myrtle groves, it had been the only thing left of his stepfather's modest fortune when he'd passed away ten years before. Stavros Theodorou had not been a wealthy man on the scale of Zeus, but he'd done well for himself with some small investments.

When Eros had first returned to Greece, shamed and broken, Stavros had energised him with plans to develop Myrtus into something bigger and better. Community work had been a huge passion of his stepfather's. But then Arcum had come about quickly and the thoughts of revenge had consumed Eros. Every time guilt forced him to cast aside time to come and begin the project, something else had come up. There hadn't been time.

Then Stavros had died and suddenly there had been no rush any more.

As he loaded up the Jeep and they scaled the steep hill that led up to the peak of the island, he felt the history threaten to engulf him.

He had been only five years old when his stepfather had bought the deserted island as a stunning jewel to add to his wife's collection of outlandish gifts. A wife he had continuously tried to bribe with luxurious trinkets and vacations. A woman who had continued to avoid her family in favour of long work trips in faraway countries. Even when she was home, she was never truly present. When Eros had developed a severe stutter, it had been Stavros who had taken him to his various speech therapies. His mother had believed he was fabricating the condition for attention.

By the time he was ten, the only time they ever spent all together was when they were on the island, but by that point every moment had been a strain on his emotional young mind. He had felt every barbed comment and raised voice acutely, and his stutter had reappeared.

It had been here on this island that his mother had served his stepfather with divorce papers. It had been here he had first witnessed the violence that could come from two people with warring hearts. There had never been physical violence but words, in his experience, could be far more deadly. And there had never been a greater weapon in his mother's arsenal than the son Stavros had adored and loved as his own.

In the last days of their marriage, Stavros had thrown

party after party to try to lure his wife home to the Greek society she had once loved. But Arista had no interest in being Stavros Theodorou's wife any longer. She had set her sights on a prize far greater.

That final loss had been paralyzing and Eros had watched his stepfather descend into the addiction that had always been there, waiting.

Suddenly this island had become his prison. The place where they'd lived during his designated time with the man who had raised him. Of course his mother had never been allowed to visit.

The affair between Arista and Zeus Mytikas had been whispered about for years until eventually it was revealed she was living with him in New York. The drama had rocked the tabloids so thoroughly and yet no one had ever suspected that there could be more to the story until it was revealed publicly that Eros was, in fact, Zeus's son. He had always known that Stavros was not his birth father, but it had never bothered him. He had been happy not knowing.

Eros watched as the great white sprawling villa came into view at the southern tip of the island and tried to block out the memory of finding out that his birth father had always known about him, but had paid for his existence to be kept secret from his high society wife. A wife who had finally passed away after a long illness, leaving Zeus childless and in need of heirs.

And nothing had been the same again.

He inhaled the cool salty breeze and tried to feel his stress melt away, annoyed at himself for allowing his thoughts to wander to such darkness. He realised with a frown that Priya had sat like a silent statue beside him for the entire ten-minute journey. She didn't gasp at the views or the stunning wildflower meadows that framed the single winding road that connected the villa to the small bay that housed the marina. He felt the tension rise in him as they passed along the sleek driveway up to the villa. Tall myrtle trees formed orderly sentries along the sides of the neatly maintained avenue.

As the villa came fully into view, like a large white castle atop the highest peak, she didn't comment on the architecture or the stunning views of the bay. With a thoroughly benign expression, she opened her own door once they stopped and took her case out before he had even taken the keys from the engine.

'As far as cages go, it's a pretty beautiful one, don't you think?' she said.

Priya stood in the courtyard and looked up at the most beautiful home she had ever seen. The whitewashed facade was embellished by cascades of pink and purple bougainvillea that covered what seemed to be small turrets at each corner.

She walked through an archway into a sun-drenched courtyard and found herself met by the most stunning view across the Aegean from their high vantage point.

Eros followed close behind her, seemingly annoyed at the fact that she had chosen to take her case herself.

Her muscles felt tight and she was on edge with the effort of watching her every move and word around him. She had to temper her awestruck reaction to the sight of the most ornate pool she had ever seen in her life. A giant circular shape, the pool was dominated by what looked like an eight-foot-tall sculpture of what appeared to be a nude man, pointing his finger up at the sky. It was an impressive place, and not an unpleasant one in which to spend an extended vacation.

She closed her eyes and pushed away the reminder, not knowing how on earth she would survive one week away from her work, never mind three. She had barely stopped moving over the past few years. Always with her eye on the next goal, the next achievement, the next step towards fulfilling whatever it was that haunted her every moment that she stood still.

Pushing away the suddenly dark turn her thoughts had taken, she waited as Eros unlocked the terrace doors and led her into an impressive open-plan living space.

All the brightness from the outside was mirrored inside with cream-coloured tiles and lush curved sofas, giving the space a modern airy feel yet still having touches that were quintessentially Greek.

The window frames on the inside were the same deep sapphire-blue as they were outside. There were no ultra-modern glass walls here. The house had clearly been renovated at some point in the past few years, yet it remained classically Greek.

She remembered Eros's words about his penthouse in New York, that he liked to keep parts of history and build around them. She might almost begin to think that he was a romantic soul.

'You are quiet.' His deeply accented voice came from behind her.

'Maybe I'm speechless with joy.'

'Quiet and now sarcastic.' He cocked his head to one side, observing her with such intensity it made her skin prickle. 'Just what every groom wants to see from his bride on their honeymoon.'

'I'm just processing things, that's all.' She shook her head, running her finger along a bookcase filled with novels in many languages and ignoring the flutter in her stomach at the thought of being on honeymoon. This wasn't that, certainly not.

'Regretting walking away from your grand society wedding?' His voice was closer, a strange tension in him that made her back away a step.

'I have no regrets.' She steeled herself, straightening her spine as she looked up at him. 'I made my commitment, as did you.'

'You know... I suppose this is technically our wedding night.' He prowled closer, that smirk once again gracing his full lips. 'Perhaps I should have written a romantic island consummation into our contract.'

Priya avoided his eyes. 'I wouldn't have signed it if you had. I am not the kind of woman easily pulled off course by anyone.'

'Am I so easy to generalise?' He cocked his head to one side, watching her with the shrewd gaze of a hunter. 'Do you often moan into a kiss like you've tasted heaven?'

'Don't flatter yourself.'

'We can try it again if your memory needs refreshing.' His pupils seemed to widen, his eyes lowering to her lips. 'I'd like the chance to sample my beautiful bride in private.'

His words lit up that same spark within her, the needy primal core that she had long buried and suppressed. She was not that girl any more, she didn't long for the protection and security of marriage to the right man. To her, marriage was the opposite of safety. Already she felt vulnerable and on edge just from him saying it out loud.

She had moved so far away from this world. From powerful, overbearing men who believed they knew better than the women they claimed to be in lifelong partnerships with.

Tilting her chin up, she met his eyes and wondered how on earth she'd managed to get herself into this situation. The man was a veritable sexual force of nature and he seemed intent on pushing her out of her comfort zone. She needed to show him that she was not some meek and mild society princess to be manipulated and cowed. She was his wife now, after all.

A shiver coursed down her spine at the thought.

Shocking herself, she took a step forward until barely an inch remained between their chests. Forcing herself to look up, she met his cerulean gaze. 'Allow me to make one thing perfectly clear. I may have agreed to marry you, but I did not suddenly transform into an object that you can own. I am not a pocket watch.'

His eyes gleamed at her words but he did not laugh. Suddenly the air between them was thick and heated. Priya felt too warm and too bare under his gaze. Mustering up the composure for one final supercilious brow rise, she turned away to continue her explorations, feeling the heat of his gaze follow her every step of the way.

CHAPTER SIX

EROS KNEW THAT Priya was lying when she said she was taking a nap a short while later, as she had got what he considered to be a full night's sleep on the last leg of the flight to Athens. He had ensured she was left undisturbed, insisting on checking her comfort himself when the staff had offered to dim the lights in the cabin. He remembered the silky feeling of her hair under his fingertips when he'd accidentally brushed against it while removing her glasses so that they didn't become damaged.

He'd reclined her seat quickly and efficiently after that, eager to step away into his own space. But he'd found his concentration lacking, his eyes continually wandering back to her and her unnatural stillness as she slept.

He'd hoped she might enter into some more verbal sparring and give him another chance to see what was truly going on behind that fiercely intelligent and serious gaze.

He wanted to know more.

The thought stopped him in his tracks, knitting his brows together with almost painful force. Had it truly been so long since he had last blown off some steam in the bedroom that he was lusting after his angry wife? She had openly admitted to despising him, and likely found him lacking compared to his paragon of a brother. That she had ever thought his brother to be some kind of avenging Robin

Hood infuriated him even more. He knew that Xander only cared for his bank account and his image, in that order.

Anger fuelled him as he deposited his luggage in the master suite and stepped into the shower, cleaning away the grime of travel with swift, angry strokes. He was becoming soft if one woman's opinion could have such a drastic effect on his mood. He shouldn't care if she liked the damn island.

He walked over to the small urn that sat atop a marble sideboard by the wide windows of the master suite. He had placed it there the day after Stavros's funeral, but then, filled with anger, he'd walked away without truly saying goodbye.

This rock had been his stepfather's prized possession and in his final days he had used it as a prison of his own making. Hiding himself away.

He had often been subjected to his stepfather's drunken diatribes about his wayward wife. He had known far too much at too young an age. Their short marriage had been so unhappy and turbulent that he remembered his relief and happiness when he'd finally found out that they were to be divorced.

His happiness had been short-lived, with him being used as a prize between two hateful and emotionally immature adults during the following years, until he'd eventually turned eighteen. His best interests had always come second to their need for control and revenge against each other. For their need to win their petty battles, not caring that he had grown up in a war zone.

The memories of endless months spent roaming this island alone were particularly difficult to revisit. But he had some happy memories here with his stepfather and this was the place Stavros had requested to be laid to rest.

By now, Arista would be beginning to piece together

his double-cross. He almost wished he had decided to give the news in person. Did that make him just as hateful as she was? Perhaps, but every ounce of hate in him had in part been created by her and the choices she'd willingly made.

He walked out into the centre of his bedroom and surveyed his reflection in the mirror. He was only thirty-four but he felt like he had lived two lifetimes already. His father's first, and now his own. If this was his second life, maybe it was time he started doing solely what he wanted. He had told Priya that she could do with time away from the city but the same could also be said for him. He had travelled non-stop over the past few years, expanding his empire. Despite his reputation as a spoilt European party boy, he couldn't remember the last time he had taken a vacation of any kind.

The effort of keeping his transactions away from Mytikas's ears had meant doing much more work in person than would normally be the case for a man of his wealth.

The thought of being forced to stay here for a few weeks in the sun, becoming reacquainted with this little slice of heaven… It was not entirely unappealing.

Except for the fact that his vacation medication came with a guest. A dark, brooding guest who wore his ring on her finger and currently bore *his last name.*

She was just another stuck-up society heiress, he reminded himself. He should hate her and everything she stood for by agreeing to become a part of the obnoxious fake world of corruption and ballgowns that his brother inhabited.

And yet something bothered him deeply about the image she portrayed.

His mind wandered back to that kiss. The pretty cherry flush of her lips afterwards and the dazed sparkle in her chocolate-coloured eyes. Something within him had growled with satisfaction the moment he'd felt her stop holding back. The moment she had broken and acknowledged the intense chemistry between them.

His body instantly reacted to the erotic image his mind created and he hissed out a low breath, fighting the urge to continue the fantasy. His skin felt too hot, every muscle in his body wound tight with tension begging for release. But not just any release. Claiming her. Bringing down those polished stone walls surrounding her and making her completely lose control.

If just thinking of making love to his wife affected him this way...

He walked out onto his balcony, not caring that he wore only a white towel draped low on his hips.

Just a few weeks, he reminded himself. Just a few weeks here and they would part ways and he would be free to go wild and satiate the incurable lust that seemed to hound him of late. Soon he would finally finish snuffing out every last piece of evidence that Zeus Mytikas had walked this earth.

Priya ducked behind the pillar of what she'd believed to be her own private balcony but in fact was an adjoining one to what was evidently her husband's suite. Eros stood half-naked, tilting his head back to the sun like he was playing a part in a damned TV commercial.

She wrenched her gaze away from her husband's impossible beauty, quietly closed her sliding door behind her and promptly threw herself face down onto her bed.

She didn't even have the luxury of screaming her frustrations into her pillow for fear he would hear her and come barging in to investigate. He had deliberately re-awoken the memory of how her body had reacted to their wedding kiss, trying to unsettle her and make her blush. The way he'd looked at her as he'd taunted her had only served to heat her blood more, as though he'd wished to devour her.

The realisation that he was attracted to her too had unlocked some hidden pocket of desire she'd buried deep, deep inside and now she was working furiously to try to gather it all back in before she completely embarrassed herself.

In the few minutes of watching him she'd been amazed at how at ease he was in his own body. She'd seen the smallest lines around his eyes as he exhaled on a long, deep sigh. Smile lines, she'd realised. This was a man who smiled so much they had left a mark on him. What did it feel like to live with that kind of abandon? For as long as she could remember, people had commented on her serious nature. Little girls were supposed to smile, Mama had urged when young Priya had abandoned the delicate country club tea parties in favour of reading or playing billiards with her father.

Her father had always allowed her to be herself, whether they had been working on his classic cars or just sitting reading side by side in the library. His sudden death had hit them all hard.

And as she'd grieved for Papa, she'd bloomed into a young woman and her beauty had become even more notable than her mind. Suddenly Mama's gentle urging her towards members of the opposite sex had become more insistent. She'd thought that it was her way of connecting, that she was simply traditional. But soon it seemed that attracting a suitable man was the only thing they'd talked about and marriage the ultimate achievement. She had no longer been allowed to play billiards or chess or to work on the cars but had been forced to attend feminine etiquette lessons and socialise with the daughters of her parents' wealthy friends. Her clothing had to be pre-approved, and her extracurricular activities cut back in favour of charity dinners and social events.

When she'd met Eric, everything had intensified. What should have been the first flush of innocent teenage infatuation had become a stage production. Both of their parents had pushed for an immediate wedding. She had been eighteen.

Looking back, she had always known there was something more behind her mother's manipulations. On the eve of her wedding day, she'd gone to her father's old office, as she had most evenings. She'd sat in his big leather chair and sobbed, thinking about how much she was missing him and wishing he were still alive to walk her down the aisle. She'd wondered why she felt so confused about something that was supposed to be a joyous occasion. She certainly hadn't felt joy.

Then she'd gone in search of tissues and come across the details of his last will and testament instead. It had all been laid out in black and white. Every last cent of his estate was left to her, including the shares he controlled in Davidson Khan. He'd left everything to her, but had locked it away, tied it up in an ironclad trust until such time as she married or turned thirty.

The last words her mother had ever spoken to her that day, once she'd stopped sobbing and begging her to reconsider calling off the wedding, would be imprinted in her mind for ever.

You will always be alone.

She had been her mother's greatest failure and once Priya had finally accepted that she would never fit into the mould Mama wished for her, she'd stepped into the role of black sheep with gusto. Cut off from all financial help, she'd left for college on her own merit after achieving a scholarship and had never looked back, accepting an internship with a rival firm in New York and throwing herself into the work that she loved.

She flung her arm over her face, feeling exhaustion creep into her bones despite having slept on the plane. She was used to travelling—she'd done a bit after graduation with Aria—but had never been able to truly relax the way her best friend's carefree spirit allowed her to. She'd watched her friend go on dates but she'd had no time for them herself. Once she'd been promoted to associate she'd accepted moves to their foreign offices and made a name for herself as a tireless force—reliable, if a little intense. She'd grown past the boundaries that had caged her in and she'd taken time to figure out who she was.

But, still, as she drifted, her mother's voice remained in the background, reminding her that she had remained alone.

Priya awoke with a start to complete darkness. Frowning, she realised she must have nodded off to sleep at some point. When she checked the slim watch on her wrist she was shocked to realise she had slept for almost four hours. After a quick shower, she dressed in her favourite pair of white skinny jeans and opted for a pale blue blouse that was embroidered with tiny seed pearls around the collar. The resulting look was smart but not too dressy, considering she had no way of knowing what the dress code might be for dinner.

It suddenly dawned on her that she had no idea who would be doing the cooking if there were no staff on the island. The question was answered the moment she entered the large kitchen at the rear of the house.

Eros stood with his back to her, stirring an array of pots and pans on the state-of-the-art cooker.

She cleared her throat so as not to alarm him. 'Do you need any help?'

He tipped his head in her direction as an acknowledgement of her presence. 'Ah, the princess has risen from her slumber at last. You can set the table, if that's not too far below your station.'

'It's almost as though you forget that you too are the heir to a large fortune.'

'Yes, but I find it funny when people comment on my birthright, whereas you get that delightful little bridge between your brows and blow air through your nostrils. Rather like an irritated horse.'

'Horse,' she repeated slowly.

'Stallion, if you prefer.' He raised one brow. 'Yes, more of a stallion than a mare, I believe. Especially if your track record in the boardroom is anything to go by.'

Priya moved to one of the drawers, selecting a tablecloth and an array of utensils before moving over to the large marble table that dominated the dining area. 'You've been investigating my track record?'

'Of course. I could hardly marry a woman without knowing how much worth she had added to her previous employer's value. Isn't that how all great fairy-tales begin?'

Despite herself, she laughed quietly at his words. 'I'm still the princess in this scenario, I presume?'

'Upon reflection, I'm prepared to offer you an apology for my earlier comments about your privileged upbringing and haughty demeanour. In fact, I feel foolish now for not realising you are much more suited to the role of Queen or Empress.'

Priya remained silent as she spread the tablecloth and finished arranging the silverware in preparation for dinner. But she could feel his eyes on her, waiting for her response.

'I assume you are the white knight in this tale.'

'Oh, no,' he said with obvious pleasure as he advanced on her with two steaming plates of food in his hands. 'I'm far too self-centred to be considered a hero of any kind.'

'You are the villain, then.'

'Perhaps. But I've always believed even the villain has his reasons for doing what he does.'

Priya thought on his words for a moment and realised that her own action of jilting her original groom might also be perceived as villainous. It made her feel uncomfortable that people would see her in such a light without knowing the truth behind the story. But wasn't that exactly how she had treated Eros?

Before she could think too much on the topic she was presented with a perfect dish of golden seafood risotto. Delivered fresh by a local fisherman, he explained. Famished, she inhaled the scent of the fresh seafood and herbs and vegetables so vibrant and intensely flavourful they had to have come fresh from the garden.

Neither of them spoke for a while as they tucked into their food. Priya tried to eat slowly but soon she found her plate was completely clear.

'A high society woman with a good appetite,' his voice teased as he leaned down to collect her plate. 'Wonders never cease.'

'Not unlike a billionaire who knows how to cook,' she retorted, mirroring his tone, at which he let out a single burst of laughter.

She suddenly realised with horror that she was quite enjoying his company and that went directly against her plans for this arrangement. It was much easier to keep an enemy at arm's length, despite the sayings to the contrary. He may be her ally in their arrangement, but in every other sense he felt more like a threat. A dangerous force, set on unravelling her orderly world.

He arrived back at the table with a second plate, this time with fresh swordfish and mixed greens. The vegetables were delightfully tender, dressed in a simple olive oil and lemon sauce. Priya fought not to moan with delight at the cavalcade of taste that exploded in her mouth on biting into the fish.

Damn him, she thought mournfully. On top of being blessed with perfect looks, he could also work magic in the kitchen. And not just throwing together a concoction of ingredients and hoping for the best, which was what she usually did. This was the kind of cooking learned from experience and pleasure.

'Where on earth did you find the time to learn how to cook in between being an internationally renowned playboy and founder of a secret empire?' she wondered aloud.

'Now you're really making me sound like a villain.' He smirked. 'I learned to cook here, actually. During my teenage years, I spent a lot of time here. The people who live here and farm the land year-round run a small restaurant on the nearby island. They taught me much of what I know. To fly a seaplane, to make wine and olive oil.'

'Sounds like an ideal childhood,' she said, noting that his expression seemed suddenly darker. 'Do you come back often?'

'Yes, if you can consider every ten years as being often.' He spoke in a gruff monotone.

'Why such a long time if you love the place?'

'My stepfather died here.'

The fleeting haunted look in his eyes was so dark she had to fight the urge to reach out and touch his arm. She knew what it felt like to lose a parent. 'Were you close?'

'Does it matter, once they've passed?' He shrugged, levelling her a crooked half-attempt at a smile that did strange things to her chest. She opened her mouth to ask more but he quickly changed the subject.

When he created two mixed drinks and invited her to follow him out onto the terrace she still felt the urge to prod and poke and find out more, then stopped herself.

Her expression must have shown her own discomfort for when she looked up it was to see him looking right back at her knowingly.

'There is no need to maintain the ice princess facade with me, Priya,' he said coolly. 'I will not jump your bones at the first sign of kindness, if that's what you think.'

'I don't know what to think of you,' she said honestly. 'That's the problem.'

'Why is that a problem?' he asked. 'Do you often need to have precise labels on all the people you are in contact with?'

'When you say things like that…' She looked away towards the moonlight that was gracing the top of the waves with silvery light. Why did he seem to see so much where others had never looked twice? No one had ever asked her why she behaved the way she did. Why she seemed to hold back her emotional reactions in favour of silent reproach. Yet from the first moment they had spoken he had *seen* her. She wasn't quite sure if that realisation made her nervous in reproach or anticipation.

Anticipation of what? she asked herself, pushing the thought away quickly. The only thing that she should expect from this man was deception and manipulation and she would do well not to forget that.

He was a world-class playboy. Working women was quite literally his bread and butter. Already she had fallen into his trap by enjoying his meal and his flirtatious conversation just like any other woman would. Disappointment flooded her at the ease with which she had fallen for it all.

'So serious, Priya,' he said, taking another sip from his drink. 'What terrible things are you thinking about me right now?'

'You are so arrogant that you presume I'm even thinking of you.'

'I presume nothing,' he said quickly. 'I can simply see when you are thinking of me. You get a particular dark look in your eyes and you make sure not to look in my direction. It's quite attractive, actually.'

She felt a flare of temper, her hands tightening on the arms of her chair, but just as she was about to raise her voice in reproach she noticed the mirth sparkling in his eyes. He was enjoying every single moment of this. Damn him. Taunting her simply to get a reaction.

'This will be a very long three weeks if that's the best you can do.' She spoke with deliberate calmness, sitting back in her seat and taking a long, languorous sip of her drink, licking the sugar from the corner of her lips, his eyes following the movement.

'You are accusing me of playing games again.'

'Aren't you?' she asked, stifling a yawn behind her hand.

To her pleasure she could see the smallest tightening around his lips. He thrived on her reaction and so logically her lack of reaction would be torturous.

Perhaps she was putting far too much stock in his investment in antagonising her for sport, but she was good at reading people, she always had been. Except when it came to the ones she loved, a small voice said. She pushed it away.

In business, she could read people. She could tell by his body language that he was barely holding onto his control.

One foot tapped idly on the floor as he swirled the liquid in his glass. He was looking away from her, probably trying to come up with a different angle from which to prod. The interactions were not unlike fencing, both parrying, stepping back and then edging forward, waiting for the right moment to strike.

CHAPTER SEVEN

EROS MEASURED HIS words before he responded, wondering why her stony exterior bothered him quite so much.

He had met plenty of women in his life who pretended to be one thing when in fact they were another, his mother being the prime example. But that was not it. He didn't care that his mother pretended to be kind on the outside when underneath she was far from it.

But with Priya he felt the compulsion to tap at that suit of armour she insisted on wearing to show her that he saw through the layer of perfectly polished ice she presented to the world. To see how far he could push to get a glimpse of what lay beneath.

'Does my attention make you uncomfortable?' he asked, gauging her reaction and knowing that if she said yes he would stop.

She looked away, hiding her expression behind the curtain of her long brown hair.

'It's inappropriate.'

'That was not my question.'

She turned and pinned him with a sharp gaze, amber eyes burning in the candlelight, and he was struck by arousal so intense it took his breath away. What would it be like to unleash that fire? What would it be like to let her burn him in it?

Almost as though he had spoken out loud, her eyes darkened and almost as if against her own volition, her tongue darted out to explore her bottom lip in a quick lick.

He felt that lick deep in his gut and lower, taunting him with the sight of her perfectly pink tongue and the glistening trail it left on her full pouting lips. When she looked at him like that, he knew he wasn't mistaken.

She had said that their relationship was to remain strictly business and he respected that but he didn't believe that was what she truly wanted.

'I am not the kind of man to play games where it counts, Priya. If I behave as though I am attracted to you it's because I am. Very much so.'

She inhaled a sharp hiss of breath, but did not cut him with a sharp retort. So, the direct approach had got her attention. He would remember that. He sat forward, placing his elbows on his knees and looking up at her from under his brows.

It was the kind of look he normally reserved for a date when he wanted things to move further. A smouldering look that usually had an intense and sudden effect on the woman he directed it upon.

Priya bit down on her lower lip, displaying the tiniest flash of her white teeth as she held back whatever words she had been about to speak.

Tell me, he silently urged, then felt irritation flare as he watched her shrink back.

'Does that usually work?' she said breathlessly, trying and failing to appear unmoved. She gestured to her face and made an impressive attempt at imitating his expression.

Eros froze for a split second, then almost lost his composure completely, his mouth cracking into the barest smirk.

'Yes, it does, as a matter of fact.'

She pressed a hand to her chest with a dramatic flourish. 'I'm honoured to be the recipient of such esteemed moves.'

'Yet you are completely immune?' he asked silkily.

She ignored his question. 'Be serious for a moment. Tell me that you don't see how utterly inappropriate all of this is.'

Eros sat back in his seat and shrugged one shoulder. 'Tell me to stop.'

'Stop,' she said quickly, still not meeting his eyes.

'Say it as if you actually mean it. Say it as if you haven't thought of what might happen if you let loose and had some fun. It could be just the kind of distraction that we both need.'

'I know how to have fun,' she protested.

'You are wound up so damn tight…' He let heat burn in his gaze as he leaned forward. 'One night in my bed, Priya… I swear I wouldn't stop until we were both boneless from pleasure.'

Her eyes widened. Her breathing became shallow and he could have sworn she blushed.

'If you're not going to steer away from this conversation, then allow me to do it for both of us.'

She stood from her seat and looked down at him with her best reproachful glower.

Eros stood too, instantly regretting pushing her so far when he saw the slight tremor in her hands. Whether it was a tremor of arousal or of discomfort he couldn't know. He caught her hand to stop her from retreating from him.

'This place turns me into a slightly darker version of myself and I apologise,' he said with complete sincerity, hating the guarded look that he had put on her beautiful face. 'If you want this to remain a strictly business arrangement, you have my word I will not bother you with any unwanted advances.'

'You seem to view flirtation as a sport,' she said, pulling her hand from his grip.

'You have my word it won't happen again.' She nodded once and he released her, taking a step away before he spoke. 'However, if you change your mind, let me know.'

'About one night of mindless pleasure?'

'It could be mutually beneficial.' He shrugged. 'No strings, no complications.'

She shook her head in disbelief. 'There I was thinking you were actually offering me a sincere apology.' Before she disappeared, she turned back once. 'Hell would freeze over before I accepted the position of night-time distraction in your bed.'

'Well, when you put it like that it doesn't sound—' he began, but quickly realised he was speaking to thin air as she had disappeared inside the house.

That had gone just about as well as he thought it would go.

He wanted her and had made that very clear from the outset. But what he could offer her was not exactly enough to risk putting a strain on their relationship and they both knew that. Still, the idea that she could so easily feign disinterest irked him.

Because *he* was distracted by her presence. And he was never distracted by women. He adored making love with them and he was always respectful when the arrangement came to an end. But his arrangements had never lasted more than a few weeks. Had never involved being trapped alone on an island together.

And none of those women had been his wife.

Business bargain or otherwise, the fact that they had made vows to one another certainly complicated things so he needed to get hold of himself. He would not proposition her again, he had made that promise. But if she came to him?

If she let those walls down and decided she wanted to

explore the attraction between them as badly as he did, he wasn't so sure he could say no. And that bothered him most of all.

Priya awoke to the sound of rhythmic banging, as if someone was pounding a hammer against the side of her bedroom wall. For a moment she was disorientated, squinting at the dawn light through the curtains.

The pounding sound stopped, only to start up again. More furious with more power. She quickly rose from bed and moved to the French doors, which she had left slightly ajar to combat the heat. The house did not have air-conditioning, simply large fans in each room and an airy layout.

She opened the doors and stepped out onto the terrace, taking a quick peek to the side to make sure her handsome neighbour was not also investigating. She didn't think she could stand another view of his perfect just-out-of-bed appearance.

But the sight that met her was even more intense. Her husband stood waist deep in the ornamental fountain with a large tool in his hand that looked suspiciously like a sledgehammer, which he was swinging in perfect strokes at the tall statue that stood in the middle.

With each arc, the muscles on his back rippled and sweat glistened on his golden skin.

Priya was entranced, her mouth going dry as she watched the unbelievable spectacle unfolding before her. For a moment she didn't even care why he was destroying what might possibly be a priceless piece of history at dawn, all she could do was watch helplessly as he unveiled the sheer devastating power of his body.

Then he paused, turning to look up at her. Their eyes met and what she saw in his gaze shocked her.

He looked like he was in pain.

Not the kind of physical pain that came from over-exerting oneself or pulling a tendon. It was as though some of his armour had come apart and she had seen through to a place she was never meant to see. He looked away quickly, a charming smile appearing on his face as he turned back and saluted her like a general with his free hand.

'*Kalimera!*' he shouted up to her.

She waved once, then moved back inside to puzzle over what she had just witnessed.

She was still trying to make sense of it by the time she had showered, dressed in olive-green shorts and a black tank top, and gone into the kitchen to see about breakfast.

Already set, the table on the terrace overlooked the sea. Her view of the destruction in the fountain was conveniently blocked by a low wall. But when she closed her eyes, she could still see the ferocious swing of his arms as he beheaded the statue and hear the guttural grunt that came from him.

'I don't remember ordering a wake-up call,' she said dryly as he walked towards her. 'I assume it was part of the plans you mentioned.'

'It was more of an impromptu task,' he said without much emotion. 'I apologise for the timing. I didn't realise it would be so loud.'

'It's fine. I had plans to get up early anyway to get started on my reading.'

'You remember our bargain?'

'I'm not planning to work. It's been a long time since I allowed myself to simply read for pleasure. I grabbed a few books at the airport and that is the full extent of my plans for the next few weeks.' She didn't mention the fact that she'd already constructed a book review tally in her planner complete with goals for maximum pages read per day. Self-consciously she tucked the personal folder further under her chair cushion.

'I'm glad to hear it,' he murmured, seemingly distracted as he stared out at the horizon. She realised he seemed different this morning. Dark shadows circled his eyes and she wondered if he had slept, then reminded herself that that was none of her business. The fact that he showed none of his usual charm and flirtation was disarming but she wouldn't rule out this being another part of his act.

She made some further attempts at banal conversation but when he politely excused himself for some business calls on his own personal satellite connection, she was almost glad to be left alone. She momentarily mourned the loss of her own mobile device but the island had no mobile service so it wasn't like she could have done much. But without the rhythm of her own schedule and goals, she felt rather adrift.

Once she'd cleared away the breakfast dishes, she took the time to explore the rest of the house that she had missed the day before. She found herself charmed by the bright interior decor and soft furnishings. Every room seemed to have a stunning view, whether it was of the pool area and the sweeping views of the Aegean or the large expanse of agricultural land that spread out behind the house like a cape of verdant green.

The sweet, spicy scents of fruit trees and the olive and myrtle groves seemed to come in through every window, mingling with the salty ocean breeze. Eros had mentioned that the housekeepers produced olive oil and she found a door leading down to a large wine cellar filled with barrels of aging wine and tall glass jars of oils and preserves.

Stairs led up from the cellar out onto a covered veranda with a homely wooden dining table covered in small tools and baskets. It was a working area but also an ideal shady spot for a nap, as was evidenced by the large hammock that had been stretched between two pillars.

It was truly like stepping back in time to a simpler pace. She ambled along the cobbled path that led back to the front of the house, inspecting all the beautiful trails of bougainvillea and jasmine that covered the whitewashed facade of the villa, inhaling their aroma and glorying in the vibrant colours.

The heat of the sun on her skin was an instant mood lifter and as she inhaled and exhaled a long breath while staring out at the waves crashing on the cliffs below, she tried to encourage serenity to settle over her. Without her phone and laptop as a distraction she felt both relaxed and strangely adrift in the moment.

Wooden steps had been built into the cliff face leading down to a viewing deck suspended just above the shoreline. The beach here was far too rocky and wild to walk along safely so she settled for spreading out her towel on the wooden planks and settling into the strange and wondrous world that existed in her novel. She had always loved fantasy adventures but once work had become a priority, leisure time had seemed non-existent.

It seemed her brain had lost its ability to concentrate on anything other than investment portfolios. Silence had always been her enemy and she felt the worries of reality looming over her like a cloud, threatening to rain at any moment. Standing up with sudden frustration, she grabbed a handful of rocks and threw them, one by one, into the water. Watching the ripples pass slowly along the surface, spreading out to disturb the previous stillness.

Unlike this barely moving sea, she had always needed a riot of waves and movement to feel anything close to calm. She felt like a ripple moving slowly in reverse, edging backwards from control into the darker corners of her mind where she tried not to look.

What happened when that ripple turned into a swirling whirlpool?

She sat down, hugging her knees to her chest, and tried to push away her visions of the water growing dark, pulling her downward into the fathomless sea of her own thoughts.

Eros continued his demolition over the next few days, only coming back into the house for meals and sleep. The manual work became a burning drive within him, almost as though he was finally keeping the promises he'd made so many years ago. It wasn't enough to undo his wrongs, but it helped with the guilt. Already plans had begun to form in his mind for how he could expand the current architecture to create Stavros's vision. It would be a huge undertaking, but it would be worth it.

If his icy bride was annoyed by his abandonment she did not mention it. In fact, she seemed to disappear entirely during the day, only resurfacing at mealtimes. He had expected a woman who'd grown up in upper-class New York to be unfamiliar with the kitchen, which she was. But, to his surprise, she had found cookbooks and insisted on trying her hand. Again, with that intense focus of hers. Other than mealtimes, the only other time he saw her was when she was in the pool.

He had tried not to look, truly he had. But it was utterly scandalous how she could make her one-piece swimsuits look quite so...sensual. It was the racer back, he decided late one afternoon at the end of their first week as he watched her toned curves cut gracefully through the water. She was all ruthless efficiency, her long limbs powering her body up and down the Olympic-length pool. He'd bet she was even timing herself. Sure enough, as she lifted herself up easily onto the ledge, she picked up the slim gold watch, which she'd left on a nearby table, and a scowl of frustration turned her full lips downward.

He fought the urge to laugh, but still she looked up as though she'd heard his thoughts. One hand moved to her hip and the challenge in her eyes was palpable as she stared him down. He allowed himself one final long, languorous look at her in all her glory before he raised his coffee cup in salute and turned to head back to his work.

He was busy cutting down trees at the rear of the property when he felt a strange prickling on the back of his neck. He turned to find Priya standing under the covered veranda, watching him. The setting sun cast an orange glow over her, illuminating the plain white tank top she wore.

'Do you need help?' she asked quietly. 'I'm not much of a gardener but I'm sure I could be relied on to rip up some plants with enthusiasm.'

'Bored, princess?' He wiped some of the sweat from his brow with his forearm, feeling a pleasurable burn in his shoulders from the labour.

'If you're going to be like that...' She shrugged and turned to take a few steps towards the cobbled path that led out into the manicured gardens.

'Wait.'

She paused, looking back at him over one newly bronzed shoulder. The look of cool challenge on her proud features was strangely alluring. He almost felt bad about how hard a time he'd been giving her. Almost.

'As a matter of fact, I am bored.' She crossed her arms and turned to face him head on. Even with the space of a few metres between them he could see the flecks of gold sparking in her dark eyes.

He smirked with his usual charm, noticing the stiffness

in her shoulders relax a little as he did so. He closed the space between them with a few easy strides, pulling off his thick work gloves with two sharp tugs. When he reached out for her hands, she instinctively pulled away and he almost growled with annoyance at the telling movement.

'Put them on.' He grunted and turned to walk back to the wild section of the garden he'd been clearing.

'What exactly is it that we are doing here?' she asked breathlessly after a while, taking a step back to wipe away some of the perspiration that had gathered on her forehead.

'This was Stavros's favourite part of the garden.'

'Your stepfather?' she asked with a hint of softness.

Eros heard the change in her tone and fought not to roll his eyes. 'Stavros Theodorou was the only father I knew. But yes.'

'How did he die?'

He heard her question but chose not to answer it. The only answer he could give her would be a lie and he did not want any more lies between them.

He could not tell her the truth. He had protected Stavros's reputation for many years and would not stop now.

'I'm sure he would be very proud of your work on the house.'

Eros felt a cruel sound slip from his lips. 'He probably wouldn't care. He hated this place as much as I did towards the end.'

'Is that why you destroyed the statue?' She paused, shaking her head. 'I'm sorry, I'm just trying to make sense of it.'

He paused for a moment, fighting the urge to simply walk away from the conversation as he usually did when it was a subject he did not like. Childish, perhaps, but that was the way he was. But something in her eyes made him stay.

'The statue was a wedding gift from Zeus,' he gritted,

hefting a large rock out of his way. 'He liked to play games. Stavros never suspected.'

'You are doing all this work yourself. You must have loved him.'

'I did, yes.' He cleared his throat. 'Does the fact that I possess a conscience surprise you?'

'Strangely, no. I know that you have an honourable streak. You wouldn't have married me otherwise.'

'I married you mainly for my own purposes,' he said gruffly, hefting the sack over his shoulder and moving across to the small pile he'd accumulated. The physical work had been therapeutic and necessary but he felt like with each swing of his hammer he was uncovering more of the childhood self he'd locked away here.

'The garden will be the only piece of this house that remains once I'm finished.' He spoke the words and watched them register on her face. Saw the frown settle between her perfectly plucked brows as she turned to look up at the historical façade of the villa.

'You can't mean...'

'That I plan to demolish the entire place? Does that surprise you?'

She was quiet for a long moment. Her hands continued to move as she cut and pruned along a particularly difficult patch of vines that covered the wall. When she spoke, her voice was deliberately calm and devoid of the emotion he realised he suddenly wanted. He wanted her to rise to him and challenge him. Tell him how terrible and selfish his plans were. To shame him just as he constantly shamed himself.

'Ah, there is no sentimentality to it after all,' she mused, half to herself. 'What do you plan to do with it?'

'Redevelop. Capitalise.' He shrugged.

'Just what this part of the world needs. Another luxury resort.'

He did not reply or attempt to put her straight. He simply stood facing her, fascinated by the play of emotions across her face as she tried and failed to disguise the obvious anger growing within her.

'You said you missed this place. Clearly there's history here, anyone could see it in the way you describe the land.'

'Priya, I don't live in the past, I move to the future. It's simply another asset that I acquired along the way.'

'Do you view everything that you acquire so coldly? Because if that's true, perhaps I should fear ruin too.'

He stepped closer, deliberately lowering his voice. 'The only kind of ruin that I would offer you is the kind that you would beg me for.'

She inhaled one sharp breath. Her amber eyes widened and her pupils dilated. 'I beg no one.'

'I believe you,' he purred, 'but I have never been able to back away from a challenge. You see, here's another secret about me… I despise being told no.'

'That's not a secret.' Her voice was barely a whisper now and there was barely an inch separating their bodies as they stood in the midday heat.

There were no shadows here. Nowhere to hide, only blistering sunlight making his skin feel even hotter than it already felt in her presence. The thrill of seeing her reaction to him made it even harder for him to concentrate on his side of their dance.

Distraction, his mind screamed. That was all this was. A delicious game to occupy himself while they were both forced to stay here together.

The memory of her lips under his had been the last thing he'd thought of every night since they'd arrived on this island. Knowing that she slept on the other side of the wall had tortured him as he had gritted his teeth and taken more than one cold shower or swim in the middle of the night to try to rid himself of the restless energy that had plagued him.

He was not alone in this. Every single day he had seen her walking the length and breadth of the small harbour below the house.

For a woman who had talked about wanting to lie back with a book and switch off, she had done no such thing. She was always moving, cleaning—more than once he'd wandered into the kitchen to find drawers rearranged. She was so wound up she was practically thrumming with excess energy. That, he could help with.

'If I kissed you right now...what would you do?' he asked on impulse.

She didn't answer him immediately, her eyes lowering to his lips before they lifted to meet his gaze. 'Eros...'

'How about now?' He stepped forward another inch. 'If I stopped right here, would you beg me to continue?'

'If anything, it seems like you would be the one to beg me,' she said breathlessly.

'You would like that, wouldn't you?' He fought the urge to move closer, knowing there was a delicate balance to their game. 'Tell me, are you imagining it right now?'

She bit her lower lip, her eyes glazing over slightly, and he became instantly hard at the idea that she might be fantasising about exactly what he was. She was quiet for a moment and he briefly contemplated simply closing the gap between them, everything be damned.

In the end, she made the decision for him, leaning forward and pressing her mouth tentatively to his.

CHAPTER EIGHT

PRIYA HAD APPROXIMATELY ten seconds of holding the upper hand before Eros growled under his breath and pulled her closer. Her own tentative kiss was commandeered and guided into a red-hot meeting of tongues and teeth that made her cheeks heat and her heart pump wildly in her chest. His big hands moved down to splay across her hip-bones, his grip tight and unyielding, holding her in place.

The rest of their surroundings fell away into the background and she was immersed in him. In his scent and his heat and the delicious taste of wine on his tongue. She thought she had kissed in the past, thought she had been kissed. But there was no comparison.

The kiss was the most wonderful, terrible thing she'd experienced. She scrambled to keep her thoughts straight, to remind herself of all the reasons why this was a terrible idea, but it was useless. She felt control slipping through her fingers with each slide of his tongue against hers. She melted into him, giving in to the roar of arousal in her ears and the tightening of need building within her.

'You taste amazing.' His voice was a husky murmur against her lips as he proceeded to quite literally taste her with a slide of his tongue. The sensation sent a jolt of heat between her legs and she squeezed her thighs together with shock.

His lips continued in their passionate onslaught, stoking the fire within her out of control. It was too much, she thought desperately. He was too much. He was a bona fide playboy and if he had any idea how inexperienced she truly was…

As though he sensed her inner battle, he pulled back and met her gaze. 'What's wrong?'

Priya could have laughed at the absurdity of the moment if she wasn't so mortified. What would he say if she told him that actually she was so anxious about the idea of her own sexual performance, she was on the verge of a panic attack. The intimacy of the moment was too much. She was too warm and too out of breath and she needed to think.

His breath fanned her cheek, his hands still splayed against her bare skin, and she felt the urge to just lean back in, to dive back into the pleasure he was stoking and try to ignore all the rest of the thoughts swirling in her mind.

But she knew too well her mind didn't work like that.

Pressing two hands against his chest, she gave a gentle push while simultaneously moving backwards. 'This is a terrible idea.'

'It didn't feel terrible to me.'

'You know what I mean, Eros.' She blew out a long breath, focusing on the hum in her chest as a centring point. 'I don't want to be a part of your games, or whatever this is.'

'That's what you think of me?' His expression became dangerously calm as he surveyed her. 'You think this is another part of my revenge?'

'Maybe.' She shrugged. 'You said yourself not to trust you.'

'Do you wish you'd married him instead, Priya?' he murmured with exaggerated softness. 'Would you have preferred to have him kissing you into oblivion right now?'

She didn't answer the question, feeling the tension emanate off his bare shoulders in waves. She couldn't even have pictured any other man's face right now if a million dollars had been on the line. All she could see and feel was Eros. If this was a part of his plan, he was an incredible actor. Suddenly she knew why she was so afraid of how he made her feel. Because for the first time in her life she knew what she wanted. Too bad that it was the one thing she couldn't allow herself to take.

Eros walked away from her and sat back in one of the large lounge chairs under the covered veranda. Tension still rolled off his powerful shoulders in waves, but he didn't look up at her.

'Goodnight,' she murmured, walking back up the steps into the house and resisting the urge to look back. Every step seemed to tighten the knot in her chest even further, the familiar burn creeping into her lungs. The climb up to her bedroom may as well have been a hike up Mount Olympus for the state it put her in.

Panic crowded her thoughts, tightening her limbs and limiting her breathing. Her fingers shook as she reached for her small medicine case. She had once resisted the idea of needing any help to manage her anxiety when it took over this way, seeing it as a weakness. Aria had been the one to make her seek help when intense college deadlines and her fragile relationship with her mother had brought her to her knees.

Now she saw her medication for what it was, a lifeline.

Spreading her blankets on the floor, she lay down and breathed deeply. She'd done enough therapy by now to know exactly why she had reacted this way, but still she asked herself the same question over and over for the next few hours until she fell into a fitful sleep.

Why had she kissed him?

But most of all, why had he been so angry when she'd stopped?

* * *

Eros woke with a start, the echoes of a woman's cries in his ears.

He allowed himself a moment for his eyes to adjust to the faint light filtering in through the open balcony doors. The air was still and silent. The sun had not yet risen into the sky but he could see the glowing blush of pink along the horizon.

Everything seemed well and yet… He watched the linen curtains blow in the gentle breeze and tried to pinpoint what had awoken him. Some inner pull had him rising from his bed and walking out onto the terrace as though he knew what he would find there.

He almost didn't see the small shape huddled up on one of the lounge chairs. Priya lay there, a blanket wrapped around her. For a moment he wondered if she had fallen asleep in such an uncomfortable position, but then her eyes opened, their brown depths so haunted it stopped him still in his tracks. She quickly recovered her expression, but he had got a glimpse under the mask for that split, unguarded second and he burned to reach out for her. To chase away those shadows in the only way he knew how.

The thought jarred him with its intensity.

'Is everything okay?' He kept his distance, remembering her words from the night before. Still, the tell-tale redness around her eyes and on the tip of her nose made something tense within him.

'My body clock is used to rising before dawn.' She shrugged. 'It's a good excuse to watch the sun rise every morning. It's…relaxing.'

'You don't look relaxed.'

'I'm fine,' she said quickly, standing up and folding the blanket into a neat square, then worrying at the corners.

He gently took the blanket from her hands, waiting until she finally met his eyes.

'I'd like the truth now. Are you so unhappy here?'

She shook her head and for a moment he wondered if she might simply walk away, back into her bedroom, and lock him out once more. It shouldn't matter to him if she kept her walls up even when she was suffering. He shouldn't care.

And yet he did.

When she finally sighed and turned back towards him, he felt a rush of triumph.

'This island is beautiful.' She shook her head, shrugging one soft shoulder. 'It's just so…quiet. I've never coped well without keeping busy. I need constant motion.'

'Like a shark,' he mused, smirking when he saw the frown lines appear between her eyes. 'Sharks need to keep swimming continuously—if they stop, they die.'

Her gaze brightened up slightly. 'So I'm a shark now? How flattering.'

Eros knew exactly how it felt to feel utterly adrift in one's own thoughts. She openly admitted to being a work-aholic, to filling in her days with projects and goals. When was the last time that she had truly stood still? Suddenly an idea took hold.

'You said you like tasks and hard work?' he asked, watching as her eyes brightened and she nodded quickly. 'How quickly can you have an overnight bag packed?'

Within the hour, Eros had driven them down to the pier and they set sail on a sleek white yacht. She looked over her shoulder, taking in the verdant green jewel that was the island disappearing into the distance behind them. All that claustrophobia and anxiety seemed to melt away with every metre they moved forward through the crystal blue waters.

Eros seemed practised and knowledgeable as he pointed

out the various other small islands dotted around them and explained that fishing was strictly limited to certain areas to protect the environment. As the sun began to rise higher in the sky, turning the dawn light pink and purple in the clouds, he brought them to a stop.

They both took a moment to simply breathe. It was impossible not to be enchanted by the stillness of the water and the complete lack of a breeze in the air. But instead of feeling claustrophobic in the absence of hustle and bustle, she felt strangely at ease. Gulls cried overhead, flying in the race to find their breakfast.

Instead of taking charge of the fishing part of the trip, Eros was surprisingly patient as he explained the difference between hooks and bait rods and reels and other terminology that she had heard previously but never actually given much thought to.

Once he had set her up with her own line, he moved to a spot at the rear of the boat and their small talk soon turned to silence. The kind of easy, companionable silence she had never truly experienced with another person. She no longer saw him in black and white, she realised. He was no longer an enemy. Yet she did not think of him as a friend, did she?

He had seen the anxiety rising in her and instead of commenting on it he had expertly redirected her attention. He had given her exactly what she needed without expecting anything in return.

She would only be lying to herself if she said that she hadn't replayed that kiss in her head over and over again since yesterday but she still knew that it had been a mistake that could not be repeated.

She stole a glance at him every now and then, watching the delicate play of his muscles as he easily managed all the various instruments. He seemed to be an expert. She, on the other hand, achieved nothing. No surprise really, considering the first time something pulled at her line she had immediately squealed and almost let the entire rod disappear into the water.

Thankfully Eros had quick reflexes and was right there when she needed him. He capably rescued the fishing rod, inadvertently grabbing her, as well.

'I would never have thought such a sound could come from such a serious, dignified woman.'

'I am still dignified,' she said quickly. 'I just have a severe dislike of surprises. All of this would be much more efficient if we could schedule the fishing. What's the point in getting up and going out at dawn with no guarantee of getting anything?'

'Oh, yes, the perfect plan. Unfortunately, the ocean does not abide by a timetable and I am unable to pre-order fish at this time.'

She tried to stifle her smile but of course he saw it.

'Did you just respond to my humour?' he purred sulkily, his blue eyes glinting in the sunlight. 'Anyway, speak for yourself, I've already got five fish.'

'What?' She walked over to his bucket and sure enough inside there were five large fish, already gutted and cleaned.

'This is ridiculous.' She sighed, moving to slap herself back down on her own bench and glower at her empty bucket.

'I imagine this is that competitive nature I've read so much about.'

'I like to succeed. Is that another strike on my score sheet?'

'You think I award women scores according to their attributes?'

She frowned. 'I think anyone is lying if they say that they don't have traits that they admire or dislike in another person.'

'And you see your competitiveness as a trait to be disliked?'

'In my experience, men prefer women to be quietly efficient. We are allowed to be capable and to progress but we are not allowed to impinge on another person's success.'

'By another person you mean a man.'

Priya didn't answer his question. She simply raised her eyebrows and went back to focusing on casting her line out again. She would catch a fish today if it killed her. Even if it was only to wipe that satisfied smirk off his face. She felt him move and sit beside her on her bench, leaning over just a fraction to expertly angle her rod in the way he had done the first time. She was grateful for the fact that rather than taking her rod or moving his hands over hers, he simply sat back and gave short clipped instructions.

He praised her efforts when she finally did it correctly and didn't so much as blink when she almost let the rod go again at the first hint of a tug. The low rumble of his voice moved closer to her ear.

'Easy now. You've got it.'

And sure enough she had. She had caught her first fish. Unabashedly she pumped her fist in the air and did a little shimmy of a dance.

'I did it! I actually caught one.' Then she dipped and carefully dropped her bounty into her bucket.

She turned to face Eros. He had the strangest look on his face and Priya felt suddenly self-conscious. She had an overwhelming urge to simply throw her arms around him. Then he stood and looked at her with such intensity and heat she felt a flush run from her toes right up to her cheeks.

'You are magnificent.'

'It was just one tiny fish.' She looked away, focusing on cleaning her hands. She felt a tension in the air that made her anxiety rise but not in the way it had before. This was a different kind of tension. Tension that came from desire. She was almost afraid to look back up at him, knowing that if there was even the slightest hint of heat there she would give in helplessly. Thankfully he moved back to his own side of the boat and set about clearing up the fishing tackle.

Priya thought of returning to the big echoing glass villa and the endless hours spent alone with her thoughts. It was a beautiful place but it was the kind of slow-paced life that only seemed to send her thoughts into a tailspin. She was enjoying the freedom of being out on the water and having some purpose.

'Are you ready for a little more adventure in your life?' He surprised her, coming to a stop by her side.

She looked up at him, seeing that delicious dimple appearing in his cheek. That little dip of mischief as he set about steering the boat towards a cluster of islands in the far distance.

'I prefer to wing it without a schedule. Are you sure you trust me, princess?'

The nickname reminded her of that first moment in the limo and how utterly infuriated she had been by this ruthless charmer...but hearing it on his lips now didn't have the same effect. In fact, it did the opposite, warming something deep inside her.

'I trust you, Eros.'

She aimed for the words to sound playful but somehow they settled heavily between them. Did she trust him? Just for today or did she truly trust him? When had that happened?

Not wanting to examine that feeling too closely, she settled back into the seat as Eros took command of the helm and they set off across the waves once more.

CHAPTER NINE

HE TOOK THEM along a scenic route that wove around a cluster of islands that speckled the Aegean Sea like golden nuggets. As they neared one of the smaller ones he surprised her by pulling in to a picturesque fishing harbour. The harbour was lined with colourful houses and dominated by a large white church at the centre.

'Welcome to Halki,' Eros's voice rose above the waves. 'The tiniest jewel in the Dodecanese Islands.'

Charmed, Priya felt like she was entering an old vintage movie as she wandered down the cobbled streets of the bustling harbour. Several quaint tavernas looked out onto the sea and after a brief wander around the town, Eros pointed towards a restaurant for lunch.

Priya looked down at her shorts and tank top combo and groaned. 'I'm really not dressed for a restaurant.'

'Dimitri would not care if you were nude, he lives for tourists. They don't get enough here.'

Eros guided her inside, greeting the restaurant owner like an old friend and presenting him with the small container of fish they had caught that morning. They took their seats on the outside terrace. She looked around and noticed the place was surprisingly quiet for Greece at the end of the summer.

'It's nice that you still know the locals, even though you haven't been here in so long.'

He looked away from her to where a fishing boat was unloading its catch.

'I haven't been back to Myrtus for ten years but I have a home here on Halki that I visit often. There was a pretty bad storm a few years back and I paid for a lot of the restoration work. Well, my stepfather's charity did, technically. Stavros was born and raised here and he was very passionate about giving aid to the smaller island communities. With such large tourist resorts scattered around, other places can really suffer.'

'That seems strange considering a large portion of your wealth comes from such large resorts.'

'I like to restore a little balance wherever I can. There is a place for my resorts and building developments but I try to make sure that my plans never take away from the existing surroundings.'

Priya was quiet for a moment, almost wanting to bite her tongue at the question she knew she needed to ask. 'So why do you insist on destroying a place you clearly adore? It has plagued me from the moment we arrived. You clearly have a beloved history on Myrtus. I just want to understand.'

For a moment, she worried that he might simply ignore her question.

'Perhaps I was not entirely honest when I told you of my plans for the island. But, you see, explaining the truth would require me to betray a trust that I long ago swore to protect. But I suppose that trust is no longer needed once I go through with my plans so perhaps it's time that I shared it.'

'Eros, I didn't mean for you to—'

'No, it's fine,' he said quickly. 'It hasn't sat right with me that you believe me to be such a cruel and callous capitalist. The truth is I don't plan to turn the island into a resort at all. It is to become a retreat centre.'

* * *

He thought back to that time in his life and even though it had been a decade since Stavros's passing, he still felt that helplessness. His stepfather's alcoholism had been nothing compared to the other invisible battle that had been waged within him every day. He had told himself that he was preserving his anonymity by not visiting and allowing him to lock himself away on the island. But really he had simply abandoned him like an unwanted problem.

When Stavros had eventually passed away, Eros had been hundreds of miles away at a week-long event in the Côte d'Azur.

Brushing off that memory, he looked back at the woman in front of him, so curious and so gentle.

'I have often heard of luxury treatment centres for addicts or even yoga retreats but I want to create a place of true retreat. Accessible to the public, but private for those who need the privacy.'

'That's beautiful, Eros.'

'Don't mistake me for a complete altruist,' he said quickly. 'I will obviously be charging exorbitant fees to any celebrities who need that anonymity.'

'I bet you don't plan on keeping that profit, though, do you?'

'You're trying to read me again, I take it,' he said quickly, taking a large sip of his ouzo. 'I am a puzzle that no woman has ever successfully solved.'

'Are you issuing a challenge?'

Was he imagining it or did he see a slight spark of interest in that dark gaze? He had thought he'd seen something in her eyes when they had been on the boat, but he'd assumed it was a remnant of whatever had plagued her in the early hours of the morning. But now, looking at her closely, he saw the tell-tale widening of her pupils and the way her tongue crept out to gently moisten her lower lip as she spoke.

'There I was thinking that I had piqued your interest from the moment you first laid eyes on me.'

Her cheeks became slightly pink and she redirected her gaze away from him. He felt his long-ignored libido spark to life, begging for satisfaction, but he kept it caged. He had made a promise that he would not pursue her. She had to come to him.

He sat back in his seat, stretching his arms above his head languorously. 'You insist that you're immune to my charms but you know that old saying—"the lady doth protest too much"…'

'It's a wonder this island has not sunk under the weight of your ego.'

'Careful, now, you don't want one of the locals to hear you talk like that.' He lowered his voice conspiratorially. 'There are many ancient ruins here, many old legends.'

She paled, frozen for a moment. 'Oh…of course. I didn't mean to…'

'The mermaids can get quite offended too.' He fought to maintain his facade but the sudden darkening of her expression had a rumble of laughter escaping his chest.

'Remind me never to take anything you say as truth.' She fought to hide her smile as she sipped her drink, eyes sparkling. 'I don't usually find it funny to be made sport of…but you are just so charming about it.'

'I don't see you as sport, Priya.' He met her eyes. 'Maybe I just challenged myself to make you laugh today. Nothing more.'

Her expression softened. 'No ulterior motives?'

He shook his head, knowing that it was the truth. He didn't see her as a game or distraction. Perhaps he never had. But that made his attraction to her even more complicated.

'If you no longer view me as a game to play, how do you see me?' she asked.

He considered his words for a long moment. 'I see you as something very rare, born into a world where so much is the same. You walked away from everything. You forged a new path and then you voluntarily chose to walk back into the fire to save people. You chose to marry me for completely selfless reasons and that is a badge that I cannot claim for myself. It's heroic.'

'Not just a vapid princess, then?'

'You hide your steel well, princess. But beneath all the beauty and polish lies a warrior.'

'A knight in a white wedding gown.' She smirked, twirling her finger around the rim of her glass slowly. 'I don't think you are quite as villainous as you try to behave. Perhaps we should just agree that we rescued one other and come to a truce.'

He opened his mouth to reply with something charming and flirtatious, as was his norm, but found he had no response. He was entranced by the softness of her lips and the warmth in her eyes. For once, he was not trying to manipulate her or charm her or any of the usual reasons that he conversed with people. Had she seen under his facade just as clearly as he had seen under hers?

He grew pensive, unconsciously letting an awkward silence fall over them. Suddenly the mood between them seemed stilted and tense, as though they were both stopping themselves from saying any more, from treading any further into the dangerous waters which they had entered.

Their food began to arrive and, sure enough, Dimitri had outdone himself with a platter of traditional souvlaki and fresh fish that would rival that of any five-star restaurant he had encountered.

He had not been lying to her when he'd said he treasured

the small village just as much as he did one of his resorts. He had even asked Dimitri to come and work for him during the off season. The man had refused, stubbornly sticking to his small-town life. Not that Eros would blame him. Halki was a tiny slice of paradise. It had somehow remained immune to the chaotic hustle and bustle of the hectic tourism that had engulfed the rest of the islands around them. But that also left the people of Halki at more risk of unemployment and poverty.

His plans to nourish and build a sustainable tourism plan for these smaller islands in Greece was a clever one. Sure, it had begun as a way for him to help hard-working men like Dimitri, but ultimately it served his purposes too. It built his own personal wealth and furthered his status as a powerful investor and developer.

Just because he had a conscience it did not mean that he was a good person. He had stolen another man's bride for revenge and he planned to take and destroy his birth father's legacy without a thought for those who relied upon it. He was not a good man.

He watched as she groaned, biting into her swordfish and took another sip of her wine. The stress and tension of the previous week seemed to melt away from her slim shoulders and, in turn, he felt himself relax.

He had not anticipated this intense attraction…or whatever it was, and he had not anticipated liking this pampered society ice queen. As far as complications went, this one was new for him.

He thought of the call he had received from his team in New York the day before to tell him that his mother had been seen meeting with Vikram Davidson Khan. Arista was a powerful legal force in the financial world but even she couldn't damage the plan he'd put in place for Priya to take control of her family business.

Still, he couldn't shake off the feeling that he had pulled the wreckage of Priya's family company from the murky waters of bankruptcy only to paint a bright red target on them. But it was pointless to worry Priya about such a vague piece of information when there was nothing that she could do. She worked herself to the bone and deserved some time to unwind before the deal was finalised and they were thrown back into reality.

Priya noticed the change in Eros as they finished up their food and he moved to the kitchen at the back to thank the chef. As the men spoke in rapid Greek, she ambled along the wall of photographs and found a teenage Eros pictured in many of them, along with an older man who must be his stepfather. Stavros smiled broadly in each photo, not betraying any of the pain Eros had spoken of.

A computer sat on a table near the entrance and Priya noticed it was open on an internet search page. She turned her head to see if Eros was still deep in conversation, wondering if perhaps this was a test to see if she was trustworthy.

She bit her bottom lip. She could email Aria…but to what end?

Surprisingly she realised that she had no real urge to contact anyone. Technically, she was unemployed for the first time in seven years and although she was about to step into the biggest position of her career to date, for now she had no obligations. No one waiting for her, no one needing her to keep things together.

She found she was looking forward to perhaps spending a day on the beach tomorrow and reading rather than busying herself around the house as she had done for the past few days. The thought shocked her.

Eros appeared by her side without warning and she

jumped. He looked down at the open computer and raised one brow.

'Apparently, unlike your island, Halki is a part of the twenty-first century.' She smiled crookedly. 'I didn't use it, if that's what you're thinking.'

'Do you want to?' he asked.

She crossed her arms over her chest. 'What about our rules?'

'I trust you.' He shrugged. 'I'm going to go run a few errands around town, you can come with me or you can explore by yourself.'

She watched him walk away, feeling something warm and indescribable blooming in her chest at his words. What was happening between them? She had enjoyed his company so much the hours had flown by. She chose to stay with the computer for a moment, just to check her messages and send Aria a quick email to let her friend know that she was fine.

The lure of freedom to explore the picturesque seaside paradise was too much to ignore and she happily spent an hour wandering along the streets and drinking it all in. She had once dreamt of travelling the world at her leisure. She had once been carefree and full of hope for her future. Her work and her ambition drove her…but was that enough? She had existed for so long in an endless pursuit of scaling the ladders of power and seeking justice for her father's hard-won legacy…

When she looped back around to the harbour, Eros stood leaning against one of the pillars looking painfully handsome as usual. She felt her breath catch as he caught her eye and let a half-smile touch his lips.

'Dimitri has just told me that there is an evening of food and dancing planned later in the town square,' he said, extending his arm to her.

'Dancing,' Priya said with mock horror. 'Oh, no, you do not want to see me dance.'

He cocked his head to one side, those cerulean eyes sparkling with mischief. 'Well, now, I quite find that I do, as a matter a fact. As your travel guide, I insist.'

'Don't we need to keep a low profile?' She bit her bottom lip, feeling the insane pull to nestle closer into his side and drink in his strength. He was not hers, she reminded herself.

'I consider Halki more my home than anywhere else I've lived.' He shrugged. 'The Theodorou family were some of the first settlers. I was thinking we could stay the night and do some more exploring tomorrow. Keep that brain of yours occupied.'

The little farmhouse Eros had spoken of owning turned out to be a magnificently restored villa and old barn with original stonework that was joined perfectly by a glass wing with perfect views down over the cliffs. She was thankful that he had advised her to bring a change of clothing, and took the opportunity to shower and dress in an olive-green jersey sundress. She surveyed herself in the mirror and felt a wave of self-consciousness wash over her.

What would his community think, seeing someone so plain on Eros Theodorou's arm? She had no make-up with her, no jewellery or hairstyling products to accentuate what she knew was an entirely forgettable face.

But when she stepped out into the courtyard of the farmhouse and was instantly pinned by his appreciative gaze, she felt a dangerous ember of hope begin to glow within her.

She took his hand and tried to ignore the delicious scent of him as they strolled down the cobbled streets towards the small town square. Evidently some kind of festival was being celebrated because the square had been lit up with rings of small lanterns and lights strung between the buildings. People stopped Eros at every turn, kissing his cheeks and engaging in animated conversations she couldn't understand.

When one person congratulated them on their marriage, Priya darted her gaze to Eros, who quickly explained that Dimitri hadn't understood it was confidential and had already spread the joyful news around the island.

She looked around, seeing all the curious eyes on her. A strange feeling settled in her gut as he took her hand once more and led her into the centre of the crowd. A band had set up in the middle on a raised platform and a makeshift dance floor was filled with locals dancing gleefully in the fading evening light.

The day had passed so quickly, she realised. A handful of stars were already beginning to appear.

'If you don't want to dance, I won't force you.' He led her to a low table and chairs at the edge of the dance floor. 'Sit here. I'll get us a drink.'

She watched him walk away and felt a weight settle in her chest. She would bet that a passionate man like him knew just how to move. She would bet that the women he usually dated were fabulous swan-like creatures who allowed him to swirl them around the dance floor in scandalously sensual positions. Unfortunately for both of them, she had absolutely no rhythm in her body and two clumsy left feet.

An older gentleman caught her eye and began moving towards where she stood motionless at the side of the dance floor.

'Good evening,' he said in husky Greek. 'Are you seeking a dance partner?'

Priya froze, turning her head in search of Eros. She spied him standing at the bar, one brow cocked playfully as he watched her awkward interaction. A slight smile played upon his lips. Damn him.

He would expect her to say no, she realised. He would expect her to be her usual stay-safe self.

Before she even knew what she was doing she had turned back to the gentleman and placed her hand in his, mumbling a quick thank you in Greek that she had learned from the phrase book she had bought at the airport.

The man was smartly dressed in a blue shirt and black tailored trousers, his shoes polished to a high shine. He was the epitome of respect as he kept one hand deliberately above her waistline and the other on her left shoulder.

She tried to focus on the quick shuffling dance and found herself genuinely enjoying it after an initially nervous start. She was painfully aware of Eros as he moved across the square and took a seat at the edge of the dance floor. Even from her moving position she could see the women around him stare, desire in their gazes. He was pure alpha male, spreading out his legs and sipping his drink as he watched her.

'An old man like me should not make your husband jealous,' the man whispered in perfect English in her ear. 'But he watches you like he fears I will steal you away.'

'No…he doesn't care what I do,' she said quickly. The music ended and Priya took a step back, smiling tightly.

The old man smiled, taking a step back as well and looking at a spot just over her left shoulder. 'I think we have tested him enough with this dance meant for lovers.'

'I think so too.' Eros's voice came from behind her.

Priya turned, ready to chastise him, but Eros smoothly pulled her into his arms and began to guide them in a slow, seductive movement. As she had expected, he had almost professional dancing expertise and made her feel rather like a stuffed animal who was being pulled along in the dance rather than a participant.

'A dance for lovers,' he murmured near her ear. 'It is a pity that he has no idea that we are sworn enemies. Still, I thought I owed my bride a first dance.'

She tried to ignore the tightness of her breath in her chest and the tingles down her hips from where his hands made contact.

The material of her dress was too thin, the air was too hot, she could feel him everywhere, and the worst part was she did not want it to stop. For a woman who hated dancing, she could have moved around that dance floor with him all night. She felt feather-light in his arms and the way he moved was utterly magical. He made her feel like she *could* dance.

His hands tightened on her waist and she looked up to find him staring at a spot over her shoulder, his jaw set like steel.

'Did I do something wrong? I'm not really good at this,' she said quickly.

'Do you always assume that things are your fault?'

'It's okay, I know I'm terrible. I was given dance lessons as a teenager and even my dance partner abandoned me. Then the dance master kicked me out.' She laughed softly, remembering the horror on her mother's face when she had returned home just a week before her cotillion.

Before she could respond to him they were interrupted by the arrival of a beautiful redhead, a sultry smile on her lips as she reminded Eros that he had promised her a dance. Something dark twisted inside Priya's stomach.

'Is that okay?' Eros looked to her.

'Of course. By all means. I'm terrible at this anyway.' Priya avoided Eros's raised brows and the beautiful wom-

an's sultry smile as she walked quickly back to the table
he had recently vacated.

This entire day had become far too much. She was supposed to keep her distance from him. Now he was teaching
her to fish, introducing her to his old friends and showing her his human side here on this beautiful island full of
history. All of this had been so much easier when she had
believed him to be an egotistical self-centred playboy, but
it was becoming clear that there was far more beneath the
surface than he chose to show.

She resisted looking back towards the dance floor for as
long as she could manage. A part of her had wanted Eros
to turn the redhead away, but he was known here. He was
one of Halki's benefactors so of course he would dance and
enjoy himself. Maybe he even knew the redhead already...
The thought was jarring enough to give her the strength to
look up, and what she saw made her stiffen with an emotion so dark and primal it made her shiver.

The beauty had coiled herself around Eros's body like
a glove and he was gazing down at her with what she recognised to be one of his trademark charming smiles. He
laughed at something the woman said, tipping his head
back to the sky and revealing the strong column of his
throat.

His hands were neutral, and there was nothing truly im-
proper about the situation.

And he was free to dance with whoever he wanted, she
reminded herself. Yes, the people here now knew that they
were married but she and Eros still knew the truth of the
matter. It was a business arrangement, a sham that should
hold absolutely no effect on her feelings or actions. So then
why was she struck by the dark urge to rush over and claim
him as her own? Was she...jealous?

He wasn't hers. He couldn't be. He had only married her

for revenge and once she had served her purpose he would discard her and dissolve their arrangement just as they'd agreed to. It wasn't personal…it couldn't be.

He'd made no secret of his attraction to her and she'd done her best to ignore it but now, watching him flaunt his dancing skills with another woman in front of her, she wondered why on earth she had ever refused his offer. Why she had been so hell-bent on denying herself adventure in all its forms.

Eros Theodorou was the living embodiment of adventure and excitement and she was suddenly so, so sick of working so hard and letting life pass her by.

Before she knew what she was doing, she had stood and begun moving across the dance floor.

'Excuse me.' She arrived by their side and gently placed her hand on Eros's bicep. They stepped apart and Priya almost backed away as she felt the heat of his gaze on her. With a deep breath, she met his eyes, ignoring the presence of the other woman entirely.

'My husband has promised me the next dance.'

CHAPTER TEN

THE OTHER WOMAN'S eyes widened at her words and she meekly moved away into the crowd. Priya watched Eros's expression darken, his lips turning into a thin line. Was he angered by her obvious display of possession over him? She couldn't deny that's what it was. She could still feel the hum of adrenaline in her veins from fighting the urge to tear him away from the dance floor. What had come over her? She felt like she was losing all control.

Eros didn't speak, he simply extended his hand towards her and pulled her into the circle of his arms. The music sped up slightly and Priya felt the change in him. His hands were tight on her hips as they moved, urgent and possessive. True to her word, she had terrible rhythm, but somehow he seemed to smooth out her movements when she second-guessed herself. His confidence was infectious, as was his natural rhythm, and she found herself following him, allowing him to lead. It was a revelation.

Had she always been attempting to lead the dance in the past? Had that always been the problem? Or maybe she'd just never had a dance partner as skilled at taking control.

She felt warm and flustered and wild and she suddenly regretted following him onto this dance floor. She had never felt such a distinct pull of temptation for any man in the past. Keeping her precious control intact had always been of far greater worth to her than any other benefit. But in Eros Theodorou's arms she questioned everything.

He made her feel small and delicate and feminine and the worst part was that she liked it. He made her want to stop fighting and simply relax into his strength for a moment and it absolutely terrified her. She looked up to find his eyes on hers, serious and questioning.

His hands moved a fraction lower on her back, the heat of his fingertips like a brand. 'You didn't like watching me dance with her?'

'I decided that the only person who should be allowed to touch my husband is me.' She spoke the words on a rush of breath. Fear and longing and confusion were all seeming to amalgamate into adrenaline. She paused, moving closer to his ear. 'Maybe it's all just a part of the act. Or…maybe I am a spoilt princess after all.'

He moved her over his arm, dipping her backwards inch by inch as the music came to a crescendo. 'Is it bad that I find this possessive streak intensely seductive?'

'I'm not possessive.'

'Oh, you are.' Using one finger to hook her hair behind her ear, he trailed his thumb softly along her collarbone. 'It's possibly the one area in which we are not polar opposites. I've been staring down every man who looked your way since we arrived.'

She shivered under his touch, hating herself and loving it all at once. Was this always how it would be with him? Would she always feel this push and pull between good and bad, wrong and right?

He was the perfect temptation, and he was everything that she should never have or want for herself. He was dangerous. She had built her life around her safe, secure path to her goals. Eros was a walking hazard sign so why was she tempted to dive off the cliff?

'If you could hear my thoughts right now you would run.' His eyes had darkened to a storm, his fingers weaving a path up her ribcage. 'You should run.'

'Tell me.'

'I want to devour you right here on this dance floor.' His lips touched her ear as he continued to lead her in the dance's slow and seductive rhythm. 'I want to see just how far I could push you. How close I could get you to climax before anyone around us would notice.'

'You once promised to ruin me.'

'You have been a good girl for far too long. Even that first day in the limo I could sense the real you hiding under all that ice, desperate for release.'

The last word was little more than a whisper in her ear. How could one word be filled with such sinful promise?

She was so tired of being a good girl. She was so tired of playing it safe and making plans and always, *always* doing the right thing. Was he right? Had she simply buried this part of herself under her icy facade? She'd never thought of herself as sensual or passionate or any of the other words he'd used to describe her in their verbal sparring. And yet, when their bodies were close, she felt it. She stopped holding back, consciously leaning into the fire that had been steadily building within her since they'd begun dancing.

She leaned in and pressed her lips to his, soft and tentative. He tasted like the sweetest sugar mixed with the hard bite of liquor. A sensual contradiction, just like the man himself.

As she deepened the kiss, he seemed to growl underneath her lips and tongue. He gave her a moment to take the lead, standing still and becoming pliant under her touch. Holding her as she devoured him, feeling whatever control she had left melt away in the heat of their embrace.

This was what she had felt, she realised. This was what

had been taunting her, building tension within her at every tense interaction they'd had over the past week. Her body had craved this man so deeply it had consumed her, even if her mind had refused to acknowledge it. As if he sensed her losing control, he tightened his hold on her waist, easing her with gentle strokes of his hands along her nape.

He broke the kiss, pulling back a few inches, and she practically growled at him to come back.

'There she is,' he purred, trailing one hand down the side of her neck and pressing lightly. 'Tell me…do you know what you want yet?'

'I want you to take me somewhere…' She felt the hitch in her breath, felt his gaze scorching her with its intensity. 'I want to explore this…whatever this madness is. Then maybe we can get back to our lives.'

'You want this to be over before I've even begun?' His fingers trailed along her collarbone and down the side of her breast. 'If you think you can keep a lid on this tightly coiled control while you're in my bed, you are very mistaken.'

Her lust-scrambled brain struggled to process his words until they began to move to the music once more and she felt his thigh press between her legs. His eyes were filled with dark promise as he moved against her and to her shock and awe she felt herself moisten.

She tried to relax, her eyes darting around to the other couples dancing, oblivious to the torrid scene in their midst. It was depraved, it was probably skirting the law…it was the most excited she had ever felt.

'What are you doing?' She breathed heavily.

'Giving you a taste of what's to come,' he murmured in her ear.

She dug her nails into his bicep, stifling the moan that wished to burst free from her lips. It was torture, delicious, sensual torture. She closed her eyes as the pressure between her legs intensified.

'Look at me, Priya. Tell me that you want this to be done quickly. Tell me that once will be enough. *Damn*, I can feel how close you are to the edge.'

She cursed under her breath and felt his chest vibrate on a growl. He was so male, surrounding her with his primal heat, and deep down she knew how dangerous it was to accept this offer. She could see now why others had never wanted it to end. He was a force of addictive sensual energy and even the sight of him dancing with another woman had got her claws out.

Who had she become?

She didn't care that there were people nearby, she didn't care about anything but holding him closer while he worked his magic, grinding the pleasure higher and higher…

'That's enough, I think.' Eros stepped away, staring down at her with a look on his face that was pure male possession. 'The first climax I give you will be for my eyes only.'

'Yes. I want that very much.' She gasped, hardly believing the words that came from her own lips. He couldn't either, judging by the stunned expression on his face. His lips were a deep swollen red from her kisses, and she shivered as they curved into a sinful smile. Taking her by the hand, he practically pulled them from the square at speed, barely pausing to wave goodnight to Dimitri.

Eros carried Priya up the pathway to his farmhouse, the only place he'd truly felt happiness, and was suddenly intensely grateful that he'd thought to stock up on protection. He'd never brought another woman here in all the years he'd owned it, but today, with Priya, he'd wanted to be prepared just in case. No matter what reputation he had on the mainland, he was not the type to use and discard women at will. He needed to feel an attraction, a sense of connection. But he had never felt anything like this.

When he looked down at the woman in his arms she beamed up at him, her face flushed from their frantic rush back from town. The feeling that had plagued him all day seemed to pulse within his chest, making him claim her mouth in another brutal kiss. The last shred of resistance within him broke completely, threatening to unleash the wildness he had been keeping locked down. But he needed to know that she wanted this too, that she wanted him and not just what he could give her.

'This has never been a game for me, Priya. Despite what you might think, I'm not the kind of man who flirts with everything with a pulse.'

'What makes me the exception?'

'I don't quite know,' he said, surprising himself with his own honesty. 'All I know is that from the moment I first laid eyes on you I have craved this. I have become rather addicted to your scent and the way you move and I want nothing more than to take you into my bed and not let you free until we are both thoroughly satisfied. But if you say no... I will walk away.'

'I don't want to say no.' She breathed deeply, stepping closer.

'Thank God for that.' He reached out, running a finger from her wrist up to the tip of her shoulder blade and feeling her shiver under his touch. 'I think it would have killed me.'

She undulated under his touch, reaching out to lay her hands flat against his chest. 'You make me not care about the rules so much and that is a dangerous quality in a man.'

'I'm a dangerous man, Priya. But not to you. Never to you.'

Without another word, he closed the gap between their

lips and felt her meet him halfway. Her hands were all over him, touching and burrowing into his unbound hair as though she had been craving it. He heard the low groan in the back of her throat and thought he might come on the spot at the delicious sounds she made.

He lifted her against him, moving faster than he'd have thought possible as she laughed against his lips. The white-washed walls and modest comfortable furniture of the living area passed in a blur as he guided them both down the hall to the master bedroom.

The sensation of her teeth scraping the bottom edge of his neck was almost enough to make him lose control entirely. *Take it slow*, he reminded himself. Something told him that she was easily spooked. For such a confident woman she seemed almost afraid of her own sexuality. She was a delicious puzzle that he felt compelled to solve, even when he knew that this was a temporary entanglement. A short-term release from the pressures of reality.

But somehow, knowing that she felt the same, hadn't given him the reassurance he'd expected. For a man who had experienced the obsessions of former partners, finding the one woman who didn't want more from him should be akin to stumbling upon heaven itself.

He ignored the thought, stroking upward along the soft, bare skin at the back of her sundress, pulling the material down at her shoulders. Priya laughed at his urgency but once her eyes landed on the impressive antique four-poster bed, she visibly froze for a moment.

'Everything okay?' he asked, fully prepared to stop.

She nodded a little too quickly, reaching up to continue his slow undressing herself. The dress was pulled down more, revealing a lacy white bra. Eros was silent as he teased one fingertip along the rim of the lace, watching as her skin turned to gooseflesh and she shivered. Priya kept her eyes closed, her breathing ragged as she undid the clasp and slowly bared herself to him. Reverently, he took both sizeable breasts in his hands.

Finally, something within him growled. Not wasting a single moment, he kept his eyes on hers as he ran his tongue along one tip.

She hissed between her teeth at the contact and then groaned, grinding her pelvis against his.

'You like that,' he murmured against her breast, using his other hand on its twin. 'You like just that little hint of hardness with the soft.'

'I don't really know what I like but I like that.'

Her words stuck in his mind for a moment as he wondered how she could not know what she liked. The thought that she'd had selfish lovers in the past infuriated him. He continued kissing and teasing the hard peak of her breast, loving each tiny sound of pleasure that escaped her lips. Every new touch and response made him want to spend hours finding out where she was most sensitive.

He stood back up to his full height, pulling her closer and claiming her lips once more. She surprised him by sliding her hands down his back and exploring his muscles.

But when he lowered his hands to her hips and slid them even lower she froze.

'Wait.'

That single word was all it took. He stepped back, sliding his arms away from her body even as everything within him growled in protest.

Her face was drawn with tension as she struggled with some internal debate. Finally, she spoke. 'I know a little of your experience, mainly that you've had quite a lot of it.'

'I don't need you to tell me how many partners you've had, Priya, that's your business.' He ran his hand down the soft skin of her arm, reluctant to break any contact between them. 'I'm here with you, not your number.'

'What if the number directly related to my…experience?' She stiffened in his arms, pulling away and turning to face out towards the sea. 'My first engagement left scars that I never quite managed to shake off. I had dated guys before Eric, I had enjoyed male attention but after… I questioned every man who showed interest in me. I questioned everybody, even friends. I isolated myself from everyone except Aria.'

He waited for her to elaborate but she seemed to visibly shrink from his gaze. He coiled a tight leash around his frustrated libido and placed his arms firmly on her shoulders, stopping the exit he knew she was poised for. Holding her in the moment before she retreated.

He would not judge her inexperience, just as he would not judge her for the opposite if that were true, but still his brain struggled to process what her words meant.

She practically exuded sexuality in the way she walked, in the way she spoke, even in the delicate way she ate her food. She was all contradictions. Just when he thought he had her worked out, she revealed another layer.

'I was young, I had this foolish notion of saving such a special moment for my wedding night and then…well, you know how that went. Afterwards, I told myself that I didn't need to date or have sex to live a fulfilling life and I don't.' She turned to face him, her lips in a hard line. 'For the most part, I've effortlessly ignored my virginity…until I met you.'

CHAPTER ELEVEN

FOR A LONG moment the only sound was the wind coming in through the tiny sapphire-blue window. Priya felt the tension in her jaw as she forced herself to remain still, to keep her feet planted and resist the urge to walk away from this conversation and the intense look in Eros's eyes as he ran a hand through his long blond hair.

'With your track record in the boardroom I'm not surprised that you've had no time for men.' The barest hint of a smile touched his firm lips. 'I'd be lying if I said I wasn't extremely turned on at being the first to tempt you.'

'I thought you were the kind of man who would be absolutely horrified at the idea he had been courting a real-life virgin.'

'As opposed to an imaginary one?'

She let out a sound that was half breath, half laugh, and closed her eyes tightly, words completely failing her. She always knew what to say, always knew how to talk herself out of every situation, but something about this beautiful infuriating man seemed to short-circuit every one of the synapses in her brain.

She felt the warmth of him even though he still did not touch her. She opened her eyes and was met with a look of dark desire.

'You may be inexperienced but you are still one of the most sensual women I've ever met. If you honestly think this changes anything for me...' He bit his lower lip, moving closer and gripping her chin gently. 'I have never wanted a woman more than you.'

She felt the tension in her body thrum when she saw the heat in his gaze. She'd expected a different reaction to her disclosure. She'd expected him to retreat, for his interest to wane. It was only now she realised how relieved she was that it hadn't.

Almost on reflex, she felt her body lean into his and heard the harsh exhalation of his breath as his lips pressed into the sensitive skin of her neck.

'I want you too,' she said quietly, leaning back to meet his eyes. 'I want you to be my first, Eros.'

Their kiss was a harsh meeting of lips and tongue, the frantic need that had been building and doused over and over now finally roaring to a blaze. Feeling emboldened by her own admission, Priya moved backwards until she was lying on the bed. He was on her in an instant, his lips trailing fire along her skin. But when he finally moved his fingertips between her legs and she tensed, he paused, the first look of uncertainty she had ever seen on his face.

'Before I told you the truth about myself, you promised to ruin me for all others.' She took his hand, slowly sliding it back to the spot he'd just vacated, hardly believing her own actions. 'I want all of you, Eros. Please don't hold back.'

After a few slow slides of his fingertips through her sensitive folds, he seemed to zero in on the most sensitive spot. Priya felt sparks of pleasure shoot up her spine and loosen all her muscles in a pleasurable warmth. He kept up a slow rhythm, all the while kissing her and whispering growls of encouragement in her ear. She could see in his eyes how much he was enjoying seeing her lose control and that realisation made her give in to him more and more with every new wave of pleasure.

When he slid one finger deep inside her she bit down on her lip so hard she thought she tasted blood. Then he added a second and all coherent thought left her. Was it possible to die from too much pleasure? Her body seemed to convulse and shake with every thrust and she was shocked to recognise the throbbing tightening sensation of an imminent climax.

He seemed to know just how to bring her back down to earth with gentle kisses and kneading of his strong hands on her thighs. Then she was pulling his shoulders, guiding him to where she needed him most. Pleasure was a drug that had them both in its thrall.

After a moment of grappling with a foil packet, he moved above her and met her eyes. The connection was so intense; she almost spoke the crazy words that had been building within her all day. Intense, passionate feelings that she knew were too much for whatever this was between them. She pushed the thoughts away, focusing on the moment, on the feel of his strong hips between her widespread thighs and the sight of his golden hands pinning her waist as he slowly thrust inside her.

To her surprise, there was no pain, only a feeling of intense pleasure she had never known she craved. He was an expert lover, whispering deep murmurs of encouragement in her ear while simultaneously building the force of their rhythm to the one she craved most. She didn't want him to be gentle and he seemed to understand without her ever voicing the words. She worked her hips, matching him and taking him deeper with each brutal thrust. She could tell the moment that he began to lose control, as his biceps clenched and he let out a low curse that was part moan.

The sight of him becoming lost to this primal force between their bodies was enough to send the fire within her burning in an upward spiral once more.

'I think I'm going to…' She could barely speak with the intensity of sensation building inside her, it was almost too much and yet she couldn't quite…

'I'll get you there,' he growled, reaching under her hips and pulling her up at an angle. Somehow he found the exact spot that she needed and pressed down, sliding slow torturous circles over her sensitive flesh.

The combination of him moving inside her and his expert touch was like lighting a hidden fuse within her. She'd never once felt anything like the trembling ripples that overcame her as she succumbed to an earth-shattering climax. And in the same breath Eros was right there with her, growling her name as he buried his face in her hair.

Eros awoke to an empty bed.

He found her sitting out in the glass conservatory that overlooked the crashing waves of the bay, the moon bathing her silk-covered figure in silvery light. For a long moment he simply breathed in the sight of her sitting in his favourite wingback chair as though she belonged there.

When she looked up, he saw the guarded look in her eyes and felt his own uncertainty take hold. They hadn't discussed what their decision tonight might mean going forward.

It had been her first time and they'd made love three times in the night. He cursed himself for being so thoughtless. 'Are you sore?'

'No. I'm…' She shook her head, biting her lower lip.

'Tell me,' he urged.

'I had to leave that bed…because I woke up and you were lying beside me and I just wanted you all over again. Is it always like that?'

He had to fight not to lose control there and then. As she looked up at him and smiled with such shy innocence, he thought, *Mine*, with such force it knocked the breath from his chest.

Had it ever been like this for him before? Tomorrow they could deal with the aftermath of this madness. Here, now, he would give in to his own selfish need to possess her. He would claim her again and again, as no other man had.

But first... First, he would make her scream his name a few more times. He lowered himself down to kneel between her thighs, pressing her back against the chair with one hand.

She spread her legs, reaching for him, and he shook his head as he skimmed his fingertips down the insides of her thighs, baring her to him. She was all woman, the perfect tapestry of caramel perfection where the glow from the moon bathed her in shadows and light.

He traced the centre of her with one finger, watching her eyes flutter closed then open again, as though she couldn't quite decide if she could watch. He began a slow path of feather-light kisses at her knee, feeling her breath catch as he neared his inevitable destination.

She met his eyes, a shy smile on her swollen lips, and suddenly he felt something he hadn't encountered since his teens. Uncertainty. His past fell away...all the accolades of his bedroom prowess, all his own bravado.

He looked into Priya's eyes, poised above her most intimate flesh, and he swallowed past the lump in his throat.

'I want to devour you.' His voice was a thin rasp in the silence. 'And I want you to watch me.'

Her breath shuddered in her chest as she nodded once and he gripped her thighs, pushing them wide. The woman seemed to set him on fire. He pressed his lips against perfect folds and felt her hips rise as though answering the motion. Such a fast learner, his little wife. He hummed his approval against her folds and heard her let out a very un-ladylike curse of pure pleasure.

'More,' she gasped, her fingers tentatively touching the hair that had fallen across his face. Touching it like perhaps she wanted to take hold and command just how much more she would like.

The image snapped his control completely, igniting the embers of his endless hunger.

Like a man starved, he commenced his feast.

The next few days passed in a blur of lovemaking and hushed conversations.

They returned to the island to continue the work on the house together, spending the days toiling under the warm autumn sun and nights consumed by a different kind of heat. The dark stillness of the night paved the way for intimate conversations Priya had never believed herself capable of. She told him about the anxiety that had always been a part of her and he shared flashes of his own difficult upbringing, revealing a vulnerability she would have never guessed at.

When the subject of her first engagement came up, she didn't brush it off as she usually did. She shared in detail the terrible deceit and pressure to marrry that had led to her running away from society. He was furious but didn't prod when she changed the subject.

She didn't feel the need to pretend around him, she didn't worry that he would take advantage of her for showing weakness, and perhaps that was the most dangerous thing of all about this illicit affair they had embarked upon.

Her joy bloomed into a weightless happiness as he continued to show her slices of adventure each day, along with unbelievable pleasure. Priya knew that she should be cautious. She knew that nothing good could come from taking this man's hand and following blindly to whatever new slice of heaven he offered.

But when she was with him…it felt good. More than that, *she* felt good. As if with every kiss and touch he was wiping away some of the darkness inside her and letting some of his glowing vitality shine in.

It won't last, that voice within whispered.

The voice was particularly strong one afternoon after she overheard Eros on the satellite phone to his legal team. He seemed agitated, pacing the floor of the villa like a caged animal. When he saw her watching him, he quickly ended the call.

'Is everything okay?' she asked, dreading the answer.

'We need to return to New York sooner than I had planned.'

'Is there a problem with the deal?' She crossed her hands over her chest and felt the simple action shift something between them. A shutter seemed to come down over Eros's eyes as he took in her anxious pose. They hadn't mentioned their arrangement once in the week since they'd first made love. It was as though they'd entered an unspoken truce.

'My mother has decided to take an interest in the proceedings. It's just best that I'm there in person while things are finalised.'

Priya nodded at his vague answer, feeling a barrage of confusing emotions threaten to overwhelm her. When his phone rang once more, she was grateful for the interruption and slipped back to her bedroom to pack her things.

How had it only been a couple of weeks since she'd come to this slow-paced slice of tranquillity?

The sun was beginning to set on the waves below, casting an orange glow over the white stone walls of the villa. She stepped out onto the balcony, breathing in the scent of bougainvillea and salt that had somehow become a balm to her soul. Eros had been right, she'd been so wound up and in need of a little adventure in her life. If that was the only positive thing she took from this time here, maybe it would be enough.

Their flight back to the mainland was quick and soon they were seated on a private charter flight out of Athens, the orange glowing lights of the city disappearing in the distance below them. Priya had felt the distance growing between them from the moment they'd left the island, neither of them wanting to be the one to speak first and say what needed to be said.

She sensed him before she saw him from the corner of her eye taking a seat across from her. 'You seem lost in thought.'

'I'm feeling grateful for the past couple of weeks, that's all," she said. "Now that it's over, I feel like I should thank you for showing me such a perfect slice of paradise.'

He froze, the strangest mixture of anger and disbelief on his face. 'Thank you?'

His expression was dark and unreadable as he stared out the window, into the distance. 'Are we talking about the island or about the sex? Do you plan to leave me a star rating somewhere? Maybe check me off on one of your lists in your planner?'

'That's not fair, Eros.' She frowned, confused and hurt at his cruelty. 'I'm trying to be logical about this.'

'Logic? That's what you want?' he asked softly.

'It's the path of least risk, isn't it?' She shrugged, not knowing how the conversation had got so tense. 'We both know we've been stupid, letting this affair go on without any rules in place.'

'I told you, I don't play by the rules,' he growled.

'Well that's one of the many reasons why we are incompatible.' She realised she was breathing hard and turned away from him with frustration. 'Because I do. I need them. I have a plan for what I need to achieve and—'

'I'm not a part of the plan. Got it.' He laughed, a low hollow sound. 'Well, you weren't a part of my plan either and yet here we are.'

A long moment passed between them. She had never seen him this way, all his bravado and charm stripped away. He seemed angry. At her.

Could it be that he wanted more?

Uncertainty kept her frozen in place. The prolonged silence was frigid and unbearable after the scorching inferno of the past week.

'I don't trust myself, Eros,' she whispered. 'If we don't draw the line now, when will it be the right time? I'm not practised in these kinds of arrangements. Especially not when the man in question is already my husband.'

'I know you're right,' he said gruffly. 'But I can't get enough of you.'

'Should I be flattered?' She attempted humour but the words that escaped her lips was tempered by fear. She was tempted by the thought of more time with Eros, but the logical side of her she had buried away was beginning to resurface. Deep down, she knew this was a terrible idea.

'You should be afraid,' he growled next to her ear, gently nipping at the skin and soothing it with his devilish tongue. 'I have no control when it comes to you. None.'

For a long moment all she could feel was his heat against her, his arms anchoring her body ever tighter to fit against him as he wrought sensual torture down her neck. The sensation of being his sole focus was intense, as he'd told her it would be. But the thought that this was all some practised act was suddenly unbearable to her.

'Is this real?' she asked on a whisper of breath. 'Why is this suddenly so different for you? Why me?'

For a moment she thought she had ruined everything. That he might turn away from her and choose to finally end whatever madness they were courting. Instead, he pressed his forehead to hers and let out a long exhalation. 'Priya… I'm not the kind of man who makes promises outside the boardroom.'

'I don't want you to,' she said quickly, knowing she wasn't being entirely truthful. But even if he did decide he wanted more than just a fling, what kind of future could they have?

His lips claimed hers in a searing kiss that took her breath away. He was all around her, consuming her, and she felt like she could have burnt for all eternity with the ferocity of the passion that rose within her. She had thought that this might have ebbed now that they'd spent the past two weeks together. But it seemed the opposite was true. The more she was with him, the more she wanted to be with him. The more he touched her, the more she craved his touch.

Suddenly the thought that she might walk away from this marriage unscathed was utterly ridiculous. He had once jokingly promised to ruin her for all other men… Right now, with his lips tracing a fiery path between her breasts and lower, she worried that he was right, and that he might have left his imprint on her for ever. That she would never stop measuring every other sexual experience she might have to this one. She would never be free of the ghost of this wonderful, perfect pleasure that he stirred up within her.

But it wasn't just the pleasure she was addicted to, it was him. It was his playful nature and the passion he put into all his endeavours. The freedom with which he shared his thoughts. He was her opposite yet in so many ways they were one and the same.

She closed her eyes, feeling emotion threaten at the back of her eyelids, and prayed that she would keep her composure. Focus on the pleasure, she told herself. Focus on the present.

But then he growled, lifting her up and putting her legs around his waist and began telling her all the beautiful things he thought about her as he walked them towards the bedroom to the rear of the plane. When he laid her down on the bed and rose over her, his blue eyes glowing in his perfect face, she thought of the fact that eventually this would come to an end and felt something freeze inside her. Closing her eyes, she pushed away the uncomfortable emotions and allowed herself to be swept away into passion.

CHAPTER TWELVE

EROS TOOK ONE last look at Priya's sleeping form in the dawn light of his penthouse. He had kept her awake half of the night and it was only fair that he let her sleep, even if he was sorely tempted to wake her up for one last kiss before he went to his meeting.

When he finally emerged out into the cool morning air of the city he opted to walk, feeling a sense of calm.

From the first moment they'd met, he'd known that she was a woman who prided herself on control. Perhaps in the beginning he had seen her as a challenge, a fortress to be breached and conquered to prove his own prowess. Or perhaps he had simply told himself that over and over to avoid investigating this deep connection between them any further.

Maybe it was some outdated male instinct that came from seeing his ring on her finger or maybe it was the fact that she'd told him she trusted him. Maybe he enjoyed her fiery wit and her open dislike of his public persona. Who knew what it was? All he knew was that he had never wanted a woman more...

She had said she didn't want to use him for sex, but he was used to being used. There was comfort in knowing where the intimacy began and ended. No games, no emotional entanglements or pain. There couldn't be a more ideal situation for two people who prized their own space. He would give her exactly what she wanted. He would show her the depths of that intense sensuality that he could feel hidden deep inside her.

He wasn't ready for this to be over just yet.

He had decided to allow his mother to name the terms of their meeting. It simply wasn't worth it to squabble over the details, not when there was so much at stake.

Eros arrived at the tall glass building that had housed Mytikas Holdings for decades, the realm of Zeus. Their investment banking headquarters spanned the top four floors of the shining tower at the centre of the financial district, and here was where Zeus had truly been treated as a god amongst men, using fear and intimidation to rule.

As the lift rose to the top floor, Eros felt the eyes of men and women on him. Though the sun had barely risen in the sky, the offices were already teeming with people. There was a reason why the Mytikas name was at the top of the chain. There had been newspaper articles documenting the hellish landscape that interns encountered here, the legacy of overworked employees and unequal opportunities. But unlike Davidson Khan, Mytikas Holdings had never been bankrupted despite countless lawsuits and accusations of exploitation.

But as he walked along the thickly carpeted halls of the open-plan office space, he was surprised to find people drinking coffee and talking at volume. The top floor looked almost…normal. These people did not look unhappy or overworked.

Priya's words came back to him, her confession that she worried over the staff employed in her father's company. For the first time he wondered what would happen to all these people once he dismantled Mytikas. He couldn't employ them all in his own company. What about the families that relied on them?

Even as the thought entered his head he pushed it away. He was not being selfish. He had waited for over a decade for this revenge, ever since Zeus had sent him away. There had once been a time when he'd dreamed of running this building as his father's right-hand man. A dream that had been taken from him.

He was shown to one of the large boardrooms that overlooked the city but there was no sign of his older brother sitting at the head of the marble conference desk. Instead, his mother entered the room alone through the door at the opposite end of the room.

Arista strode into the room with her usual confidence, leaning one hip against the tabletop as she levelled him with a look of pure disdain.

'Lovely to see you, darling. I hear congratulations are in order. You didn't think to tell your own mother about your plans?'

This close, he could see that fine lines had finally begun to appear around her eyes and the perpetually youthful glow she exhibited had begun to dim. She was still beautiful but she suddenly looked her age. Above all…she looked miserable. For the first time he actually believed that the death of her long-time lover had truly had an effect on her. That it wasn't just an act. She looked like a woman in mourning.

'I couldn't risk you double-crossing me,' he shrugged, refusing to feel any pity for this woman who only ever seemed to cause him pain. 'Where is Xander? I want to see his face when he realises he's set to lose everything.'

'He's on his honeymoon,' Arista said in a flat tone. 'But he was kind enough to fire me before he left.'

Eros fought to keep his expression neutral, not wanting to give her one ounce of pity. Because that was the only reason she was here. She wanted to manipulate him. The fact that his brother was on his honeymoon meant absolutely nothing… Unless…somehow… Xander had managed to beat him to the altar. It was impossible. Wasn't it?

'When was the wedding?' he gritted through his teeth.

'The same day as yours. Almost to the minute.' Her face hardened, a look of distaste on her polished features.

'I will contest him in court. This—this means n-nothing.' He froze at the familiar sense of his mouth moving slower than his thoughts. He felt pain in his jaw from gritting his teeth, the effort of controlling his mouth. Of keeping his stutter from resurfacing in his mother's presence. His mother narrowed her eyes for a moment but didn't comment.

'You have an important choice to make now, son.'

Her use of the word *son* jarred him, and for a moment he thought she looked almost remorseful. He shook off the sentiment. 'I will contest him. I won't stop until this company is in the dust.'

'I'm tired of these games, Eros. I'm tired of this life, aren't you?' Arista said, a frown pulling her mouth downward as she turned her face to look out at the clouds moving in over the city. Another thunderstorm, no doubt.

'It was never going to be yours, Mother.' Eros surprised himself by speaking the words with relative softness. 'Zeus was never going to see you as his equal. The man was a chauvinist as well as a control freak.'

'You cannot choose who you fall for, Eros.' Arista stood up to her full six-foot height once more, pulling a pristine white handkerchief from a hidden pocket in her skirt. 'Despite his myriad faults, we loved each other…and I believe that he loved you too, in his own way.'

Eros laughed, a sound so sharp and devoid of warmth he saw his mother flinch.

'Your dealings with your brothers and the inheritance

clause are between the three of you now. I'm sorry I ever got involved.' She shook her head softly. 'But once I knew you had married the Davidson Khan heiress, I began digging…'

His mother watched him for a moment before shaking her head sadly and sliding a slim folder across the marble table. Eros scanned the contents and felt his stomach drop, his heart thumping in his chest as he realised what his mother had done. 'Why? She didn't deserve to be dragged into our war this way.'

'Believe me or not, but I did this to protect you. To stop you from being ruined by association. You've built so much for yourself.'

'She has waited for this for years,' he growled. 'It was my job to protect her.'

'I've never seen you this way. Eros…do you love this woman?' Arista's eyes gleamed with an uncharacteristic show of emotion.

The question jarred him, making him feel the same cloying madness he'd felt on the plane when Priya had said they needed to end things. It was an infatuation, he told himself. Nothing more.

He stood up, turning away from his mother's knowing gaze. This change in her was far more discomfiting than anything her old calculating self had done. He needed to think, to try to figure out a way out of this tangled mess where he was forced to choose between his own desire for revenge or Priya's entire future.

He could walk away from revenge or he could walk away from her.

She had never been meant to factor into his plan at all. She had simply been a pawn to use for his own aims. When exactly had she become more? At what point had she come to influence his decisions? When had she begun to matter so much to him?

Looking at that folder filled him with such rage it was as though someone had directly threatened him. She was his wife so perhaps he could fool himself by saying he feared for her reputation, being associated with such boundless corruption. She would still have her inheritance to do with as she wished.

But suddenly his plans for revenge seemed hollow when it came at such a cost. He did not wish to cause her pain. The terrible truth of it all was that he would rather go through the pain himself to avoid her having to endure it.

She had been poised to embark upon a new life, finally in control of the empire she had been born to run. She was a princess about to step into the role of queen. He tried to figure out a way through this that didn't involve risking her walking away from him for ever.

'Does anyone else know about this evidence?'

'You haven't heard the news yet?' Arista said quietly. A look that could almost pass for guilt crossed her face. 'I thought that was why you were here. It wasn't in my original plans. But I was legally obligated to forward what I found.'

'What did you do?' Eros growled, fear clutching at his chest.

'Her uncle was arrested last night and all assets seized. Davidson Khan is being shut down.'

Eros was already moving towards the door, mentally mapping the quickest journey across town to his penthouse before Priya found out. She couldn't be alone when she heard this news…she needed to hear his side first.

'I'm sorry, Eros.' His mother's words flew at his back but he kept moving, barely registering the uncharacteristic emotion in her voice as he focused on getting to his wife.

The elevator doors opened and Priya walked into the spacious, polished mahogany corridors of Davidson Khan Financial. She remembered being a small child and roaming these halls, chased by her father, his voice booming after her.

This place had been his home—that workaholic tendency had not come from nowhere. She smiled sadly to herself as she took in the small empire where her father had once been king.

The office was empty. Papers lay scattered on desks, chairs pushed back from half-opened drawers. It was like a scene from a disaster movie where people see the tornado coming through the windows and they just dropped their papers and ran.

The phone call from Sorelli, their family lawyer, had come an hour before.

Your uncle was arrested last night. Everything is gone.

It had taken a few minutes for his words to sink in as she'd lain frozen in the bed that still held Eros's warmth. The older man had calmly informed her that while she had been distracted in Greece, a pre-purchase investigation had been launched by Arcum Investments that had unearthed a vast array of secrets her uncle had been hiding. The resulting findings had been passed to the authorities and had now wrought irrevocable damage. If she tried to lay claim to the company as it sank, it would only take her own name down too.

She had rushed through the morning city traffic, panic and disbelief sending her heartbeat wild. There had to be a logical explanation for it all but when she had arrived at the office building she'd found that they had all left, every single one of them. So much for fighting for the people. Her heart sank as she walked down the centre aisle towards the executive suites at the end. The larger corner offices were usually where the higher-ups behind their desks made the big decisions that would impact everyone. She felt anger build within her as she neared the largest office of all. The place that was supposed to be hers.

Her birthright.

She eased down into the wingback chair that had once been her father's favourite spot to sit and think or bellow orders across the room. Could it all be true? Could he have been a part of such fraudulent acts? She thought of the countless secret meetings that had taken place at their home in the Hamptons, the late-night phone calls. Was it possible that she had seen only what she'd wanted to see? Her father may not have been perfect but she refused to believe he was a bad person. Surely he did not deserve to have his life's work erased?

She did not deserve it either. As she watched the busy New York streets below she found she had no energy for anger. All she felt was the crippling black hole of betrayal she had fallen into. It was so like that moment all those years ago. Another office, another time when she'd had her trust brutally shattered by someone she'd loved. Only this time she'd given herself to Eros willingly. Body and soul.

Of course she hadn't learned from her mistakes. Of course she had fallen in love with him, she realised with a pitiful sob. She had always laughed at people who claimed they had fallen in love at first sight, but she had been entranced with him from the beginning. Been pulled under his spell. Could it really be that he had been planning to find a way out of their bargain?

In the two weeks they had spent together on that island there had been countless moments when he could have mentioned his concerns about the firm. She was not so obsessed with becoming CEO that she would have ignored fraud at this level. She would have listened. But maybe this had been the point all along, a dark voice spoke from deep down. Maybe he had never intended to obey the terms of their deal. He liked to break and bend the rules to fit his own needs, he'd even said as much.

Something broke within her as she realised that all the evidence pointed to Eros's deception and the only hope she clung to was influenced by that foolish girl within her who just wanted to believe she hadn't been fooled again.

The realisation that she had only been out of the city for such a short time was startling. It had felt like another world. Could she be so utterly changed in such a short space of time? The old Priya would have run out of this place fuelled by anger and rage, ready to wreak revenge. But she felt deflated, as if with this final blow he had knocked all the fight out of her. She had let her guard down, she had left herself open for a breach of this nature. But she was so tired of fighting.

She had never been a coward in her life. She hadn't even truly run from her mother once she'd found out about her deception and had walked away from her first wedding. She had moved away to college when the time was right. If she'd been invited to an event she had attended with her head held high, always knowing that she would return and take back what was rightfully hers.

But the idea of ever seeing Eros again and having to face what he had done was more than she could bear.

She closed her eyes, praying that the tears would not come, praying that she could stand up and walk out of this room with her head held high. She had no idea what she was going to do. She had no idea who she was without the goal of continuing her father's legacy. She still had his money; it would become unlocked soon. But she had never wanted it. Perhaps, deep down, she had known it was not an entirely honest fortune.

She took the same elevator that she had taken two

weeks before and emerged into the foyer, standing and staring at the spot where she had first laid eyes on Eros Theodorou.

I'm here to ruin you.

His words from that first day haunted her, their eerie prophecy more than she could bear. He had achieved his goal. She had never felt such destruction of her defences. It was only once she stood out on the pavement and felt the first raindrops hit her head that she realised she had absolutely no idea where she was supposed to go. Not back to his penthouse anyway. He could keep her clothes, he could keep everything, she just…she wanted to be alone.

Her stomach dropped as a sleek black limo came powering up the street and stopped directly in front of her. *Not him. Not now*, she prayed silently.

But of course it was him.

He stepped out into the rain, all blue eyes and powerful grace. She didn't have to ask if he knew what had happened. She could see it in his face.

'Get into the car.' His voice was deep, filled with an emotion she couldn't quite name. It certainly wasn't guilt anyway. He had told her himself, he never felt shame for completing business.

'Go to hell.' She spoke the words on impulse and saw him flinch as though she'd hit him. He didn't respond immediately; she saw his throat work as he exhaled a long, slow breath.

'Priya…if you would just let me explain.'

'Did you start the investigation?' She shot the question at him, not giving him a chance to charm his way around his actions. She was done being lied to and manipulated by the men around her. 'Yes or no?'

'Yes, I started it.'

His admission struck her squarely in her chest and she

looked away, praying that she could finish this and get away without losing her composure.

'It's standard practice at Arcum but then my mother got involved, intent on sabotaging our arrangement, and... I never intended it to go this way, I promise you.'

'Forgive me if your promises don't hold a lot of weight with me.' She steeled her jaw, needing to get away from him before she crumbled entirely. 'You see, I upheld my part of our deal by marrying you and cutting myself off from the world for weeks. I even threw some great sex into the bargain free.'

'Don't do that. Don't negate what we shared over this... This is just—'

'Business?' she finished for him. 'Am I to believe I've crossed the threshold into your personal life now?'

'Could you honestly doubt it?' His eyes seemed so sincere. 'Priya, none of what we shared was a lie. I was too afraid to admit it at the time because...well, because I knew I had messed up. I knew I had to fix this if we had any chance.'

'A chance for what, Eros? For another few weeks of sex until you grow tired of me? You know what? It doesn't matter.'

'Of *course* it matters.' He raised his voice, one hand reaching for her as though he might simply grab her and kiss her into submission. 'Priya, your father's company was just as corrupt as Zeus's. I've been in your position. I found out about my father's corruption and I tried to take him down. Xander stood in my way and I ended up punished severely for my efforts. It almost broke me. I didn't want that kind of pain for you.'

'You could have trusted me to do the right thing. That was my choice to make. How dare you take that from me?' She breathed heavily, feeling despair turn her to ice once more. 'What is to stop me from ending this marriage right now and taking your revenge from you? What have I left to lose?'

He froze, his brows lowering as he nodded once. 'That would be your choice. I wouldn't stand in your way.'

Divorcing now would erase everything, including any claim Eros had on Zeus's empire. Her own inheritance hadn't yet been unlocked either. Without Eros, it would be impossible for her to rectify whatever mess had been made of the firm, but she had already decided she needed to walk away from Davidson Khan once and for all. The evidence that the firm had been built on bad deals and corruption from the start was painful to accept but she could not allow herself to fight for a legacy of lies.

'So that's it?' Eros asked. The rain was plastering his hair to his proud face. 'You've made your decision already? There's no need for me to say my piece?'

'What else is there to say?' She pushed down the sadness at her own words, resisting the urge to listen to his empty defence of actions she could not forgive. To hope that he might not be the cold, calculating bastard she had accused him of being. 'Chalk it up as a bad business venture.'

His head snapped back slightly at her words, his jaw so tight she feared it might break. 'If you walk away from me now, Priya, I won't follow you.'

She felt tears fill her eyes as she nodded once.

'We both know it wouldn't make a difference.'

She began to walk away and stiffened as she felt him move to her side, covering her with his umbrella. She hardly breathed as she lowered herself into the car, every cell of her being screaming at her to forget her pride and common sense. But she knew that was just her broken heart talking and right now she needed her head to stay in control if she had any hope of surviving this.

She looked out at the murky street through the rain on the tinted windows. Eros stood with his hands in his pockets, watching her for a long moment before he turned and walked away.

CHAPTER THIRTEEN

PRIYA ONCE AGAIN stepped into the beautiful building that had once housed Davidson Khan Financial and fought the wave of melancholy that threatened to overtake her. In the week since her world had come crashing down, she had spent sleepless nights trying to come to terms with everything and formulate a new way forward.

Despite the gilded building having been in their family for over a hundred years, her uncle had apparently mortgaged the premises at high cost. The initial papers she had signed to begin divorce proceedings had not affected her inheritance, but it would likely take months for her to have the means to put any kind of stop to the sale. So now the property had been sold at auction and she was being forced to clear out the remnants of memorabilia and private documents before the relevant authorities came and formally repossessed everything.

Hours passed and she found the work oddly soothing as she sorted through framed photographs of her father on his various charitable projects. Seeing the evidence of his good side did not excuse the bad but she had to find some way to make peace with the memory of the man she'd loved.

The evening light had begun to wane just as she finished packing various files and mementos into boxes. As she looked around the warm wood-panelled walls she felt a lump of emotion in her throat. Who was she, without this as her goal? She had spent so long preparing to step into a place that was now simply…gone. Her investment firm in London had kindly asked her to distance her name from theirs while her uncle's case was still ongoing, so she had begun tentatively considering the possibility of her own start-up. It would be a risk, but she found she had become a little less averse to the idea of an adventure.

Pushing her thoughts away from the image of the man who had brought about so much change in her, she paused as she heard the distinct but distant roar of an engine come to a stop outside. It was Manhattan, of course there were plenty of cars out on the streets, but this was the kind of engine that made her car enthusiast's mind stop and take notice. The kind of vehicle that was usually driven by someone wealthy and powerful.

Her heart skipped a beat and she rushed to the window, looking down to see a sleek red sports car parked out front.

Before she could think through her actions logically, she took the grand polished oak staircase that sloped down to the main entrance of the building. However, it was not Eros who stood in the gleaming parquet foyer but his mother.

She had seen the elegant blonde the week before through the spyhole of her apartment door, hand-delivering the relevant documentation necessary to begin divorce proceedings. She hadn't opened the door. She had signed and returned the forms via courier, knowing that the dissolution would likely not be finalized for months but at least the process had begun.

'Don't worry, I'm not here to cause trouble,' Arista Theodorou said with a smile.

'How did you know to find me here?' Priya frowned.

'I didn't.' The other woman spoke with authority, her eyes moving to take in the details of the space around them.

'I tried your apartment first but you didn't answer so I decided to take a chance. I do hope you haven't cleared everything out already.'

'Why wouldn't I?' Priya crossed her arms over her chest. 'It's not mine any longer. I don't think it ever was.'

'What if there was a chance to take it back for yourself?'

'I've considered every possibility. I would know if there was one.'

'I'm here on behalf of the person who just bought the building at auction. I've been authorised to sign over the deeds with immediate effect for your purchase. If that's something you would be interested in.'

'Of course it is.' Priya frowned. 'But—'

The older woman cut across her protest with a single raised hand. 'I can expedite the access to your full inheritance, a sizeable amount from my understanding, and the transaction would be done in full.'

'Why would you…?' She paused, realisation dawning. 'Eros sent you.'

'I've begun doing some consultancy work for Arcum. He thought you might take the offer better from someone else.'

Priya turned away, hiding the wave of sadness that came from knowing he had bought the entire building just to give her exclusive access to purchase it herself. A memory rose, unbidden, of lying in his arms as the dawn light filtered through the windows, telling him of all the strategies and ideas she'd had in preparation for taking over the company.

He had been impressed with her ideas, even taking notes to adapt some of his own practices at Arcum. He had called her an innovator. He'd believed in her. No matter what mistakes he had made, she knew that much was true.

Now…she was without any purpose for her innovation. She had no idea who she was.

Arista's heels clicked across the floor, drawing Priya's attention back to the present.

'Was it always a wealth management firm?' she asked, considering one of the ground-floor conference rooms with gleaming oak floors and an impressive antique chandelier.

'The building has been in my family since it was built more than a century ago. They were in the steel business at first, I believe. It's been reinvented a few times since then.'

'Reinvention is good, trust me. I've recently found myself in a similar position. A place like this could provide a very grand landing space for women like me who mostly travel with our work. I don't fancy sharing office space with a bunch of loud digital nomads.' She surveyed the surroundings once more. 'I've been on the hunt for a sophisticated alternative to renting hotel suites.'

Priya felt the suggestion seep into her consciousness. It was a good idea. A great one, even. She knew she wasn't ready to begin a large business just yet or take on a lot of staff. She wasn't even sure what kind of approach she'd take, with her own name on the door. The idea of starting up shared office space as she began her own company was clever.

'Thank you,' she said, meaning the words.

Arista waved it off. 'It's the least I can do after all the trouble I caused.' The other woman pursed her lips, her eyes darting away for a moment before she finally spoke. 'I assume that Eros has already told you the part I played in everything?'

'He mentioned it.'

'I'd like a chance to explain myself, if I may.' Arista's tone was flat and to the point as she continued, explaining that she had, in fact, been the reason that Eros had even set his sights upon revenge in the first place. She could hear the regret in the older woman's voice and then the anger as she spoke of finding out that Eros had double-crossed her. She apologised, revealing that she had already had an inkling of Vikram's corruption but hadn't realised her influence would become the catalyst behind the investigation into Davidson Khan, which had turned into a runaway train of sorts.

'He should have told me about all of this.' Priya turned to stare out the glass doorway to the lights outside. 'Why didn't he just tell me? He allowed me to vilify him rather than explain.' Or had he tried? She thought back to their painful moment on the rain-soaked street. He had mentioned his mother but she had been too hurt to hear it.

'He is a very proud man. Always has been.' Arista shrugged. 'I have treated him poorly in the past. He was such a sensitive child and I was a selfish mother. I want to put that right now…if he'll let me. I always compared him to Zeus but they are nothing alike.'

'No, they are not,' Priya snapped. 'He is so much more than anyone believes him to be, and I include myself in that.'

'Spoken like a woman in love,' Arista said softly.

Priya fought the sudden emotion clawing at her throat. 'I do love him. I know that now and I wish things had been different. But maybe this is the best way.'

'I had a feeling you might but I wasn't sure…until you sent me back the divorce papers without your signature on the dotted line.'

'That's impossible. I remember signing them. I was…' She thought back to that day, sitting in her apartment and staring at Eros's name on the white sheets until the tears had eventually stopped pouring and she'd fallen asleep.

'I have them right here, you can of course sign them right now again. If you actually want to?'

Priya felt an explosion of something dangerously close

to hope bloom somewhere in the centre of her chest. She had never been a firm believer in signs or destiny but she had to admit this felt…right.

'If you're about to ask me where he is, technically I'm not supposed to know.' Arista swirled her car keys on one long, slim fingertip. 'But if I *were* the type to keep tabs on my son, I would tell you that he is currently about to board a plane out of the country, never to return.'

'Never to return? But what about Mytikas Holdings?'

'He walked away from all that. He decided he no longer wanted anything to do with Zeus's legacy. He only stayed in town this long to ensure that you got this building. Once he knew that had been done he arranged the first flight out of here.'

Arista took a step towards her, placing her car keys firmly in the centre of Priya's shaking hand. 'The flight leaves in twenty minutes. Go catch your husband.'

Eros stepped onto his jet and took a seat nearest the drinks bar.

The decision to finally leave New York had not been easy, hence the alcohol. If he hadn't remained slightly drunk for most of the previous week, he probably would have hunted Priya down and forced her to hear him out. But his own pride and the memory of how easily she'd presumed the worst of him still stung. He'd believed they had achieved a level of trust between them. Apparently he'd been wrong.

He'd barely slept in the days it had taken to settle his affairs with Xander and try his best to put things right before he left the country for good. During a single, tense phone call with his brother, he had almost felt compelled to ask how married life was treating him, but the weight of the past was still too heavy between them. Xander hadn't known of Priya's uncle's corruption, just as he hadn't known that Priya had not consented to her uncle's wish to sell. He had seemed genuinely remorseful for the way things had panned out, not that Eros had stayed on the line for very long to chat.

Perhaps one day he might try to mend the relationship with his older brother, but for now, staying anywhere near New York was out of the question. Priya's scent on his sheets had haunted him—even driving past Central Park had made him think of her.

But returning to Myrtus or Halki was equally out of the question. Too many memories. He had settled on the plan to return to Athens first and focus on work, then maybe expand into the Asian market ahead of his original schedule. Yes, Asia sounded ideal, he thought as he downed an entire tumbler of whiskey in one go. Thousands of miles of physical distance seemed necessary when it came to Priya Davidson Khan.

He wondered if she'd got the papers that gave her the right to purchase the Davidson Khan building yet. He knew that in clearing the way for her to gain access to her own fortune, he had completely removed any other need she might have for him. But he had wanted to set her free from their bargain and he just hoped that clearing his own conscience would be enough for him to move on and forget.

It had to be.

'What's taking so long?' he called to the cabin attendant, seeing that the door of the aircraft was still ajar. 'What are we waiting for?'

'We were told to wait for important documentation.' The young man shrugged.

'Told to wait by whom?' Eros frowned, staring out at the busy airport.

It was fast approaching nightfall and a light fog bathed

everything in a silvery glow, but as he squinted he could see a set of headlights advancing across the tarmac towards them at high speed. As it came closer, he saw it was a sleek red sports car, not unlike the one his mother drove. In fact, it *was* Arista's car, he realised as the licence plate came into view. Cursing under his breath, Eros clenched his jaw, approached the door of the jet and steeled himself for whatever could possibly have warranted his mother delaying his flight.

But when the door opened and a familiar curvaceous shape emerged, he felt his breath catch. He knew those curves so well he could have picked them out in a darkened room. Priya stepped out into the cold evening air and visibly shivered as a gust of wind sent her hair flying around her face. She wore the remnants of a sleek black suit, seeming to have forgotten to put on whatever blazer or jacket came with it.

'I didn't know if I could make it on time.' She spoke loudly over the hum of the airport around them, biting her lower lip. 'Your mother told me you had walked away from everything, that you were never coming back to New York, and I—'

'Why did Arista come to you? Was there an issue with the building?'

She shook her head, taking a few steps closer. 'No. I own it outright now, just as you arranged. Thank you for that.'

'You came all this way and delayed my flight just to thank me?'

The silence stretched between them but Eros forced himself to stay still. He had made a fool of himself once, he would not do it again.

'She came to tell me that apparently I failed to sign the divorce papers correctly.' She gestured to the sheaf of papers she held in one hand and moved to the bottom of the steps, looking up at him as she slowly ascended. 'She asked me if I truly wanted to divorce you.'

He could smell the scent of her perfume on the air as she came to a stop a few steps down from him. Her hands seemed to be trembling.

'What did you tell her?' he asked, feeling his heart pound uncomfortably in his chest.

She took a breath, a nervous smile touching the corners of her lips. 'I don't think I actually answered her, now that I think of it. I pretty much just drove straight here. You said you wouldn't follow me…but I don't think I believed you. And now…now you're just leaving?'

'Priya… I couldn't trust myself to even be in the same room to sign my name on the documents that would begin to end this marriage. I wanted to make sure that our union would be dissolved cleanly, without pressure from me. I wanted you to make your own choices.'

'That's the thing.' She shook her head. 'I think, even in all of my anger, I couldn't bear to sign my name on a document that would break my heart even further.'

He felt her words hit him square in the chest. 'I never meant to break your heart. Trust me, if I could have shielded you from the pain of losing the company—'

'It wasn't just sadness about losing the company. I was losing you too.' A sheen of moisture shone in her dark eyes and when her voice broke, Eros felt his body move of its own volition. He was down the steps and holding her in his arms before he had as much as taken a breath.

'Don't,' he rasped. 'I've been trying to do the right thing by leaving you alone. I won't be able to walk away if you're crying. I can't bear it.'

'I don't want you to leave me alone.' She looked up at him, teardrops glistening in her eyelashes. 'I'm sorry that my own fears and anger blinded me to the fact that you were only ever trying to protect me. You said you were a selfish bastard but... I only ever felt cared for when we were together.'

'Priya...' He whispered her name like a prayer, holding her against his chest with so much force he feared he might break her. 'If anyone should apologise, it's me. I may have started out with bad intentions but I assure you my regrets are enough to keep me company for decades. I know that I don't deserve your forgiveness, but it doesn't stop me craving it... It doesn't stop me craving you. I don't deserve you.'

'Don't say that. That's not how love works, Eros. We are both deserving, no matter what mistakes we make.'

He stilled, looking down at her. 'Love?'

Uncertainty marred her brow for a moment before she finally spoke. 'You may have stolen your bride at first, Eros, but I fell in love with you quite willingly. Even this past week when I told myself that it was over... I can't seem to stop loving you.'

'Don't stop. Please, don't stop.' He leaned down, claiming her lips like a drowning man getting his first gasp of air. That's what this woman was to him. Vital. He pulled away after a moment, running his fingers down the silky length of her hair. God, he had missed touching her, holding her, just being near her.

'You aren't panicking? I know how you feel on the subject of love,' she said quickly, running her fingertips in an idle circle over the middle button of his shirt.

'I knew from the first moment that what I felt for you was more than just a passing attraction. But that day on the fishing boat...and then our first night in Halki...' He shook his head, feeling her hands tighten their grip on his shirt. 'It terrified me. You came into my life and tore down every wall I had and reminded me who I truly am. I love you so much it's driven me halfway to madness over the past week to think of my world without you at the heart of it.'

A small sob escaped her lips as she reached up and claimed his lips once more, their kiss becoming something frantic and primal. Like two souls trying to merge into one.

'Does this mean you will stay my wife?' he asked, between kisses. 'Because I'm not opposed to starting from scratch and wooing you all over again.'

She paused, raising one brow. 'I might amend our new terms to include a very romantic, very lavish proposal.'

'I think we need to finalise this negotiation somewhere a little more private, don't you?' he murmured silkily.

Without warning, Eros picked his wife up and climbed the rest of the staircase into the aircraft. She squirmed and kicked in jest, all the while beaming up at him with so much love in her eyes he feared his heart might burst. He smiled back at her, feeling the air crackle around them with something wild and filled with promise.

His lips couldn't seem to release her for more than a second at a time as he navigated the length of the plane. Priya's laugh was like a balm to his soul as their bodies finally landed in a tangle on the lavish bed in the private cabin.

'Are you stealing me away again, Mr Theodorou?' she asked breathlessly.

Eros framed her face in his hands, feeling a rush of emotion so primal it made his throat clench. 'Always, *agape mou*. Always.'

EPILOGUE

EROS GUIDED THE Aqua Hawk into a smooth landing on the water's surface and moved the vessel gently into the island's unusually busy harbour. He frowned as he scanned the dock, noting it was filled with yachts. The Stavros Theodorou Centre for Rehabilitation was into its second year of business now but it still took his breath away every time he returned to see the evidence of his hard work.

Even before he had finished tying off and securing the vessel he heard the sound of a familiar engine descending the hill at speed. His wife was a veritable speed demon.

A soft smile touched his lips as the white Jeep came to a stop and Priya jumped out of the driver's seat. He moved like lightning down the marina and within minutes she was in his embrace.

'Never leave us for that long again.'

'Agreed.'

He breathed in the vanilla scent of her hair, smoothing his hands down the familiar curves and dips of her body. Long moments were lost as he took her mouth in a deep sensual kiss, showing her exactly how much he had missed her, body and soul.

She tried to move away and with a gentle growl he lifted her legs around his waist, pulling her even closer against him.

'Eros!' she squeaked, and yet she moved herself even

tighter in his arms. 'There are people setting up for the charity dinner on the terrace. But, God, I missed you. I missed the quiet of this place but it's not the same without you.'

'I assumed you'd be kept distracted enough.' He raised one brow.

They both smiled knowingly. Her old wish for constant distraction had become a joke between them, because Priya had not set foot in the New York office in more than six months. For a very good reason.

'Where is my other ferocious she-wolf?'

'Sleeping.' Priya smiled, that familiar warmth entering her gaze every time she spoke of their five-month-old daughter Amara. 'The whole family has already arrived, as you can see. Your mother has not let her granddaughter out of her sight and insists on being called Gia-gia now. I think we may have created a monster.'

Eros smiled, glad that he had chosen to invest time into mending his relationship with Arista. Priya had shown him that sometimes love meant looking past mistakes and choosing forgiveness. It had been tough, but he'd believed in his mother's remorse. They had even scattered Stavros's ashes together here on the island, laying to rest their grief and ill will.

'I'm not quite ready to share you yet,' Eros rasped, running his hands down her sides and pulling her close. Already he could feel himself responding to her. Pregnancy and new parenthood had only seemed to increase the ferocious hunger he felt for his wife. Watching her grow their child and give birth had been the most intense, powerful experience of his life. And all the while she had continued to grow her own empire from the dust of Davidson Khan Financial and make a name for her own small consulting firm and the sophisticated shared work spaces she'd begun to invest in around the globe.

'Always so greedy.' A sparkle of mischief entered Priya's eyes as her gaze moved to where the seaplane still bobbed and swayed against its moorings. 'You know…we never did get around to christening the newest model.'

She took him by the hands and began a slow, seductive walk down the whitewashed pier. One look in her eyes and he knew she was thinking of the jet-black privacy windows and the long bench in the back. He wondered just how many scandalous things they could do in the small block of time they had before they needed to return to the house.

Eros had barely stopped to close the door of the plane behind them before he had her under him. She pulled off her tank top with one smooth movement and spread her knees wide as he settled between her thighs.

'No time for play?' He teased his words against her lips, laughing low in his throat as he felt her hands moving frantically lower on his hips, hurrying him on to what they both needed. There would be plenty of time for slow lovemaking later.

But when he finally slid inside her and felt her warmth surround him, he fell silent and still, needing a moment to simply feel the connection. Priya's eyes held him captivated, the emotion in them echoing the sudden tightness in his chest.

'Every single time…' he said with wonder, capturing her moans with a deep kiss.

He moved slowly at first, wanting to savour having her under him after their time apart, but soon he gave in to the overpowering need to claim, to possess.

Much later, as their guests began to depart, Priya watched as the evening light began to fade over the grounds of their private domain and small lamps lit the place up. The sprawling villa they'd built on the southern end of the island was an ideal base to keep watch on the centre and hold events for their growing charitable organisation, but the farmhouse on Halki was still their true home.

A small cry grabbed her attention and Priya felt a lump in her throat as she watched the man she loved cradling the tiny life they had created together. Amara was the little spark of joy she had never known she was waiting for. Her pregnancy had come as a complete surprise to them both, the result of a much-needed wild weekend spent on the island after months of crazy working hours and very little sleep.

She felt peace spread through her entire being as she watched her husband coo over the difference in his daughter's size, in her expression, delighting in every moment of her upbringing. This was the story they were weaving together, the family that they were building.

He took a step towards her, cradling them both close. A deep rumbling sigh escaped him when their eyes met and she knew that he was feeling exactly the same thing without words passing between them.

This was true happiness, she thought with sudden clarity, just as she had done countless times over the past four years since this man had come into her life. Since she had taken a leap of faith, believing that happy ever after was in her future after all.

She couldn't have picked a more perfect partner for the adventure.

* * * * *

ITALIAN'S SCANDALOUS MARRIAGE PLAN

LOUISE FULLER

MILLS & BOON

To my mum x

CHAPTER ONE

STANDING ON TIPTOE, Juliet reached up and shoved her small suitcase into the overhead locker.

It was difficult, though, what with all the other passengers pushing past on their way up the plane. Frowning, she shoved again. But it was catching on something—

'Here. Let me.'

The voice had a definite Italian accent, and it was male—very definitely male. As strong hands made space for her bag she was suddenly aware of the pounding in her heart and the onset of panic.

'There.'

Turning, Juliet felt her panic die and her cheeks grow warm as she gazed up into a pair of eyes the colour of freshly brewed arabica coffee.

'Thank you,' she said quietly.

The man inclined his head and then smiled. 'It was my pleasure. Enjoy the flight. Oh, and let me know if you need a hand getting it down. I'm just back here.' He gestured to several rows behind her seat.

'That's very kind of you.'

Heart still pounding, she slid into her seat. Her skin was tingling. Stupid, *stupid*, *stupid*, she thought, glancing out of the window at the dull grey runway. Not for thinking it was Ralph but for wishing it was—for letting her romantic dreams of love momentarily overrule cold, hard facts.

Her husband was cheating on her and, aside from the legal paperwork, her marriage was over.

Only, unlike her famous namesake and her Romeo, they hadn't been torn apart by warring families. They had been the ones to destroy their own marriage.

But then they should never have been together in the first place…

Her hands were suddenly shaking and, needing to still them, she leaned forward and pulled out the safety instructions card from the pocket in front of her. She stared down at the cartoonish pictures of a young woman jumping enthusiastically down an inflatable slide.

That was exactly what she had done.

Leapt into an unknown, trusted in fate, stupidly hoping that, despite all the odds stacked against her, everything would be all right. That this time the promises would be kept.

Some hope.

Blood flushed her cheeks for the second time in as many minutes as she thought back over her six-month marriage to Ralph Castellucci.

They had met in Rome, the city of romance, but she hadn't been looking for love. She'd been looking for a cat.

Walking back from the Colosseum, she'd heard it yowling. Just as she'd realised it was stuck down a storm drain it had started to rain—one of those sudden, drenching January downpours that soaked everything in seconds.

Everyone had run for cover.

Except Ralph.

He alone had stopped to help her.

And got scratched for his efforts.

In the time it had taken to walk with him to the hospital and get him a tetanus jab she had found out that his mother was English and his father Italian—Veronese, in fact.

She had also become *innamorata cotta*—love-struck. And it had been like a physical blow.

Wandering the streets of Rome, she'd felt dazed, dizzy, drunk with love and a desire that had made her forget who and what she was.

All it had taken was those few hours for Ralph to become everything to her. Her breath and her heartbeat. She had craved him like a drug. His smile, his laughter, his touch...

They had spent the next three weeks joined at the hip—and at plenty of other places too.

And then Ralph had proposed.

It had been at the hospital that she had first noticed the ring on his little finger, with its embossed crest of a curling *C* and a castle, but it had only been later that she'd discovered what it meant, who his family were—who he was.

The Castelluccis were descended from the Princes of Verona, and from birth Ralph had lived in a world of instant gratification where his every wish was immediately granted, every desire fulfilled.

Her skin tingled.

And he had desired her.

Whatever else had proved false since, that was undeniable.

Right from that very first moment in Rome the heat between them had been more scorching than Italian summer sunshine.

What she hadn't known then was that wanting her wouldn't stop him from wanting others—that for Ralph Castellucci sexual nirvana wasn't exclusive to the marital bed.

It was just what rich, powerful men had been doing throughout history, all over the world. Taking one woman as their wife, and then another—maybe even a couple more—as their mistress.

Only, idiot that she was, she had been naive and smug and complacent enough to believe that the heat and intensity of their passion would somehow protect her. That they were special.

Remembering the agonising moment when she'd spotted her husband climbing into a car with a beautiful dark-haired woman, she tightened her fingers around the armrest.

It wasn't as if she hadn't been warned.

It was what they did—his set.

She'd heard the gossip at glossy parties, and then there were the portraits dotted around his *palazzo*…pictures of his ancestors' many mistresses.

As an outsider, with no money or connections, she had got the barely concealed message that she was lucky even to be invited through the front door. She certainly didn't get to change the rules.

Rules that had been made perfectly clear to her.

For the Castelluccis, as long as it was kept away from the media and out of the divorce courts, adultery was acceptable and even necessary for a marriage.

Not for her, it wasn't.

Her stomach twisted.

Maybe if Ralph had been willing to have a conversation she might have given him a second chance. But he'd simply refused to discuss it. Worse, after she'd confronted him, he'd still expected her to get dressed up and join him at some charity auction that same evening.

And when she'd refused, he'd gone anyway.

Her body tensed as she remembered the expression on her husband's face as he'd told her not to wait up.

Now there was only one conversation left to have. The one in which she said goodbye.

But first there was the christening to get through.

A shiver ran down her spine.

When Lucia and Luca had asked her to be Raffaello's godmother she had been so pleased and proud. Unfortunately for her, Ralph was Luca's best friend, so of course they had asked him to be godfather. He would be there in the church and then at the party afterwards, so she was going to have to see him.

There was no way around that, and she had accepted it. But as for the ball...

She breathed out shakily.

The Castellucci Ball might be the highlight of the Veronese social calendar, but a herd of wild horses couldn't drag her there.

She would act the good Castellucci wife for the sake of her friends at the christening, but her cheating husband could go whistle.

Her mouth twisted.

Ralph would never forgive her for not going.

Good. That would make them equal.

The thought should have soothed her, but even now—five devastating weeks after she had fled from the glittering palace in Verona—it hurt to admit that her marriage was over. And with it her dreams of having her own baby.

An air steward had begun running through the pre-flight safety demonstration, and as she fastened her seat belt she curled her fingers into her palms.

More than anything she had wanted a baby. Ralph had too. She'd been planning to come off the pill. Only fate had intervened...

Her father-in-law, Carlo, had been rushed to hospital, and somehow she had simply kept on taking it out of habit.

She hadn't told Ralph—not keeping it from him intentionally...it just hadn't come up. How could it when they never had a conversation?

And later she had been scared to stop taking it.

With Ralph absent so often, and without a job of her own or any real purpose to her days, it had been the one area of her life where she'd still had some control.

And then she had seen him with his mistress, and suddenly it had been too late.

She had been tempted to do what her mother had done. Get pregnant and live with the consequences. But she was one of those consequences and she'd had to live with the aftermath of her mother's unilateral decision. And unhappily married couples, however wealthy, didn't make happy parents...

The flight arrived in Verona on time. It was a beautiful day and, despite her anxiety, Juliet felt her spirits lift. A baby's christening was such a special occasion, and she was determined to enjoy every moment.

She held out her passport to the bored-looking man behind the glass at Immigration.

It would be awkward seeing Ralph, but she was willing to play the wife one last time, for Lucia and Luca's sake.

'Grazie.'

As she headed towards the exit she slipped her passport back into her bag and pulled out a baseball cap and a pair of sunglasses. Cramming her hair under the hat, she slid on the glasses.

She would behave.

And Ralph would do the same.

Her husband might be a philandering liar, but first and foremost he was a Castellucci. And more than anything else his family hated scandal.

There was no way he would make a scene.

'Scusi, Signora Castellucci?'

Her brown eyes widened in confusion as two uniformed

officials, both female, neither smiling, stepped in front of her, blocking her path.

Plucking off her sunglasses, she glanced at their badges. Not police…airport security, maybe?

'Yes. I'm Signora Castellucci,' she said quickly.

The younger woman stepped forward. 'Would you mind coming with us, please?'

Her heart started to race. It had been phrased as a question, but she didn't get the feeling that refusing was an option. 'Is there a problem?'

There wasn't.

There couldn't be, because she had done nothing wrong.

But, like most people confronted by someone in uniform, she felt instantly guilty—as though she had knowingly broken hundreds of laws.

'Do you need to see my ticket? I have it on my phone—'

Her cheeks felt as though they were burning. After weeks of speaking nothing but English she knew her Italian was hesitant, and it made her sound nervous…guilty.

The second woman stepped forward. 'If you could just come this way, please, Signora Castellucci.'

Juliet hesitated. Should she demand an explanation first? Only that might slow things down, and really what she wanted to do was get to her hotel and have a shower.

Her shoulders tensed as the first woman turned away and began speaking into a walkie-talkie.

Even though she looked nothing like a Castellucci wife, there was just a chance that somebody would recognise her, and the last thing she wanted right now was to draw attention to herself.

Perhaps she should call Lucia first and ask her to…

What? Hold her hand?

Lucia was a good friend, and during the first few months of her marriage, when everything had been so strange and scary, she had been a lifeline—at times literally holding her hand.

But she was a big girl now, and Lucia had an actual baby to look after these days.

Besides, she knew her friend. If she called her now, Lucia would insist on coming to the airport. And what would be the point of that? Clearly this couldn't be anything but a mix-up.

'Follow me, please,' the second woman said.

Stomach flip-flopping nervously, Juliet nodded.

They left the arrivals hall and began walking down a series of windowless corridors. People passing glanced at them curiously, and some of her panic returned, but surely it was too gloomy for anyone to recognise her.

'This way, please.'

She walked through a pair of sliding doors, blinking at the sudden rush of daylight.

And then she saw the car.

It was sleek and dark, both anonymous and yet unnervingly familiar—as was Marco, the uniformed chauffeur in the driver's seat.

But it wasn't the car or the driver that made her heart lurch.

It was the tall, dark-haired man standing in the sunlight. Even at a distance, the cut and cloth of his dark suit marked him out. He had his back to her, and she stared at the breadth of his shoulders, her nerves jangling.

No. Not him. Not here. She wasn't ready.

There was no need for her to see his face. She would know him in the darkness, would find him in a crowd with her eyes blindfolded. It was as if she had some invisible sixth sense that reacted to his presence like a swallow following the earth's magnetic fields.

Ralph.

But it made no sense for him to be here.

She had told no one which flight she was catching. Even with Lucia she had kept her travel plans deliberately vague.

Yet here he was. Her husband. Or rather her soon-to-be ex-husband.

She stared at him in silence. Not so long ago she would have run into his arms. Now, though, a voice in her head was urging her to turn and run as fast and as far away from him as she could. But every muscle in her body had turned to stone and instead she watched mutely as the younger official stepped forward.

'*Vostro moglie, Signor Castellucci.*'

Your wife, Mr Castellucci.

Her breath hitched in her throat and then her hands started to tremble with shock and disbelief.

She was being delivered.

Like a parcel. Or some mislaid luggage.

Her fingers twitched against the handle of her bag as Ralph slowly turned around.

'*Grazie.*'

His eyes flickered across the Tarmac and he inclined his head, just as if he was dismissing a maid from the tennis-court-sized drawing room of his fifteenth-century *palazzo*.

As she stared at him in silence, she was dimly aware of the two officials retreating. It was five weeks since she had last seen her husband, and in that time she had transformed him into some kind of pantomime villain. Now, though, she was blindsided by the shock of his beauty.

Eyes the colour of raw honeycomb, high cheekbones and the wide curve of his mouth competed in the sunlight for her attention. But it wasn't just about the symmetry and precision of his features. Plenty of actors and models had that. There was something else—something beneath the flawless golden skin that made everyone around him sit up and take notice.

He had a specific kind of self-assurance—an innate, indisputable authority that had been handed down invisibly over hundreds of years through generations of Castelluccis. It came from an assumption that the world had been set up to meet *his* needs. That *his* happiness took precedence over other people's.

Her shoulders tensed. *Even his wife's.*

He was moving towards her and her eyes followed his progress as though pulled by an invisible force of nature. She felt her heartbeat jolt.

She hadn't forgotten the smooth lupine grace with which he moved, but she had underestimated the effect it had on her.

Only why?

Why was she still so vulnerable to him?

Why, after everything he'd done, did this fierce sexual attraction persist?

He stopped in front of her and she felt her breath catch as he tipped her chin up and plucked the cap from her head.

'Surprised to see me?' he said softly.

Mutely, she watched as he lifted his hand in the imperious manner of a Roman emperor, and then the chauffeur was opening the door for her. More out of habit than any conscious intention to obey, she got in.

The door closed and she waited as Ralph crossed behind the car. Then the other door opened, and he slid in beside her.

Moments later, the car began to glide forward.

She felt her stomach muscles clench as he shifted into a more comfortable position.

'Good trip?' he said softly.

His words flicked the tripwire of her nervous anger. He

made it sound as though she'd been on holiday, when they both knew she'd run away.

The note she'd left for him when she'd fled Verona five weeks earlier might have been brief and vague.

I need some space...

But the voicemail she'd left him a week ago had been less ambiguous. She'd told him she would be returning to England after the christening and that she wanted a divorce.

Afterwards she had cried herself to sleep, and during the days that followed she'd been awash with misery, panicking about his possible reaction.

But she needn't have bothered.

Ralph clearly didn't believe she was serious.

To him, all this—her leaving, asking for a divorce—was just a storm in an espresso cup that required only a little of the famous Castellucci diplomacy. And so he'd turned up at the airport to meet her, assuming she would back down as every other Castellucci wife in history had done.

Fine, she thought savagely. If that was the way he wanted to play it, so be it. Let him realise she was serious when he got the letter from her solicitor.

Tamping down her anger, she forced herself to meet his gaze. 'Yes, thank you.' She kept her voice cool. 'But you really didn't need to do this. I'm perfectly capable of taking care of myself.'

'Clearly not.'

Her eyes narrowed. 'What's that supposed to mean?'

'It means that, despite knowing the risks, *bella*, you didn't follow the rules.' His gaze was direct and unwavering. 'If I hadn't intervened you would have walked out of the airport unprotected and—'

'And caught a taxi.' She glared at him. 'Like a normal person.'

Something flared in his golden-brown eyes. 'But you're not a normal person. You're a Castellucci and that makes you a target. And being a target means you need protection.'

Her heartbeat accelerated as a flicker of heat coursed over her skin like an electric current. She did need protection, but the man sitting beside her was a far bigger threat to her health and happiness than some random faceless stranger.

He stretched out his legs and the effort it took her not to inch away from him fuelled her resentment. 'If you've finished lecturing me—'

'I haven't,' he said calmly. 'By not following the rules you're not just a target, you're also a liability. You make it harder for the people responsible for your safety to do their job.'

Heat scalded her cheeks and she felt a wave of anger ripple over her skin.

But he was right.

It had been one of the first conversations they'd had when he'd finally told her about his family—how being a Castellucci was a privilege that came with enormous benefits, but that there were some downsides to being an ultra-high net worth individual.

She could still remember him listing them on his fingers. Stalkers, robbery, kidnapping, extortion…

Cheeks cooling, she edged back in her seat. Except the risk today was minimal, given that he'd clearly had her followed the entire time she was in England.

How else would he have known that she was catching this flight?

Her heart bumped behind her ribs.

Besides, if he wanted to talk about rule-breaking, she

could name a few he'd broken. Like the vows he'd made at their wedding when he'd promised to be true to her.

'People in glass houses don't get to throw stones, Ralph,' she said crisply.

He held her gaze. 'But I don't live in a glass house or any other kind of house, *bella*. I live in a palace. As do you.'

For a few half-seconds she thought about the beautiful home they had shared for six months. The timeless elegance of the vaulted rooms with their frescoes and sumptuous furnishings, the creeper-clad balconies overlooking the formal gardens and the rest of the *palazzo*'s estate.

And then she blanked her mind.

Did he really think that was all he had to do to get their marriage back on track? Remind her of what she would lose? Didn't he understand that she'd already lost the only thing that mattered to her? His heart.

Battening down her misery, she reached up and slowly twisted her hair into a loose ponytail at the nape of her neck. 'Why are you here, Ralph?' she said quietly.

Honey-coloured eyes locked with hers as his mouth curved at one corner. 'I take care of what belongs to me.'

She looked at him incredulously. How could he say that after what he'd done? He had broken her heart.

But in the grand scheme of things the compensations of being a Castellucci more than made up for a little heart-break and a bruised ego.

Or that was what everyone kept telling her.

Only none of those things—his wealth, his connections and social status—were what mattered to her. They never would. That was why she had left and why she would be leaving again.

And this time she wouldn't be coming back.

'You have people here. They could have done it for you,' she persisted.

He shrugged. 'I wanted to meet my wife at the airport.' He held her gaze. 'You are still my wife, Giulietta,' he said softly.

Her chin jerked upwards, his words jolting her.

Everyone else called her Letty. He alone called her by her full name, but in the Italian form, and the achingly familiar soft intonation felt like a caress.

The narrowed gaze that accompanied it, on the other hand, felt like sandpaper scraping across her skin.

Her eyes found his. The anger and the bruised ego were there—she could see it simmering beneath the surface.

But that was the problem. He would never show it. He was always so in control.

Glancing across the seat, she felt her pulse skip and her breasts tighten as her body, her blood, responded to the memories stirring beneath her skin.

He was not always in control. Not when they made love.

Then he was like a different man. Every breath, every touch, unrestrained, urgent, unfeigned.

Her breathing slowed as images of his naked body moving against hers crowded into her head. She felt her skin grow warm.

Back in England she had felt so certain, so sure that it was all wrong between them, but being alone with him now was making her second-guess herself.

Only there was nothing to second-guess.

She had seen it with her own eyes.

He was having an affair.

Heart thumping against her ribs, she stared at him mutely, the knot of anger hardening in her stomach. He had deceived and betrayed her, lied to her face. And, judging by the fact that he'd not even attempted to get in touch with her over the last five weeks, he'd clearly been having far too much fun with his dark-haired lover to care about her absence.

The thought of the two of them together made her feel sick, and suddenly she was done with playing games. What was the point of delaying the inevitable? Why not confront him now?

Lifting her chin, she met his gaze head-on. 'Not for much longer.'

There was a long silence.

Glancing up, she saw the glitter in his eyes and it made a shiver run down her spine.

He raised an eyebrow. 'You think?'

A tiny part of her wished she already had the paperwork from her solicitor, so she could throw it into his handsome, arrogant face. The rest of her was too busy trying to ignore the effect his casual question was having on her nerve-ends.

'Did you not get my message?' she asked.

'Ah, yes, your message…'

Slouching backwards, he nodded slowly, as though he was a record producer and she had sent him a particularly uninspiring demo.

'It was all so sudden. I assumed you were being…' He paused, frowning and clicking his fingers for inspiration. 'What's the word? Oh, yes, dramatic. London's theatreland rubbing off on you.'

She held his gaze. 'I want a divorce.'

If she was looking for a reaction she didn't get one.

He merely inclined his head. 'That's not going to happen, *bella*.'

His voice was soft, but there was an unequivocal finality to his words.

'It's not up to you, Ralph.' She was battling with her anger.

He stared at her steadily. 'Now you really *are* being dramatic.'

She wanted to hit him. 'I want a divorce, Ralph. I don't want anything else.'

It wasn't just words. She really didn't want anything from him. It was going to be hard enough getting over her marriage as it was. It would be so much harder if there were reminders of him everywhere.

'I'm not looking for any drama or some cash prize. I just want a divorce.'

His expression hardened, his eyes trapping hers. 'And what are you expecting me to say to that, Giulietta?'

'I'm expecting you to say yes.' Her fingers curled into her palms. 'Look, we both know this isn't working. *We* don't work as a couple.'

Probably because they weren't a couple any more, she thought dully. Now there were three of them in the marriage.

'And that's what you do, is it? When something doesn't work.' His eyes locked with hers. 'You just discard it.'

She stared at him incredulously, feeling an ache spread through her chest like spilt ink. How could he say that after what he'd done? After what he'd thrown away.

Her eyes blazed. 'Our marriage hasn't meant anything to you for months.'

'And yet you're the one who's walking out,' he said slowly.

She took a breath, trying to control her escalating temper. 'Because you are having an affair!'

Even just saying the words out loud hurt, but his gaze didn't so much as waver.

'So you said. And I denied it.'

Her head was pounding in time with her heart. 'Look, I've made up my mind, so you can stop lying to me now—'

His eyes narrowed almost imperceptibly. 'I didn't lie. I told you I wasn't having an affair. That was true then, and it's still true now. Only you chose, and are still choosing, not to believe me.'

She stared at him, the memory of that terrible argument replaying inside her head. Although usually an argument required the participation of more than one person...

Remembering her angry accusations and his one-word denials, she felt a beat of anger bounce across her skin. 'There was no choice to make, Ralph. I believe what I believe because I saw it with my own eyes.' She drew a deep breath. 'Now, are we done?'

'Not even close.' His jaw tightened. 'You didn't see what you thought you did.'

'Of course I didn't.' She hated the bitterness in her voice, but it was beyond her control. 'So explain it to me, then. What exactly did I see?'

He was silent for so long she thought he wasn't going to answer.

Finally, though, he shrugged. 'She doesn't threaten you—us.'

His reply made her breathing jerk. 'Oh, I get it. You mean it's not serious?' She shook her head, her chest aching with anger and misery. 'And that's supposed to make it all right, is it? I should just put up and shut up.'

'You're twisting my words.'

Her head was hurting now. She was so stupid. For just a moment she'd thought that finally she'd got through to him. But it was all just the same old, same old.

'You know what, Ralph? I'm not doing this with you. Not here, not now.' Leaning forward, she tapped on the glass behind Marco. 'Can you drop me at this address, please?' Glancing down at her phone, she read out a street name. 'It's near the hospital.'

'What do you think you're doing?' His voice had become dangerously soft.

Forcing herself to hold his gaze, she took a deep breath. 'I'm going to my hotel.'

He raised an eyebrow. 'Hotel?'

'Yes, Ralph. It's a place where people stay overnight when they go away.' Watching his eyes narrow, she gave him a small smile. 'I think it's for the best if we keep our distance from one another.'

He stared at her for a long moment. 'You mean you're worried you won't be able to resist me.'

Her skin prickled. 'No, I just don't want you turning up at the christening with a black eye,' she said stiffly. 'But you don't need to worry. I'll play my part at the ceremony, and the party, and I made the hotel reservation in my maiden name.'

Something primitive darkened his expression. 'Show me,' he demanded.

Feeling all fingers and thumbs, she tilted the screen towards him.

'I don't know this hotel.'

Of course he didn't. For Ralph, like all his family and friends, there was only one hotel in Verona. The five-star Due Torri.

She shrugged. 'It's only for one night. I just want somewhere clean and quiet.'

'I'm sure it's both, but…'

He paused and she felt a shiver of apprehension. There was something wrong—a disconnect between his reasonable tone and the glitter in his eyes.

'But what?'

'But if it isn't it won't matter.'

As his gaze drifted lazily over her face a chill began to spread through her bones.

'Because you won't be staying there.'

Her eyes clashed with his. 'Oh, but I will. And there's nothing you can do about it,' she added hotly as he started to shake his head.

He met her gaze with equanimity. 'It's already done. I've had someone cancel your reservation. It's time to come home, *bella*.'

CHAPTER TWO

WATCHING HIS WIFE'S brown eyes widen with shock, Ralph felt a savage stab of satisfaction. *Good*, he thought coolly. Now she knew what it felt like.

Although there was obviously no comparison between her shock and his...

Gritting his teeth, he replayed the moment when he'd walked into their bedroom and seen the envelope on his bedside table. Even now he could still feel his anger, his disbelief, at returning home and finding his bed empty and his wife gone.

Although, in the scheme of things, that was one of her lesser crimes.

He glanced over at his beautiful, deceitful wife. An oversized linen blazer disguised the curves beneath her dark jeans and white T-shirt, and she was make-up-free aside from the matt nude lipstick she loved.

She looked more like a gap year student than the wife of a billionaire. But, whatever she might say to the contrary, she was still his wife. And that wasn't about to change any time soon. Make that *ever*.

It was five weeks since she had bolted from his life, leaving no clue about her motives or plans except a two-line note. But he hadn't needed any note to know why she had fled. She'd still been steaming over that row they'd had. A row he knew he could have done more to mitigate.

Except why should he have to mitigate anything?

He had told her the truth. Vittoria was not his mistress. Their relationship was complicated, but completely innocent. As his wife, Giulietta should have believed him. In fact, she shouldn't even have asked the question.

Most women in her position—his cousins' wives and his aunts for example—would have understood that.

But his wife was not most women.

He glanced over at her, watching the flush of anger colour her sculpted cheekbones.

When he'd first noticed Juliet Jones on that chilly afternoon in Rome, it hadn't been for those glorious cheekbones, her bee-stung lips or glossy tortoiseshell hair. In fact, her hair had been hanging down in rat's tails and she hadn't looked that different from the half-drowned cat she'd been trying and failing to rescue.

No woman he knew would have been out in that downpour, much less halfway down a storm drain.

But then Giulietta was not like any other woman he knew.

He had fallen for her beauty and the fire in her eyes— fallen deeper for her smile and her laugh. And then she had made *him* laugh. There had been no doubt, no hesitation in his heart. She was his soulmate. He knew what she was thinking, what she was feeling...

Or he had thought he did.

Remembering the empty packet of contraceptive pills in the bin, he felt his jaw tighten. It didn't make any sense. They'd been trying for a baby—

Except apparently they hadn't.

Hadn't she known how much it meant to him to have a child?

Had he not made it clear how important it was to him to have a son or daughter of his own?

It made no sense, her behaviour. She'd wanted a baby

as much as he did—had been eager to start trying. Or so she'd said.

But women—some women anyway—were very good at keeping secrets.

'You had no right!' She practically spat the words at him, her eyes flaring with fury.

'To protect my wife?' He frowned. 'Most husbands would disagree with you.'

She scowled at him. 'Well, it doesn't matter anyway. I'm just going to rebook it.'

With her hair tumbling free of its ponytail and her flushed cheeks she looked the way she had in Rome that first day, when they had kissed their way upstairs to her room.

His stomach muscles tightened. He'd missed her—missed her fire and her spirit—and for a moment he considered running his finger over her soft, flushed curves.

But he still had scars from the last feral cat he'd cornered…

'I thought you might,' he said mildly. 'So I took the precaution of booking all the available rooms.'

Her eyes widened with shock, and then she rallied. 'Then I'll book another hotel.'

'You can try.'

She stared at him, her mouth an O of disbelief. 'You can't have booked out the whole of Verona, Ralph.'

For a moment he thought about toying with her, stringing her along as she had strung him along for months now.

'I didn't need to,' he said finally. 'In all the excitement you appear to have forgotten that the opera festival starts this weekend. You'll be lucky to get a manger in a stable.'

His people had reserved the few remaining rooms that had still been available, but he would have booked every room in the city if it had been necessary. He had the wealth and the power to surmount any obstacle in his path. And when it came to his wife he was prepared to use any and all means at his disposal to get her back where she belonged.

Sighing, he pulled out his phone.

'I suppose you'd better stay with Lucia. I know she has her family and Luca's there. And, of course, she's got Raffaelle's christening to organise, but…'

He watched the emotions chase across her beautiful face, ticking them off inside his head.

Confusion.

Outrage.

Then, last but most satisfying of all, resignation.

'Okay, then.' It was almost a shout.

Snatching the phone from his hand, she threw it onto the seat between them and slid as far from him as physically possible.

'Does that mean you've decided to come home with me after all?'

Momentarily the flicker of fury in her dark eyes reminded him of the flickering candles in the simple trattoria where she had treated him to dinner the night they'd first met.

'I hate you.'

'I'll take that as a yes,' he said softly.

Shifting back against the cool leather, he let his gaze skim over her rigid profile, then down to her tightly closed fists.

She wasn't exaggerating. She really did hate him.

And maybe if they'd been anywhere else in the world he might have been worried. But this was Verona, a city where hate and love were inextricably linked. All he needed to do now was remind his Juliet of that fact.

* * *

'Buongiorno, Signor Castellucci. Benvenuto a casa, Signora Castellucci.'

They had arrived at the Palazzo Gioacchino.

Striding into the imposing hallway, Ralph nodded at the small, balding man who was waiting for them.

'Buongiorno, Roberto. Signora Castellucci and I will take coffee on the terrace.'

Giulietta had followed him inside, but now he felt her hesitate. A ripple of irritation snaked over his skin. She had no idea what she had put him through these last few weeks, or how hard it had been to give her the space she'd requested. But he had done it. He'd made himself wait.

Knowing the mistakes his father had made with his mother, how could he not have done?

His hands curled into his palms. He had given her a week, thinking he was doing the right thing, and then two. Two had become four, then five, and then suddenly she was asking him for a divorce.

A divorce.

Listening to her message, all he'd been able to think was, *This cannot be happening. This can't be what she wants.*

Even now it blew his mind—and he knew they would have a short, edifying conversation about it soon. But it would have to wait until after the christening. Luca and Lucia didn't need their special day overshadowed by some bump in his marriage.

And, whatever Giulietta might think to the contrary, that was all this was. A bump.

There would be no divorce. Not now. Not at any point in the future.

'Is there a problem, *bella*?' he said roughly.

She was staring at him as if he'd suddenly grown an

extra head. 'You mean other than you forcing me to stay here?'

Anger and frustration clouded her features, and if she'd had a tail it would have been flicking from side to side.

Frowning, he glanced pointedly round the opulent hallway. 'This is your home. I shouldn't need to force you to stay.' He let his gaze rest on her face. 'But if that's how you feel, *mia moglie*, then maybe you need to rethink your priorities.'

Her priorities.

That was the problem.

Surely her priorities should run in tandem with his? She'd certainly led him to think that was the case.

But the empty blister pack he'd found said otherwise...

He heard her take a breath, could see the pulse jumping at the base of her throat as she glared at him.

'You have to be kidding. You know all those beautiful Venetian mirrors in the drawing room? Well, you need to take a good look at yourself in one of them. Because it's not me who needs to rethink their priorities.'

If she'd been angry before, she looked as if she wanted to hit him now. Only why? He'd given her the space she'd demanded. Why couldn't she do the same? Why couldn't she back off and just accept what he'd told her? That what she'd seen didn't threaten their marriage.

But, no, she had to go flouncing back to England.

He shook his head slowly. 'And yet you are the one behaving like a petulant child.'

Her mouth dropped open, but without giving her a chance to reply he spun on his heel and walked away from her.

As he strode through the rooms, past the rare French and Italian tapestries on the walls, he tugged off his jacket and tossed it onto a chair.

'In what way is that true?' She had followed him. 'Tell me.'

They were outside now. She blinked in the sunlight.

'What? I'm being childish because I had the effrontery to get upset that you cancelled my hotel room?'

'Which I did for obvious and understandable reasons.'

Her eyes flared. 'In other words, you were protecting the Castellucci brand.'

His jaw tightened, but he resisted the urge to tell her that as her surname wasn't ever going to change *she* was part of that brand.

'My decision to cancel your booking had nothing to do with my family.' Why was she so determined to think ill of him? 'I was thinking about our friends and how they would feel if their son's christening got turned into a circus by his godparents.'

He took a step towards her.

He had been thinking, too, about his wife.

His chest tightened. It had been hard enough when she had been in London, but knowing she was here in his city, sleeping in some strange bed instead of by his side...he couldn't let that happen.

'I was careful,' she said.

But the colour had drained from her cheeks and he could hear the catch in her voice.

'Not careful enough,' he said quietly.

Even after six months as a Castellucci she still didn't get it. She still hadn't accepted that her life was not like other people's. And, like his mother, apparently she wanted something different—something more.

The thought made his stomach muscles tighten painfully. 'What if the taxi driver had recognised you? Or someone at the hotel? That's all it would take.'

There was a long silence. She was biting her lip.

'I thought it would be awkward...me staying here.'

He studied her face: the full, soft mouth, the dark arch of her eyebrows, the eyes the colour of molten chocolate. Eyes that had lost their anger.

A pulse of heat danced across his skin as the silence lengthened. Did she know how beautiful she was? How much he wanted her? He didn't even need to touch her to get turned on.

But that didn't mean he wasn't interested in touching her. He was.

He was very interested.

As though reading his thoughts, she lifted her chin and their eyes collided. Around them the air was pulsing in time with his blood surging south.

Reaching out, he touched her cheek, let his hand slide through her hair, feeling the glossy weight. 'Does this feel awkward to you, *bella*?'

Heart pounding, Juliet stared at him, shivers of anticipation tingling across her skin. One second she had been standing in front of him, blinded not just by sunlight but by anger, the next his hand had been caressing her cheek.

Stop this now, she ordered herself, her hands pushing against his chest.

Except they weren't pushing.

Instead, her trembling fingers were splaying out, biting into the cool cotton of his shirt.

And now time had stopped, and everything was fading into the background, and she was conscious of nothing but the man and the pulsing wayward urges of her body.

Her heartbeat accelerated as she silently answered his question. *No*, this part of their life had never been awkward. Not even that first time—her first time.

Her skin tightened as she remembered those magical hours in Rome.

The tangle of sheets and their bodies blurring over and over again in that stuffy little bedroom.

Before Ralph she'd done things with guys, but always something had stopped her from going all the way. Her nerves, their clumsiness, a lack of the chemistry she assumed would and should be there. But mostly it had been an unspoken need for her first time to matter. Or, more accurately, for *her* to matter.

That was the difference between her and her friends. Obviously they had wanted their first time to be a good experience too, but they'd grown up believing they mattered, so for them it had been more about getting their virginity 'out of the way'.

It had never been in the way of anything she wanted.

Her pulse dipped.

Until she'd met Ralph.

And he had been worth the wait.

From that first caress everything had flowed like water. At some point they had become one, and by then there had been no barriers between them.

Remembering his smooth, sleek skin, and the tormenting pleasure of his touch, she felt her body grow warm. She had known that sex could be quick or slow, tender or passionate, but she hadn't known that it had the power to heal. That it could make you feel whole.

Her eyes fluttered over his body. He had taken off his jacket and he was close enough for her to see the definition of hard muscle and the hint of hair beneath his immaculate handmade shirt.

So close that she could feel the heat of his skin.

Feel the heat racing along her limbs.

But she was over him.

Wasn't that why she had walked out of this glittering palace and away from their life? Why she had told him she wanted a divorce? So she could walk away for ever and move on with her life.

And yet she could feel herself leaning closer, feel her body starting to soften, her pulse to slow. It would be so easy to move nearer, to thread her fingers through his tousled hair, sink into his body and feel that perfect curving mouth against her lips.

There was the clink of china behind her back. For a moment she felt her body sway like a pendulum, and then she took a step backwards, glancing over to where Roberto was putting down a tray on the glass-topped table.

The skin on her palms felt as though it had been burned. Her cheek, on the other hand, felt cool without Ralph's hand there. She took a shaky breath, her pulse ragged with shock and exasperation.

One touch! Was that all it took to make her forget all sense of self-preservation? *Clearly she had been out in the sun too long.*

'Would you like me to pour the coffee, *signor*?'

'No, it's fine, Roberto.' Ralph was shaking his head, but his eyes stayed locked with hers. 'We can manage— can't we, *cara*?'

We.

She felt her stomach flip over. His choice of word was deliberate, and she waited impatiently, nerves jangling, for Roberto to leave the terrace.

'Won't you join me?' he asked.

She turned, her eyes narrowing, as her husband dropped down into a chair and sprawled out against the linen cushions.

'What are you doing?' she said hoarsely.

'I'm sitting down.'

'I meant before. What was that all about?'

He stared at her steadily, his face impassive. 'You said

we didn't work as a couple. I was just reminding you that we do.'

She glared at him, the truth of his words only making her angrier with both him and herself. 'We don't.'

'So what was that, then? And please don't tell me it was a mistake,' he said softly.

'It was nothing.'

She wanted to move further away, to get more distance between them, but that would simply suggest that the opposite of what she was saying was true.

'Nothing happened and nothing is going to happen,' she said stiffly.

His golden gaze was direct and unwavering. 'You can't fight it, *bella*. It's stronger than both of us.'

His cool statement made her breathing jerk.

It scared her that he might be right. That years from now, maybe decades, she would still crave Ralph as she did now. It didn't matter that she would never admit that to him—she couldn't lie to herself.

And what made it worse—*no*, what made it wrong—was that her hunger for him was unchanged even though she knew he'd been unfaithful.

Surely that should have diminished her desire? Eased the ache inside her?

The fact that it hadn't scared her more than anything else. She didn't want to be that woman—to be vulnerable.

Only she was vulnerable where Ralph was concerned.

She knew how easy it would be to give in to the heat of her hunger, to go where he wanted to take her, just as she'd done at the airport.

Her hands tightened into fists.

But it was bad enough that Ralph had betrayed her. She didn't need to betray herself too.

'That doesn't make it right,' she said. 'Just because you

want something—*someone*—it doesn't mean it's okay to act on that desire.'

She felt a spasm of pain, remembering the moment when she'd seen Ralph guiding his mistress in the street, the intensity of his gaze, the urgency of his hand on the car door.

Lifting her chin, she locked her eyes with his. 'But obviously I can see why you might find that a difficult concept.'

Watching her face, Ralph felt his shoulders tense. On the contrary, he thought. He'd spent five weeks *not* acting—five long weeks tamping down his anger. Now he could feel it rising to the surface.

He wanted to shake her.

Gazing up at her flushed face and the glossy hair spilling free of its ponytail, he felt his groin harden.

Actually, no. He wanted to kiss her.

Here, now, he wanted to pull her into his arms and cover her soft mouth with his, to strip her naked and make her what she had been before and would be soon enough again.

His.

But he resisted the temptation to act on his desire. There was plenty of time. What mattered was that she was here and not in some shabby hotel on the outskirts of the city.

Everything was going according to plan.

Tomorrow they would arrive at the christening together.

Afterwards they would leave together.

Later in the week she would be by his side like a good wife, welcoming guests to the Castellucci Ball.

And then he would get answers to the questions that had been swirling like storm clouds inside his head.

But for now he would be patient.

Not that his beautiful, baffling wife would believe that was possible...

He stared at her steadily, his mind searching its own corners for words that could douse her fire and fury—temporarily at least.

But why did he need eloquence? Simple and honest might actually work best.

Sighing, he gestured towards the sofa. 'Look, I get that you're angry with me, and we clearly need to talk, but could we just put this particular conversation on hold? For our friends? For Lucia and Luca?'

Her face was stiff with tension, but he could see she was listening.

'It's their son's christening. Our godson's christening. And we might not be in agreement about much right now, but I know neither of us wants to do anything that might impact on Raffaelle's special day.'

There was a beat of silence as her dark eyes searched his face, and then she sat down stiffly on the sofa opposite him. He felt a rush of triumph, and relief.

'Coffee?' he said.

She nodded slowly. 'But, so we're clear. Just because I've agreed to stay here, it doesn't mean I'll be sharing a bed with you.'

Sitting down, he picked up his cup and took a sip of coffee, deliberately letting the silence swell between them.

The Castelluccis had been, and still were, one of the most powerful families in Italy. For that reason alone most women would have burned a path across the earth to share his bed.

Not his wife, though.

His pulse skipped a beat.

It was tempting to haul her across the sofa's feather-filled cushions and demonstrate that a bed wasn't necessary for what he had in mind. But, much as he wanted to do so, what mattered more was that she came to him willingly, wantonly, as she had before.

Remembering the softness of her skin, the urgency of her touch, the smooth dovetailing of her body with his as she melted into him, he felt his groin tighten. And then, blanking his mind, he shrugged.

'That won't be a problem. There are twenty-five bedrooms here, *bella*. I'm sure one of them will meet with your satisfaction.'

Roberto would have had her case taken to their room, but that was easily resolved. The butler had worked for the Castellucci family for thirty years. He was both quietly efficient and discreet when it came to family matters—as were all members of the household staff.

'But you will dine with me tonight?' he said.

He held her gaze…could almost see her brain working through a flow chart of possible outcomes.

Finally, though, she nodded. 'I suppose we both have to eat.' Smoothing down her jeans, she stood up, her eyes dark and defiant. 'I'm going to freshen up. I'll see you at dinner.'

Forty minutes later she was staring at her reflection and wondering why she hadn't just said no.

It was crazy.

She could easily have had a tray sent up to her room.

But, then again, she was going to have to see him at the christening anyway, and it was clear she needed to practise pretending that everything was fine between them.

Blotting her lips, she checked her reflection again.

And she wanted to prove to herself and to Ralph that what had happened out on the terrace had been a one-off. A moment when the past and present had overlapped.

Picturing the up-curve of his mouth and the familiar

blunt expression on his face as he'd stared down at her, she felt her breath hitch in her throat.

She knew time couldn't stop or stand still, but just for those few seconds it had felt as though the laws of physics had been disrupted and they were back at the beginning, before everything unravelled.

Her mouth thinned.

And maybe that was a good thing.

Those few seconds had amply proved just how naive she had been, assuming an explosive sexual chemistry like theirs could simply be switched off.

Looking back at the mirror, she adjusted the neckline of her dark blue sleeveless shirt dress.

But, as she'd told Ralph, it wouldn't happen again— whatever she wore tonight needed to reinforce not undermine that message, and this dress was perfect.

For a moment she considered putting a thin cardigan over the top, but that might imply that she needed additional barriers between them.

Plus, it would remind her of Rome…

Her lip curled. *No.* Rome was the past.

If she thought about Rome then it would be all too easy to let good memories persuade her that his betrayal had been a momentary lapse. Particularly now that she was here in Verona…in the home they shared.

Only it wouldn't be her home for much longer.

She swallowed against the lump in her throat. It hurt to let go of the past and the passion. But there was no point in holding it close. In thinking that things would change. That people changed.

Her body tensed.

Been there, done that.

And not just once, she thought, closing her eyes.

For a few half-seconds she let herself go back…let memories float up through the darkness.

Other children had been raised by their parents. She had been forged. So often she had been out of her depth, and always it had felt as if she was waiting and hoping. Waiting for the inevitable. For things to go wrong, for the latest set of promises to be broken. Hoping that this time would be different. Only that had just made the disappointment worse.

She opened her eyes and stared at her pale, set face in the mirror.

Ralph had been right.

Some things were too relentless, too immutable to fight. And, no matter how much she wanted to stay and keep fighting, she knew from experience that the only way to survive mentally, emotionally, was to walk away.

So, however much it hurt, however desperately she wanted to hold on to the dream of her marriage, that was what she was going to do.

Walking downstairs, though, took more courage than she'd thought. Her beautiful home seemed both different and yet familiar, so that she felt as if she was sleepwalking in a dream.

'*Buonasera, Signora Castellucci.*' Roberto greeted her as she walked into the drawing room. 'Signor Castellucci is waiting for you on the terrace.'

'*Grazie*, Roberto.'

She walked outside, her breath tangling in her throat. They hadn't often eaten alone in the evening. He'd worked long hours—longer after Carlo had been taken ill. And on the rare occasions when they hadn't been attending a party or a charity event there had been numerous family commitments.

Her heart twisted.

It was ironic that only a few months ago she'd actually longed for an evening when it would be just the two of them.

She felt her pulse stutter as she spotted Ralph. He was standing with his back to her, as he had at the airport, his gaze directed towards the yellowing lights of Verona. Gone was the dark suit of earlier. Instead he was wearing pale chinos and a dark brown polo shirt that hugged his broad shoulders.

As he turned towards her, she stared at him mutely. The Castelluccis might live in palaces, but they had a horror of the baroque or flamboyant. Ralph's clothes were a masterclass in the kind of high-end stealth-wealth camouflage loved by his family. Inconspicuous, logo-less, but eye-wateringly expensive.

She hadn't realised that in Rome. She'd been too smitten, too dazzled by his beauty and confidence to think about his clothes. He'd told her he was taking a few days off and his jeans and sports jacket had reflected that.

Now, though, she knew that, however casually her husband was dressed, he was rarely off duty or off guard.

She walked towards him, her skin tightening as his gaze drifted slowly over her dress down to her sandaled feet.

'You look beautiful,' he said quietly.

She accepted his compliment. Her plan was to stay cool, but polite, to eat, and then to excuse herself as soon as possible. 'Thank you.'

'What would you like to drink?'

'Sparkling water would be lovely.'

She was careful to avoid his fingers as she took the glass from his outstretched hand.

Glancing across to the table, she felt a flutter of relief. There were candles, but there was still enough daylight to offset any seductive overtones from the fluttering flames.

'Shall we?' Ralph gestured towards the table. 'Unless you—?'

'No, let's eat,' she said quickly.

The sooner this was over the better.

He stood behind her, waiting while she sat down. And, nerves tightening, she held her breath until he was safely seated opposite her.

'So, how was England?' he asked.

She had half thought he might pick up their conversation from where he'd left off earlier, but if he wanted to talk about England that suited her fine.

Ralph's chef, Giancarlo, had run an award-winning *cantina* in Venice, and his food was innovative, quintessentially Italian and delicious. But her stomach was tight with nerves and each mouthful of her ravioli with lobster and saffron was harder to swallow than the last.

'Relax, *bella*. It's just some pasta in a sauce.'

His lazy smile made her chest ache with an unsettling mix of regret and longing.

'But don't tell Giancarlo I said that. He still hasn't forgotten when I asked him to make a Hawaiian pizza for my seventh birthday.'

Her laugh was involuntary. 'Did he make it?'

'Of course. I always get what I want,' he said softly.

Her blood turned to air as he reached over and lightly traced the curve of her mouth.

'You have such a beautiful smile. I'd forgotten just how beautiful, and that's my fault.' His mouth twisted. 'All of this is my fault. I know that. But I want you to know that I can change, and if you give me a chance I will prove that to you.'

The pull of his words was making her breathless. She so wanted to believe him, but—

She batted his hand away. 'I'm sorry, but that's not what I want.'

'And *I'm* sorry, but I don't believe you.' His eyes didn't leave her face. 'Giulietta, we have something special.'

'*Had* something special,' she corrected him.

Or maybe they hadn't. She didn't know any more. That blissful certainty of finding her one true love had been no more than pyrite—fool's gold—and she would be a fool to go back to the pain of loving him again.

'Please, Ralph, there's no purpose to any of this.'

'No purpose to fighting for our marriage?' He frowned. 'We promised to be there for one another, for better and for worse.'

She opened her mouth, then closed it again. She didn't want to think, much less talk about their wedding day, or the vows he had unilaterally broken. What was the point?

'Giulietta—?' he prompted her.

'*What*, Ralph?' Her voice was vibrating with reproach and accusation. 'What do you want me to say?'

His eyes hardened. 'Look, I know this has been a tough time, but all marriages go through rocky patches.'

She knew they did. A lifetime in and out of foster care was proof of that.

But, looking at his face, she felt her heart twist. This wasn't about reconciliation. It was about pride and power. Ralph Castellucci simply didn't understand the word *no*.

She stood up from the table and took a step back 'They do, but not everyone wilfully steers the boat onto the rocks.'

Ralph stared at her in exasperation.

Moments earlier she had smiled a smile he remembered and missed…a smile of such sweetness that he could almost taste it in his mouth.

And, watching her, he had felt a sudden rush of hope

that maybe he didn't have to be alone with the truth any more. That maybe he could finally confess to her and then everything would go back to how it used to be.

But how could he tell her the truth? She wouldn't even meet him halfway, even though she was the guilty party. She had lied and deceived him, only apparently all this was his fault.

'It's not me who steered the boat onto the rocks. I can sail with my eyes shut.'

Her eyes narrowed. 'I'm not talking about the *Alighieri*.'

'Neither am I,' he said softly.

She glared at him, her teeth bared. 'What's that supposed to mean?'

It was on the tip of his tongue to tell her. To upend her world as she'd upended his. But he wanted time and privacy for this conversation. Fortunately, he had just the place in mind.

For a moment a strained silence hung between them, and then she took another step backwards. 'I think we're done here, don't you?'

Watching her stalk back into the house, Ralph picked up his glass and downed the contents.

They weren't done. Far from it. But he could afford to let her go. Afford to wait until the time was right. And then he would prove to her just how seriously he took his marriage vows.

CHAPTER THREE

'*EHI*, CASTELLUCCI! OVER HERE!'

Glancing over the heads of the guests gathered outside the beautiful Romanesque church, Juliet felt her lips curve upwards as she spotted a smiling Lucia holding Raffaelle. Beside her, Luca was waving and grinning.

She looked up at Ralph. 'They're over—'

'I can see them.'

Her body tensed as his hand caught hers, but he was already tugging her forward. 'This way.'

How did he do this? she wondered. There was an incredible number of people milling around in the square, and yet the crowd was parting like a Biblical sea as he guided her towards Lucia and Luca.

Following in his footsteps, she had the usual feeling of being both protected and horribly conspicuous—as if every eye was tracking her through the crowd, judging her hair, her clothes, her weight, her suitability as a Castellucci bride.

She had never really got used to it—no more than she had got used to the bodyguards who were an integral part of life for the super-rich. And now, after five peaceful, anonymous weeks back in England, she felt extra naked.

Not a particularly relaxing sensation to have around Ralph, she thought, feeling his gaze and his fingertips on her back.

'*Amico!*'

As Luca grabbed Ralph in one of those complicated one-armed man hugs, Lucia kissed her on both cheeks. 'Letty, you look beautiful. I love that dress.' Her eyes widened. 'And those shoes!'

Glancing down at her dark red heels, Juliet laughed. 'I'm happy to swap. Truly. I nearly broke my neck just walking here from the car.'

Lucia breathed out shakily. 'I'm so glad you're back. Promise me you won't disappear like that again.'

It was a simple exchange between friends, and yet Juliet could feel a tingling warmth creeping down her spine. From somewhere over her shoulder, she was aware of Ralph's gaze boring into the back of her head.

She hesitated, not wanting to lie, but also wanting to reassure her friend. Only the stubborn need to remind her husband that he wasn't calling the shots forbade her from doing so.

'I didn't disappear,' she said quickly, sidestepping the question. 'But I did miss you and...' she glanced down at Raffaelle '... I missed this little one too.'

Reaching out, she gently stroked his cheek, feeling something unravelling inside her as the baby grabbed her fingers with one chubby hand. With his dark, silky hair and huge brown eyes, he was utterly gorgeous.

'Hey, *ometto*...'

Even without hearing his voice, she knew that Ralph was standing beside her. She could feel his eyes picking over her face, looking at her hand in Raffaelle's, and the sharp ache in her heart made her feel faint.

Watching the baby's lips flutter into a smile, Juliet felt her heart contract. She'd wanted a baby so badly. Ralph even more so. Although perhaps it might be more accurate to say that he'd wanted an heir.

A sharp pulse of pain made her press her fingers against

her forehead. Was all this her fault? Would it have been different if she'd got pregnant?

Yes. No...

Truthfully, she didn't know. But she did know that if she'd kept on playing by his rules their child would have grown up in Ralph's gilded world. Heir to a fortune, and surrounded by unimaginable luxury and opulence.

Except that wasn't enough.

Not if that world required her son or daughter to grow up as she had—surrounded by lies and compromise and broken promises.

Gazing down at the baby, she felt her throat tighten. She knew how painful that was—knew too that you could never outrun the damage it caused.

Why else had she married a man like Ralph?

A man whose carelessness with people's feelings matched—no, *surpassed* that of her parents.

As a child she'd had no control over her life. She hadn't understood then that her parents' choices had required her to give up something of herself. But she did understand now that if her marriage continued she would be pitched back into the pain and uncertainty of her childhood.

Only she wasn't a child now. She was an adult. And she couldn't—she wouldn't—go there again.

She wouldn't be trapped in a loveless marriage.

Not even for Ralph.

Shifting the baby in her arms, so that Ralph could kiss her, Lucia grimaced. 'He's not so little now. He's actually the biggest baby in our mother and baby group,' she added proudly.

'That's because he takes after his *papà*.' Leaning forward, Luca blew on his son's neck, grinning as the baby squirmed and giggled in delight. 'We Bocchetti men inspire superlatives.'

'Yes, you do.' Ralph grabbed his friend round the shoulders. 'Like dumbest and most uncool.'

Lucia burst out laughing, but Juliet barely registered the joke. It was the lazy smile pulling at Ralph's mouth that had captured her attention and was holding it with gravitational force.

Around her, she felt the women in the crowd crane forward, like flowers turning towards the sun, and despite her resentment she completely understood why.

It was a smile that promised and delivered unimaginable pleasure.

Other promises, though, he found harder to keep.

And yet seeing him with his friends made it hard to remember that.

Her heart began beating a little faster.

She hardly ever saw this side of him—perhaps only ever with Luca, his childhood friend…the one person he seemed able to relax around.

With his family—particularly the older members—he was serious and formal. And his cousins Nico and Felix were too in awe of his status as heir, too anxious both for his attention and his approval to fully relax with him.

Perhaps he had been different with his mother?

But Francesca Castellucci had died just over a year ago, and although Ralph had told her about his mother's illness he hadn't offered any insights into their relationship.

Her heartbeat accelerated. It was something they had in common, that reluctance to talk about their mothers. Although not, she was sure, for the same reasons.

She had no desire to talk about any of her parents. Not her numerous foster parents and particularly not her biological ones.

Nancy and Johnny had collided when Nancy was just seventeen. Their marriage had been an unhappy mix of easy sex and complicated emotion, and almost exactly nine months from the day they'd met they'd become parents.

Juliet felt a familiar nausea squeeze her stomach.

By then there had already been fault lines in the relationship, and they'd got deeper and wider after her arrival.

For weeks at a time, sometimes months, it would work. But sooner or later it had always fallen apart, and she had always been waiting for that moment to happen, body tense, all five senses on high alert, trying to anticipate every potential flash point.

An empty milk carton.

Money missing from a purse.

A dropped call.

She swallowed. Telling Ralph about her childhood hadn't been an option. She had shared the bare bones with him, but she knew he would never understand the chaos, the lack of control, the insecurity.

How could he? He'd grown up in a palace, the pampered heir to a fortune, and he was part of a large and close family.

Correction: they were close to *him*. To her they were polite, but clearly baffled as to why someone like Ralph had chosen someone like her.

Her stomach churned.

And, judging by his behaviour, Ralph was starting to agree with them.

'Are you ready?'

She turned at his voice. Ralph was looking down at her steadily, the corners of his eyes creasing, and she felt suddenly as if the crowds had parted again and it was just the two of them, standing outside in the mid-morning sunlight.

As usual, he looked ridiculously handsome. Like every other man there he was wearing a suit—handmade, dark, Italian design, of course—but Ralph looked nothing like any of them.

For starters—perhaps thanks to his mother's genes—he was taller. His hair was lighter too, and of course he had those incredible golden eyes.

And yet it was more than just his physical appearance that set him apart.

Around him everyone was talking expansively, hands moving, gesticulating, heads tipping back to roar with laughter, but Ralph was quiet and calm: the eye of the storm.

He had been her one place of safety—only that wasn't what she needed to be thinking right now.

'It's time to go,' he said softly.

'Yes, of course.' She nodded, then felt a rush of panic bubble up inside her as he held out his hand. But this wasn't the time or place to be proving a point and, ignoring the pulse of heat that jumped from his skin to hers as their fingers entwined, she joined the guests walking into the church.

The service followed its usual pattern, and then the priest smiled at Lucia and Luca and it was time for the christening.

Taking a breath, Juliet walked towards the font.

Although she knew it was a simple ceremony, she was slightly worried about saying her lines, but everything went perfectly. Raffaelle was utterly angelic, gazing solemnly at the priest and not even crying when the water was poured over his head.

It was beautiful, she thought, tears pricking her eyes.

And then suddenly it was over, and they were back in the midday sunshine, and everyone was smiling and clapping.

'Thank you.' Lucia was hugging her. 'Both of you.' She hugged Ralph. 'He's such a lucky boy, having two such wonderful godparents.'

Juliet smiled. 'It's an honour to be asked.'

'And you're coming in the car with us,' Lucia said firmly. 'I love my family, but after two solid days of living with my mother, my sisters and…' leaning forward, she lowered her voice, '…my *mother-in-law*, I just need a few minutes to recover.'

Tucking her arm through her friend's, Juliet laughed.

The christening reception was being held at the Casa Gregorio Hotel, twenty minutes outside of Verona. Although the word 'hotel' didn't really capture the magic of the Gregorio, Juliet thought as she slid into the cool, air-conditioned interior of the limousine.

Set in idyllic countryside, the exclusive, exquisitely renovated monastery offered a tranquil retreat from the bustle of city life, and these days the legendary kitchen garden was being put to mouth-wateringly good use by two Michelin-starred chef, Dario Bargione.

'Just sit back and enjoy the party,' she advised her friend. 'Everything is under control. You don't need to do a thing.'

Eyes suddenly bright, Lucia reached over and squeezed her hand. 'I know, and we're so grateful to you and Ralph for making this reception possible. It was so generous of you both.'

'It was our pleasure.'

Juliet felt Ralph's words skimming across her skin. You could hear it in his voice, she thought. Hundreds of years of Castellucci patronage.

How had she ever thought they would work?

Paying for Raffaelle's christening party was no big deal to him, whereas she felt uncomfortable when strangers thanked her at fundraisers and charity balls.

But then, when it came to money, the Castelluccis were in a league all their own. And, thanks to his talent for unearthing tiny start-ups that turned into commercial behemoths, Ralph had personally redefined the concept of wealth.

As well as the *palazzo* in Verona, he owned a villa in the French Riviera and penthouses in Rome, New York and London. For him money was almost irrelevant. Put simply, there was nothing he couldn't buy.

Except her.

'No, we mean it, *amico*. We can't thank you enough.' For once Luca's face was serious.

Juliet opened her mouth, but before she could speak Ralph said, 'But you have. You chose us to be godparents to Raffaelle. You're trusting us to help raise your beautiful son.' He paused. 'Aside from love, there's no gift more precious than trust. Don't you agree, *mia moglie*?'

Her heart thumped against her ribs as his eyes locked with hers. She knew he wasn't talking about Lucia and Luca.

He was talking about her.

More specifically, he was talking about her refusal to trust him, to take his word over the evidence of her eyes.

Her breath caught in her throat. *Trust.* It was such a small word and yet it encompassed so much. Confidence. Security. Hope. *And betrayal.*

Ignoring the misery filling her chest, she held his gaze.

'Ralph's right. Trust is the most precious gift.' She forced a smile onto her face. 'So thank you, both, for trusting us.'

Snatching a glass of prosecco from a passing waiter, Ralph stared across the heads of the other guests, his eyes seeking out his wife like a wolf tracking a deer.

His gaze narrowed as he caught a flash of dark red.

There she was.

His stomach tightened.

All through the ceremony she had avoided his gaze, focusing instead on the priest and then on Raffaelle. But as she'd made her vows her eyes had met his, and suddenly he had been fighting the temptation to reach out and touch her—to press his lips against hers.

Gritting his teeth, he stared across the terrace to where his wife was talking to Luca's mother. It was a cute dress— pleated, one-shouldered, with a flippy little skirt. From a distance the print looked floral, but it was actually tiny cherries.

And then there were her shoes…

Shiny patent red heels, the colour of the Marostica cherries that grew on the hillsides in the town down the road in Vicenza.

For a moment he let his gaze drop, and felt his body hardening exponentially as his eyes drifted slowly down the length of her legs, then back up, drawn to the hollow at the back of her neck that was just visible beneath her smooth chignon.

Even now it caught him off balance. Not her looks— in his world beauty was the norm, although with that hair and face, *those legs*, it was hard not to feel as though the floor was unsteady beneath his feet—what had got under his skin that first day they'd met in Rome, and what still blew his mind even now, was how she drank in life, lived so completely in the moment.

A pulse of heat beat across his skin. Even when she was soaking wet, with her head stuck in a storm drain.

And look at her now.

Glancing across the terrace, he watched as she leaned forward to choose a canapé. He had seen her look at beautiful jewellery with the same attention and excitement. It was a quality he'd never encountered in anyone but Giulietta. The unique ability to free herself from time and place and other pressures to edit her emotions, her actions, her thoughts.

In contrast, he was both burdened with the past and preoccupied with the future. He had grown up in a world where nothing had been what it seemed. There had been mirrors that were doors, and windows that were walls, and the people had been the same.

Giulietta was different. Transparent. He had *known* her—

His mouth twisted. Except clearly he hadn't.

He watched as she caught Lucia's arm, gestured. Even at a distance it was clear that she was offering to take the baby, and his heart thumped as Raffaelle took the decision into his own hands by lunging towards his wife.

Watching her tuck the baby against her body, he felt his anger and frustration rise up inside him like mercury in a heatwave.

How could she have lied to him about wanting a baby? And why had she deceived him?

The same questions had been burning inside his head for weeks now, and he still had no answers.

Soon, he promised himself. Just a couple more hours. But first...

His shoulders tensed.

His wife was walking away from Lucia back towards the hotel.

Without so much as a beat of hesitation he began moving smoothly after her, tracking her progress through the guests mingling in the sunshine.

'Signor Castellucci?'

Ralph swore silently as Giorgio, the hotel manager, popped up beside him, smiling nervously.

'I hope you're enjoying the celebrations, *signor*. I just wanted to check that everything is to your satisfaction.'

Ralph nodded. 'It is. Thank you.' Despite his irritation, his voice was even, his smile polite.

'No, thank *you*, Signor Castellucci, for choosing Casa Gregorio for this most special of celebrations.'

Still smiling, Ralph darted his eyes over Giorgio's shoulder. If this carried on they would still be standing there thanking one another at Raffaelle's eighteenth birthday party.

'I look forward to returning very soon. Now, if you'll excuse me, I need to speak to my wife,' he said firmly.

'Ah, yes, Signora Castellucci has taken the baby to have a nap. As you requested, we have reserved a suite for that exact purpose.'

The suite was on the first floor, away from the noise of the party. He didn't need the room number. The two dark-suited bodyguards on either side of the door told him that was where he would find his wife.

He nodded to them briefly and opened the door.

After the heat of the terrace, it was blissfully cool. But it wasn't the drop in temperature that made him stop mid-step—it was the sound of his wife's voice.

She was singing softly, some kind of lullaby, and the sound was so intimate, so tender, that he felt as if he was intruding.

For a moment he almost retreated, but the softness in her voice pulled his legs forward with magnetic force.

The room was decorated in a style that might be described as 'minimalist luxe': clean lines, a neutral colour palette, and artisan furnishings with impressive ethical credentials.

A simple iron bed with a canopy of ethereal white muslin dominated the room. Through a doorway, he could see the cot that had been set up for Raffaelle.

But the baby was not in the cot.

Giulietta was holding him.

He stared at his wife in silence. Her face was soft with love and she was gazing down, entirely absorbed. Holding his breath, he stood transfixed, fury and confusion merging with desire in a maelstrom of emotion.

He was sure that he'd made no sound, and yet something made her turn towards him—and as she did so her face didn't so much change as turn to stone.

The creamy skin of her bare shoulder tugged at his gaze like a headstrong horse, and the rise of her small, rounded breasts transformed her from tender to sexy.

'What do you want?' she said hoarsely.

Behind her, a light breeze riffled the muslin, giving him a glimpse of a crisply folded sheet, and he felt his body harden with an almost unbearable hunger.

I want to take you bending over that bed, and then against the wall, and then again on that desk, didn't seem like a reply he could make.

'Luca said I need to start pulling my weight.' It wasn't quite a lie. Luca had teased him about never having changed a nappy. 'So I thought I'd see if you needed any help.' He glanced over at the sleeping baby. 'I also thought this might be an opportunity to hold him without it turning into a circus, but I can see he's settled.'

There was a moment's silence. Then, 'You can put him down if you want.'

'I'd like that,' he said quietly.

She didn't meet his eye as she handed the sleeping baby over to him, but he could feel the tension in her body as he briefly brushed against her.

Despite what Lucia had said about his size, Raffaelle seemed incredibly small and light to him. He felt his heart contract as he looked down into the baby's peach-soft untroubled face, and a primitive, unbidden instinct to protect surging through his veins.

Leaning over the cot, he gently laid the baby on his side. 'He's so perfect,' he murmured, gently touching one of the tiny thumbs.

Giulietta had followed him into the room.

'He is, isn't he?' Her eyes found his.

He smiled. 'It's hard to believe he's going to be like Luca one day.'

Personally, he thought Raffaelle looked more like Lucia. But it was the first time she had willingly agreed with him about anything since returning to Italy, and he didn't want to lose this fragile connection between them.

'Perhaps he won't be.' She gave him a small, stiff smile. 'Not everyone grows up to be like their parents.'

She turned and walked out of the room and he stared after her, his spine tensing, picturing the handsome, patrician face of his father, Carlo Castellucci, and his mother, Francesca.

Guilt rose up inside him—guilt and shame and an anger that he couldn't seem to shift.

No, not everyone did grow up like their parents.

Blocking his mind against where that thought would lead, he followed her out of the room, leaving the door slightly ajar.

Someone had loosened the thick linen curtains, so the room was half in shade, and Giulietta had chosen to stand in the darkened half.

His chest tightened. Was that why she wanted a divorce? Did she think she could hide from him? From the truth?

'Well, in Raffaelle's case it wouldn't be a bad thing, would it?' he said.

She didn't answer, and he felt a rush of irritation.

'Is that it? You're done with the small talk?' He shook

his head. 'And I thought one of your jobs as godparent was
to lead by example. It's not a promising start, is it?'

Her eyes narrowed. 'It's not just small talk, Ralph. I'm
done with talking to you, full-stop. And as for setting an
example—I'm not sure cheating on your wife is the kind
of life lesson Lucia and Luca are hoping you'll share with
Raffaelle.'

Swearing softly, he crossed the room in two strides, so
fast that she took a clumsy step backwards. 'For the last
time, I did not cheat on you.'

'I know.'

He stared at her in confusion. 'I don't understand—'

Her eyes were fixed on his face. 'I didn't understand
either at first. I thought you were lying to me. But you
weren't. You're not even lying to yourself.'

She lifted her chin, and now he could see that her eyes
were dark and clear with hurt and anger and determination.

'You actually believe that adultery is a part of marriage.
That having a mistress doesn't cross any boundaries. But
I don't think like that and I can't live like that. So can we
just agree to end it here—now?'

Slowly he shook his head. 'No. Not here. Not now. Not
this side of eternity, *bella*.'

Her hands curled into fists. 'But I don't want to be your
wife any more.'

'*Too bad.* You see, I'm not the only one who made promises. And I'm not talking about *till death us do part*.'

He took a step closer. '*"Indivisa, etiam in morte."* The
Castellucci family motto. It means "Undivided, even in
death".'

Holding his breath, he pushed back the memory of his
father weeping at his mother's grave.

'And that's why you want to stay married?' Giulietta
asked. 'Because of some stupid medieval family motto?'

Her voice was shaking, and he could see the pulse at the base of her neck hammering against the flawless, pale skin.

'It's one of the reasons, yes.'

She was staring at him incredulously. 'Well, it's not enough. It doesn't count—it's not a real reason.'

'And that's what you want, is it?' Goaded, he closed the gap between them. 'You want something real? I'll give you real.'

And, lowering his mouth to hers, he kissed her.

He felt her body tense, her hands press against his chest, her lips part in protest—but then, even as he moved to break the kiss, her fingers were curling into his shirt and she was pulling him closer.

His hand wrapped around her waist and for a few half-seconds he was conscious of nothing but the hammering of his heart and how soft her lips were. And then he was closing the gap between them, his hand anchoring her tightly against his torso.

Oh, but she tasted so good. Soft and sweet, like *dulce de leche*. And her body was soft too…soft and pliant…so that it felt as if she was melting into him.

And where she was soft, he was hard.

Harder than he'd ever been in his life.

He groaned, sliding his fingers through her hair, his hands at her waist, pushing her up against the wall. He felt her fingers tighten in his shirt, her nails catching on the fabric as she pulled it free of his waistband, and he breathed in sharply as her hands splayed against his bare skin—

There was a sharp knock on the door.

Beneath his hands, he felt Giulietta tense.

'Excuse me, *signor*, but the nanny is here.'

He closed his eyes, wishing he could block out the body-guard's voice as effortlessly. *Not now.*

But it was too late. His wife was pushing away from him, smoothing her hair back from her face in a gesture that was an unmistakable shorthand for *We're done here*.

'Giulietta—'

He reached for her, but she sidestepped him with such speed and agility that he was still tucking in his shirt when he heard the door open and her voice telling the nanny to 'go on in'.

Breathing shakily, Juliet pulled out her phone and checked the time. The taxi firm had said twenty past and it was a quarter past now.

Her heart felt as though it was going to burst through her ribcage.

What had she said to Ralph? *'Not everyone grows up to be like their parents.'*

Obviously *she* had.

She moaned softly. Wasn't it bad enough that she had let Ralph kiss her? Had she had to kiss him back?

Remembering how she had pulled at his shirt, how her hands had pressed against his skin, she felt her face grow hot.

And not just kiss him...

Quelling a bout of panic, she checked her phone again. Just one minute to go. And then this would all be over.

Her flight wasn't for another three hours, but once she was at the airport she could check in and then— She felt her pulse accelerate.

Oh, thank goodness. It was here. The taxi was here.

Holding up her hand in greeting, she watched, relief flooding through her, as the car came to a halt.

'*Ciao.* The airport, please.'

She opened the door—but as she leaned into the taxi a hand closed over her wrist.

'Not so fast.'

In one smooth movement Ralph had slammed the door and pulled her away from the car.

The next moment one of the bodyguards stepped forward, bending down to the driver's window. Before she'd even had a chance to open her mouth in protest the taxi had sped off.

She shook herself free. 'What do you think you're playing at?'

His face was impassive, but there was a dangerous glitter in his eyes. 'I could ask you the same question. Only there's no need. You're making quite a habit of this, *bella*. Sneaking off without saying goodbye.'

He was right. She was sneaking off. But how could she have stayed after what had just happened? After what she'd let happen?

'It's got nothing to do with you.'

'Wrong. You're my wife. I think you sneaking away from a christening party for *our* godson has got everything to do with me.' He shook his head in mute frustration. 'How do you think Lucia and Luca would feel when they realised?'

Her stomach twisted with guilt. She couldn't meet his eye. Of course she had wanted to say goodbye—but then she would have had to tell them that she was leaving Italy for good.

'They'd understand,' she said, cringing inside at how callous she sounded.

He clearly thought so too; the contempt on his face made hot tears burn the back of her eyes.

She took a step backwards. But how dare he try to shame her? 'You know what, Ralph? You're so keen to keep reminding me that I'm your wife, but maybe if you hadn't forgotten that you're my husband this wouldn't be happening.'

His face hardened. 'Really? You want to do this now? Here?'

'I don't want to do it anywhere,' she snapped. 'I want to go the airport.'

He was staring at her as if she had said she wanted to go to the outer ring of Saturn.

'You want to leave? You want to go back to England? After what just happened?'

Her pulse accelerated. 'Why wouldn't I? What happened didn't change anything.'

He swore softly. 'I kissed you. And you kissed me back. You wanted a reason to stay and I gave you one.'

She felt pinpricks of heat sweep over her body. 'Well, you probably confused me with someone else. Like your mistress. I certainly confused you with someone else. Someone with scruples. Someone who wasn't going to lie to my face.'

'I'm not lying,' he said quietly.

She watched, frozen with misery, as he lifted his hand and, seemingly out of nowhere, a familiar sleek dark limousine drew up beside them. A second car followed a beat behind.

'Please get in the car, Giulietta.'

Planting her feet firmly on the Tarmac, she lifted her chin. 'I told you—I'm going to the airport.'

A muscle flickered along his jawline. 'Fine. My car is here, ready and waiting.'

She straightened her back. 'And it'll carry on waiting unless you tell me who she is.'

'I've told you she's no threat.' His voice was expressionless.

'Just tell me. Do you love her?'

His silence wrapped around her throat, choking her. She couldn't breathe. The ache in her chest was swallowing her whole. No pain had ever felt like it.

Suddenly she felt exhausted. It was over. All this was just her fighting the inevitable. Fighting the knowledge that she was the problem. She had failed as a daughter, and now she had failed as a wife.

But she couldn't fight any more. She was done.

'Goodbye, then, Ralph.'

She spun on her heel, but as she started to walk away he blocked her path.

'She's not a threat,' he said again. And then he closed his eyes, as if he too had stopped fighting.

Suddenly she didn't want to hear the truth. She didn't want to hear about this woman who had captured his heart and broken hers.

'Don't, Ralph, please...' she whispered, turning away.

Swearing softly, he spun her round, his hand tipping up her chin. 'She's not my mistress. She's my sister.'

She looked at him for one long, excruciating moment and then she pushed his hand away. 'You don't have a sister.' She shook her head, rage mingling with misery. 'You don't have any siblings.'

His skin was stretched taut over his cheekbones, like a canvas on a frame. 'She's my half-sister.'

Half-sister.

She stared at him mutely. That couldn't be true—but why lie?

'What's her name?'

He hesitated, then sighed. 'Vittoria. Her name's Vittoria Farnese.'

She felt a rush of confusion, almost like vertigo. The name sounded familiar.

'So why hasn't anyone mentioned her?' Her tone was

accusatory. 'Or am I supposed to believe your entire family is suffering from some kind of collective amnesia?'

'They don't know about her.'

There was tension in his frame now, as though speaking each sentence required an effort of will.

She looked at his face, trying to fill in the gaps, to make sense out of what made no sense at all, unless... 'Are you saying—do you mean Carlo had an affair?'

He shook his head. 'It was my mother. She had the affair.'

Her heart hammered against her ribs. 'So Vittoria is her daughter?'

There was a stretch of silence and then he shook his head again. 'No, Vittoria is my half-sister on my father's side.'

He stared past her, letting his words sink in.

'But you said your father didn't have an affair...' she said slowly.

'He didn't.'

And now she could hear the pain in his voice.

'But Carlo Castellucci is not my biological father.'

CHAPTER FOUR

FOR THE SECOND time in less than twenty-four hours Juliet found herself climbing into the limousine on automatic pilot. But this time it was not so much habit that propelled her as shock.

She watched numbly as Ralph leaned into the driver's side window to talk to Marco. Her head was spinning. Questions were bubbling inside her so fast and so violently that she felt as though a dam had burst and she was being carried along in the surging water.

Breathing out shakily, she tried to put her thoughts in some kind of order—but it was hard to do that when she felt as though she'd been kicked in the stomach.

Her fingers tightened around the smooth leather armrest as Ralph sat down beside her. She was stunned... confounded by what Ralph had told her. But most of all she felt swamped with guilt for not having been there for him.

For weeks now, she had been so sure that he was having an affair. And, given that she'd spent most of her married life waiting for their relationship to fall apart, it had been easy to stay sure even when he'd denied her accusations repeatedly.

Her pulse shivered.

Easy to convince herself that his denial was simply the reflex of a wealthy man not used to having to justify his actions. After all, the Castellucci male's right to variety in his marriage was not just hearsay. It was well-documented in art and history.

But if what he said was true then she was wrong.

Her husband hadn't been unfaithful.

She breathed in against a sharp rush of adrenaline.

And, perhaps more shockingly, Carlo was not his father.

Glancing at Ralph's set face, she felt her heart begin hammering inside her chest.

And as the silence stretched out in the air-conditioned chill of the limo she knew there were no 'ifs' or 'buts' about it.

It was true.

She could see it in the tension around his jawline and the rigidity in his shoulders.

And in that moment her own anger and hurt were instantly superseded by the emotions she knew her husband must be feeling.

How had he discovered the truth?

And who was his real father?

Gritting her teeth against the weight of questions forming in her throat, she said quietly, 'When did you find out?'

His hesitation was so brief she might not have registered it had it not been for the slight tensing around his eyes. Then he turned to face her.

'My mother told me. Not long before she died.' His eyes locked with hers. 'She'd wanted to tell me sooner, only she never found the right time.' Pain, mostly masked, shimmered for a moment. 'I think she realised she'd run out of time.'

Juliet stared at him mutely, the strain in his voice pinching her heart. She'd had difficult conversations with her own mother—the last one in particular had been in a class of its own. The only positive was that she had initiated it, so that the time and place had been of her choosing.

Pushing aside the memory of that appalling day, she said hesitantly, 'Does anyone else know? Does your father—?' She stumbled over the word. 'Sorry. I mean, does Carlo know?'

Carlo Castellucci.

She could still remember the first time she had met her father-in-law. Her stomach lurched at the memory. Would it have been any less intimidating if she'd known then what she knew now?

Probably not, she concluded. At the time she'd been dazed—dazzled, really—by the glamour of the Castelluccis and the lives they led. And as the resident patriarch of the family, Carlo's unlined face and languid, cocktail party smile had perfectly embodied that glamour.

He had kissed her on both cheeks, welcomed her to the family, but despite his words she had sensed his well-bred disbelief.

Her hands curled in her lap, her fingers grazing the huge yellow diamond that Ralph had given her to make up for the lack of an engagement ring.

Part of her hadn't blamed Carlo. After all, Ralph was his adored son. Only now it appeared that he wasn't.

She felt again that same shock of something fundamental being turned on its head, like a storm of hailstones beating down on a sunny beach in July.

Her heartbeat stuttered as Ralph shook his head.

'No one knows except me and Vittoria. And now you. My mother didn't—' his jaw tightened '—couldn't tell my father.' His voice sounded as if it was scraping over gravel. 'She knew how much it would hurt him. '

'And she didn't think it would hurt you?'

The words were out of her mouth before she could stop

them, propelled by a spasm of anger that had nothing to do with Francesca Castellucci's infidelity. It was an anger that came from having had to deal with adult truths at an age when she had been ill-equipped to deal with them.

Chest tightening, she smoothed a crease from the skirt of her dress. But when would any child be ready for something like this? It was the most basic, essential truth—one you unthinkingly took for granted. Your mother and father were your parents. To learn that was a lie…

His expression didn't change, but something flickered in his eyes. 'She thought it was important that I knew the truth.'

Now Juliet felt a sharp pang of empathy for Francesca. Telling the truth sounded so easy. All you had to do was say what was in your head or your heart. But countless family therapy sessions had taught her that it was a whole lot more complicated than just opening your mouth and talking.

In practice, it was more like balancing an equation—facts had to be weighed up against the feelings they inspired, and often the process had to be done in the blink of an eye.

She watched as Ralph glanced away to where the sun was starting to dip down into the hills. His head didn't move. 'She wanted to give me the chance to get to know my biological father, Niccolò Farnese. If that was what I wanted.'

And was it?

A sudden silence filled the space between them. Inside her head, her heartbeat was deafeningly loud as a mix of panic and misery mingled uneasily in her stomach.

Once she'd thought she knew instinctively what Ralph wanted, but for months now she'd had no idea what he was thinking, and she didn't understand what mattered to him or why. It was as if there was some invisible barrier between them, blocking that immutable private bond they had once shared.

Correction: that she'd *thought* they had once shared.

She took a breath, needing to process her thoughts, his words.

Niccolò Farnese. That name was definitely familiar, and now she was putting a face to the name…the face of a handsome, smiling man, waving to the crowds…

She stared at Ralph, the image frozen in her head. 'Are we talking about Niccolò Farnese the politician?' Politician, philanthropist and media tycoon.

He nodded. 'We are.'

His slightly accented voice was quiet, but firm. He had a beautiful voice…

Glancing at his profile, she felt her breath tangle in her throat. Before bumping into Ralph in Rome, she'd spent a few days on her own, exploring the city. Rome was bursting with things to see and do, and she had devoured all the sights as greedily as she had the *supplì*—the deep-fried rice croquettes sold in pizzerias across the capital.

It was truly the eternal city. Everywhere she'd looked she had seen ancient ruins rubbing up against modern concrete curves. She had been smitten…speechless. But it had been the ceiling of the Sistine Chapel that had left her reeling. It was mesmerisingly beautiful. Each time she'd looked up, something else had held her captive.

Her eyes fluttered across the car. Only in comparison to Ralph even the artistic power and brilliance of Michelangelo felt muted. He was so close, so solid beside her…

She breathed in and felt her stomach muscles tighten, responding to the pull of his beauty and the hint of leashed power. Her body was remembering the feel of his mouth on hers, the way he kissed, touched, caressed—

Her heart began beating unsteadily.

And he hadn't been unfaithful.

She reached across the seat and took his hand, felt a pulse of hope ticking over her skin as his fingers tightened on hers.

Maybe she'd had to push him, kicking and screaming, into doing so, but he was talking to her now—talking in a way that he had never done before.

Her pulse dipped. Her marriage wasn't over. They could work this out.

She squeezed his hand. 'And is it what you want? To get to know him? Niccolò?'

He made an impatient sound. 'You don't need to worry about that.'

'But what if I did?'

His features tightened. 'I wouldn't tell you. This is my problem and I will find a solution.'

He looked across the car but his expression was distant—as if he wasn't really seeing her. Watching him lean back in his seat, she felt her a trickle of ice run down her spine. He might not be Carlo Castellucci's biological son, she thought dully, but the casual dismissal in his voice was a pitch-perfect match of the man who had raised him.

Replaying his words in her head, she felt her mouth tighten. Surely he wasn't being serious? They needed to talk about this. Didn't he want to talk to her about this? She was his wife…

For a few half-seconds she thought back to their wedding ceremony and how his eyes had meshed with hers as he slid the single gold band onto her finger.

Her throat tightened and she thought of the blind, limitless happiness of their wedding day bleaching out to nothing.

She might be his wife, but he couldn't make his message any clearer short of parading in front of her with a placard.

As far as he was concerned, she knew *enough*. Everything else was beyond her pay grade.

He'd given her the basic facts, just as he might to a child. But she wasn't a child. She was an idiot.

A chill was creeping over her skin, and with it the unwelcome but inescapable awareness that, far from being a turning point in their relationship, this was simply another example of how far apart they were.

His confession had never been about confiding in her. It had been an exercise in damage limitation.

Glancing helplessly down at her hands, she took a deep breath, hating him, and hating herself for being so naive as to think that he could change…that he even *wanted* to change.

'You're right,' she said. Smiling thinly, she slipped her hand free of his. 'It's none of my business.'

She stared down at her dress, remembering how she had smoothed out the pretty cherry-printed fabric just before the sky fell in. Just before it had become clear that he was willing to commit them both to this marriage for no better reason than—what? Pride? The need to maintain a public façade?

She was done with this. With him. There were no more questions she needed or wanted to have answered. Not any more. And not because she didn't care, but because she did. And it was too dangerous to let herself keep caring about this beautiful, baffling man.

Caring was a hoax. Her parents had taught her that. It was a game played by the heart to distract the head from looking too closely at the facts. Or, in this case, one diamond-hard fact that she had chosen to ignore.

Her fears about Ralph's infidelity had simply been a distraction from the bigger picture. From their fundamentally different beliefs about what made a happy, healthy marriage.

She felt the car slow.

Outside, the sounds of the real world bumped against the solid body of the car. Men shouting…some kind of machinery humming…

As she looked up, her eyes clashed with his.

He raised an eyebrow. 'None of your business, *bella*? How so? You're my wife.'

So now she was his wife?

She could feel anger rising in waves inside her. Marriage was supposed to be a partnership of equals. But with Ralph everything had to be played out on his terms. He got to make the rules and change them as and when it suited him to do so.

Catching sight of her wedding band, she felt her heart being squeezed as though by a fist. She'd kept it on, telling herself that she had to for appearances' sake. But the truth was that, despite telling him she wanted a divorce, a part of her had still been hoping that she could make her marriage work.

Now, though, she knew nothing she did or said could make that happen.

She forced herself to speak past the frustration twisting in her throat. 'Fat lot of difference that makes.'

His golden gaze bored into her. 'Meaning?'

'Meaning that wives are not just for sex and providing heirs. Not this wife, anyway. So when I get back to England I will be filing for divorce.'

She reached for her wedding ring, struggling to loosen it from her finger.

His hand covered hers. 'Leave it on.

Pulling her hand free, she glared at him. 'Why? I'm not staying married to you, Ralph.'

Tilting his head back, he stared at her in silence. The silence stretched and stretched, and when finally he spoke she could hear a note of exasperation in his voice.

'Enough of this, Giulietta.' His voice rose. *'Enough.'*

He made a gesture that was familiar to her. It was the same gesture he made in a restaurant, when he dismissed a waiter. Like waving away a particularly persistent fly.

'There will be no divorce—as you very well know. You made accusations and you were wrong. But fortunately for you I'm willing to forget your behaviour.'

She gaped at him mutely, a ripple of anger, smooth and hot like lava, snaking sideways across her skin. 'Well, I'm not willing to forget yours,' she said slowly.

His gaze was direct and unwavering. 'Did you not understand anything of what I just told you? I haven't been having an affair—'

'I know.' She cut him off. 'And I'm sorry that I thought you were. But it doesn't make any difference—'

Now he cut her off. 'You're kidding me?' His mouth curved upwards at the corners, but there was nothing humorous about his smile.

As she started to shake her head he pressed his hand against his eyes, as if doing so might change what he was seeing.

'Let me get this right. You spend days accusing me of being unfaithful with another woman. Not only that, you storm off to England for *five weeks* because you need "space".'

His voice was quiet—soft, even—but it crackled with an authority that made it impossible for her to look away.

'According to you, nothing I say or do matters except the truth. So I tell you the truth. Only now you're saying it makes no difference.'

He practically chewed the words and spat them out at her.

'It doesn't…'

Her heart was racing with panic and pain. He was right. When she'd gone to London she'd thought all she cared about was finding out for certain if he was having an affair. Threatening to divorce him had been the only thing she could think of that would push him into telling the truth.

But in these last few minutes she'd finally accepted that what they'd shared had never been strong enough to survive outside of that small hotel room in Rome.

Marriages needed solid foundations.

They needed transparency and trust.

Ralph didn't trust her, and she sure as hell didn't trust him.

Not with her heart or her future.

Nor could she risk giving him a second chance—not when she knew first-hand how easy it was for that second chance to slip into a third, and then another and another.

But one look at his face told her that trying to explain that to this man would be a fruitless exercise.

'There's no point in trying to do this here…now. Let's leave it to the lawyers.'

Ralph would have access to some of the finest legal brains in the world, but she had everything she needed with her. Her passport was in her handbag. She wanted nothing from the house. Her broken heart was all the reminder she needed of her failed marriage.

As she opened the car door she heard him call her name, sensed him reaching out for her.

But it was too late.

It had always been too late.

Stepping out onto the kerb, she froze, her mouth hanging open. She had been so preoccupied by their conversation that she had barely glanced out of the window during the journey, but naturally she'd assumed they were heading to the airport.

But they were not at the airport.

Nor were they in Verona.

They were at the marina in Venice.

She gazed up at the huge, gleaming white yacht, her skin prickling with shock and disbelief.

Not just any yacht.

Ralph's yacht. The *Alighieri.*

Ralph had got out of the car.

She spun round to face him, a wave of fury cascading through her body. 'You said you were taking me to the airport.'

He shook his head. 'I think you'll find that I didn't. Besides, why would you want to leave now? We're in the middle of a conversation.'

'We are not in the middle of anything. We are at the end,' she snapped.

Her voice was rising, and on the other side of the road a couple of men loading equipment onto another boat turned towards her, their eyes sharp with curiosity.

'So, unless you want me to cause a truly memorable scene that will make your illustrious ancestors roll over in their graves, I suggest you take me back to Verona right now.'

Although she knew there was every chance she would miss her flight…

'That's not going to happen.'

His face was impassive, and his cool, untroubled expression made her want to scream.

Stomach curling with apprehension, she glared at him. 'I'm warning you, Ralph. I won't hold back.'

He stared at her for a long moment, his golden eyes locking with hers. 'Oh, I know, *bella*,' he said softly. 'You're always very vocal...'

She felt her breath catch, her pulse fluttering. Ralph knew exactly how to make her lose control.

Only she didn't need reminding of that now.

'We're not doing this, Ralph,' she said stiffly.

'Really?' He raised one smooth dark eyebrow. 'I thought you weren't going to hold back?'

His eyes gleamed with the satisfaction of having proved a point, and suddenly she hated him more than she had ever hated anyone.

How did he always manage to make it so that she ended up on the wrong foot? If only for once she could get under his skin, make him see red, lose his head, lose control...

But she didn't have to stand here and wait for him to stop playing his silly games. She was perfectly capable of getting herself back to Verona. Alone.

She spun round, but as she started to walk away, he blocked her path.

'We need to talk,' he said softly.

He sounded calm, but there was something flickering in the dark gold gaze. Like a warning beam from a lighthouse. *Danger. Rocks ahead.*

But she was too awash with misery and humiliation to care. 'I gave you a chance to talk and you threw it in my face.' Her eyes narrowed, her body vibrating from the close proximity to his. 'And, frankly, I don't have anything left to say to you,' she hissed.

'That suits me fine.' His voice was infuriatingly calm. 'It means I can talk without interruption.'

And, without missing a beat, he plucked her handbag from her fingers, tossed it to his bodyguard and scooped her up into his arms.

* * *

Gritting his teeth, Ralph ignored his wife's flailing fists and, shifting her body, tipped her over his shoulder.

'Put me down!'

'Oh, I will—just as soon as you're safely on deck.'

She had threatened to make a scene. If that was what she wanted, then that was what she was going to get, he thought savagely, tightening his grip.

'Let me go! You can't do this!'

'Apparently I can,' he said softly.

After he'd stepped on deck he moved swiftly through the boat, nodding briskly at Franco, the skipper, and the crew members.

They reached the master cabin and he walked across the room and dropped her onto the bed.

She swore graphically.

He frowned. 'I'm not sure if that's anatomically possible.'

From somewhere down below a low hum rose up through the boat as the engines started.

Her eyes narrowed as she looked past his shoulder at the open door.

'Don't!' he said warningly.

'Or what?' she raged. 'You're already kidnapping me.'

He shrugged. 'I'm not asking for a ransom, so technically it's more of an abduction—'

As she swore again, he watched her, like a cat with a mouse.

Actually, he thought, this was retribution. It was payback for the hypocrisy of her behaviour. She had no idea what she had put him through these last few weeks, but she was going to find out now.

Her chin lifted pugnaciously, and despite his own simmering anger he couldn't but admire her defiance. And the indignant swell of her high-riding breasts...

'You had this coming, *bella*.'

'Why? For having the temerity to want more than you're offering?'

Fighting an urge to pick her up again and toss her overboard, he narrowed his eyes. Was she serious? Was that what this was about?

'You live in a palace,' he said coolly. 'You have access to a private jet, this yacht, a limousine. You have an unlimited expense account. Do you know what most women would give to have your life?'

'Well, they can have it—and you.' She glared up at him. 'There's more to life and marriage than palaces and private jets, Ralph.'

Yes, there was. A whole lot more.

Her soft brown eyes were muddied with anger and resentment, and the set of her jaw held more or less the same message as her eyes. But, glancing down at her, he felt his heartbeat quicken and his groin tighten.

Probably it was her hair, he thought distractedly. Gone was the smooth chignon. Now her long tawny hair fell about her shoulders in disarray. Like it did in bed. When she rode him. Head thrown back, small upturned breasts bared to his gaze, face taut with the fierce, animal passion that would melt away into surrender at the moment of climax.

He felt his breath catch.

In the time it had taken for his brain to conjure up that picture, his body had hardened as if in a forge, and the speed at which his anger had turned to hunger did little to improve his temper.

Ignoring the ache in his groin, he stared at her steadily. 'Like what?'

She scrambled to her feet, her glossy hair fanning out behind her. 'Like honesty.'

Honesty?

The word vibrated in his head.

Ma che cazzo!

His fingers twitched. He wanted to shake her. Or kiss her. Maybe both.

How could she look him in the eye and talk about honesty? She had been lying to him for months. Not in words, maybe. But in her actions. Pretending that they were trying for a baby when she'd known the whole time that it would never happen.

He took a step towards her. 'I have been honest with you. I have told you about Vittoria.'

And she had no understanding of how hard that had been. How impossible it had been to say the words out loud.

His family were not like other families. The Castellucci name was not just a name, it was a brand. They lived in the public eye. Every birth, marriage and death was given round-the-clock news coverage and everything in between was meticulously managed.

And this scandal would not just be about him, but his entire family.

He had kept the secret to himself to protect the people he loved most in the world and he'd been so careful.

But then Giulietta had seen him with Vittoria. And it hadn't mattered what he'd said—she wouldn't let it go.

She should have trusted him. Like he'd trusted her.

His pulse twitched and he thought about the empty blister packet in his pocket. He'd been carrying it around with him for months now—carrying around the pain and shock of her deceit, waiting to confront her as she had confronted him.

She was staring at him, her lush eyelashes flaring around her widened eyes.

'Only because I made you tell me,' she said.

Her hands were clenched—not into fists, but as if she were trying to hold on to something.

'I don't understand...' The words sounded as if they were caught in her throat. 'You're acting like there's some kind of need-to-know basis and I don't have clearance.'

The catch in her voice snagged at something in his chest. He had hurt her, and he didn't like how that made him feel. But she was wrong. He had been planning to tell her the truth.

Not at the beginning—not when they'd first met in Rome. Later, though, in those first few months of their marriage, the honeymoon period, he'd fully intended to tell her. Only each time something had happened. First Carlo had been rushed to hospital with a kidney infection, and then Raffaelle had been born by emergency C-section.

For a split second he replayed the moment when he'd noticed the gleam of silver in the bin, remembering his confusion, and then the headrush of shock, the pain of betrayal.

Another betrayal.

And this one worse, somehow, for not being refracted through his father.

After that there had been no way he could trust her with the truth about his parentage.

His throat tightened. He still didn't understand why she'd done it. Why mislead him like that? Why let him think they were trying for a baby?

He thought back to that moment in the hotel when he had seen her holding Raffaelle. It had been like a painting brought to life, everything in the room retreating so that it was just the woman and the child illuminated in the early evening sunlight.

Her gaze had been fixed on Raffaelle's face, her eyes soft with love and longing, and in that moment he had known with absolute conviction that she wanted a baby of her own.

But that meant there was only one possible explanation for why she had been taking the contraceptive pill.

His fingers curled into fists. She didn't want a baby with *him*.

Had that been how his mother had felt about Carlo?

Having realised too late that she'd married the wrong man, had she deliberately chosen to get pregnant? To keep a piece of her lover for herself?

The thought of Giulietta having a baby with another man made him want to smash the cabin to pieces with his bare hands.

'What else is there to know?' he asked. His voice echoed harshly round the room, but anger had stifled all other emotions.

'What else?' she repeated. 'Oh, I don't know, Ralph... How about what you're thinking. What you're feeling.'

His feelings. He felt his chest tighten. *No way.*

To share how it had felt to have his whole life upended, to watch history being redacted and rewritten? His history?

Ever since that day it had felt as if he was walking through a minefield. Every step carried an unseen risk. Nothing was what it seemed. Looking at his reflection, he felt like an imposter. An actor hired to play Ralph Castellucci.

The one constant in this storm of uncertainty should have been Giulietta and the child they would make together. Her child and his. Only now, thanks to his wife, it turned out that his dreams for the future were as shifting and ephemeral as his past.

And now she wanted him to share his feelings.

His jaw tightened. Why shouldn't he let her know what it felt like to be kept in the dark? 'I don't know what benefit that would serve.'

She was staring at him, her eyes blazing.

'But that's not what marriage is about, Ralph. You can't choose which parts of yourself you get to share. We're a couple. We're supposed to share everything—especially the truth.'

'It's good advice.' His eyes locked with hers. 'What a pity you don't apply it to yourself.'

She stared at him, the pulse in her throat leaping against her skin like a startled rabbit. 'I don't know what you're talking about.'

'You don't?' He reached into his pocket. 'Then allow me to refresh your memory.'

Stalking towards her, he tossed the blister pack onto the bed.

'These were in the bin in our bathroom.'

He watched her face stiffen with shock.

'You want to talk about honesty, *bella*? Then perhaps you'd like to explain why you've been *pretending* to try for a baby for months.'

CHAPTER FIVE

JULIET STARED AT Ralph in silence.

Shock was clawing at her, swamping her. Beneath her feet she could feel the *Alighieri* moving smoothly through the lagoon. Soon it would reach the choppier waters of the Adriatic, but she was already adrift and starting to drown in a treacherous sea of her own making.

She tried to speak, but her throat was dry and choked.

Heart pummelling her ribs, she glanced down at the packet. There were empty spaces where the pills had once been and now they gazed back at her like twenty-eight accusing eyes.

In her head, she had rationalised her behaviour. She had got married in haste to a man who had turned from soul mate to stranger in front of her eyes. It had broken her heart, but she'd decided she could, and would, live with her mistake.

But, no matter how badly she'd wanted a baby, she couldn't allow herself to bring a child into the world.

How could she? When every day she had felt herself and Ralph slipping further apart from each other? Watched the pure white brilliance of their love fading into darkness like a dying star?

Only now, faced with his real and justifiable anger, she felt her certainty fade. 'I can explain—'

'You said you wanted a baby.' His eyes narrowed and the cabin seemed to shrink in on her as he took a step closer. 'We talked about it three months ago and we decided that it was the right time. *We* decided that, Giulietta—not me. You said it was what you wanted.'

His hands—those beautiful long-fingered hands that had made pleasure pulse through her body—clenched at his sides. She swallowed past her panic, ripples of guilt spreading out over her skin like the wake from the *Alighieri*.

They had talked about having children.

She could remember the conversation almost word for word. It had been the exact opposite of the conversation they were having now. Easy, smooth-flowing, punctuated by laughter and smiles and kisses. So many kisses... Warm, sweet, soft at first, then more urgent, the heat of his lips demanding a response she had been more than happy to give, her body melting against his...

She pushed the memory away.

'I know I did. And it was what I wanted...' She faltered, her voice dropping.

It still is, she thought, an ache spreading through her chest. Holding Raffaelle at the christening party had been both a joy and an agony. But, if anything, she and Ralph were further apart now than they had ever been—like the earth from the sun at aphelion in its orbit.

He frowned down at her. 'Strange, then, that you would carry on taking a pill whose sole purpose is to stop that happening.'

His voice was rough-sounding, but it was the serrated edge to his gaze that made her skin feel as though it was being flayed from her body.

'I'm sorry.'

She meant it. She'd hated misleading him. But her words sounded meagre and inadequate even to her. As if she was speaking by rote, not from the heart.

Ralph clearly thought so too.

He swore beneath his breath. 'For what?' he asked

abruptly. He was staring at her in disbelief, his handsome face harsh in the fading light of the cabin. 'For deceiving me for months? Lying to me?'

Her heart was pounding and she could barely breathe. The diamond ring on her finger felt like a leaden band.

'I didn't lie.'

He stared at her for a long time, as if he didn't know who she was. 'Only because I didn't actually ask if you'd come off the pill,' he said slowly. 'Idiot that I am, I didn't think I needed to. I just assumed you had.' His gaze didn't waver. 'Just out of interest, would you have told me the truth if I'd asked?'

How could she explain?

How could she put into words how she had felt?

The sliding panic, the sense of losing her grip, spinning out of control, and the creeping dread of knowing that she was moments away from impact but powerless to stop it.

To have done so would have meant talking about a life she had not just abandoned, but buried. It would have meant confessing more secrets, more lies—or 'unspoken truths' as she preferred to think of them.

When could she have told him about Juliet Jones? The small, scared, brittle child who had waited in her bedroom for the shouting to stop and waited in the playground, hoping someone would remember to pick her up after school. How could she have explained about living in a house where there had always been alcohol but no food?

She shivered inside.

Talking about it would have made it feel real again, and she couldn't have coped with that. That was why she'd fled to England five weeks ago. To put as much distance as possible between herself and those feelings.

'I don't know,' she said quietly.

There was another silence, thick and heavy like the silence that preceded a storm.

He took a breath, ran a hand over his face, swallowed.

For a moment she thought he was trying to think of a suitable response, but when finally he looked at her again she knew why he'd hesitated.

He hadn't been thinking. He was just too angry to speak. Not just angry, but coldly furious and barely hiding it.

She tried again. 'I didn't mean—'

'Di che diavolo parli!'

This time he swore out loud, and the anger in his voice sliced through the panicky drumroll of her heartbeat.

'"I didn't mean to" doesn't fly in this situation. You were taking a contraceptive pill. Fifty-six pills, in fact. That wasn't an accident or a mistake, Giulietta. It was deliberate.'

A dark flush of anger was highlighting his beautiful curving cheekbones.

'You didn't want to be pregnant.'

He shook his head.

'All these weeks you've been sitting in judgement of me, accusing me of being dishonest, when all the time you were playing me for a fool. You're such a hypocrite.'

Her breath caught in her throat. She took a step backwards, her panic giving way to anger. 'That's not fair,' she said, stung by his words, by their truth and their injustice.

His face was a hard mask. 'No, what's not fair is making me believe there was a chance you might be pregnant when you knew definitively that there couldn't be.'

She flinched inwardly. He was right, but he was ignoring his part in why she'd acted that way.

'I did want a baby when we talked about it.' Her fingers curled into her palms. 'But then everything changed. You changed.'

Even before she had seen him with Vittoria he had become different. Gone had been the man who had taken her to the Trevi Fountain to watch the sun rise over the city and then produced a breakfast picnic of *maritozzo* and *ciambella* with fresh cherries.

They hadn't been able to get enough of each other...

But then everything had begun to change. Her husband had never been at home, and when he had been they'd hardly spoken.

His eyes were dark with frustration. 'So it's my fault you lied?'

She stared at him. 'No, that's not what I'm saying. I'm trying to tell you how it was. How we ended up like this.'

Her voice was rising now, and the tension and unhappiness of the last few weeks was enveloping her. It felt as if she was playing snakes and ladders—a game she loathed. Every time they seemed to be getting somewhere she landed on a snake and went slipping back to the start.

They would never sort this out.

The only way they had ever managed to communicate successfully was physically.

But sex couldn't resolve anything but lust.

Nor would having a baby tackle the raw emotions and complex issues they'd spent months circumnavigating.

A lump formed in her throat. 'You're not the man I married, Ralph.'

The silence tautened between them. Heart pounding, she watched his shoulders tense. There was a strange light in his eyes and his breathing wasn't quite steady.

'Finally,' he said quietly, 'we have something we can agree on.'

And before she could react, much less form a sentence, he turned and strode through the door.

Walking back through the boat, Ralph thought his hammering heart was going to break through his ribcage. He had waited so long to confront Giulietta, only nothing had gone according to plan. In fact, he couldn't have handled it any worse if he'd set out to do so.

In his head he'd played out various scenarios, and in all of them he'd stayed calm, coolly presenting the facts of her betrayal like a prosecuting lawyer. But the last forty-eight hours had made staying cool an impossibility.

His shoulders tensed.

More specifically, *his wife* had made staying cool impossible on so many levels.

He wasn't sure if it was her continued insistence that they get a divorce or the fact that after five weeks of abstinence his body was in a state of almost permanent discomfort, but as he'd carried her on board all his good intentions had been swept away by a toppling wave of anger.

It had been like nothing he'd ever known—a feeling so pure and absolute it had wiped out everything: all dignity and decorum and understanding.

His chest tightened.

He'd wanted answers, not a screaming match. He'd failed on both counts.

His stomach was tight, and aching as if he was hungry, but when he walked out onto the spacious on-deck lounge area he headed to the bar.

Leaning over the marble countertop, he reached for a bottle of his favourite whisky—a thirty-year-old single malt Laphroaig.

But maybe he should eat.

He glanced at the intercom. It would be no trouble to call downstairs and get the chef to prepare him a light supper. Then again, after his performance earlier the crew were probably hiding in the lifeboats.

And he also knew the ache in his stomach had nothing to do with lack of food. It had been there since Giulietta had fled from the *palazzo*.

Pushing aside the memory of that night, he snatched up a tumbler and made his way over to one of the huge sofas. His wife might be the most infuriating woman on the planet, but he wasn't quite at the necking-it-from-the-bottle stage yet.

He unscrewed the top of the bottle, poured out two fingers of whisky and drank it in one gulp. It was a crime not to savour it, but right now he needed the hit of alcohol to dull his senses and the feeling of failure.

Then, maybe, he might be able to think about—

He frowned. What was it she had said? Oh, yes—how they had ended up like this.

Gritting his teeth, he poured another glass. This time, though, he rested it on the arm of the sofa.

Who was it who had said that people lost things that they wanted to lose? For him, meeting Giulietta in Rome had been the opposite. He had found the one woman he'd wanted to find.

Beautiful, smart, and free from the expectations of the world he lived in, she had wanted him for himself. Not for his wealth or his name or his connections. For her, he had been enough.

Or so he'd thought.

He still couldn't accept that he had got it wrong. But it wasn't just up to him.

His fingers tightened around the glass and he had to stop himself from tipping the contents down his throat.

'You're not the man I married.'

He breathed out unsteadily, her words replaying in his head. Had he changed? Yes and no.

When they'd met in Rome it had been a little over five months since his mother's deathbed confession. Six months since Vittoria had come to the house and tearfully confronted him with the letters she'd found.

His heart began beating faster. Love letters from *his* mother, Francesca, to *her* father, Niccolò. Intense, passion-filled letters that he'd struggled to read but found impossible to ignore. Particularly the one in which she begged Niccolò to meet her so that she could tell him her news.

At first his mother had refused to discuss it. It had only been in those last few days that she had finally confirmed what was hinted at in the letters.

Niccolò, not Carlo, was his father.

His mouth twisted.

And ever since then he'd been trying to decide what to do next. That was what the trip to Rome had been about. Getting some space from the family, from Verona, from the life that had been mapped out for him as heir-in-waiting to the Castellucci empire.

He'd wanted—needed—to do the right thing. The trouble was that then he hadn't been sure what that was. He still wasn't.

Saying nothing to Carlo was the simplest option—only that would mean living a lie for the rest of his life.

On the other hand, telling the truth would have devastating consequences.

The Castellucci name would be lost. Worse, the man who had raised him from birth and earned the right to be called his father would be without a son and heir.

Picking up his glass, he took a sip, holding the whisky in his mouth to savour the smoky, peaty flavour, the hint of lime and the salty sharp cleanness.

Ever since birth he'd been surrounded by family. Five hundred years of history flowed through his veins and the progression of his life had had an almost mathematical certainty to it.

But suddenly he'd never felt more alone, more hesitant, more unsure of himself.

And then he'd met Giulietta, and he'd seen a way forward to a shared future with a family that would share his own bloodline.

Closing his eyes, he blew out a breath.

'Is that a good idea?'

His heart kicked against his ribs and, opening his eyes, he glanced across the deck to where his wife was hovering by the bar. She was still wearing the cherry-patterned dress, but she had taken off her make-up and her feet were bare.

So she could run away faster? he thought, his pulse accelerating.

Aware that one wrong word would send her storming back to her cabin, he raised an eyebrow. 'Breathing?' He raised an eyebrow questioningly. 'I suppose that depends on if you'd rather be a widow or a divorcee.'

'I was talking about the whisky.'

As she took a step forward into the light he saw that she wasn't smiling. But she hadn't walked away. He watched her in silence, waiting...

'I'm sorry,' she said quietly. 'For what I said before. About you. I wasn't talking about Carlo not being your father.'

His fingers pressed against the glass. Hearing the truth spoken out loud made it suddenly shockingly real. And yet somehow it was a relief to finally admit even a fragment of his feelings.

He held her gaze. 'It's a bit of a sensitive subject.'

She bit her lip. 'And I'm sorry for not telling you I was still on the pill. I didn't plan to keep taking it,' she said slowly. 'I was going to stop when I came to the end of the cycle. Only then Carlo was ill—' She stopped.

'I remember.'

It had been less than a year after his mother's death. Carlo had been taken to the same hospital where she'd died. For over a week he'd been stricken with fear that he would lose his father too, and torn over whether to tell him the truth.

'Things were difficult.'

Looking back, he knew that he'd been distracted, distant—not just emotionally, but physically, in that he'd often stayed overnight at the hospital in case...

His throat tightened.

But he hadn't just been worried about Carlo. The thought of losing his father had made his plan to start a family of his own seem even more important—urgent, in fact. He hadn't meant it to, but it had taken over everything.

'It's been a long day.' Tilting his head back, he kept his voice steady and walked over to the bar. 'Why don't you join me?'

He had meant it innocently enough but, looking over at her, he saw that his remark had backfired.

'So that's it, is it?' she asked. 'We're just going to sit down and hit the bottle? I thought you wanted to talk.'

Her hands were clenched at her sides, and her glorious eyes were flashing with poorly concealed irritation.

'I mean, that *is* why you dragged me here in the first place, so I would have thought the least you could do is not walk off in the middle of a conversation,' she said hotly.

'Really? I could have sworn you said we were at the end of everything,' he said slowly.

'Don't get smart with me, Ralph.'

Her chin was jutting forward, and with her bare feet and her clenched fists she reminded him again of that cat he'd pulled from the storm drain. His finger brushed against the puckered skin where it had bitten him. What little patience he'd started the day with had almost completely gone.

'Oh, I'm not smart, *bella*. If I were I wouldn't have been hoodwinked by you into thinking you wanted a baby.'

He heard her breath hitch.

'I did want a baby. But babies aren't just an accessory.' Her eyes darted to his wrist. 'They're not some expensive watch. They're tiny little humans with feelings. They need love and security.'

'Are you seriously suggesting I wouldn't love my child?'

She raised her chin. '*Our* child, Ralph. Not yours—ours.' Her gaze locked with his. 'But I don't count, do I? That's the bottom line here.'

The gentle slap of the waves against the boat's hull filled the sudden silence on deck. Far out at sea, the sun was slipping beneath the horizon, the daylight transmuting into darkness.

'You're being foolish.'

She was impossible. Stubborn. Difficult. And scared.

A thought jolted him.

Just like his mother had been.

His shoulders tensed. He'd read those letters and he knew how trapped Francesca had felt in the first few months of her marriage to Carlo. Like Giulietta, she had fled. But not from the country. Instead she had sought comfort in the bed of Niccolò Farnese.

The idea that history might repeat itself—that he might drive his wife into the arms of another man—filled him with a fear and anger he found difficult to control. Anger with her, but mostly with himself.

He'd been a fool not to follow her to England.

A muscle bunched in his jaw. This time he wouldn't let her escape.

She took a step towards him, her hair spilling over her shoulders. 'No, this is foolish. Us trying to make our marriage work.'

His eyes clashed with hers. 'Our marriage worked just fine until you started making false accusations.'

'How can you say that? Our marriage was in pieces. That's why I thought you were having an affair.' She breathed out shakily. 'You were never there. You were either working or on this bloody boat.'

It was true. His father's illness had given him new responsibilities over the family's various charitable foundations, and, of course, he had to look after his aunts and his cousins.

And all the time, at every board meeting or lunch with his aunts, he'd felt a creeping sense of guilt...of being a fraud.

He glanced across the smooth wooden deck. It had only been here, on the *Alighieri*, that he'd felt 'at home'. Here, drifting out at sea, the rootlessness he'd felt on land had seemed to dissipate.

'I found it hard...being in Verona.'

She was staring at him in silence, and he realised that he had spoken out loud.

Juliet felt her breath catch. His words had startled her. Not their meaning, but their directness.

For weeks now they had been butting heads metaphorically. Or rather she had been butting her head against the brick wall of Ralph's refusal to discuss anything.

Looking up at his face now, she felt her heart contract. He looked tense, troubled, his features tight, and she felt some of her anger fade. 'You were upset.'

Doubly upset, she thought with a pang of guilt.

It would have been unbearable for him to see his father so ill, and so soon after his mother's death. And, of course, he'd also been carrying around the burden of when—*whether*—to tell Carlo the truth.

Ralph might seem strong and unbreakable, but she knew that the worst wounds were the ones beneath the surface.

His eyes found hers. 'I should have told you about my father.' He hesitated. 'I was going to, only then I found the pills, and you saw Vittoria with me, and everything got out of hand.'

And she had fled to England.

It was such a mess. All of it. And it was a mess of their own making. Both of them had held back when they should have opened up with each other.

A lump filled her throat. She felt suddenly helpless—the same kind of helpless she had felt as a child, when everything had been beyond her control. When nothing she'd said or done had seemed to make any difference to her situation.

She held her breath, held on to the panic rising in her chest. It was ironic but the only time she'd felt in control of her life had been with Ralph in Rome—before he'd even proposed to her, when they had been nothing more than lovers.

Except that 'nothing more' made it sound ordinary or just adequate, when in fact their being lovers had been the purest state of all.

Her hands felt clammy. And they had ruined it by rushing into marriage.

She turned to him and said, a little breathlessly, 'Has it ever crossed your mind that this can't be fixed?'

He stared at her for a long moment, and then he shook his head. 'We'll get through it,' he said.

'How?' She felt angry tears prickle her eyes. 'How can we get through this? Everything is wrong between us. Nothing works.'

She felt her heart thud against her ribs. He was standing so close she could feel the heat of his skin, see the heat in his gaze.

There was a long, burning silence.

'Not true,' he said softly. His eyes were fixed on her mouth, and they lingered a moment before rising to meet hers.

The sea was smooth, and beneath her bare feet the smooth wooden deck was solid, but suddenly she was fighting to retain her balance.

'Giulietta...'

He spoke her name gently. His hand when he touched her face was even more gentle. She was afraid to move, almost afraid to breathe. But the temptation to move closer, to touch and trace the shape of his beautiful mouth, made her shake inside.

'Giulietta...'

This time when he spoke her name his fingers slid through her hair, moving with a caressing slowness that stalled her heartbeat. His hands were tangling through her hair and he was tilting her head back, slanting his mouth over hers. She felt something unfurl inside her, like a flower opening its petals towards the sun, as she waited for his kiss.

His lips brushed against hers, their warm breath mingled, and then she leaned in closer, her mouth finding his, unable to tear herself away.

'Trust me, *bella*,' he whispered. 'We work.'

She felt his mouth drop to her neck, to the shadowed hollow at the base of her throat. *We.* That word again. Only this time she was honest with herself—could admit that she had come back to Verona not just for the christening but for this.

For him.

For the touch of his hands and the soft press of his lips on hers.

Head spinning, she stared at him. And then she ran her tongue along his lips.

He made a rough sound, half-growl, half-groan, and then, reaching down his hands, cupped her bottom and lifted her in one movement and carried her to the sofa. He laid her down and, lowering his head, took her mouth again.

'Ho voglia di scoparti qui adesso,' he said hoarsely.

She wanted him too and, reaching up, she clasped his face in her hands and pressed a frantic kiss to his mouth, her teeth catching against his lips.

He leaned into her and she felt the hard press of his erection against the softness of her belly. A moan rose in her throat. Sliding her arms over his shoulders, she pulled him closer, arching her spine, pushing her pelvis upwards, squirming against him, trying to ease the ache that was throbbing between her thighs.

He was reaching for the zip of her dress, but she batted his hand away. She didn't want to wait. She wanted it to be just like it had been in Rome that first time, when they had done it standing up against the bedroom door with his body supporting hers.

'I need you now,' she whispered.

Encircling her waist with his arm, he raised her slightly, and her body clenched as he slid his hand beneath her panties and drew them down over her bare legs. She whimpered, and his mouth found hers and he kissed her thoroughly, his tongue pushing deep into her mouth.

And then she was pulling him closer, her nipples brushing against the hard muscles of his chest, fingers tugging at his zip. Pulling him free, she tightened her hand around him and felt his control snap.

Holding her firmly, he thrust inside her, and she cried out in shock and relief as he began to move.

Her eyes closed. Heat was uncurling inside her, faster and faster, in time with his hips, and she was wrapping her legs around him, holding him close, her hands gripping his shoulders, her body convulsing around him as he erupted inside her with hot, liquid force.

CHAPTER SIX

RALPH WOKE WITH a start, his heart racing, muscles stretched taut. Opening his eyes, he stared around the cabin. It was still dark, but there was a silvery opalescence in the air and he guessed that it was not quite dawn.

For a minute or so he steadied himself, willing the panic to recede. Finally, he managed to breathe. He felt as though he'd been fighting, but it was just a dream. The same vivid dream, part nightmare, part panic attack, that had woken him on and off since his mother had told him the truth about his father.

A dream that seemed to be getting more intense, more vivid, more terrifying...

It always started the same way, with him walking into the Palazzo Gioacchino after work. Everything looked normal—except his mother was still alive and he could hear her and Carlo talking in the drawing room.

But when he walked into the room his father was alone, and instead of welcoming him home Carlo said, 'You shouldn't be here. You're not my son.'

His fingers tightened against the sheet, the memory of the terror and the guilt pressing down on his ribs. So far, so familiar—but then this time in his dream his father had turned into Giulietta, who had shaken her head and said, 'You shouldn't be here. You're not my husband.'

From somewhere outside the sharp cry of a gull cut through his heartbeat and he felt a rush of relief, for even though he knew it was just a dream it had felt paralysingly real.

Beside him, he felt Giulietta shift in her sleep, and his body tensed as she rolled towards him. But as she settled against him he felt some of his tension ease.

It was called 'grounding'. Using something solid and certain to pull yourself back to reality.

And Giulietta was real. He could feel the heat of her body and the steady beat of her heart, her breath against his bare chest.

She was real and she was here with him.

Against her will?

His hands clenched and then he breathed out slowly. On the boat, yes. But in his bed, no.

His groin tightened at the memory of her touch. It had been almost a rerun of that first time in Rome. There had been no time to savour any preliminaries, no slow, teasing exploration. They hadn't even taken off their clothes. It had been raw and urgent and necessary—a consummation of desire. She had wanted him as much as he'd wanted her.

But last night had to be more than just some mechanical satisfying of hunger.

Why else would she have led him back to this cabin? To this bed.

Thinking back to the moment before they'd kissed, he felt his breathing slow.

He had brought her onto the *Alighieri* wanting answers, wanting to punish her for her hypocrisy, for running away, for deceiving him, for wanting to abandon their marriage.

They had already argued twice—once in the car and then again after he'd tossed onto the bed in their cabin. But neither round had ended satisfactorily, and they had been squaring up to one another again, both of them simmering with rage and frustration.

And then she had looked up into his face and he had seen not just her anger, but her fear.

Her confusion.

Her uncertainty.

It had shaken him, for he understood all those feelings.

And somehow, in his understanding, the bitterness and all the *misunderstandings* of their shared history had dissolved, and they had come together as man and wife. Equals in the face of a shared and potent sexual attraction.

They had made love again and again. In the past, perhaps even in that moment, he would have told himself that sex—the one-of-a-kind sort of sex they shared, anyway—was enough. Should be enough to smooth the tensions in their relationship.

He knew now that it wasn't.

Trust was the issue here.

Giulietta's behaviour had surprised and angered him, and there was still a degree of anger beneath the surface. But the spark of his anger had been lit before they even met.

It had started to flicker way back, when his mother had first told him that Carlo was not his father and his place in the world, the person he'd believed himself to be, had vanished.

A pale pinkish-yellow light was filtering into the cabin now and, gazing down at her sleeping face, he felt his jaw tighten.

It was easy to understand the mistakes he'd made.

Betrayed by the past, feeling trapped in a present where he was torn between continuing to live a lie or ruining the lives of those he loved most by telling the truth, he had become fixated on the future. On having a child.

Only by not telling Giulietta the truth he had forfeited her trust and self-sabotaged his right to the baby he craved so badly.

It was all such a mess of lies and half-truths and secrets. His body tensed.

And he was still holding back.

Understandably. Trust worked both ways.

And, yes, it didn't sit well with him, the part he'd played in making Giulietta think that her only option was to flee. But the fact was she had chosen to abandon him instead of fighting for their marriage.

His chest felt tight. It had been humiliating, trying to explain her absence to his family and their friends, and the threat of scandal had been the last thing he'd needed.

She moved against him again, her hand splaying out over his stomach, and he felt a kick of desire just below where her fingers lay twitching against his skin. He ached to pull her closer, to caress and kiss her awake.

It was an admission of sorts, her being here. Only he would be a fool to think that last night had resolved anything except a mutual sexual hunger.

She might be back in his bed, but he wanted her back in his life.

For good.

So he needed to work out how to persuade her that last night hadn't just been a one-off sexual encounter but the first step in their reconciliation.

Feeling calmer, he curved his arm around her waist, anchoring her against his body as he drifted back to sleep.

When he woke again, the bed was empty.

Rolling over, he picked up the remote control by the bed and opened the blinds, blinking as daylight flooded the cabin. It was a perfect day. In the flawless blue sky an apricot sun was already warming the air.

He glanced across the rumpled sheets, his pulse out of sync with his breathing. But where was his wife?

His shoulders tensed, and a rush of irritation flared over

his skin. Did she really think she could run from this—from him?

His body had sung at her touch, and he knew he had made her feel the same way, but still she seemed bent on denying that fact.

It took him longer than he'd expected to track her down. She wasn't eating breakfast in the sunshine, or relaxing by the pool. Instead, he found her on the top deck.

He stopped in the doorway, his stomach clenching. Giulietta was less than five feet away. She was wearing peach-coloured shorts and a loose vest with a crossover back. Her hair was in a high ponytail and he could see the gleam of sweat on the lightly tanned skin of her shoulders.

But it was not her hair or her clothes or even her skin that made his breath catch.

It was her pose.

She was on her knees, leaning forward, with her arms stretched straight ahead and her bottom raised as though in supplication or surrender.

He knew it was a perfectly legitimate yoga position, designed to stretch the spine in both directions. But, predictably, it still took his brain less than three seconds to come up with a modified version of the same pose…this time involving him as well.

Pulse quickening, he found his eyes snagged on the cleft of her buttocks, and he struggled silently against the urge to reach and caress her there, as he had done only hours earlier.

He hadn't thought he'd made any noise… But maybe she had the same inbuilt radar as he did when it came to sensing each other's presence, because the muscles in her back and legs suddenly stiffened, like a deer catching the scent of a predator.

There was a stretch of silence as she rolled up her spine

and sat back on her haunches, and then she stood up in one smooth movement and turned to face him.

He stepped out into the light. *'Buongiorno,'* he said softly. 'Or should I say *namaste*?'

The fringe of her dark lashes fluttered as she tilted her head back, her mouth moving into an approximation of a smile. *'Buongiorno* is fine.'

His fingers twitched. Last night he had felt as if she was his again, and it was tempting to reach out and pull her close, take her mouth with his. But, despite the clamour of his pulse, he stayed where he was.

'That pose looked familiar. It was the Melting Heart, wasn't it?'

She nodded slowly but, judging by the wary expression on her face, her heart hadn't been similarly affected by last night's encounter.

'That's one of the names for it. My teacher calls it the *anahatasana*. It's supposed to be good for tension.'

His eyes rested on her set, pale face. In that case, it wasn't working. She looked tense—nervous, even—and he was pretty sure he knew the reason why. It was the same reason she had not stayed in bed and waited for him to wake this morning.

Clearly they needed to talk about last night.

But they were on a boat in the middle of the Adriatic. Here, they were unmoored from the landlocked constraints of time. Surely he could wait a few moments?

Besides, he thought, as the smell of freshly brewed coffee drifted up from somewhere on board, he'd realised he was ravenously hungry.

'I'm guessing you haven't eaten,' he said slowly. 'Why don't you go and shower? Then we can get some breakfast.'

Fifteen minutes later she joined him on deck. She had

changed her clothes, and her hair was still damp from the shower, but the wariness of her expression hadn't changed.

Keeping his expression intentionally bland, he waited while she served herself some fruit and muesli. 'Tea or coffee?' he asked.

'Tea, please.'

Leaning forward, he poured out the tea and added milk, his gaze drifting over the toned curves of her shoulders and arms. He liked what she was wearing. The sleeveless white shirt knotted at her waist and the flirty printed skirt reminded him of some Hitchcock heroine—Grace Kelly or Eva Marie Saint, maybe.

Except he couldn't imagine his wife as a cool, glacial blonde. She was too easy to stir to passion. And to anger.

Impulsively he leaned forward and tucked a stray tortoiseshell curl behind her ear. He felt her tense and, watching the flurry of conflicting emotions chase across her face, he felt his own body tighten too.

It was always there, simmering beneath the surface. One touch was all it took to remind both of them. The difference was she was still fighting it.

Lowering his hand, he leaned back in his seat. 'This is all very civilised,' he said softly.

Her eyes flickered up to meet his. 'You know what would be even more civilised? You turning the *Alighieri* round and taking me back to Venice.'

He held her gaze, letting the silence that followed her remark drift into the warm air.

Her lip curled. 'Doesn't it matter to you that I don't want this?'

'To be on the boat?'

'To be with you anywhere,' she snapped.

He let the silence that followed her remark deliberately

lengthen. Then, 'In that case, I think now might be a good time to talk about what happened last night.'

Not just last night, Juliet thought, feeling heat feather her cheeks and her throat. They had reached for one another again and again as night had slipped into a new day.

She felt her pulse stumble.

How could she describe what had happened last night? It had been both inevitable and yet miraculous. Like adding potassium to water and standing back to watch it explode.

She didn't remember falling asleep, and when she'd woken she had momentarily thought that the warm pressure of Ralph's body next to hers was just a dream—some kind of hyper-realistic wish-fulfilment fantasy.

But of course it had been all too real.

She stared at him in silence. Even if she had any it was too late for regrets. But how could anyone regret such blissful sensual fulfilment?

Shifting in her seat, she thought back to the moment when she had finally stopped fighting the inevitable. Except that made her sound passive. Made it sound as if he had plundered her against her will like the heroine of some old Regency romance novel, when in fact their desire had been mutual.

She had matched his hunger. Shaking with eagerness, she had kissed him, pulled him hard against her and inside her aching body. It was she who had led him to their cabin.

It had been a fast and urgent no-holds-barred mating. With mouths, hands, reaching unashamedly for one another, bodies responding to an impulse as old as time.

And it had felt so good.

Glancing across the table, she felt her skin twitch as she remembered what lay beneath that pale blue striped knitted polo shirt and those faded linen shorts.

He had felt so good.

Hard where she was soft, his muscles smooth and taut, his skin warm and sleek. And she had wanted all of him. Skin on skin, the unthinkable freedom to taste, to touch, to savour the teasing, the slow foreplay and the swift passion.

Her eyes dropped to the deck. During her five weeks of self-inflicted celibacy she'd thought she was learning to live without him. She'd been wrong.

But it didn't matter how much she craved him, she was going to have to try harder to learn that particular lesson.

Her shoulders tightened as the words she'd thrown at him last night bumped into one another inside her head.

'Everything is wrong between us. Nothing works.'

He had proved his point: on one level they worked perfectly.

But to acknowledge that Ralph had the power to render her boneless with desire was to prove another point entirely. That sex was both the cure and the cause of their marital problems—an irresistible quick fix for when words failed as a means of communication.

A slow fix too, she thought, her cheeks heating as she remembered what had happened when they'd finally reached the cabin. Kisses had become caresses and their anger had grown formless, transfigured into passion of a different kind that overcame everything.

Last night's encounter was all part of the pattern of behaviour that had characterised their relationship from the start. It was hardly the basis for a good marriage. And as for having a baby—

Her heart jerked to a halt as a new, devastating thought barged to the front of her mind.

Around her, the warm air pulsed like a bass guitar at a rock concert and she gripped the arms of her chair. She felt suddenly breathless, dizzy, and something of what she was feeling must have shown in her face because he started to shake his head.

'Let me guess,' he said slowly. 'You're going to tell me that what happened was a mistake. That it means nothing and that it won't happen again.'

Actually, she wasn't.

A knot of panic was unravelling inside her chest.

So many times in the past she'd questioned how her mother could have made so many mistakes.

Now she knew.

She stared at him, not trusting herself to speak.

But she couldn't lie. Not after everything they had been through these last months. Not about this.

Her eyes found his. 'I'm not on the pill any more,' she said slowly. 'I stopped taking it just before I went back to England...' Her voice trailed away into silence.

She'd been in such a state—upset, angry, both hating him and missing him. When her period had finished it had felt like fate forcing her to choose a future.

Dazedly, she did some calculations in her head. *It might be okay...*

Heart pounding, she did the calculations once more. *Then again, it might not.*

'I'm about twelve days into my cycle.' *Make that thirteen this morning*, she corrected silently.

He was staring at her, his eyes steady, but she could sense his mind working swiftly through the implications of her words.

'You're saying you could be pregnant.'

He put the emphasis on 'could', but she still felt her pulse accelerate.

Yes, that was what she was saying. And, despite her panic, a shot of pure, shimmering happiness, bright as sunshine, more intoxicating than prosecco, flooded her veins.

She nodded. 'I don't know the odds, but it's definitely possible.'

Her heart thudded. She sounded like some clueless teenager. Worse—she sounded like her mother.

A cool spiderweb of shame wound over her skin. She'd spent so many years trying not to be Nancy Jones, smugly believing herself to be smarter, more stable, better... But she was worse. At least her mother had been only a teenager when she'd had unprotected sex and got pregnant.

She was twenty-five.

There was no excuse for behaving so irresponsibly.

But it had been so fast she hadn't been thinking straight. Truthfully, safe sex had been the last thing on her mind. Fast sex, slow sex, urgent sex, tender sex—but not safe sex.

His expression was unreadable. 'Why did you come off the pill?'

'I don't know.' How was she supposed to explain the chaotic, topsy-turvy flow of her thoughts back then? 'I suppose because I didn't think I needed to be on it any more.'

She watched his face harden infinitesimally, her stomach churning. More implied meanings...more unspoken truths.

'And if you are pregnant?'

His Italian accent was stronger now, muddying his vowels and softening his voice, and she felt her body start to hum beneath his steady gaze.

'Then we'll be having a baby—'

Her words stalled. It was still what she wanted, despite everything. Only it terrified her too—the idea that she might have replicated her own haphazard conception.

'You know nothing would make me happier if you were.'

He was staring at her, and his golden eyes were so incredibly gentle that it was all she could do not to cry. It was too easy to remember their shared hope in those few months of their marriage. Only so much had happened...so much had been revealed as fragile and illusory.

'I might not be,' she said quickly.

The silence stretched away from them, across the sparkling blue sea.

'There's only one way to find out for sure.'

Pushing back his seat, he stood up and pulled out his phone. She watched him walk away, nerves twisting in her throat, and then she stood up too. It was impossible to stay sitting. Her heart felt as though it might burst through her chest.

Trying to steady her breathing, she walked across the deck and braced herself against the handrail, her gaze fixed on the rippling jewel-coloured water.

She should never have come back to Verona. Then none of this would be happening.

Her whole body tensed.

Except then she might not be possibly pregnant, and even now, when she was awash with panic, she felt not just love but a yearning for the baby that might already be embedding itself inside her.

Her heartbeat stuttered as she remembered that moment at the christening when Luca had reached for Lucia, wrapping his arms around her and Raffaelle. Around them guests had stood chatting and laughing, and waiters had offered prosecco and canapés, but they'd had everything they needed.

She held her breath, feeling a tug in her belly like a magnet, and on its heels a swift, shameful envy at being untrammelled by doubt.

Her throat burned with tears.

But that was the difference. Lucia and Luca were meant

to be together. They did not and never would know what it felt like to have a child with the wrong person. Or to be that child.

And what if she couldn't pull off being a mother?

The thought stabbed at her. She had tried and failed to be a good daughter and wife—why would being a mother be any different?

'That's sorted.'

His mood had shifted like the breeze coming off the water. The softness had faded from his eyes and his voice had the familiar cool authority of a man used to snapping his fingers and getting his own way.

Her fingers tightened against the cool metal. Abruptly, she turned and faced him, her chin jutting out. 'What are you talking about?'

'That was Dr de Masi. I've made an appointment at her clinic. She says she can do a pregnancy test when you come in.' His gaze held hers. 'Apparently you can do one as early as eight days after conception.'

Eight days.

So soon.

Needing to stop the panic rising in her throat, she resorted to anger. 'And that sorts everything out, does it?' She shook her head. 'Either I'm pregnant or I'm not and then life goes on?'

His gaze didn't shift from hers. 'That's not fair,' he said quietly.

It wasn't. But knowing that only made her feel more defensive.

'Yes, it is.' She couldn't stop the bitterness entering her voice. 'I know you, Ralph.'

'Clearly not.' Taking a step towards her, he caught her wrists, eyes locking with hers. 'If you did, you would know that I wasn't for one moment suggesting that life will just "carry on". But we do need to find out if you're pregnant.'

Her heartbeat stumbled. She couldn't fault the simple logic of his statement. Or his motives for contacting Dr de Masi. Monica de Masi was the obstetrician of choice for wealthy Veronese families. She had met her once and liked her.

But something inside her baulked at the idea of her and Ralph going to the clinic. It made it feel as if this was something they'd planned together as a couple, when actually the reverse was true.

'Can't we just get one of those tests you buy at a pharmacy?' she said, tugging free of his grip.

Their eyes met.

'The Clinica Filomena has an excellent reputation,' he said smoothly. 'And if the test is positive then we will have expert care on hand to advise us and answer questions.'

That was true—and again she couldn't fault his logic. But she knew that the real reason Ralph wanted to go to the clinic had nothing to do with expert care and advice.

He didn't trust her to tell him the truth.

Her fingers curled into fists, guilt and regret jabbing at her. She couldn't blame him. Certainly if their positions had been reversed she would have felt and acted the same way.

Only it hurt.

Not just the fact that he felt that way, but the fact that her actions had let distrust and doubt colour what might be the first few hours of their baby's life.

'I don't just want to buy some kit from the pharmacy,' he said quietly. 'I want to do this properly.'

She bit her lip. 'How can we do that? We've just blundered into it.'

Her mind twisted and turned away from the thought of her own careless conception. She knew that the setting had been somewhat shabbier—a bathroom at a raucous house party rather than a floating palace—but the occasion had shared the same reckless mix of sex and stupidity as her encounter with Ralph.

It made her feel sick.

'I was irresponsible and you were ignorant,' she said flatly.

Ralph's face was expressionless, and then a flicker of frustration crossed it. 'That's one way of looking at it,' he said. 'The other is that we wanted each other. Absolutely and unconditionally.' His thumbs bit into her shoulders. 'Do you know how rare that is, Giulietta? How incredible?'

Despite herself, she felt his words reach down deep inside her. Even now her body still sang from his touch. But that kind of passion carried a sting in the tail.

'It's not that rare.' Her mouth trembled. 'My parents felt like that every single time they had sex.'

She was talking too loudly, and too fast, and she wanted to stop but couldn't seem to call a halt. It was as if the words were like oil gushing from an uncapped well.

'It was what kept them together for so many years—even though their relationship was a disaster and they were completely wrong for one another.'

Ralph heard the break in her voice. It matched the one in his heart.

The thought that Giulietta could be carrying a child… their child…almost undid him. It was what he'd wanted for so long—ever since his mother's bombshell confession had cast him adrift.

It had been a double loss. Losing his mother and learning the truth about his father. He'd been numb with grief… eating standing up, barely sleeping.

It had only been after the funeral that he had been able to register the full extent of the damage, and in those terrible, endless, unnumbered days his life had collapsed like a house of cards.

Everything he'd taken for granted—familial bonds, ancestors stretching back five hundred years, a name that not only opened doors but took them off their hinges—all of it had been proved false.

He'd realised that the gleaming palace of his life had been built on the frailest of foundations. On his ignorance of the truth. But the instant that Giulietta had told him she might be pregnant he had felt as if an anchor had dropped to the seabed.

Not to know for certain was killing him.

He glanced over at her face, but she wouldn't meet his eyes.

Only he knew this wasn't just about him. Or even the possibility that she was pregnant.

He could see there was an exhaustion beneath her panic, as though she had been struggling with something for a long time. *Struggling alone.*

The thought jolted him.

He knew very little about her family or her background. So little, in fact, that what she had told him could be summed up in three sentences.

Her parents were separated.

When her mother had struggled to cope she had been placed with foster parents.

She had left home at sixteen and got a live-in job in the kitchen of a country house hotel.

At the time he hadn't given her reticence much thought. He'd been too distracted by his own unravelling family tree. But clearly it was the parts she'd edited out that mattered most.

Keeping his voice even, he said carefully, 'How long did they stay together?'

She hesitated, then shrugged. 'On and off for about ten years.'

Her eyes were still avoiding his. 'A decade is a long time to stay together,' he said quietly. 'Surely there must have been more to their relationship than sex.'

'There was.' Now she looked at him. 'There was anger. And resentment. And endless misunderstandings. But everything started and ended with sex.' She cleared her throat. 'You know, for a long time I thought that was what people meant by "foreplay"—arguing, making accusations, storming off.'

He heard her swallow.

'I wasn't planned. My parents barely knew each other when my mum got pregnant.'

Her shoulders were braced, limbs taut like a sprinter on the starting blocks, and he wanted to reach out and pull her close, smooth the tension from her body. But he didn't want her to run from him again.

'It was a disaster. They should never have been together. They certainly shouldn't have had a child. And I didn't want to be like them... I didn't want us to be like them. Only it's happened anyway.'

The ache in her voice swallowed him whole. For a few half-seconds he thought about the fears he'd kept hidden, and then he stopped thinking and caught her by the shoulders.

Her body tensed and she jerked against his hands, but he held her still. 'None of us get to choose our parents, *bella*. We don't get to choose how or when or where we're conceived.'

She stopped struggling.

'But we can choose how to live our lives—and you and

I…we're not like your parents or mine. And we don't have to make a binary choice between fighting and breaking up.'

Watching her eyes widen, he steadied himself, and just for a moment he considered telling her more about his mother's affair.

But he couldn't bring himself to do so.

Instead, he captured her chin and tilted her face up so that she had to meet his gaze. 'We're going to do this our way, Giulietta. And whatever it takes I'll make it work. I promise.'

Her hands clenched. 'It's not that simple, Ralph.'

'Sure it is.' He spoke with a calmness he didn't feel. 'We go to the clinic. You take the test. And—'

'And then what?'

'I don't know,' he said simply. 'I don't have all the answers. But I do know that if you are pregnant then we can't be constantly at war. We need to be able to talk…to have a relationship for the sake of our child.'

He was choosing his words with the care of a violinist tuning his instrument.

'I know we have a lot of unresolved issues. But if I take you back to Verona then we'll have failed at the first hurdle.'

Something shifted in her eyes, like sunlight on water, and she stiffened for a heartbeat. And then he felt her relax just a fraction.

He relaxed a little too then. 'Look, we have a week until you can take the test. Why don't we spend it here?'

'Do you really need to ask that?' Her brown eyes widened and she twitched free of his grip. 'You brought me here against my will.'

He studied her face. Beneath the defiance she looked incredibly fragile. His heart was hammering his ribs. He felt like a diver standing on the edge of a board. It was all or nothing now. *Crunch time.*

'I can't change that. But if it's what you want then we can turn the boat around now. I'd prefer it if you stayed. Only this time, of your own volition.'

Her eyes flared. 'Why? So we can have sex again?'

Sex.

The word reverberated between them and, watching the pulse in her throat jump out at him, he had to stop himself from closing the gap between them and pressing his mouth against hers.

'That's not going to happen,' she said.

She sounded adamant, but as she spoke she swayed forward slightly, her body momentarily contradicting her words. He stared down at her, seeing his own hunger reflected in her eyes and in the flush of her cheeks, in the shiver running over her skin.

She was fighting for control.

He was too, his body reacting instantly, viscerally, to the quivering tension in the air.

Pulse trembling, he moved towards her, close enough that all it would take was one more step for him to curl his arm around her waist and join his mouth with hers. He wanted to pull her close as he had last night, as he had so many times in the past, but for this to work he needed to take sex out of the equation.

'You can have your own cabin. There'll be a lock on the door.' His body tensed in revolt, but the need to reassure her took priority over his hunger. 'In nine months' time we could be parents, *bella.* Surely we can call a truce and spend eight days together?' he said softly.

There was a pause. Then, 'Okay.'

Her voice was still taut, but her shoulders had relaxed and he felt a flood of relief. It was a long way from *till death us do part*, but they could start with that.

'I'll stay.' Her eyes clashed with his. 'But this doesn't change anything.'

She was right. Nothing had changed.

Whatever that test said, she was still his wife.

And eight days alone on a boat in the middle of the ocean should be plenty long enough to remind her that he was her husband.

CHAPTER SEVEN

SHRUGGING OFF HER ROBE, Juliet kicked off her flip-flops and dropped down onto one of the teak loungers that clustered around the on-deck pool like animals around a watering hole. She knew she could go for a dip, but it was her brain, not her body, that needed occupation, and she had come prepared.

Picking up her book, she flipped it open, tilting the spine back to avoid the glare of the sun. According to the blurb on the cover, it was 'a pulse-pounding thriller' promising 'an escape from reality'. But, glancing down at the first page, she felt a rush of frustration.

It was going to take a lot more than a fast-paced holiday read to match the drama of her own current situation, she thought, gazing away to the sparkling blue waters of the Adriatic. And as for escaping it...

Her mouth twisted. Right now, a lifeboat might be her best option.

It was just over an hour since she had agreed with Ralph that she would stay on the *Alighieri*.

It was only for eight days.

Hardly a lifetime.

But already she was wondering if she had made yet another mistake by agreeing to stay.

Only it would sound so juvenile to insist on going back now, when she was going to have to see him at the clinic anyway.

The clinic.

She felt her pulse stumble and her fingers twitch. But there was no point in reaching for her phone to check the calendar again. The facts hadn't changed.

They'd had unprotected sex yesterday.

And this morning.

More than once.

And at the time in her cycle when the chances of conception were at their greatest.

So, theoretically, she could be pregnant.

But, since it would be at least a week before she could confirm if she was having Ralph's baby, she was just going to have to wait.

Shifting against the cushions, she steadied her breathing. She hated waiting—hated feeling so uncertain about everything. It reminded her of being a child, shuttled between foster homes, her stomach cramping with hunger and a nagging unspecified dread.

She had learned to manage the feeling by living in the moment, and that had worked well for her. After moving out of her last foster parents' home she'd made a life for herself. She'd had friends, a rented flat, and her hobby—blogging about food—had turned into a job she loved.

Only then she'd fallen in love. And suddenly the past and the future had been all that mattered: Ralph's past, their future...

Just like that, all her doubts and fears had suddenly been unleashed again, so that for weeks—months, even—she'd felt out of depth.

But she'd never felt more confused than she did right now.

Lifting her arm to shade her face, she squinted across the deck at the docile blue sea.

Her head felt like a slot machine. Each time she thought

she had a handle on what she was thinking and feeling something else happened and sent her thoughts spinning.

Her heartbeat skipped.

Like earlier.

They had been talking about her parents. Something he had said had caught her off balance and she had ended up unloading about her past.

She shivered in the sunlight. Not everything. Not the whole sordid story. Nobody needed to hear that. Just the part about the rows and the sex and the fact that she had been conceived without thought.

It was the first time she'd shared the ugliness of those years with anyone. Even just thinking about it had always made it seem too real again, so she'd buried the memories in the deepest corner of her mind.

But this morning, with Ralph, the truth had come tumbling out.

Heart hammering against her ribs, she thought back to that moment when he'd caught her arms, his golden eyes joining his hands to hold her captive.

'None of us get to choose our parents, bella. We don't get to choose how or when or where we're conceived.'

We.

Her shoulders tensed as she remembered how it had angered her at first, him talking about them in the first-person plural when they were, in effect, estranged.

But this time it hadn't angered her.

Instead it had been as if the last few months had never passed. She had wanted to hold and comfort him, had wanted his arms to close around her.

Picturing the defensive expression on his face, she felt a sudden rush of shame burn through her.

It wasn't hard to imagine his feelings—then or now.

To learn that the man who had raised him from birth

was not his father would have been huge. Like an A-bomb detonating in his living room. And she should have been there to support him, but he'd been alone.

They had both been alone with their fears—both been caught up in the events of their pasts. Was it any surprise they had each been swamped by doubt and misunderstandings?

She closed the book.

It made her wonder how different things might be now if they had even once tried to face the past together as a couple, rather than separately as two individuals. If he hadn't kept the truth from her, and she had been able to trust him, would it have made a difference?

Hating that the answer to that question might possibly be yes, she blanked her mind and glanced across the deck. The boat was skirting the coastline now, and as her gaze snagged on a cluster of wildflowers clinging heroically to the cliffs she felt her pulse dart.

It was one of the many advantages of having your own private yacht. Space, independence, incomparable views... And, of course, if you wanted to, you could stake a claim to one of the many beautiful sandy beaches that were only accessible by water. Just like that you'd have your own completely private idyllic retreat, far from the chattering crowds of tourists.

Her heart beat a little faster as she thought back to the first time Ralph had taken her out on the *Alighieri*. They had driven across the country from Rome, picking up the *Alighieri* in Rimini and then drifting up the Adriatic coast towards Venice in the cool winter sunshine.

Sometimes they'd made it up on deck, but often they'd just stayed in bed, eating, talking, playing cards and making love as the coastline changed from the unbroken stretches of sand to dramatic eroded cliffs.

They'd dropped anchor in the early evening, just south of the resorts of Rimini and Riccione. From the boat, the beach had been just a teasing sliver of gold, like a crescent moon. Up close it had been magical...otherworldly. A tiny scallop-shaped curve of sand overlooking an iridescent sea the colour of an abalone shell.

Beneath a flawless white moon they had swum in the cool aquamarine water, lost in the magic of being completely alone with each other, and then he had rolled her under him on the wet sand, his body covering hers as the foaming waves spilled over them...

There was a shout from the lower deck, a burst of laughter, and she was back on the *Alighieri* with the sun burning the air.

It wasn't fair.

It wasn't fair that she could recall it all so clearly.

She didn't want or need to be reminded of how it had felt. It was over, gone, lost... *Wasn't it?*

As the question fizzed inside her head a shadow fell over her face and, looking up, she felt her spine tense with an almost audible snap.

Ralph was standing beside the lounger, his phone in his hand, his body edged with sunlight.

She felt her stomach muscles curl as his gaze roamed over the three triangles of her rose-coloured bikini.

'Hi,' he said softly.

The air felt as though it was electrically charged. Suddenly all her senses were burning.

She cleared her throat. 'Hi.'

It was hard to look at him, but impossible to look away from his preposterously photogenic face.

'Luca called. He sent his love. And these.'

As she gazed up at him he nudged one of the other loungers closer to hers and sat down on it, resting one leg on the other with a familiar masculine confidence that made a pulse of heat tick over her skin.

Her fingers bit into the cover of the book.

She couldn't fault his dark blue swim-shorts or accuse him of underdressing. They were perfectly respectable. And yet they seemed deliberately designed to showcase his superb body: the taut chest, broad shoulders, curving biceps. And the skin that tasted as good as it looked.

She felt Ralph's eyes on her face and her heart thudded hard against her ribs as he held out his phone.

'Here. They're from the christening.'

Grateful for a reason to drag her gaze away from his powerful frame, she took the phone.

She knew hearts couldn't melt but, glancing down at the screen, she felt as if hers was turning to liquid.

Slowly she swiped downwards.

People always said the camera didn't lie, and as far as Lucia and Luca were concerned that was true. They both looked radiant with a happiness that shone from within. But, gazing down at a picture of herself, Juliet wondered at her calm expression. She had been so tense all that day, yet there was no sign of the chaos churning beneath her skin.

Bending lower over the phone, she began scrolling down again—and then her fingers scuffed against the screen and a fluttering mass of butterflies rose up inside her stomach.

It was a photo of Ralph. He was holding Raffaelle and his face was serious. Solemn, almost, as if he was taking a private vow.

Her pulse jumped. She'd told herself there was nothing left between them but a physical attraction. Only gazing down at the photo she knew that it was more complicated than just passion and possession.

With a hand that shook a little, she held out the phone. 'He's a good photographer.'

He stared at her steadily. 'Yes, he is.' His eyes flickered over her bikini again. 'I might take a dip in the pool before lunch. Would you care to join me?'

Her skin felt as if it was suddenly on fire. Being half naked on a lounger was one thing. Being half naked in a pool with Ralph in swim-shorts was something else entirely.

She managed a small, taut smile. 'I'll think I'll just read my book.'

There was a short pulsing silence as his eyes flickered over the cover and then he shrugged. 'Okay.'

Heart pounding, she watched as he tossed his phone onto the lounger and stood up. Relief washed over her as he executed a perfect dive into the pool and disappeared beneath the water.

An hour later it was time for lunch.

Forking the delicious antipasti of stuffed peppers, parmigiana and tiny pink prawns into her mouth, she was surprised to find she was really quite hungry. It was her favourite kind of food. Simple ingredients cooked well. But she knew it was more than the food.

It was easy being with him—easier than it should be, she thought. Easier than it had been even a few weeks ago. Easy, too, to see why she had fallen so deeply under his spell.

And might do so again?

She stared down at the cutlery, her eyes tracing the intricate embossed pattern on the handle of her spoon.

All she had to do was say the words. Only she'd felt like this before and been wrong. What if she was wrong again?

As they waited for their plates to be cleared away Ralph lounged back in his seat, tilting his face up to the sun. 'I was chatting to Franco earlier, and he told me about a place just down the coast where we can drop anchor.'

Her heart skipped. Could he read minds? Had that night beneath the stars stuck in his mind too? Or was it just co-incidence?

His eyes met hers. 'I thought maybe we might go ashore.'

She held his gaze. 'You're not worried I might run away?'

A faint smile tugged the corners of his mouth. 'Should I be?'

They both knew it was a hypothetical question. She would need crampons to climb the cliffs that hugged the patches of sand edging this stretch of the coast. But she knew that he wanted to gauge her mood. To find out if their truce was holding.

Glancing past him, she focused her attention on the plunging sandstone cliffs. There was a part of her that was relieved to have a respite from fighting him.

She looked up to find him watching her, and suddenly she was conscious of every breath, of the heavy pulse pounding through her body.

He was on the other side of the table, but it felt as if there was no distance between them. She felt hot and tingly, as if his golden gaze had set off firecrackers beneath her skin.

No, Ralph didn't have to worry about her running away—but she should be worried about why she'd stayed.

Forcing herself to hold his gaze, she shook her head. 'Of course not. We made an agreement. I said I'd stay until the appointment with Dr de Masi, and that's what I'm going to do.'

Later, as they sped across the translucent water to the cove Franco had told them about, Ralph replayed her words in-side his head, frustration swelling up inside him like the curling bow wave at the front of the dinghy.

She didn't trust him. Still.

But was that such a surprise? It required time to repair and restore trust.

He felt a rush of panic. What if he ran out of time, like his mother had?

His hands clenched. He wanted to scoop Giulietta into his arms as he'd done at the marina. Only this time he didn't want to let go of her.

But everything was so finely balanced at the moment. He didn't want to do anything that might risk them going backwards.

The cove was deserted—and beautiful. Powder-soft ivory-coloured sand, clear shallow water and the occasional piece of bleached driftwood.

He had hoped she might swim with him, but instead she lay down on the comfortable oversized cushions the crew had brought over earlier and began reading her book.

The water was perfect and, closing off his mind, he swam until his muscles ached.

Finally he'd had enough, and he made his way up the beach, his eyes fixed on his wife. She'd changed position. Now she was sitting with one arm curled around her knees, her tawny hair framing her face.

He felt his heart contract. She looked so young, and yet there was a tension to her shoulders as if she was carrying the weight of the world.

When he dropped down beside her she didn't look up from her book and, rolling onto his side, he sighed. 'I've got to say, this isn't doing much for my ego.'

There was a pause and then she lifted her face, frowning. 'What do you mean?'

'I'm not used to playing second fiddle—particularly to a book. Must be a real page-turner,' he prompted, sitting up.

There was another pause, and then she shrugged. 'Actually, I haven't managed to get past the first chapter.'

He raised an eyebrow. 'Really?' Ducking his head, he tipped the cover towards him. 'It says here it's "gripping, pacy, and utterly addictive".'

He watched the corners of her mouth lift.

'It probably is. I just can't concentrate.'

'Why not?

'I've got a lot on my mind.'

'So what's bothering you?' He screwed up his face. 'I mean, other than being abducted and possibly getting pregnant by a man you want to divorce.'

They stared at one another in silence, and then she smiled, and suddenly he was smiling too.

Then her mouth started to tremble. 'You make it so hard for me to fight you,' she said shakily.

The sheen of tears in her eyes made his body tense in shock. He'd never seen his wife cry. And he hated it that he had been the one to change that fact.

'That's because I don't want to fight with you any more, *bella*.' He kept his voice deliberately steady. 'I want to start again. Go back to the beginning.'

The beginning: Rome.

Memories of those first few days together moved smoothly inside his head like the picture strip in a spinning zoetrope.

It had been perfect.

Heat and passion.

Skin on skin.

And an all-encompassing need.

They might have met in Rome, but he didn't need to be in Verona to know that she was the one, his Giulietta. In that moment it was as if he could see the rest of his life with her at the centre. Only, through arrogance and stupidity, he had not just let her go, he had driven her from their home.

'Do you think we could do that, Giulietta? Do you think we could start over?'

His heart stumbled when she started shaking her head. 'I don't know if we can. I don't know if *I* can…'

Something in her voice reminded him of their conversation earlier, when she'd told him about her parents and their rows and their making up. There had been the same note of fatigue—defeat, even—and he felt suddenly out of his depth. He hadn't even managed to sort out his own problems. Why did he think he could help soothe her pain?

Because you're her husband, he told himself fiercely. *That's why.*

He took a breath. 'When did you last see them?' he said quietly. 'Your parents?'

She was silent for so long he thought he'd lost her, but then he realised she was searching for something to say that would be enough but not too much.

He knew that feeling well.

'I don't know,' she said finally. 'My dad was never really there. He was always coming and going. Mostly going.' Her lips twisted. 'I suppose I was probably about nine when he stopped coming back.'

She glanced past him, looking upwards, her eyes tracking the contrails of a plane across the sky.

'I don't remember the exact day, but it was October and it was foggy. He went out for bread and never came back.' Despite the heat of the sun, she sounded shivery. 'It was like the fog just swallowed him up…' Her words drifted into silence.

'And your mum?'

Now her eyes clashed with his, the brown dark and defensive.

'Why are you asking all these questions?' She had

scooted away from him and she was holding the book in front of her chest like a shield.

'Because you're my wife,' he said quietly, reaching over and capturing her hand. 'And because I should have asked you when we first met.'

It hurt, admitting that to himself—to her. But at the time her past, her background, had been secondary to his. Or rather secondary to the earth-shattering repercussions of finding out that everything he had taken for granted was a lie.

He'd arrogantly assumed that nothing in her ordinary little life could be as devastating as finding out he wasn't a Castellucci.

He felt a rush of self-loathing. He'd had so much in his life, an excess of everything—*even fathers*—and yet he had failed to give his wife the reassurance and support she needed.

Across the beach, the waves were tumbling onto the sand, each one washing away the lacy patterns of the last. If only he could so easily erase the mistakes he'd made.

But, then again, maybe this shouldn't be easy.

Clearly she thought so too.

She pulled her hand free. Her mouth was trembling. 'But you didn't.'

'No, I didn't.' He pushed back against the regret. 'And that's on me. I let you down, and I hurt you. And I know I can't change what I did, but I will do everything in my power to earn your trust back.'

He could see the conflict in her eyes, the longing to believe his words vying with the hurt, and he hated it that he had so carelessly lost her trust.

She breathed out shakily. 'This isn't all on you. I was wrong too. I wouldn't have told you anything even if you had asked me about my parents. I didn't want you to know about them…about me.' Her voice was trembling now. 'Talking about it is so hard. It makes it all feel real again.'

He reached out and caught her hand again. 'Makes what feel real?' he asked gently.

'How it felt, living like that.'

This time, her fingers tightened around his.

'It wasn't just the rows. They were alcoholics. If they weren't out getting wasted, they were hungover and hopeless. When my dad left for good, my mum just gave up. One day she took some pills—'

The words sounded stark, ugly against the soft beauty of the beach. And there was a seam of pain in her voice now that made his stomach twist with rage. She had been nine years old…just a little girl.

'What happened?'

'I tried to dig them out of her mouth but she wouldn't wake up. So I called an ambulance. She was okay, but there was no one to look after me so I went to stay with Rebecca and Tim.'

She was curled over now, her shoulders hunched, as if she was surrounded by a pack of wolves. Maybe she felt that way.

'They were my first foster parents.'

First. For such a small word it packed a hell of a punch.

He stared at her small, tense body, his heart aching with emotions that felt too big to be contained. 'But there were others?'

She nodded. 'Lots of people like me…they just slip through the net. So I was lucky, really.'

He watched her fingers bunch into a fist. The gesture made his whole body hurt.

'I suppose it was just not knowing each time if there would be anyone there to catch me that was so terrible…'

His ribs ached.

For her, love had proved dangerous. What should have been solid—the love of her parents—had been consistently weak and unreliable, and yet she had not given up. Despite all those betrayals of her childhood she had let herself feel again, let herself love him.

Unlike him, she had faced her fears, her doubts, head-on, trusting to love, *trusting him*.

'What about now? Do you have anything to do with her?'

She cleared her throat. 'Not since I was sixteen. That's when we last spoke. She texts me sometimes, but I made the decision to cut her out of my life.'

She was looking at him, but not quite meeting his eyes.

'I know she's my mum, but being around her makes me feel so out of control, so powerless, and it scares me...'

Her voice wavered, and he had closed the gap between them and pulled her into his arms before he'd even realised what he was doing.

A sob caught in her throat and she crumpled against him. He held her tightly, stroking her silken hair and telling her over and over again that everything would be all right, swapping back and forth from English to Italian until finally she was calm.

'That's why you went back to England,' he said hoarsely. 'I'd made you feel powerless.'

He felt her shiver.

'I panicked. I thought it was something in me—something I was doing—and that was why you wanted someone else.'

Cupping her chin, he tipped her face up to his, fearing and knowing that he hadn't made his feelings for her sufficiently clear. 'I didn't want anyone else. I never have. I want you—all and every possible version of you.'

He felt her hands flutter against his chest and, looking

down, felt heat flood his veins. Her eyes were wide and soft, her body pressing against his was softer still, and he was on the verge of kissing her.

But something held him back. The need to demonstrate that he wanted her for more than just sex. That he *needed* to be there for her.

And he needed her to be there for him.

His stomach clenched.

Could he tell her? Could he share his fears?

The dark, clammy panic rose inside him like an intruder, pinning him down and suffocating him. Heart swelling, he glanced down at her tear-stained face. Another time, maybe. This was about her, and her needs, not his, and she needed to know that she was deserving of love—his love.

'You don't need to be scared any more, *bella.* I'll always be there to catch you. Always.' Leaning down, he kissed her on the forehead, his hand moving over her cheek. 'I think we should get back to the boat now.'

Away from this secluded little beach, where he might be tempted to give in to lust or, worse, to the need to unburden the misery in his heart.

Stepping out of the shower, Juliet tucked the plush towel around her body, knotting it above her breasts. It wasn't late—not much past nine—but after a light supper she had retreated to her cabin, claiming tiredness.

And it was true. She felt exhausted and dazed. Just as if she'd just finished a race she had been training for all her life.

For so long she had dreaded talking about her childhood—had spent years avoiding the subject or telling a carefully edited version of her past. And yet she'd done it. She'd told Ralph the truth. And, although it had been distressing having to remember it all, it had been easier than she'd expected.

He'd made it easy for her.

Her heart bumped against her ribs.

She still couldn't quite believe everything that had happened since she'd returned to Verona. So much had changed in such a short time.

They had changed.

Take today. They had fought—*again*—but the difference was that this time they had finished the conversation. And they hadn't ended up having sex.

No thanks to her.

Remembering the moment when he'd told her he wanted her, she felt her skin grow suddenly warm.

Pressed against his beautiful bare chest, she had felt so weak in the face of her need for him that she had been seconds away from pulling his head down to hers and forgetting about the consequences.

Again.

Without thinking she moved her hand to her stomach, to the possible consequences of the last time she'd given in to just such an urge.

Her fingers trembled against the towel.

She might not be pregnant, but the possibility had broken the impasse between them. It had shown both of them that although they might be flawed, change was not just possible but in their hands.

Their hands.

His hands.

She felt her body tense and soften at the same time. He had the most instinctive sense of touch, reading her body like a healer. Only it wasn't her body she was talking about. He had helped heal the scars on her soul.

She felt calmer. But it was more than that. It was as

though someone had shifted a burden from her shoulders so that she no longer felt like that unloved—worse, unlovable—little girl.

Her throat was suddenly so tight it was hard to breathe.

Not someone.

Ralph.

Pulse pounding, she walked over to the connecting door between their cabins and gently pushed it open.

Ralph was standing by the bed. He too was naked, except for the towel wrapped around his waist. He was rubbing his hair with another towel.

Glancing over at her, his face tensed. 'Giulietta—is something wrong?'

Dropping the towel, he crossed the cabin in two long strides.

'No. I...'

As her eyes slid over the powerful muscles of his chest she was momentarily lost for words. His body was just so perfect.

'Did you want to talk to me?' He was looking down at her, his beautiful golden eyes trained on her face.

She blinked, tried to refocus her brain. But she couldn't seem to think straight. Only why did she need to think at all? No thought was required for what she wanted—and she did want him, with an intensity and a freedom she had never felt before. Not even in Rome.

Then she had been...

Her heart was pounding so hard she thought it might burst. Taking a step forward, she leaned into him, her hands reaching up to capture his face. Tilting her head slightly, she brushed her lips against his.

'Kiss me.'

As she breathed the words into his mouth she felt him tense for a fraction of a second, and then his hands were sliding beneath the towel, fingers splaying against her back, his lips so warm and urgent that she felt a pit of need open up inside her.

Parting her lips, he kissed her more deeply, and then he pulled her closer, close enough that she could feel the thick outline of his erection pushing against her stomach.

She felt her breath tangle as he lifted her hair from her shoulder, tugging it sideways to expose the curve of her throat. And then he was licking her skin, running his tongue along her clavicle to the pulse leaping beneath the skin.

'La tua pelle sembra sete,' he said hoarsely. His eyes found hers, the pupils huge and shockingly dark against the gold of the iris. 'You want this.'

It was a statement of fact.

Licking her lips, she nodded slowly. 'Yes.'

He groaned as she began moving against him. *'Mi vuoi...'*

She shivered inside. Her body was tense. Hot. Damp. Her breasts felt heavy. She ached for his touch.

'Si,' she said softly, her hands reaching down to where the towel hugged his abs. *'Ti voglio così tanto.'*

CHAPTER EIGHT

HOOKING HER FINGERS beneath the damp fabric, she tugged gently, her pulse jumping in her throat as the towel slid to the floor. Now he was naked too. Naked and aroused. *Very* aroused.

'My turn,' he whispered softly.

Her mouth went dry as he reached out and pulled at the knot between her breasts. His face stilled, and she felt her muscles clench as he reached out to caress first her cheek and the curve of jaw, then lower to her taut ruched nipples.

She moaned softly as his fingers teased first one then the other. Her body tightened with need. She was so hot and hungry for him.

Her hand twitched against his skin. He was looking down at her in silence, his eyes like molten gold. 'You like that?' he said softly.

She nodded slowly, feeling an answering wetness between her thighs as he gently cupped her breasts in his hands and kissed her slowly and deeply.

Breathing out raggedly, she reached down and wrapped her hand around his hard length, a sharp heat shooting through her as he grunted against her mouth. Head swimming, she caressed the velvet-smooth skin, feeling him pulse in her hand.

'You're killing me, baby,' he groaned.

Batting her hand away, he lifted her up and lowered her onto the bed.

* * *

Gazing down at her, Ralph felt as though his skin was going to catch fire. She was so beautiful, and she was his to explore, to pleasure.

Leaning forward, he drew first one and then the other taut nipple into his mouth, his body tensing as the blunt head of his erection brushed against where she was already so wet for him.

He touched her lightly between her thighs. She felt slick and white-hot. Shaking with need, he ran his hands over her body as she arched upwards to meet his touch. For a moment he admired the smooth, flawless skin, the small breasts and the curve of her belly, and then, lowering his face, he kissed a path from her stomach to the triangle of fine dark hair.

Her fingers tightened on his head. She was moving restlessly, squirming against his mouth, and he slid his hand beneath the curve of her buttocks, lifting her up. He could feel tiny shivers of anticipation darting across her skin as he stroked her trembling thighs with his thumbs, inhaling her salty damp scent.

She was already swollen and, flattening his tongue, he began licking her clitoris with slow, precise strokes, again and again, until he was no longer conscious of anything but the pulse beating against his tongue and her soft moans.

Suddenly her hands jerked. 'No, not like this.' She was panting. 'I want you inside me.' Her eyes flared. 'You need a—'

'I'll get a condom.' His voice was husky.

They'd both spoken at once.

He rolled off the bed and Juliet watched dazedly, her breath trapped in her throat, as he tore open the foil. The need to touch, to taste, overwhelmed her and, cupping him in her hand, she leaned forward, flicking her tongue over the smooth polished head.

He made a rough sound in the back of his throat. Gripping her hair, he let her take him into her mouth, and then she felt him jerk away and he grabbed her wrist.

'Next time.'

With fingers that shook slightly he rolled the condom on, and then, dropping down on the bed, he pulled her onto his lap. She kissed him hungrily, nipping his lips with her teeth, and then he was holding her hips, raising her up, guiding himself into her body. His groan mixed with her gasp of pleasure as he slid into her.

Pulse hammering, she felt Ralph grip her waist, clamping her body to his as she started to roll back and forth.

Threading his fingers through her hair, he tipped back her head, baring her throat to his tongue and his lips. His hand moved to her clitoris, working in time with her frantically arching pelvis.

Juliet felt her pulse soar. 'Yes…' She moaned the word against his mouth, turning it from one syllable to five. Her skin was so hot and tight—but not as tight as she felt on the inside.

His thumb was pushing her to the edge, the fluttering ache between her legs was now impossible to ignore, and she shuddered helplessly, muscles rippling, her body gripping him, becoming his.

And then she cried out as he tensed, slamming into her, and there was nothing that mattered except Ralph and the power of his hard body driving into hers.

The shout filled her head and, jolted from sleep, Juliet struggled onto her side. The last thing she could remember was Ralph burying his face in her hair, his arms curving around her, anchoring her to his body as her heartbeat slowed.

Now her heart was hammering inside her ribcage.

She reached out.

In the darkness beside her Ralph was shuddering, his arms pushing against the covers.

'Ralph!'

She felt him tense as her voice echoed sharply round the silent cabin and, reaching out again, she fumbled for the light.

By the time she turned round he was sitting on the edge of the bed, his head in his hands.

'Ralph,' she said again, more softly this time. 'It's okay. You were having a nightmare but it's over now.'

He flinched as she touched his shoulder. His skin felt warm, but he was shivering as if he had a fever.

She stared down at him uncertainly. Ralph had always been a bad sleeper. But this didn't seem like the aftermath of a nightmare. He seemed barely aware of her presence and his breathing sounded jerky.

Sliding onto the floor, she knelt in front of him. 'You're going to be fine.'

Gently she reached up and took his hands in hers. He didn't reply, but she felt his fingers tighten around hers.

'It's okay, I'm not going anywhere. I'm going to stay right here,' she said quietly.

He still hadn't spoken, but he hadn't let go of her hands either and so, keeping her voice calm and fluid, she carried on talking.

She talked about the food they had shared that evening, and the pictures Luca had sent of the christening, until finally she felt his breathing grow steadier.

'Would you like a glass of water?' she asked.

For a moment she didn't think he would respond, but then he nodded.

'Wait a second,' she whispered.

Standing up, she went to the bathroom and filled a glass with water from the tap.

'Here.' She handed him the glass.

He took it without looking up. 'Thank you.'

His voice sounded frayed, as if he had torn it by shouting, and she felt a sudden rage at whatever it was that had crept into his dreams.

'How are you feeling now?' She sat down beside him, keeping her movements small and her voice steady.

'Better.'

She watched as he ran a hand over his face.

'I'm sorry,' he said quietly.

'For what?' She hesitated a moment, then took his hand again.

'For waking you up like that. I didn't hurt you, did I?' Now he looked at her, his eyes desperately searching her face.

'No, of course you didn't hurt me.'

'I could have done. I didn't know what I was doing.'

He sounded distraught.

'You didn't do anything. You were just moving about and then you shouted something—'

But he was shaking his head. 'I'll sleep next door.'

He made as if to stand up, but she caught his arm.

'No, Ralph. You're not sleeping next door. If you do, then I'm coming with you.'

He stiffened, but didn't resist as she tugged him gently down onto the bed. His body was still trembling and, reaching round him, she grabbed a sweatshirt from the chair by the bed.

'Here—put this on.'

She watched as he pulled it over his head, breathing shakily into the silence of the cabin.

'It might help...' She hesitated, catching sight of the shuttered expression on his face, then tried again. 'It might help to talk about it.'

Her words hung in the air.

He glanced over at her and shook his head, then looked down at his hands. 'There's no need. It was just a nightmare...a bad dream. You said so yourself.'

She felt her heart beat faster.

Ever since she'd known him Ralph had slept badly, shifting restlessly and often waking in the night. The only exception to that pattern had been during those first few weeks in Rome—but of course then he had been on holiday.

This was different.

He had seemed disorientated, almost unaware of her and his surroundings. And scared. As if the nightmare hadn't stopped when he'd woken up.

She knew that feeling well.

'Is that what you think it was? Just a bad dream?'

Her question was level-toned, but she felt him go still. The silence echoed round the cabin.

Normally at this point he would either kiss her until she couldn't remember having asked the question, or give her one of those cool, enigmatic smiles that meant he was about to change the subject.

But this time he kept staring down at his hands. 'I don't know.'

She could hear the heaviness, the despair in his voice.

'I don't know,' he said again. 'I think it starts out as a bad dream.'

Starts.

So it wasn't a one-off.

'And then what happens?' she asked, and gazed away, giving him time.

The cabin was silent for a moment, and then he shrugged. 'I wake up and there's this weight crushing my chest.' He pressed a clenched hand against his breastbone. 'It feels as if something is sitting on me—like in that painting.'

'*The Nightmare*,' she said quietly.

Like most people, she knew the Fuseli painting. The image of a beautiful sleeping woman draped across a bed with a hunched creature with the face of a gargoyle crouching on her stomach was enough to give anyone nightmares.

She felt him shudder and, reaching out, prised his fingers apart and took his hand in hers again.

'I try to push it off me, but I can't, and then I realise I'm still asleep, and that I'm never going to wake up.'

It sounded terrifying. Doubly terrifying for an intensely physical man like Ralph.

She glanced down at the sculpted muscles of his thighs. He might be a billionaire businessman, with a highly trained security team tracking his every movement, but Ralph could take care of himself. Not only did he work out regularly, but he had been trained in the Russian martial art Systema.

'But you do wake up?' she said gently.

He nodded slowly. 'But I can't breathe. It's like I'm choking. The first time it happened I thought I was having a heart attack.'

It obviously hadn't been a heart attack, but it hadn't been just a bad dream either.

'Oh, Ralph…' As she whispered his name he turned to look at her, a muscle flickering in his jaw, and she felt her own heart twist.

'I thought it would stop.'

His eyes looked desperate and she nodded quickly.

'It will.' They were the only words she could force past the lump in her throat. 'But panic attacks don't go away on their own. There's usually a trigger.' She hesitated. 'What's the dream that starts it about? Or can't you remember?'

The sudden tension in his body told her that she was on the right track.

'I can remember it,' he said flatly.

There was a long silence, and then he inhaled sharply.

'It's always the same. I come home after work and everything seems normal, only my mother is still alive, and I can hear her and my father talking.'

Her throat was tight. No matter how bad her own pain had been, nothing could compete with hearing his…feeling his. It felt like a vice around her heart.

'I walk into the drawing room, but my father is alone, and he turns to me and he says, "You shouldn't be here. You're not my son. You'll never be my son."'

He ran his hand over his face, and with a shock she realised that he was close to tears.

'You *are* his son,' she said fiercely. 'You've been his son for thirty years. His face lights up when you walk into the room. He loves you so much.'

'And I love him.' His voice was rough. 'And I don't want to keep lying to him. But I don't want to hurt him either.' He looked exhausted all of a sudden. 'He's already lost his wife. If I tell him the truth it'll be like losing her all over again.' A tremor started in his hands. 'If I tell him the truth he'll lose his son and heir too. He'll be the last of the Castelluccis.'

There was a long, dull silence. Juliet felt her pulse accelerate. She hadn't really registered the wider implications before, but Ralph was right. Without him, the Castellucci name would disappear.

Gazing over at his taut profile, she felt her heart twist.

It must have been hard enough finding out his mother had been unfaithful and his father was not his father, but this was bigger than Ralph.

What he chose to do would have an impact on his entire family.

No wonder Francesca had held her secret close for so long. And yet something had pushed her to confess the truth...

'What did your mother want you to do?' she asked carefully. 'I know she couldn't bear to tell Carlo herself, but surely she wouldn't have told you if she didn't want him to know eventually.'

There was another silence, this one longer.

Then, 'She didn't want to tell me.' He met her eyes and his mouth twisted. 'Vittoria told me. She found some letters my mother wrote to her father, Niccolò, and she came to the house. She was so upset, making all kinds of accusations... Luckily I was there on my own.'

His hand clenched painfully around hers.

Luckily in some ways, she thought. But it would have been better for Ralph if Francesca and Carlo had been there. Then he would have been spared all these months of carrying the burden of guilt and uncertainty.

'Did you look at the letters?' she asked.

His beautiful mouth curved into a grimace. 'Yes. I don't know why. Maybe I shouldn't have. I suppose I wanted to prove her wrong, but I recognised her handwriting and it was clear that they'd been having an affair.'

He was silent again.

Gazing up at the smooth planes of his face, Juliet tried to imagine what it must have felt like to read those letters. The shock, the pain of betrayal, the burden of knowledge...

'Is that when you talked to your mother?' she said quietly.

He shook his head. 'That was the day they got her test results back from the hospital. They were both stunned... devastated... I couldn't—' Tears pricked the back of her eyes and he breathed out unsteadily.

She tightened her grip on his hand. 'Of course you couldn't. No one could.'

He was looking down at his hand in hers, his eyes locked on the signet ring on his little finger. 'Sometimes I think I should have just left it alone. Kept what Vittoria told me to myself. Only I couldn't. I think I knew that there was more to it.'

Juliet stared at him in silence. It was easy now to understand why he had found it so hard to confront the problems in their marriage. Look at what had happened last time he'd tried: his whole world had come tumbling down.

Her throat was tight and aching. It ached for him.

'What did she say when you did talk to her?' she asked.

'Nothing. She wouldn't talk about it.' There was a heaviness in his voice now, a note of finality. 'Not until the end. That's when she told me that Carlo wasn't my biological father.'

He looked up at Juliet and she saw his eyes were full of unshed tears.

'I knew that anyway by then. I'd taken a DNA test. I just wanted her to say it to my face, so I could remember her telling me the truth.'

'And she did tell you the truth.' She spoke firmly, her hand tightening on his.

It felt like it had in Rome, when they had been so in tune with one another—only then it had been physical. This time he had stripped off more than just his clothes. He had bared his soul.

'She told you everything. The whole truth. Not just that she had an affair. But that Carlo wasn't your father. She didn't have to do that, but she did. Because she wanted you to have the choice. The choice she took from you before you were born.'

'But I don't want to choose.' His mouth twisted. 'I just want to do what's right.'

'You're already doing that,' she said slowly. 'You run your business. You take care of your family, your father—'

'I didn't take care of you.' The pain was there again, at the edges of his voice. 'I hurt you so badly you ran away.'

'We hurt each other—and I came back.'

His eyes found hers. 'For the christening.'

She held his gaze. 'For that too.' Reaching up, she cupped his face. 'Whatever you choose to do will be the right thing.'

She could feel his pain so acutely that it made her own eyes fill with tears, and without thinking she slid both arms around him and pulled him close.

He breathed out shakily. 'I miss her so much... I don't want to lose him as well.'

Light was starting to squeeze around the blinds and, her heart pounding, she took a breath. 'You can't lose him, Ralph. Carlo raised you, and he loves you, and no test can change that.' She forced a smile. 'DNA makes a baby, not a father. Trust me—I know.'

He pulled her closer, holding her tightly. 'You deserved so much better. You *deserve* so much better than this... than me.'

She could feel his heart beating in time with hers.

'I'm sorry...' He struggled with the words, a muscle working in his jaw. 'I'm sorry you had to see me like this.'

Pulling away slightly, she looked up at him. 'You're my husband. We took vows, remember? I know bad dreams and panic attacks aren't mentioned specifically, but I reckon they're covered by "in sickness and in health" or maybe "for better or worse".'

He looked up at her in silence, and her heart performed a perfect somersault as she felt the full impact of his beautiful golden eyes.

'What?' She frowned. 'What is it?'

He slid his hands into her hair and tilted her face up to his. 'That's the first time you've acknowledged that I'm your husband since you got back from England,' he said softly.

Watching her face, Ralph held his breath. There was a silence. Their eyes met.

She blinked, then looked down. 'I suppose it is.'

The cabin fell silent.

'So, I was wondering,' he said slowly, 'and hoping that maybe you might have changed your mind...'

As she looked up at him the glow from the bedside lamp lit up her face, emphasising both its softness and its strength.

'About getting a divorce. You see, I meant what I said on the beach about us trying again.' Reaching out, he touched her stomach gently. 'I want to spend the rest of my life with you. Have children with you. Grow old with you. Do you think we could do that, *bella*? Do you think we could try again?'

She held his gaze, and then slowly she nodded. 'Yes, I think we could.'

Her words—so simple, so honest—made his heart turn over and emotion shudder through his body. He leaned in to kiss her, sliding his tongue over her lips and then into her mouth.

Her hands slid over his stomach, and he sucked in a breath and then tugged the sweatshirt over his head and reached for her...

* * *

When he woke, the sun was already high in the cloudless blue sky.

Giulietta was still asleep.

He stared down at her, holding his breath.

Her hair was a dark, swirling storm cloud on the pillow, and with her eyelashes feathering the curve of her cheekbone she looked exactly like an illustration in a book of fairy tales. A beautiful sleeping princess, trapped in a tower, waiting to be rescued by her prince.

His chest tightened.

Except that last night it had been he who had needed rescuing. He had been the one drowning in panic, and Giulietta had chased away his demons.

He dressed noiselessly and, resisting the urge to wake her with a kiss, made his way out onto the private deck beside their cabin.

It was another beautiful day, but as he walked into the sunlight he felt a rush of emotion that had nothing to do with the warm air or the sea or the sky. It was as if he had woken not just from a long sleep but from a living nightmare. He felt calmer than he had in months.

And it was all down to Giulietta.

His fingers tightened against the handrail.

Up until a few hours ago he'd barely been able to acknowledge the breathless, heart-hammering episodes that had been plaguing his nights, much less give them a name. But Juliet had done both. And more. She had agreed to give their marriage a second chance.

'Ralph...'

He turned, his heart missing a beat.

Juliet was standing in the doorway. Her hair was spilling over her shoulders in untidy curls and she was wearing the T-shirt he'd been wearing yesterday.

'Why didn't you wake me?' she said huskily.

Glancing down at her bare legs and imagining them wrapped around his waist, he felt his body harden.

Good question.

'I thought you needed to sleep.'

'Did *you* sleep?'

Hearing the concern in her voice, he felt his heart contract. 'Yes, I did.' He took a step towards her and pulled her against him. 'Thanks to you.'

He kissed her gently on the mouth, the tip of his tongue parting her lips briefly, and the hitch of her breath made him feel vertiginous with equal parts of hunger and relief.

'What was that for?' she asked.

'Lots of different things,' he said softly. 'Looking better in my T-shirt than I do.' Leaning forward, he kissed her again. 'Looking after me last night. And for agreeing to give us—*me*—a second chance.'

His words brought her eyes back to his. Gazing down at her face, he tightened his hands around her waist, his emotions almost too raw to contain so that he was suddenly afraid he might weep.

How could he have let it happen? That distance between them? He had come so close to losing her. To losing the one person who saw beneath the perfect façade...the one woman who knew him completely, inside and out.

And he knew her. He understood her now. He knew about the lonely little girl who had been raised by strangers and he understood her mistrust and her self-doubt.

That she had survived was miraculous.

Only she hadn't just survived. She had triumphed. And he was in awe of her strength, her determination, her courage.

There was nothing he wouldn't do for her, but mostly he wanted to hold her close, to wrap his body around hers.

Suddenly he was struggling to fill his lungs with air. He was so hungry for her. More than anything, he wanted to trail his lips along the warm silken skin of her throat, to savour that frantically beating pulse, to slide his hands beneath that T-shirt and skim his fingers over the peaks of her breasts. No boundaries. No restraint. No inhibitions.

He took a breath. 'I wish we could stay on the *Alighieri* for ever,' he whispered. 'Just you and me, sailing into a new dawn each day and drifting into the sunset at night.'

But... He didn't say it. He didn't need to.

'But we need to get back,' she said softly.

Watching his face still, Juliet felt her stomach flip over, and just for a few heart-stopping half-seconds she let her hands splay against his back as she felt the rigid press of his erection against her belly.

Heat was radiating through her body— the familiar, electrifying rush of desire for skin on skin, for his taste, his touch.

Only it was so much more than that.

On waking, she had felt memories of what had happened in the early hours of the morning fill her head. Their lovemaking, his panic attack, their conversation...and of course their reconciliation.

The last few days had changed so many things. She had talked to Ralph about her past—really talked—and his unconditional support had helped her to see herself and him in a different light.

But it had been seeing him so desperate, so distressed, or rather the fact that he had let her see him like that, that had blown away all thoughts of divorcing him.

He was her love, her life, her future—with or without a baby in her womb.

In a little over forty-eight hours they would be hosting the biggest party in town *together*—and this time it wouldn't just be an appearance of unity. This time it would be real.

Brushing his lips with her own, she tipped her head back and met his gaze head-on. 'We need to get back for the ball.'

She felt him tense.

The opera festival was a huge deal in Verona, but the Castellucci Ball was legendary in its own right. Not only was it a charitable fundraiser that raised seven-figure sums, it also gave guests a chance to mingle with celebrities from the world of art, fashion, film and music. It was the most important date in the family's social calendar. But she knew that wasn't the reason why his back suddenly felt like a rigid wall of muscle.

'Is Niccolò Farnese going to be there?' she asked quietly.

She knew he would be even before Ralph nodded. The Farneses were a powerful family—not as old as the Castelluccis, but still with connections stretching across Italy and beyond.

'With his wife.' He rubbed a hand across his eyes as if he wanted to block out the facts. 'And obviously Carlo will be there too.' His mouth twisted. 'It feels dangerous…all of us being there together. Like tempting fate.'

Hearing the strain in his voice, she felt a rush of self-loathing that she had considered letting him face this ordeal alone. 'Nothing is going to happen,' she said fiercely. 'I won't let it.'

His arms tightened around her. 'It feels like a betrayal… being there with both of them, neither of them knowing the truth…'

'You're not betraying anyone.' Her heart felt as if it was going to burst. She loved him so much that his pain was her pain. 'This is an impossible situation—nobody would know how to handle it, and most people wouldn't try. They'd just run away and hide.' She could feel his heart beating in time with hers. 'You're not doing that.'

He shifted against her, moving back slightly so that he could see her face.

Tilting her head back, she met his gaze. 'You're putting your feelings aside for Carlo and your family. You're going to smile and greet your guests and give them an evening to remember. And I'll be right by your side.'

He nodded slowly, his fingers curving over her belly. 'I'd like that.'

Her arm brushed against his. 'It's going to be fine. I promise. And when you're ready…when you've figured out how to say what you want to say…you can have a conversation with your father. Both of your fathers,' she said softly.

There was a silence. In the limitless sky above them the sun looked like a child's drawing. She heard him breathe out shakily.

'Thank you for doing this.'

She frowned. 'Doing what?'

He hesitated. 'Putting your feelings aside. I know you don't really enjoy the whole social scene, and that's partly my fault. No, it *is*,' he said as she started to protest. 'It was a lot to take on for anyone—much less someone who didn't even speak Italian.'

Reaching out, he pushed her hair behind her ear.

'Only I didn't think about that. I was so caught up with not being a Castellucci and I projected that onto you. I'm sorry.'

'I know you are.'

It was enough to know that he cared. She squeezed his hand, and saw his face relax a little.

'So, are you ready to turn the boat around?' she asked.

A shiver ran along his jaw as he glanced past her at the horizon, but then slowly he nodded.

She leaned into him, her heart beating in time with his.

The ramifications of his mother's affair had not been forgotten, but they would deal with it together. One day at a time.

The past was not going to come between them ever again.

CHAPTER NINE

TURNING ON THE SPOT, Juliet gazed into the mirror, her eyes moving critically over her reflection. She turned to the petite dark-haired woman beside her. 'What do you think?'

They were standing in the ornate master bedroom at the *palazzo*, but for once the gilt and marble setting was taking a back seat. Instead, it was the rail of jewel-bright dresses that held centre stage, their intricate beading and lustrous fabrics catching the morning sunlight and spraying rainbows across the room.

'I think you look exquisite. But it's what you think that matters, *cara*.'

Juliet grimaced. 'But I don't know what I think, Gia. That's why I have you.'

Before becoming a personal stylist, Gia Marazzi had worked for two of the largest fashion houses in Italy. Preternaturally calm and exceptionally pretty, Gia was the chicest woman she had ever met. She was also one of the nicest, and had become a friend as well as an advisor.

Gia shook her head. 'You have me because you don't like shopping.'

The look of disbelief on the stylist's perfectly made-up face as she spoke made Juliet burst out laughing. 'So would you if you had to go everywhere with a quartet of heavily armed over-muscular men tracking your every footstep.'

But that wasn't the only reason.

Before she'd met Ralph she'd never had enough money

to really enjoy spending it on clothes. Marrying into the Castelluccis had obviously changed that, but even after she'd married Ralph she'd still felt completely out of her depth and horribly conspicuous, so that even thinking about walking into the designer boutiques on Milan's Via Montenapoleone had been a toe-curlingly daunting prospect.

Back then she'd been so unsure of himself.

Or maybe sure only of one thing.

That it was simply a matter of time before Ralph realised the mistake he had made in marrying her. That sooner or later he would see her for who she was, and her fashion choices would just speed up the inevitable exposure.

Her heart bumped gently against her ribs.

Except he had seen who she was.

Sitting with her on that tiny little patch of sand, he had peeled back the layers she wore to protect herself against the world.

He knew who she was now.

He knew her and he wanted her.

The good, the bad, and even the ugly.

Ignoring the fluttering rush of unease that accompanied that resolute thought, she twisted round to face the mirror, holding out the full, heavy skirt.

This dress was the opposite of ugly.

In fact, it seemed ridiculous to criticise something so unspeakably lovely.

But… 'It just feels a little too structured, too emphatic.' She screwed up her face apologetically. 'Sorry, Gia. I know it's your favourite.'

'I do love it.' The stylist laughed. 'But *I'm* not going to be wearing it.' Running her hand lightly over the exquisite lace, Gia narrowed her eyes. 'And I do know what you mean. It's a dress that makes an unequivocal statement.'

'Yes, it does.'

The deep voice made Juliet stop mid-twirl. Glancing over her bare shoulder, she felt her mouth dry. Ralph was leaning against the door frame, his golden gaze fixed on her face, a smile tugging at the corners of his mouth.

Heat scuttled over her skin. Any ordinary man wearing black jeans and a charcoal-grey polo shirt would have looked underdressed beside all the glittering, embellished couture gowns. But that was the difference between Ralph and every other human. He didn't need a stylist or a rack of jaw-droppingly expensive clothes to make heads turn.

'It says my wife is unequivocally the most beautiful woman in the world.'

Juliet watched him walk towards her. 'You like it?' she asked. Her breath hitched in her throat as Ralph touched her lightly on the hip and she turned to face him.

They had arrived back in Verona yesterday afternoon. It had been a strange sensation, walking back into the *palazzo*—a kind of *déjà-vu*. Her home had seemed so familiar, and yet it had felt inexplicably different. Everything had felt lighter, brighter—almost as if it had been aired and redecorated in the time they'd been away.

But of course nothing had changed in a physical sense. It was just that so much had happened...so many things had changed between her and Ralph.

She felt a shimmer of pure happiness, warm like sunlight on her skin. It was as if the misery and uncertainty of the last few months had been erased and they had gone back to the beginning. Only the difference was that this time they were not stumbling around blindfolded. The past was an open book now.

It had been painful to admit their frailties and their fears, but they had come through the fire together and now they were stronger, wiser.

Closer.

She leaned into him, panic clutching at her stomach as she remembered how close she had come to walking away, to leaving this man who was her life blood, her breath, her heart, her soul.

'I like it a lot,' he said.

His fingers splayed against her waist. They were warm and firm and she felt her panic fade.

'It's a beautiful dress.' He stared down at her appraisingly. 'But I think the fabric is too rigid and the blue is too dark. You need something with a little more fluidity... *and heat.*'

Their eyes met and she sucked in a sharp breath as he brushed past her. Heart pounding, she watched as he pulled out a soft, swirling mass of primrose-coloured silk from the rail.

'That was my first choice,' she said softly. 'And I do really like it. But we thought it was a bit too sunny...'

'And you want moonlight?' he said softly, his eyes locking with hers. 'And music, and love, and romance? Isn't that how the song goes?'

Her stomach flipped over. When he looked at her like that there was no need to go to the opera. She could almost hear an orchestra playing.

'So...' his hand rested on a long silk jersey dress the colour of ripe Morello cherries '...how about this one?'

'Now, that was my first choice,' Gia purred approvingly.

Five minutes later Juliet was staring at her reflection again, and this time she didn't need to ask anyone how she looked. She could see the heat glittering in Ralph's eyes, and feel an answering heat flickering low in her belly as his gaze drifted over the smooth red silk.

'Yes,' he said quietly as she turned slowly on the spot.

The air hissed between them.

Yes, she thought silently.

From the front the dress looked simple enough—modest, even, with its long sleeves and boat neckline. But from behind the fluid fabric was cut to a tantalising bottom-skimming V.

It was Gia who broke the pulsing silence. 'I think we can all agree that in this instance less is definitely more,' she said, with undisguised satisfaction.

Picking up her handbag, she sashayed across the room, kissed Juliet, and lifted her face for Ralph to graze her cheek.

'Clearly my services are no longer required, so I'll see you both at the Arena.' She paused. 'Unless you need help with your accessories?'

Shaking her head, Juliet took hold of Ralph's hand, a small smile tugging at the corners of her mouth. 'Thanks, Gia, but I already have the best accessory.'

There was a slight click as the door closed behind her. Ralph took a step forward and caught her against him, his hand low and flat on her back. Slowly she looked up into his face.

'Hi,' he said softly.

'Hi,' she whispered.

And then his mouth found hers and she felt her body turn boneless as he kissed her softly.

When they broke apart she caught his arms, her fingers pressing against the heat of his skin. 'I missed you.'

His lips curved up at the corners. 'I missed you too.'

Pulling her close, he rubbed his face against hers. The heat of his body and the warm, clean scent of his skin was making her head spin.

'I don't know how I'm ever going to go back to work,' he murmured. 'I can't bear being apart from you.'

The steady burn of his gaze made her an ache grow in her stomach. 'I can't bear it either.'

She could say that now—could admit her need for him without fearing that it was all they shared.

Which was lucky. Because right now it was a need that was making her feel as if she was melting from the inside out.

'I'd better get this dress back on the hanger.' Lifting the skirt with her foot, she flicked it to one side and cleared her throat. 'Could you help me?'

There was a slight pause, and then he nodded. 'With pleasure,' he said softly, moving closer.

His hands were gentle but firm as he turned her away from him, and her skin twitched as his fingers slid over the smooth fabric to the concealed zip.

As he pulled the dress down over her shoulders she felt her pulse accelerate. 'Wait a minute.' Grabbing the frame of the bed for balance, she bent over. 'Let me take my shoes off—'

He caught her wrist. 'No, keep them on.'

Ralph held his breath as she looked up at him, her soft brown eyes wide with longing, her cheeks flushed with the same hunger that was turning his body to stone.

He'd been on the phone all morning, going over the last-minute arrangements for the ball tomorrow. When he'd gone looking for Giulietta he'd actually forgotten that she would be trying on dresses with Gia. He'd just wanted to see her…to hear her voice. To touch base.

Only now he was with her he wanted to do so much more.

He wanted to kiss and caress and lick and stroke and tease.

Reaching out, he slid the dress slowly down over her stomach, holding her steady as she stepped free of the silky fabric. Now she was naked except for her simple white panties, and his eyes abseiled jerkily down her thighs to her skin-toned patent high heels.

For a moment he forgot to breathe. His body ached—
hell, even his teeth ached because he wanted her so badly.

Her breasts were quivering slightly, the nipples already
taut beneath his gaze, and as the blood surged down to his
groin he thought he might actually pass out.

Almost without conscious thought, he slid one hand to
the nape of her neck. The other moved to cup her breast as
he kissed her softly, then more fiercely as he felt the slide
of her tongue against his own.

His fingers moved from her breast to her hip and then,
pushing past the waistband of her panties, he parted her
thighs and with the delicate, measured precision of a *mae-
stro pasticcere* found the nub of her clitoris.

He bit back a groan as her hand found his and she
pressed his fingers against the damp fabric. She was already so wet for him.

Dropping to his knees, he slid his hands beneath her
panties and pulled them gently down her legs. He took a
breath, inhaling her scent. Then, resting his head against the
cotton-soft skin of her thigh, his hands gripping her bottom
to hold her steady, he traced a path between the dark curls,
his flattened tongue merciless as she opened herself to him.

Her hands caught in his hair and he heard the sudden
hitch in her breath, and then she was pulling him closer,
crying out as she spasmed against his mouth. 'Let me!'

His erection was straining against the front of his jeans
and she unzipped him, and then she was pushing him ur-
gently onto the bed, her fingers wrapping around his fully
aroused length.

'Ah, Giulietta…'

He breathed out her name, his fingers moving automati-
cally to grip her hair as she knelt down in front of him and
he felt her mouth slide over the swollen, heavy head of his
erection.

Looking down, he felt his breath hiss between his teeth as he watched her guide him in, inch by inch.

When she ran her tongue over the raised ridge of his frenulum, he grunted. His head was swimming and his body felt as if it was dissolving, unravelling, the tug of her mouth acting with the gravitational force of a black hole.

He pulled out, panting, his heart raging, and then, standing up unsteadily, he turned her so that she was bending over the bed. Gazing down at the curve of her back, he felt his body tighten unbearably. He gripped her hips—and then he remembered.

'Don't move,' he said hoarsely. 'I'm just going to grab—'

'No.' She caught his hand. 'No. I don't—we don't need to. I don't want to.'

Her eyes were soft and dazed.

'Are you sure?'

She gave him an open-mouthed kiss by way of assent, and he kissed her back fiercely, drawing her up against his body.

Shivers of anticipation were rippling over her skin and, heart hammering, he pressed his erection against the soft cushion of her bottom. He lifted her hips and she backed up to meet him. Reaching under her stomach, he found her breast, brushing a thumb over the nipple, feeling it swell and harden.

Her soft moan acted like gasoline on the flames of his desire and, shifting slightly, he eased into her in one smooth movement. As her slick heat enveloped him he felt his control snap. His hands splayed against her back and he began to thrust inside her.

Moaning, she rocked against him, meeting his thrusts, her breath staccato, her whole body shaking now. He thrust harder and she gasped. He felt her jerk against him, and then he felt her fingers cupping him, squeezing gently, and he was jerking against her, a jagged cry jamming his throat, his body spilling into hers with molten force.

Breathing raggedly, he eased out of her and they both collapsed on the bed together.

He understood the significance of what they had just done—what she had allowed him to do.

It was a sign—a physical demonstration of her commitment to him, to their future, and the fact that she felt that way made an ache swell behind his ribs. The fact that she trusted him enough to show him so candidly, so passionately, almost undid him.

'What are you thinking about?' she asked,

Her hand was pressed against his shirt and, looking down, he saw that she was searching his face. In the past when she'd asked him that question he'd usually changed the subject. Or kissed her. Sometimes both. But now he gently smoothed her hair from her face and met her gaze.

'I was thinking about us. About how we met. About why I stopped that day.'

Her mouth tugged up at one corner. 'You're a gentleman and you saw a woman in distress.'

He frowned. 'No, that can't be it. I wasn't actually sure you were human, let alone female.'

'Hey!' She punched him lightly on the arm and he started laughing.

'To be fair, you looked like a drowned cat.' He caught her arm and pulled her closer. 'But you're right—I did think you needed help.'

His heart turned over as he remembered the electrifying jolt that had gone through his body, the absolute, unshakeable certainty that she was *the one*.

Reaching down, he brushed her cheek with his thumb. 'Only I was wrong. You were rescuing me.'

His life had been in a tailspin. But this woman—this

beautiful, strong, loyal woman—had faced her own fears to stop him crash landing.

She stared at him steadily. 'We rescued each other.'

He brushed his lips across hers. 'And one very savage and ungrateful cat,' he said softly, gathering her against him as she buried her face in his shoulder, shaking with laughter.

For Juliet, the past twenty-four hours had seemed to pass in the space of a heartbeat, and now they were fast approaching the hour when the beautiful mirror-lined ballroom would be filled with guests.

But right now the room was empty.

The team in charge of staging the ball had worked almost non-stop to get everything in place, and from the polished parquet floor to the frescoed ceiling it all looked quite magical.

After the frantic efforts of the last few days, the silence now was intense, almost vertiginous. Or maybe that was guilt, she thought, glancing at the Rococo clock that stood at the end of the room.

Everyone else was busy getting ready. Glancing down at her cashmere robe and slippered feet, she bit her lip. She should be getting ready too. But she had wanted a private sneaky peek.

Turning slowly on the spot, she felt a rush of satisfaction.

Burnished silver bowls were filled with the palest pink roses, chandeliers glittered and the huge velvet curtains were beautifully swagged. All of it looked perfect.

Somewhere in the house a door slammed, and her heart started beating a little faster.

This year it needed to be more perfect than ever.

This year would be the first time in thirty years that the ball for three hundred carefully selected guests would not be hosted by Francesca and Carlo Castellucci.

This year she and Ralph would have that honour.

She felt a lurch of panic, as if the marble floor she was standing on had turned to ice.

Panic was understandable, she told herself quickly. It was not just an honour, but a responsibility.

Her breath caught in her throat. She should be feeling happy, and she had been happy back on the *Alighieri*, a kind of sweet, piercing happiness that had felt unassailable.

Her hand curved against her stomach. Whatever the future held, they would face it together.

Together.

Except the word seemed slippery, treacherous, unsteady— as if she was holding something that was too big for her hands, so that it was always on the verge of sliding between her fingers.

She glanced nervously up at the paintings above the mirrors, feeling the cool, assessing gaze of Ralph's ancestors.

It had been building, this feeling, as the hour of the ball had got ever closer. The familiar shifting doubts had been closing in on her like early-evening shadows. And now they were rising up and threatening to swallow her whole.

Turning away from the paintings, she glanced down at the name cards on the nearest table, her heart pounding as she read the beautiful italic writing.

Il Signor Castellucci
La Signora Castellucci

She took a deep breath, striving for calm.

It was crazy to feel so insecure, so inadequate.

She was married to the most glamorous man in the world—a man she loved, a man who loved her. And they had a seamless, innate understanding of each other, like skaters moving together with smooth synchronicity across a frozen lake.

Her chest ached sharply, as if she'd run out of breath.

Of course it was easy to spin and turn and leap when it was just the two of you on the ice. It would be harder when there were other people around to get in your way and trip you up.

But Ralph would be there to catch her if she fell. He had told her that—just as he had told her that he wanted *every* possible version of her. There was nothing to fear. Not from their guests and certainly not from a bunch of oil paintings.

From somewhere inside the house she heard the sound of voices coming from where Roberto was briefing the assembled waiting staff.

Her stomach fluttered. What was she doing? Standing here half-dressed with her hair in rollers, unpicking herself?

Tonight was a celebration. Plus, Anna was probably already upstairs, waiting to do her hair and make-up.

Blanking her mind, she turned and made her way back through the *palazzo*.

Forty minutes later the rollers were gone and in their place was a sleek, sculptured chignon.

All she had to do now was put on her dress.

Heart hammering, she checked her appearance in the mirror in their bedroom.

'It's got the night off.'

A ripple of quicksilver ran down her spine and she turned to where Ralph stood, watching her. Heat pulsed across her skin.

The first time she'd seen him in an evening suit she'd felt as though the world had tilted on its axis. And nothing had changed, she thought, her fingers gripping the chest of drawers to steady herself.

He wore a dark classic single-button tuxedo with peaked lapels, a white French-cuffed dress shirt, and superbly tailored trousers that hung perfectly to graze the tops of his handmade black Oxfords.

She frowned. 'I don't understand...'

He walked slowly towards her, his face unsmiling. 'The mirror. Not that you need to ask.' Reaching out, he touched her cheek gently. 'You are the fairest in the land.' His eyes held hers and then he smiled. 'But I think there's something missing.'

Reaching into his pocket, he pulled out a small square box. Her pulse stumbled as he flipped it open to reveal a pair of dark red pear-cut ruby earrings.

'Ralph, you didn't have to,' she whispered, touching them lightly. 'Oh, but they're so beautiful.'

He stared at her steadily. 'No, *you're* beautiful. They're just baubles.'

As she put the earrings on her eyes met his in the reflection of the mirror, and the slow, lambent burn of his gaze made her skin feel hot and tight.

Reaching out, he flicked one of the delicate jewels with his finger, and she felt her pulse beat in time with the oscillating pendant.

'You're going to be the belle of the ball tonight. But you're always my *bella* Giulietta.'

She felt her stomach clench. More than anything she wanted to believe him. To believe that she had a right to be here, to be his wife. *Unconditionally.*

Smiling back at his reflection, she cleared her throat. 'You scrub up pretty well yourself.'

His answering smile seemed to press down on her pubic bone and suddenly, illogically, breathing made her breathless.

'Thank you for these, Ralph.'

He was standing behind her, so close she could feel his

warm breath feathering the nape of her neck. The weight of his hand felt sensual, intimate, possessive…

'It's my pleasure,' he said softly.

She felt his fingers splay against the bare skin of her back and lightning skittered down her spine. It would be so easy to move her head a little, to turn into him and seek his lips, to lose herself and her fears in the firm, insistent press of his mouth…

He groaned. 'Don't look at me like that, *bella*.'

She bit her lip. 'Sorry.'

'No, I'm sorry.' A muscle tightened in his jaw. 'I'm just a bit tense.'

'It's going to be fine.' The desperation she'd heard in his voice, his willingness to share his fear, made her fingers tighten around his. 'I'll be there to make sure it is.'

It hurt her—hurt with a debilitating relentless intensity—to know that she had come so close to breaking that vow that she had let her fears and insecurities come between them.

'I wish—' He screwed up his face, stopped.

'Wish what?' She looked up at him, and kept looking until he shook his head.

'It's stupid. I just wish we knew about the baby already.'

She felt his words, and the longing in his eyes, tug at her heart. She felt the same way. The thought of walking into the Verona Arena knowing that she was carrying Ralph's child almost undid her. She wanted it so badly.

They both did.

As he pulled her against him his phone buzzed from across the room. It would be Marco, letting them know that the car was ready for them.

'I'll tell him we need a bit longer,' she said quickly. Her head was buzzing. Her throat felt as though it was closing up.

'No, it's fine.' Catching her hand in his, he lifted it to his mouth and kissed it gently. 'I'm ready if you are.'

For one wild moment she wanted to ask him whether this was real. Whether all this intimacy and certainty would fade like it had before, after Rome.

But she was being stupid.

Ralph had made it clear that he loved her—every version of her.

He'd told her that.

And, yes, they were just words, but they had come from the heart and she needed to trust in them. To trust in him and their incredible intuitive understanding of each other.

Stomach lurching, she steadied her nerves and forced a smile. 'I am.'

The journey into the city was surprisingly swift. As VIPs, the Castelluccis had a police escort, and they were waved past the lines of traffic.

The opera was packed—a sell-out, in fact. Fourteen thousand people waiting excitedly for a performance of *La Traviata*.

She had never seen so many people—so many beautiful, well-connected people—but she didn't care. There was only one face that mattered to her.

But she could sense that her husband was searching the crowd for one face.

Her pulse accelerated. She knew that, for him, tonight was not just about 'moonlight and music and love and romance'. It was about putting ghosts to rest and making a silent, heartfelt prayer for the future.

She felt Ralph's hand tense in hers as Carlo Castellucci stepped towards them, handsome in his dark suit.

'*Ciao*, Giulietta, *mia cara*, you look divine. Ralph, *mio figlio*.'

Watching the two men embrace, she felt her tears sting her eyes. Whatever their DNA might say, they were father and son, and she knew that nothing, not even the truth, could come between them.

But would that be true for her and Ralph?

Suddenly she was struggling not to cry, and it was a relief when the orchestra began to tune up and they took their seats.

Darkness fell, and the hum of voices settled into silence It was time to light the *mocoleto*—the candles handed out to the audience in homage to the ancient history of the Arena as a place of entertainment.

'Here.' Ralph bent forward, lighting her candle with his.

'Ralph, I just need to—'

'I know I don't—'

They both spoke at once.

She stared at him, her heart beating fast and out of time. 'You first,' she said quickly.

Their eyes met above the tiny, fluttering flames.

'I know I don't say it enough,' he said, 'but I love you, Giulietta. You…our baby…' he rested his hand against her stomach '…you're everything I've ever wanted.'

In the flickering circle of light, his face was so serious, so beautiful, so essential to her. She could hear the hope, the yearning in his voice, and then she thought about the excruciating loneliness she'd felt in London.

Her mouth was dry, her throat tight.

She couldn't ask him now if he'd meant what he said— couldn't break the spell of his words.

Instead she leaned into him, their mouths fusing as the beautiful, sweeping score by Verdi rose from the orchestra pit and soared upwards to the starry sky.

CHAPTER TEN

GAZING AROUND THE crowded ballroom, Ralph knew he should be feeling satisfied with how the evening was progressing—and part of him was more than satisfied.

Everything was going exactly as planned.

The tables from dinner had been cleared away and waiters with trays of drinks were moving smoothly between the women in their shimmering dresses and the men in their monochromatic evening wear. Beneath the ornate Venetian glass chandeliers people were dancing and talking and laughing.

All that remained was for him to introduce the auction. But tonight was always going to be about more than giving people a good time and raising money.

This was Francesca Castellucci's event.

His mother had started it in the first year of her marriage and, thanks to her, it had grown from being a small soirée for family and friends to a major social event.

Glancing across the room, he felt his shoulders tense.

His mother had not only been beautiful and vivacious, she'd made things happen—only for months now he'd been struggling to come to terms with some of those things.

But stepping into her shoes this evening had made him understand her more, had made him realise that she hadn't been just his mother. She had been a woman with strengths and flaws.

And he missed her. Every day.

Only thanks to the woman walking towards him now he'd been able to face the past and move forward in his life to embrace the wonderful present.

He glanced over at Giulietta, his eyes lingering on her flat stomach beneath the clinging silk of her dress. Being here with her tonight was not just about the present, but the future—a new and exciting future. A future that might already be growing inside her.

His heart began to beat a little faster.

He'd wanted a baby before, but back then it had only been a possibility. Here, tonight, at the ball founded by his mother and with both his fathers in attendance, it felt more real, somehow, and more insistent. It was a wordless, elemental need to have something of his own—a continuation of his bloodline.

'Are you okay?' Her hand found his.

He was having to lean into her to make himself heard above the hum of laughter and conversation, and as her warm breath grazed her throat he felt a flicker of corresponding heat in his groin.

He had a strong urge to scoop her into his arms and carry her upstairs. To lose himself in the heat and intensity of their coupling.

But he was a little bit older and wiser now.

Refusing to face the past had nearly destroyed his marriage and he would not make the same mistake again. And his past was here in this room.

Both the *passato prossimo* and the *imperfecto*.

His gaze travelled from Carlo Castellucci to where Niccolò Farnese stood, with his wife Marina and his daughter Vittoria—Ralph's half-sister—his head bent in conversation with the lead tenor from the evening's performance.

As though sensing his gaze, Vittoria looked up and smiled across the room, but then his heart bumped against his ribs as he realised that his half-sister wasn't smiling at him, but at Juliet. And his wife was smiling too.

Reaching out, he caught her by the waist, his thumbs gently brushing over the smooth silk of her dress. 'I'm better than okay,' he said softly.

There was a clinking of silver on glass, and a hush fell on the room. Turning, Ralph saw that Carlo was standing slightly apart, a glass and a knife in his hand.

'I know this year I've taken a bit of a back seat in the arrangements for our family's annual ball, but I hope Ralph won't mind if I say a few words before the start of tonight's auction.'

It wasn't on the running order, but Ralph shook his head. 'Of course not, Papà.'

Carlo smiled. 'Thank you—and thank you to all of you for coming here tonight. As you know, the money raised goes to the charitable foundation set up by my late wife, and it really does make a difference to people's lives.'

He waited for the enthusiastic applause to die down and then began speaking again.

'I miss Francesca,' he said simply. 'And I don't think I will ever not miss her. But it's not Francesca I want to talk about tonight. It's my son, Ralph, without whose strength and support I would have gone under.'

Ralph felt a tug at his heart as Carlo turned to face him.

'I'm in no need of charity, but he makes a difference to my life every day, and I don't think I've made that clear enough. So I'd like to remedy that now, if I may.' Holding up his glass, his father smiled across the room. 'To Ralph. For making a difference to me.'

As everyone lifted their glasses and repeated the toast Ralph felt a sharp sting of love and guilt for the man who had raised him.

Voices were buzzing in his head. Suddenly it was an effort to breathe. He felt dizzy—nauseous, almost.

He hid it well. His handsome face was smooth, and a smile pulled at his mouth so that nobody would know he was deeply moved.

Except Giulietta.

Without thinking, he leaned into her soft body and kissed her.

'It's okay,' she whispered softly against his mouth. 'It's okay.'

He pulled her closer, his fingers seeking the curve of her spine like a rock climber searching for a handhold. The pain in his chest felt as if it would never leave.

'Ralph...'

It was Carlo, smiling, calm.

'Sorry, Giulietta. I wonder if it would be possible to have a quick word with my son? I promise not to keep him long.'

Beside him, he felt Giulietta nod.

'Of course. There's someone I've been meaning to speak to all evening,' she said quickly, squeezing his hand before she let it go. 'Take as long as you need.'

As long as you need.

The words echoed inside his head as he followed Carlo into the drawing room, where he'd imagined them talking so many times in his dreams. But how long would it take before he would be ready to honour this man with the truth?

He shut the door, expecting his father to sit down, but instead Carlo walked over to where someone—probably Roberto—had put out a decanter of whisky and two glasses.

Clearly his father had planned this... His heart began to pound. Except Carlo didn't drink whisky as a rule.

'Here.' His father held out a glass. 'I hope you don't mind me taking you away from the party—it's just that we haven't seen much of one another lately, and…well, tonight is your mother's night. It always will be.'

Ralph nodded, his chest tightening at the hollowed-out note in his father's usually polished voice. 'I know, Papà.'

Carlo smiled unsteadily. 'I let her down, Ralph.'

'No!' The word exploded from his lips as he shook his head. 'You loved her, Papà. You took care of her.'

'Yes, I did.' His father nodded, his smile fading. 'But I still let her down. You see, she asked me to do something… something important…and I haven't. I couldn't. I was too scared. Too scared of losing you too.'

Ralph frowned. His head felt strange, flimsy and thin, as if it were made of paper. 'I don't understand, Papà.'

Except he did.

Around him the room seemed to fold in on itself, and he gripped the back of an armchair to get his balance back.

'You know,' he said shakily.

'That I'm not your biological father? Yes.'

There was a brightness to Carlo's eyes as he nodded.

'Your mother told me just after she found out she was pregnant with you.' His mouth twisted. 'I know you're angry with her, and that's completely understandable. But please don't judge her. She made a bad choice and she was so ashamed. That's why she found it so hard to talk to you about it.' Carlo's gaze was clear and unflinching. 'But we were both at fault, Ralph.'

Ralph met his father's eyes. 'I believe you.'

Marriages might look balanced to an outsider, but he knew from his own experience that they were a perpetually shifting equation of power and need and expectation.

'But we never stopped loving one another, and both of us wanted to make our marriage—*our family*—work.' Carlo took a deep breath. 'That's why we decided not to tell you until you were old enough to understand. And, of course, Niccolò and Marina had started their own family.'

'Vittoria...' Ralph said quietly.

'Yes, Vittoria.' Carlo gave him a small, stiff smile. 'When she came to the house your mother was devastated. She had no idea that Niccolò had kept those letters.' Reaching out, Carlo gripped Ralph's arm. 'She hated it that you found out that way. It was wrong, and unfair, and we should have told you. I know that now, and there's no excuse except that we both loved you so much and were scared of how you'd react.'

Ralph saw that tears were sliding down his father's handsome face.

'Before she died she made me promise to tell you everything—only I couldn't make myself do it.'

'I should have come to you.' Ralph didn't even try to hide the emotion in his voice. 'I should have talked to you.'

'*No.*' Carlo was shaking his head. 'You've grown into a fine young man but I'm the adult here, and you'll always be my child...*my son.*' He took another breath. 'That is if you still want to be.'

Ralph couldn't speak, but words were unnecessary for what he needed to say and, stepping forward, he embraced his father.

Carlo's arms hugged him close. 'I want you to know that I will support you in everything you want to do—including getting to know Niccolò.' Loosening his grip, he smiled shakily. 'And your mother felt the same way.'

'Thank you, Papà.'

'No, thank *you, mio figlio.*' His father squeezed his shoulder. 'And believe me when I say that you *are* a Castellucci, Ralph. Our family bond goes beyond blood and that in the end is all that matters: family.'

Ralph felt his heart swell. More than anything, he

wanted to tell his father that Giulietta might be pregnant. It would be the perfect gift to repay Carlo's love and loyalty. A chance to demonstrate his own love and commitment to the family that had raised him.

But he would need to run it past Juliet first...

After Carlo and Ralph had left the ballroom, Juliet turned and walked over to where a dark-haired woman with eyes like her husband was looking up at a beautiful Titian.

'Vittoria,' she said quietly.

'Juliet.'

There had been no need for introductions as both women had reached out to embrace each other.

As they stepped apart, Vittoria held on to Juliet's hand. 'I'm so sorry for the trouble I've caused. When I found the letters I freaked out. I thought Ralph was the only one who would understand, and he was so kind and patient.'

She screwed up her face.

'Only I didn't think about how it would look. I didn't think about anything or anyone but myself.'

Her fingers tightened around Juliet's.

'Do you think you can forgive me?'

'Of course I can forgive you,' Juliet said gently.

How could she not?

Up close, the similarities between the half-siblings were subtle, but irrefutable—the shape and colour of their eyes, the line of their noses...

'You were thinking about your family. And, actually, you did me—both of us—a favour.'

Breathing out shakily, Vittoria glanced over her shoulder. 'I should be getting back. My father wants me to bid on that BVLGARI bracelet. It's a surprise for my mum so he's taken her out to see the gardens.' She smiled. 'But perhaps we could go out to lunch one day.'

Juliet took a quick breath, steadied her voice. 'I'd like that. I'd like that very much.'

She watched Vittoria leave, then turned back to look up at the Titian. She had been terrified to approach Vittoria, but now she was glad she'd done it. Perhaps they might even become friends.

'There you are...'

Ralph was by her side. 'Ralph, I was—' she began, but he caught her hand.

'I need to talk to you.'

She searched his face, his eyes, and knew without having to ask that he had told his father the truth.

Heart hammering, she let him lead her through the house and up the stairs to their bedroom. As he pushed the door shut he turned and clasped her face, his thumbs stroking her cheeks as he stared down at her.

Her hands gripped his arms. His whole body was trembling. 'You told him, didn't you?' she said gently. 'About not being his son.'

She felt his shoulders shift, the muscles in his chest tighten.

'I didn't have to. He already knew.'

'I don't understand...' She stared at him, blinking.

'My mother told him right at the start when she found out she was pregnant. She told him she'd had an affair, and that she wanted to try and make things work between them.'

She bit into her lip. 'And they did.' Tears filled her eyes. 'They must have loved each other very much.'

'They did.' His mouth twisted. 'You know that was the hardest thing for me—thinking that it had all been a sham, an act. But it wasn't.'

She gripped his arms more tightly. 'I'm so happy for you, Ralph—and for Carlo.'

He breathed out shakily. 'They did think about telling

me the truth, but then Niccolò and Marina had Vittoria, and everyone seemed happy.'

She nodded. 'I talked to Vittoria. She's really nice.'

'She is. She found it hard at the beginning…' He paused, his eyes locking with hers. 'But she's like all the women in my life. Strong and smart.'

She shook her head. 'You did this, Ralph, not me. It was you and Carlo.'

'No, I couldn't have done it without you. I would have just kept on burying myself in work and pushing you away.' His arm tightened around her waist. 'You pushed back. You made me realise that if I didn't deal with my past I'd lose everything.' He touched her stomach lightly. 'And I have so much to lose.'

His eyes on hers were bright with unshed tears of love and longing.

'Not just our marriage, but our future.' He breathed out shakily. 'It was so hard not telling him that you could be pregnant. I didn't say anything, but I know it would mean so much to him. I thought perhaps we could call him from the clinic.'

The eagerness in his voice made her shake inside. But, forcing a smile to her face, she nodded, and he slid his hand round the nape of her neck, drawing her close.

For a moment they just leaned into one another, his tears mingling with hers. She couldn't breathe. Her throat seemed to have shrunk, so that it felt as if she was having to squeeze her words out.

'So, how does Carlo feel about you talking to Niccolò?'

'He understands why I'd want to, and I will talk to him…'

'But not tonight?'

Their eyes met and he shook his head, his mouth tipping up at one corner. 'No, not tonight. I have other priorities—'

He broke off, his face tensing as he glanced down at his watch. 'Like the auction.'

'So go.' She pressed her hands against his chest. 'Go on. I'm just going to tidy myself up a bit and then I'll follow.'

'Are you sure?' He looked uncertain.

'Of course. I'll be down in a minute. Go.'

Left alone, she walked into the bathroom and held her hands under the cold tap. Thanks to Anna, her mascara hadn't run, but she could feel her pulse leaping in her wrists.

Lifting her head, she stared at her face. Like most girls growing up, she had pored over pictures of her favourite celebrities, thinking that if only she could look like them her life would be different...*better*.

Now, though, staring at her own glossy lips, her smoky eyes and artfully flushed cheeks, she knew that anyone could look the part. It was how you felt on the inside that mattered.

And she felt as if everything was crumbling to dust... all her hopes and certainties.

She turned off the tap, watching the water spiral down the plughole. For so long she had been scared of the past. Scared of repeating her parents' mistakes, of becoming a person she didn't want to be against her will.

Now, though, she could see that the past wasn't the threat. It was the present. The here and now. The person she was.

And if that person wasn't carrying Ralph's baby, what then?

Her heart pounded like a cannon against her ribs.

Earlier in the ballroom, before the ball had started, she'd reminded herself that Ralph had told her he loved her— every version of her.

And he'd been telling the truth. She knew that. Speaking from the heart.

But what his heart wanted more than anything was for her to be pregnant.

Only what would happen if she wasn't?

They had grown so close in the past few days—surely nothing could come between them.

Except it had after Rome.

And how could she be sure that it wouldn't again?

How could she be sure of anything?

Her whole life had been spent second-guessing her parents, and how many times had she got it wrong?

She couldn't breathe. Everything was tangling inside her.

If only she could talk to someone.

Not Ralph. She couldn't bear even thinking that she might see doubt in his face, distance in his eyes.

There was no one. She was alone.

'*Sold!* To Signor Gino Rosso. *Grazie*, Gino.' Smiling, Ralph banged the gavel down as a ripple of applause filled the ballroom. 'And now, I'm going to hand over to my cousin, Felix. But please keep bidding, people. Remember, it's all for a very good cause.'

Still smiling, Ralph made his way through the tables and chairs, his eyes fixed on the huge double doors at the end of the room. But as he left the ballroom his smile faded. After the noise of the ball the house felt oddly silent, and he glanced down at his watch, frowning.

It had been at least thirty minutes since he'd left Giulietta upstairs, and he'd half expected to meet her on her way to find him. Only the hallway was empty.

His shoulders tensed. Surely it couldn't take her that long to tidy herself up?

There was no reason to think that anything was wrong, but he still took the stairs two at a time.

Their bedroom was in darkness and, switching on the

lights, he saw that it was empty. The bathroom was empty too, and for a moment he stood in the doorway, unsure of what to do.

And then a chill slid over his skin as he realised the doors to the balcony were open.

And then he was walking swiftly, fear blotting out all thought.

'Giulietta,' he said hoarsely.

She was sitting on the marble floor, hugging her knees, face lowered.

His limbs felt like lead, but his thoughts were spinning uncontrollably. *Had she hurt herself? Was she ill?*

He was by her side in three strides. Crouching down, he touched her gently. 'What is it, *bella*? Are you okay?'

As she looked up at him a tear rolled down her cheek. He felt her pain inside him, and it was more terrible than anything he'd ever experienced because it was *her* pain.

He sat down beside her and pulled her onto his lap. Holding her close, he let her cry, his fingertips drawing slow circles against her hair until finally a shuddering breath broke from her throat.

'Tell me what it is and I will fix it,' he told her.

She shook her head. 'You can't fix it, Ralph.'

Her voice sounded small and cramped, and a thin sweat spread over his body. 'Then I'll fight it.'

He stared at her, the muscles in his arms bunching. He was desperate to do something—anything—to take away the pain in her voice.

Shaking her head again, she breathed in a shaky breath. 'You can't fight it. It's me.'

His heart jumped. There was something about her posture, the way she was curled in on herself, as though she was trying to hold on to something. Or had already lost it.

'Has something happened?'

She looked up at him, her gaze searching his face. 'You mean with the baby?'

'I suppose I do,' he said quietly. 'But if something's happened to the baby, then it's happened to you too, *bella*.'

Reaching out, Ralph stroked her face gently. Fresh tears spilled down her cheeks.

'Nothing's happened,' she said. 'But what if it had? What if it does?'

She looked down, biting her lip. 'I know how much you want this baby to be real, Ralph. I know how important it is right now for you and your father, for your family…'

He brought her closer against him. 'I do want this baby to be real for my father, and for us, but—'

He swallowed, remembering what it had felt like to walk into their bedroom and find it empty that first time, and then again tonight. Seeing her curled up in a ball like that had been even more devastating.

Burying his face against her hair, he breathed out shakily. 'But when I found you I wasn't thinking about the baby. I thought you were hurt,' he whispered. 'And I didn't care about anything else. You're all that matters to me.'

It was true.

Downstairs, with Carlo, the idea of a baby had seemed so urgent to him, so imperative—only now he realised that this woman, their love was enough.

'But what about…?' She hesitated, her eyes seeking his. 'Will you mind if I'm not pregnant? I mean, I know that's the reason—'

'It was never the reason.' He cupped her face in his hands and kissed her softly. 'You're the reason, *bella*. I love you. Yes, I want you to be pregnant, but if you're not then we'll try again. And if you can't get pregnant then we'll adopt.' His expression gentled. 'In fact, we should do that anyway.'

* * *

For a few seconds Ralph rested his forehead against hers, and she felt her heart slow in time with his.

'My life is so blessed already, and I'm sorry that I made you feel that it wasn't—that you weren't enough. Because you are.' His hand moved gently through her hair. 'And I'd give up all of this in a heartbeat, for you.'

She glanced out at the beautiful moonlit grounds. 'You don't need to go that far,' she said, letting a teasing smile tug at the corners of her mouth.

The answering gleam in his eyes seemed to push through her skin.

Reaching out and gripping his jacket, she drew him closer. 'I love you. Ralph. I never stopped loving you, even when I didn't want to—even when I was scared to love you.'

Above them, the sky was starting to grow pale.

His golden gaze drifted slowly across her face, searching, seeing everything. She felt his love warm her skin, filling her with heat, and she closed her eyes against another hot rush of tears.

'E ti amo, Giulietta,' he said softly, drawing her face close to his. 'You're my sun, my light, my life. Whatever happens, you're all I need. For ever.'

Juliet gazed up at his face…a face that was as familiar, as necessary to her as the sun now rising behind the hills.

And her love for him was as eternal as his for her. Feeling the first rays of light reach over the balcony she leaned into his body, closing her eyes as his mouth found hers.

EPILOGUE

'THERE YOU ARE.' Lucia rushed forward. 'We were getting worried. I thought we might have to send out a search party.'

Shaking his head, Luca shifted Raffaelle from one arm to the other. 'I wasn't worried.'

Smiling, Juliet leaned in to kiss her friend. 'Sorry. Honestly, everything that could go wrong did. We woke up late. I dripped nail polish on my dress. Then Charlie wanted a feed…' She held up her face for Luca to kiss her, and then bent down to kiss Raffaelle. 'Hi, Rafi. And then we had to change him.'

'By "we" she means *me*.'

Turning, Juliet felt a rush of love. Ralph was standing beside her. But it wasn't just her tall, dark, handsome and dangerously tempting husband who was making her heart swell.

It was the beautiful dark-haired baby in his arms.

She felt Ralph's gaze on her face, the tight focus of his clear, golden-eyed love, and with it a vertiginous rush of happiness brighter and more vivid than the stained-glass windows of the church.

It was nearly a year since that week when she and Ralph had found their way back to one another. A week that had started with doubt and despair and ended with hope and reconciliation.

But not with a pregnancy.

Remembering that moment in the clinic when Dr de Masi had told them the test was negative, she drew a breath.

She had wept. But Ralph had held her close and told her how much he loved her and needed her, and that when it was meant to happen it would.

And it had.

Two months later she'd been pregnant.

And nine months after that Charles Francesco Castellucci had been born.

And today was his christening.

Not the usual Castellucci christening, with half the world's media tripping over themselves for a photo, but a small, private ceremony for just close friends and the family.

And they were her family too.

Ralph had been determined to make that happen—determined, too, to build on the positives from his own experience for the next generation of Castelluccis.

At that moment, the youngest member of that generation gave a short, imperious shout.

She bent over her son, breathing in his scent. He stared up at her, his small fist pressed against Ralph's shirt, his golden eyes widening as she dropped a kiss on his forehead.

'Are you ready?'

Looking up, she met Ralph's gaze. They had come so far, she thought. A year ago they had been separated by doubt and mistrust, facing their fears alone. Now they had no secrets. They talked all the time. And they still hadn't run out of ways to say, 'I love you.'

Leaning into him, she caught his arm. 'Yes, we should go in.' She smiled. 'Your fathers will be waiting.'

Ralph put his hand lightly on her hip bone and drew her against his body.

His fathers.

A year ago he had been falling apart. Everything he had

taken for granted in his life had been in question. He'd felt torn, conflicted, guilty—and excruciatingly lonely.

Living what had felt like a lie, but terrified of the truth, he'd avoided his family and pushed Giulietta to the point of leaving him.

But she had made him fight for what he wanted.

And she had fought with him. For him. For them.

Without her he would still be lost at sea, running from a past he couldn't change and in the process destroying the future he craved.

Now, though—thanks to her—he had not one but two fathers waiting in the church for the ceremony to start.

It had taken some time before he'd been ready to reach out to his biological father, but he was glad he had. He liked Niccolò a lot, and Marina had been generous in giving them the space they needed to connect.

So now he felt like the luckiest man alive.

His eyes locked with Giulietta's and he felt his heart turn over.

He was the luckiest man alive.

She was the sexiest, strongest, smartest woman in the world, and together they had made a beautiful, healthy son.

Chest tightening, he glanced down at Charlie. His son was so soft and small he fitted into his arm with room to spare, but his love for him was boundless. As it was for his wife.

'Do you want to take him?'

Juliet turned to Ralph. 'No.' She shook her head. 'He's happy where he is.'

'And you? Are you happy where you are?' he asked softly.

Juliet met his eye. 'I'm happy where *you* are.'

He held out his hand. Smiling, she took it, and they walked into the church together.

* * * * *

MILLS & BOON

Coming next month

SECRETS OF CINDERELLA'S AWAKENING
Sharon Kendrick

Almost as if he'd read her mind, Leon caught hold of her and turned her round, his hands on either side of her waist. She held her breath because his touch felt *electric* and he studied her upturned face for what felt like a long time, before lowering his head to kiss her.

It was…dynamite.

It was…life-changing.

Marnie swayed in disbelief, her limbs growing instantly boneless. How was it possible for a kiss to feel this *good*? How could *anything* feel this good? At first there was barely any contact between them – just the intoxicating graze of his mouth over hers.

He deepened the kiss and began to stroke one of her breasts. Her nipple was pushing against her baggy T-shirt dress towards the enticing circling of his thumb. Was it that which made her writhe her hips against his with instinctive hunger, causing him to utter something in Greek which sounded almost *despairing*?

The sound broke the spell and she drew back – though in the faint light all she could see was the hectic glitter of his eyes. 'What…what did you just say?'

'I said that you set my blood on fire, *agape mou*. And that I want you very much. But you already know that.'

Well, she knew he wanted her, yes. She wasn't actually sure about the blood-on-fire bit because nobody had ever said anything like that to her before. And although she liked it her instinct was not to believe him because even if they were true, she knew compliments always came with a price.

Yet what was the *point* of all this if she was just going to pepper the experience with her usual doubts, and spoil it? Couldn't she have a holiday from her normal self and shake off all the worries which had been weighing her down for so long? Couldn't she be a different Marnie tonight – one who was seeking nothing but uncomplicated pleasure? She had always been the responsible one. The one who looked out for other people – with one eye on the distance, preparing for the shadows which inevitably hovered there. Wasn't it time to articulate what *she* wanted for a change?

She cleared her throat. 'Would you mind speaking in English so I can understand what you're saying?'

She could hear the amusement which deepened his voice.

'Are we planning to do a lot of talking then, Marnie? Is that what turns you on?'

Something warned her she'd be straying into dangerous territory if she told him she didn't *know* what turned her on because she'd never given herself the chance to find out. But while she didn't want to lie to him, that didn't mean she couldn't tell a different kind of truth.

'*You* turn me on,' she said boldly and something about the breathless rush of her words made his powerful body tense.

'Oh, *do* I?' he questioned, tilting her chin with his fingers so that their darkened gazes clashed. 'So what are we going to do about that, I wonder?'

Continue reading
SECRETS OF CINDERELLA'S AWAKENING
Sharon Kendrick

Available next month
www.millsandboon.co.uk

COMING SOON!

We really hope you enjoyed reading this book. If you're looking for more romance, be sure to head to the shops when new books are available on

Thursday 10th June

MILLS & BOON

LET'S TALK
Romance

For exclusive extracts, competitions
and special offers, find us online:

MILLS & BOON

THE HEART OF ROMANCE

A ROMANCE FOR EVERY READER

ODERN — Prepare to be swept off your feet by sophisticated, sexy and seductive heroes, in some of the world's most glamourous and romantic locations, where power and passion collide.

TORICAL — Escape with historical heroes from time gone by. Whether your passion is for wicked Regency Rakes, muscled Vikings or rugged Highlanders, awaken the romance of the past.

EDICAL — Set your pulse racing with dedicated, delectable doctors in the high-pressure world of medicine, where emotions run high and passion, comfort and love are the best medicine.

ue Love — Celebrate true love with tender stories of heartfelt romance, from the rush of falling in love to the joy a new baby can bring, and a focus on the emotional heart of a relationship.

Desire — Indulge in secrets and scandal, intense drama and plenty of sizzling hot action with powerful and passionate heroes who have it all: wealth, status, good looks…everything but the right woman.

ROES — Experience all the excitement of a gripping thriller, with an intense romance at its heart. Resourceful, true-to-life women and strong, fearless men face danger and desire - a killer combination!

To see which titles are coming soon, please visit

millsandboon.co.uk/nextmonth